WHEN THE GODS ARE AWAY

Book Design and Layout by Rob Carroll
Cover Design by Rob Carroll

ISBN 978-1-958598-47-4 (paperback)
ISBN 978-1-958598-69-6 (eBook)

darkmatter-ink.com

WHEN THE GODS ARE AWAY

ROBERT E. HARPOLD

DARK
MATTER
INK

WHEN THE GODS ARE AWAY

ROBERT E. HARPOLD

Dedicated to my wonderful wife, Julie. Thank you for your constant support, encouragement, and love.

ONE

BLASPHEMER'S WEEK ALWAYS began with bloodshed.

Virgil bit into his baklava, the taste of sugar mingling with the aroma of corpse in a pleasantly familiar alchemy. Flakes of pastry fluttered to the tiled kitchen floor and settled beside the subject of today's investigation, the former Nicholas Manikas. The body lay before the food-stained refrigerator, eyes open, mouth twisted in pain. One hand clutched a tub of butter and the other a corresponding knife, neither of which had proven effective in countering his assailant. Dried blood led from a pool on the tile to the gaping wound in his dark-green house tunic. Probable cause of death: spear to the chest.

Not a typical death for a former police officer. The killer could expect a lethal reprisal of the most protracted sort, which characterized him as either ignorant and unprepared, or dangerous and cunning. Virgil adjusted his short-brimmed hat. Dangerous and cunning, then.

Virgil crammed the remaining pastry into his mouth and knelt beside the body, trying to recall the appropriate procedures for an investigation. Everything went blank, all the notes and practice sessions disappearing as though he had sipped from the river Lethe. His professor would have been furious at all the time wasted on Virgil.

The thought of blood flooding the capillaries in Professor Lambros's face gave Virgil the answer: examine the spear wound. His thumb covered the diameter of the slit skin, which resembled a tunic's burst seam. As he probed the wound's perimeter, his finger rode up and down the jagged edges as though driving along hills. Inconclusive results, then: several spear designs could have made such a shape.

As he wiped his finger on the victim's tunic, thick boots clicked on the tiled floor. Virgil started, reaching his hands behind him to prevent himself from toppling backward. Chief Dimitriou had arrived.

Chief Dimitriou wasn't tall in the conventional sense, but walked like he was, all weight and swagger. He wore the blue uniform of the Arestia Police Department, its golden badge depicting a skull pierced with a spear. The chief had probably come to remove Virgil from the investigation as he had for the previous six cases, always within minutes of the assignment. Maybe the removals weren't strictly legal, and maybe Virgil should have protested more, but he hesitated to provoke someone with the city-state police department's all-time kill record.

The chief glowered at the corpse. "Well?" The question ended there, as though complete without content or context.

Virgil opened his mouth to speak, but no sound emerged. A bad start to his seventh first case.

The chief folded his arms across his chest. "What have you got for me, Virgil?"

Virgil spread the bottom of his loose tunic across his slacks. "He died from a spear wound..."

"Obviously." The chief's voice sounded as though it had bathed for days in disdain before oozing forth. He glanced at Manikas's remains with an expression of either paternal sadness or revulsion. "I hope our priest gives us more leads than 'he was killed by a spear.'"

"Priest?" The more progressive city-states near Athens used priests to aid investigations, but Virgil had never expected it from Arestia.

"Someone killed one of our own." The chief kicked the victim's bare leg in a friendly, bruising fashion. "Even if it was just Nicholas, we will have retribution."

Virgil continued to crouch, expecting his investigation's death sentence at any moment. As the moments passed and the chief's expression remained unchanged, Virgil began to feel something foreign deep within his chest that might have been…hope. He gathered his nerve, as though preparing to leap from a cliff into icy waters below.

"I need more…" But the chief had already turned away. "Time."

The chief exited the kitchen. Maybe he would be more receptive to Virgil's work for once.

Yeah. And maybe Zeus will give me a pony at the next solstice celebration.

The chief seemed unusually interested in finding this murderer. Maybe it was because the victim was a former police officer. Or the chief might have an ulterior motive. The thought reminded him of something Professor Lambros would have said: "Trust no one, not even yourself."

The professor would also have beat him about the head for not checking the body's stiffness earlier. Virgil grabbed the victim's arm above the spindly wrist, applying a slight pressure to bend it upward. As the arm rotated, the butter knife slipped from Manikas's cold hand and clattered to the floor.

Virgil's face burned. He had disturbed the crime scene and contaminated the evidence. *Why am I even here? Why did anyone ever allow me to work on an important task like this?* He imagined stabbing his leg with the knife over and over until the shame disappeared.

No. He couldn't think like that. These negative thoughts were one reason his sister Chrysanthe had pressured him to start therapy. He had his first appointment tomorrow. Virgil sighed. Therapy hadn't even started, and it already wasn't working.

Virgil forced himself to focus on the corpse. Analyze the posture and tension. Muscles tight in the client's face and neck. *Stiffness in the arm? How stiff are arms normally?* Virgil felt his own. Manikas's was stiffer, but not rigid. *Rigor mortis peaks after, what, twelve hours?* That figure put the time of death between three and six hours ago. The opening hours of

Blasphemer's Week, when people indulged in vandalism, theft, and murder, without fear of reprisal from the gods.

Virgil took hold of Manikas's arm, returned it to its original position, with the palm facing upward, and slid the knife between thumb and fingers. *Close enough.* He rubbed his sore eyes, wishing he had managed to sleep for at least a few minutes before the chief's early-morning call.

"Virgil!" Even from two rooms away, the chief's voice sounded as though it came from a spot beside Virgil's ear. "Get your pudgy ass in the living room!"

As Virgil crossed the apartment's entryway, two uniformed figures emerged from the living room and pushed past him. One applied a vigorous shoulder, sending Virgil stumbling into the wall.

"Sorry," said Virgil.

Neither officer glanced at him. Schirra, a tall woman with prominent muscles, carried a hammer and a rolled-up canvas under her arm as she strode to the front door. Stathis, one of the typical muscular goons the department preferred to hire, held a hammer and a fistful of nails. Both officers wore regulation Helios sunglasses despite being indoors.

Virgil eyed their tools. "What are—"

"Quiet." Stathis didn't turn as he took a position opposite Schirra.

Virgil tried to remain still as he observed them. This activity wasn't typical police work.

Schirra unrolled the canvas and handed one end to her partner. "I can't believe we're nailing crap to the door. Waste of time and talent." She accepted a nail from Stathis and placed it against the canvas's upper left corner, above the doorframe. "Remember that shoplifter we caught the other day?"

Stathis grinned. "Yeah. I like it when they struggle."

Schirra hammered the nail in place, the echoes of metal against metal reverberating in the entryway. Stathis attacked his own nail with an approach based more on force than efficiency.

Virgil covered his ears and examined the canvas. It looked like several plain goatskins sewn together. Maybe the temple priests had performed some sort of prayer over it to make it more receptive for whatever it was supposed to do. A holy goatskin or an arcane goatskin or something. "Oh! This is for the ritual."

"Do you think we'd be nailing goatskin to a door otherwise?" Schirra hammered a nail into the bottom corner, just under the lower doorframe, as Stathis finished his first corner.

"The priest, Patroklus, said it would catch emotions or something." Stathis knelt to nail the final corner into place. "He said it worked in other city-states. I guess the chief's trying everything on this case. Still sounds like a bad idea to have priests involved in law enforcement. Or detectives."

Stathis locked eyes with Virgil while hammering in the last corner. The officer didn't look away, even when the hammer hit his thumb.

Virgil winced. "I think—"

Schirra laughed. "When have you ever thought? Here's something to think about: Nicholas might be alive if he hadn't been fired to make room for you."

Is that true? Virgil had been surprised his hometown police department had hired him, and he'd heard rumors that the Alliance had forced individual city-states to employ detectives, but he hadn't known the department had fired someone to create an opening for him.

Even when he tried to do something good, he ruined someone's life. He owed a debt to Manikas.

"Um," said Virgil. "Was he the worst officer or something? Was that why he was fired instead of someone else?"

Schirra and Stathis stared at him as though he had just shat on their shoes.

"Sorry." Virgil took a step toward the living room. "I shouldn't have said that. I don't know what I was thinking. I'm just stupid."

The officers continued staring.

"Um," said Virgil. "Do…do you think the priest's spell will work? You know it's Blasphemer's Week and th—"

"Ask Patroklus if you're really that curious." Stathis set his hammer down. "Now get out. Just looking at you is pissing me off."

When Virgil hesitated, Schirra pointed to the doorway. "You're dismissed."

Virgil nodded. "Sorry. I'll go now. I'll just be..." He sidled from the entryway and into the living room.

Manikas had decorated the living room in typical Spartan fashion: no wall art and few furniture items. It had a table and two severe wooden chairs, the kind that haunted the dreams of chiropractors. Chief Dimitriou occupied the nearest one. Spears, maces, and other weapons hung from the walls, positioned for easy retrieval. No vacant hooks or shelves, which meant the murderer had either brought his own weapon or had returned the weapon to its proper place after use. Training weights rested in a corner. Given the victim's physique, Manikas must have used them for décor.

"Get over here!" Chief Dimitriou slammed a fist into the table.

"Sorry!" Virgil hustled to the spot beside the chief, though he didn't know why Dimitriou insisted on hurrying. The ritual wasn't ready yet.

"Schirra!" No matter how much the chief shouted, his voice never grew hoarse. "Get in here, and bring Stathis! Assuming your woman genes will let you stop interior-decorating." He chuckled to himself.

A moment later, Schirra and Stathis entered. Schirra's expression could have melted iron, but the chief didn't seem to notice. She and Stathis took places standing opposite Virgil.

"I love this time of year." The chief glared with the same effort bodybuilders put into weightlifting. "This is always our busiest week. Ever since I was elected chief, we've had a murder on the twenty-ninth day of Hera. Always early in the morning on the twenty-ninth, too, like the murderers were just waiting for this week."

"My favorite time of year is the autumnal equinox," said Stathis.

The chief grimaced. "Son, no one gives a shit."

Stathis hid his hurt expression almost as it formed. Virgil might have felt sorrier for him if not for their previous conversation.

The chief glanced at his watch, and his frown deepened. "Stathis, text Patroklus and tell him to hurry up."

Before Stathis could pull his phone from his pocket, shadows wavered against the far wall. Without even the shuffle of clothing or the tap of feet against stone to announce his entrance, a man emerged like the breeze from an open window. He wore a long red robe that flicked across the floor and created the illusion that its occupant glided atop a cushion of air. The man's golden hair fell below his shoulders, swaying in time with the undulation of his robe. His eyes seemed to focus on some distant ethereal vision as he traversed the distance to Virgil and the others.

Patroklus. Virgil had seen the priest on occasion in the police headquarters hallways, but had never worked with him.

Patroklus didn't speak when he reached them, nor did he acknowledge their presence. Instead, he took the remaining seat across from the chief and produced a mixing bowl from his voluminous sleeves. A burnt-sponge odor rose from the bowl, reminding Virgil of the herbs used when he had attended sacrifices to Ares as a child. Patroklus set the bowl on the table without making a sound.

The chief glared at the new arrival. "Ready?"

"I am." The priest's reply had less inflection than a computer tone.

"Good. Find me someone to kill."

"This procedure," said the priest, "will locate and display any strong emotions within this apartment. Those emotions will have belonged to the occupant, as he has spent much time here and his feelings will have infused the walls of this place. Those emotions might be hatred, sadness, or love, and will likely provide a clue as to what happened here. The procedure will not, however, indicate who should be killed."

"Whatever. Just hurry."

"Very well." Patroklus removed a spoon from one of his pockets, stirred the bowl's contents, then set the spoon beside the bowl. "Please join hands."

The chief slammed his hand into Stathis's, who took Schirra's hand. Patroklus enveloped Virgil's hand, applying only the minimum pressure necessary to maintain contact. The chief paused and scowled before taking Virgil's other hand, completing the circle.

Virgil had never seen functional magic before. Only pop magic, like fireworks or smoke shapes at festivals. He wondered if the priest's magic would feel more or less impressive than those colorful tricks.

"Relax," Patroklus intoned in a soporific voice. "Free your mind and feel at peace. As the ties binding you to your body gently dissolve, close your eyes."

Virgil watched as his coworkers obeyed, then realized he should do the same. At least with their eyes closed, they hadn't noticed the lapse. If they suspected a of lack of faith...

Patroklus continued speaking without pause, his words washing over Virgil like waves at the beach. "Become as one with the world around you. Let your flesh feel the air, its warmth and pressure. Feel the power flowing through every molecule." As Patroklus spoke, a thin current of electricity traveled from Virgil's shoulder to his fingertips, jumping between the hairs on his arm. Another line trickled down his other arm, then over his legs and chest until tingles danced atop every square centimeter of skin. Virgil squirmed and felt relieved to hear the officers shift position, too. Patroklus gave no indication he noticed the sensation.

"We are part of the world. This one and the next. The seen and the unseen. The physical and the spiritual. We have broken the barriers separating us. All is one."

A gust of wind shook Virgil's clothes and threatened to tear his hat from his head. He opened his eyes to slits. His colleagues were struck by the gale as well, though the curtain, shelves, and weapons throughout the room remained in serene repose. Much more impressive than festival spells.

If the ritual works during Blasphemer's Week, though, how can anyone believe the gods have anything to do with it? Virgil closed his eyes again and buried the thought.

"We may speak with the gods," said Patroklus in a whisper. Virgil shivered, more from the tone and events around him than at the notion of speaking to beings who might not exist.

"Wise Athena," Patroklus droned, with a voice as soothing as a seashore breeze, "goddess of truth and wisdom, hear our supplication and accept our offering. Guide us that we might learn and so bring justice to the fallen and glory to your name. Grant us the sight of powerful emotions experienced within this household so that we may better understand the tragedy that has befallen the victim."

A dim roar crescendoed from nothingness until it filled Virgil's ears, like the deep thrumming of an engine. Brightness beat upon him until he opened his eyes again. A faint spark popped near the priest's head, followed by another and another until they surrounded Patroklus, shimmering.

"Our prayer has been heard," said Patroklus. "We give thanks to Athena." In an instant, the dim roar, the wind, and the thin electric charge disappeared as though they had never existed. Virgil lifted his head to see Patroklus's hand float free from the circle and produce a pinch of powder from within his robe. Spreading his fingers, the priest let the powder fall into the bowl.

Once the first granule came into contact with the herbs, a blinding light burst from the bowl. Virgil shut his eyes, letting the afterimages play across the backs of his eyelids. The images faded a moment later, and he could see again.

The chief grunted. "Schirra, Stathis, check the canvas."

The two officers jumped to their feet, Stathis following Schirra to the entryway.

A thin, disagreeable odor remained, along with a tuft of smoke rising from the herb bowl and dissipating in the air. Patroklus emptied the bowl into one of his robe's side pockets before returning it somewhere within his sleeves.

Virgil wondered what Schirra and Stathis would find upon the canvas. Patroklus had mentioned powerful emotions, but not whether they would manifest as pictograms, words, colors, or something else.

"Things are changing too quickly." The chief cracked his knuckles. "When I joined the force, we didn't have women officers. The priests prayed for us and interceded with the gods on our behalves, but they didn't interfere in the investigations. And we didn't need 'detectives' to figure out who committed crimes; we figured it out ourselves. This is all Zeus-shit. We live in Arestia, Ares's own city-state. We should act like it."

Virgil refrained from commenting on the accuracy of the previous criminal investigations; the chief responded to criticism like dynamite to a fire. Patroklus seemed unfazed by the remarks.

Stathis burst back into the room. "Nothing."

Schirra followed, carrying the canvas, and fixed her eyes on Patroklus as she spoke. "No burnt images, no scratches, nothing. The canvas wasn't even touched." She set it before the priest. Virgil leaned forward to examine it, but Patroklus collected it before Virgil could see any details.

"This can be reused." Patroklus rolled up the canvas and placed it on his lap.

Why were there no powerful emotions here? How strong do emotions need to be for the spell to consider them powerful? Did the priest make an error during the ritual? Intentionally? Or, does the spell not work during this week due to the gods' absence?

A horrible bellow shattered the silence. Virgil turned to see the chief slam a fist into the table.

"Unacceptable!" The chief's face had twisted like a scroll amidst flames. "I will not let Nicholas go unavenged."

Virgil started to raise his hand. "We're not—"

"It's been ten years since the last time an officer was killed. Because of the example we made of that killer, we haven't lost anyone else until now. I am going to enjoy finding this one."

Stathis nodded, mouth tightened. Schirra's eyes gleamed.

"Schirra. Stathis." Chief Dimitriou gestured to the kitchen. "Coin him."

"Yes, sir." Stathis grinned. He and Schirra began swaggering toward the kitchen.

"Wait!" Virgil found himself saying.

For a moment, silence. Stillness. Then, narrowed eyes focused on him, confirming that he had spoken, that he hadn't imagined it, that he had contradicted the chief's order. Virgil stared at the floor.

"What do you want, Virgil?" The chief spat out the name as though it were profanity of the most unsavory sort.

"Should we go ahead and coin Nicholas, anyway?" Stathis asked from the doorway, bobbing in sycophantic excitement.

"No. Let's hear what pressing concerns our homicide detective has."

Virgil tried to swallow, but had no saliva. "Nothing. Sorry. I didn't get any sleep last night. I shouldn't have said anything."

The chief's muscles bunched. "You directly challenged my order. You had damned well better have had a better reason than that you were *sleepy.*"

The department had fired Manikas in order to hire Virgil. If Manikas had remained employed, maybe he wouldn't have come into the circumstances that cost his life. Like Schirra had said, Manikas's death was Virgil's fault. Virgil owed it to Manikas to find the murderer.

"I'm not done with my investigation," Virgil said in a voice barely audible even to him. "I don't think the coins should be used yet. I want the soul to still be attached to the body while I'm examining it; I think that will help…with the spells?"

He looked to Patroklus. The priest remained silent.

"Um…does that make any sense?"

Patroklus nodded. Virgil felt his stomach twist.

"That's sick." Schirra wrinkled her nose.

"Yeah," said Stathis. "I hope you're not in charge of investigating *my* murder."

Chief Dimitriou stared into Virgil's eyes, an intense gaze that likely stole several years from Virgil's life, probably the best ones. What the man sought and what he found, Virgil didn't know, but after an interminable period, the chief nodded.

"Fine. We'll try it your way for now. But…" The chief leveled a finger at Virgil. "You're done when I say you're done. And when you're done, the *coins go in.*"

"Okay." Virgil winced as his voice cracked. "Thank you."

What happened? Why did the chief let me continue on the case? What if I don't find the murderer?

The chief peered about the room as though assessing what most needed to be smashed. "Schirra, Stathis, take the body to the lab. Let's clean up and get out of here."

The officers resumed swaggering to the kitchen. The chief breathed through his nostrils, forceful as a bull, and turned to Virgil.

"You'd better come up with something soon, Virgil. My killing hands are getting itchy."

TWO

VIRGIL PAUSED BEFORE the police headquarters records room. He had something else to do, something important, but he had forgotten what it was.

He sighed. He would likely remember tomorrow, when it was too late for anything but regret. *Regret is scheduled for tomorrow, then. Today, solve a murder mystery.*

Without leads or suspects, Nicholas Manikas's police record offered the best starting place for further searching. Unfortunately, the police had hidden the records room in a dark basement hallway. Virgil could only speculate on their reasons. He wrinkled his nose at the stench of mildew emanating from somewhere beneath the wall's cracking paint and grabbed the rusty door handle.

It refused to budge.

Virgil remembered Manikas lying face-up on the kitchen floor, eyes brimming with reproach. If it hadn't been for Virgil, Manikas would still be alive. All Virgil could offer as recompense was a target for vengeance, and he couldn't even give that meager offering if he couldn't get this door open.

He twisted the handle harder. This time, his palm tickled, and a dusting of green sparkles rained onto his hand.

The sparkles disappeared. Magical lock. Any other country in the world would have used a mechanical lock, but the Greek Alliance insisted on magic. And somehow, the police department had forgotten to update the spell to recognize Virgil.

Or maybe it hadn't been an oversight. Alliance laws and departmental regulations about Virgil's access privileges remained hazy, giving the police ample legal leeway to refuse him entry to the records room. He hurried to his office and returned a few minutes later with a screwdriver. The door handle slipped loose once he removed its screws. He caught the pieces before they fell, and lowered the metal jumble to the floor.

A soft click, like the tap of a pen against a distant wall, came from behind him. Virgil turned, but could see nothing other than flickering lights and empty hallway.

Is someone watching me?

No. No one cared about him.

The sound could have been thermal shifting of the building's pipes or walls. Or it could have been imaginary. Virgil hadn't slept in over thirty hours. Hallucinations would be a reasonable expectation at this point.

The handle's removal had left a circular hole in the door through which he could see the lock's mechanical remnants. Virgil reached a finger inside and squeezed one of the dangling pieces. Metal rubbed against metal and wood. He stepped back and, wincing at the squeal of rusty hinges, pulled the door open.

The records room was a nightmare, a Tartarus for clerical workers who had committed grievous offenses against the gods. Filing cabinets were stacked vertically, horizontally, sideways, front-to-back, five deep, wherever space existed, until they threatened to spill into the hall. No labels anywhere, unless one counted the obscene phrases and images etched into metal. Searching for Manikas's file could take days.

The search gave him a good opportunity to gather more data for his ongoing experiment. Praying to the gods for activities in their purviews hadn't consistently worked for him, so, when he had turned fourteen, he had begun choosing a different god each week and praying to that god for everything: good grades, finding good produce at the market, whatever felt necessary during those seven days. By tallying the successes and failures of the chosen god for that week, he could compare the efficacy of each god. None of them had fared well over the past nine years, which fueled the suspicion he couldn't vocalize in public. Of course, it could also mean none of the gods wanted his worship.

This week, it was Hebe's turn. The goddess of youth. Perhaps not a fair test, given the gods' absence this week, but the results could serve as a control for the experiment. He closed his eyes, offered a quick prayer for expediency in his search, and turned to the filing cabinets.

The first cabinet didn't have Manikas's file, nor did the one on top of it, nor the one labeled, "My dick is my spear," but the one directly behind it did. Good start for Hebe.

From the other files within the drawer, including Virgil's, he realized this was the "active duty" cabinet. Somehow, the officers hadn't removed Manikas's file yet, though Manikas had lost his job two weeks earlier. Virgil could understand them not wanting to search through this horrifying room or enter the disease-ridden hallway more than necessary, but someone must have had to do it to put Virgil's folder in the drawer.

Virgil reached for Manikas's folder, but then paused and pulled out his own folder instead. It contained one page, with his basic biographical information and physical descriptions, like his height and weight. It also included a note stating "he has the sex appeal of a turd," and listed his job title as "Playing at Being a Real Officer."

If he hadn't known before what the officers thought of him, he did now. He returned his folder and removed Manikas's, opening it on top of the cabinet. He hadn't known so much disappointment could exist in a container this small. The folder held only a few pages with the barest details. Manikas had been born in Arestia in 5385. His parents, Paulus and Clymera, and his older brothers, Boris and Alexandros, were still living. He had achieved mediocre scores in the police academy and led an unremarkable career as a police officer. Virgil scanned the reports attributed to Manikas: shoplifter, vandalism, some tickets for driving under the speed limit... No case with a severe enough punishment for the lawbreaker to consider murder an appropriate revenge, or at least none included in the official record.

The file felt so...blank. As empty as Virgil's, with the exception of the arrests Manikas had made. A real person had so much more depth: motivations, fears, failed dreams. Virgil tapped his fingers against the file cabinet. If he were going to solve this case, he needed to get inside the victim's mind so he could understand what Manikas would have done to provoke murder. Maybe Manikas's family could provide some insight.

Thinking of family reminded him of his sister. He hadn't seen her since—

Chrysanthe had a show tonight. That's what he had forgotten earlier.

He'd missed her first shows while studying at Klasistratos Academy in Athens, but now he had returned to his hometown and had promised to attend this show. This was Chrysanthe's first time doing choreography for the Arestia dance company, as she had explained several times at high speed over the phone, which added to the event's importance. And it was before some politician's speech, so she thought it might garner a crowd.

But with a case to solve, Virgil couldn't attend. He knew Chrysanthe would understand. She was always understanding of his failures.

After their mother died, Virgil had started oversleeping. He had been unable to force himself to wake up before the afternoon. That habit quickly cost him his grocery store cashier job. Though he'd been punctual the first two months of his next job, stocking, he had then returned to his pattern. For some reason, he couldn't bring himself to return to a job where no one wanted him and where he could make no meaningful contribution. Four more jobs ended the same way.

Most families would have abandoned Virgil, but Chrysanthe rescued him. When he began his gyro delivery job, she demanded to see his schedule every week. Every day, she would call him before his shift to make certain he arrived at work on time. Eventually, he started waking up before her calls. She had prevented him from ruining his life, maybe even from dying. *Am I really going to refuse to do something as small as seeing her show when she saved my life?*

He had gotten Manikas killed, though. That was the greater debt. Virgil had never made a positive contribution in his life, but his negative impacts had culminated in a murder.

Manikas's folder lay on the cabinet. The file contained one final stapled packet of papers. An arrest record, but Manikas wasn't the arrester. Virgil examined the cover page, which listed the date, time, offense...

Nicholas Manikas was the victim. He had been beaten up by his brothers only a few hours after he'd been fired.

Police rarely made arrests in domestic disturbance circumstances. They would tell the wife to apologize to the husband and to stop provoking him. Given that all the participants in this case were male, maybe the police had wanted to protect the victim.

At least this irregularity provided a potential clue. Manikas had a feuding relationship with his brothers. That relationship could have led to murder. Virgil looked for the names of the officers who had made the arrest. Kostas and Collias.

After flipping through the pages of photographs and statements, Virgil closed the folder. Maybe he should speak to the officers to find out what had made them suspicious enough to act against precedent.

When Virgil reached the front desk downstairs, Officer Tektón tapped the cracked stone counter with an oversized knife while talking to Michaelides. "Yeah, Patroklus weirds me out, too. All the time, I'm just sitting there, and I turn around and *bam*! He's right behind me. Creepy as Hades."

Michaelides swirled the wine in his glass, his bulk straining his chair as he leaned back, and glanced at Virgil. "What?"

Virgil averted his eyes to the scuffed tile floor. "Um, do—"

"Before you answer that," said Michaelides, leaning forward, "tell me this: you ever get a call, middle of the night, about a home invasion? You show up and see some hulking guy threatening a woman and her kids with a spear? Husband's on the floor, bleeding, probably dead."

Virgil blinked. "N—"

"And then the big guy sees you, and you know it's just you and him? And in that moment, you know only one of the two of you is going to walk out of that house alive? And you know if it's not you, that woman and her kids aren't coming out, either? You ever do anything like that?"

Virgil swallowed. "No."

"Of course you haven't. Well, I have. So what I don't get is why anybody decided you ought to come to our department and start telling us what to do. We already solved crimes before you came along. Plenty of times, there wasn't any evidence, but we knew who did it. You can always tell. I caught one just the other day. He was robbing people's houses. Had a nice spree going. He'd still be doing it if we had to wait for people like you to find evidence on him. You didn't even get your little detective degree, did you?"

"No."

"Something happened there," said Officer Tektón. "I forget what it was. School closed down or something."

"Sort of," said Virgil. "It was just the first year of the program. We only had one professor, and he got murdered partway through the second semester, so...they closed the program and gave us participation certificates."

Michaelides grinned. "Hilarious. Well, after you prove you're worthless, we can go back to solving cases the right way. Anyway, what do you want?"

Virgil wished he could hide. If not for the debt he owed to Manikas, he would have. He pressed his hands flat against his slacks. "Sorry, just, do you know where Kostas and Collias are? I wanted to talk to them."

"That's *Officers* Kostas and Collias to you." Michaelides shrugged and leaned back in his chair. "They're on the way back from arresting someone. Whether they'll talk to you, though..."

"Okay. I'll wait." Virgil stood with his back to the counter, trying to look natural while he listened to the officers, hoping Michaelides would say nothing more to him.

"Anyway," said Tektón. "You know, Manikas was pretty vocal about priests not belonging in law enforcement. You think Patroklus might've...?" Tektón mimed a spear thrust.

Michaelides laughed. "That would be hilarious. Patroklus with a spear? I guess he might've gotten someone to do it for him, though. You can see it in his eyes. There's something wild in there."

Virgil had seen no such thing in the priest. *Does that mean Michaelides is really perceptive? Or that I'm not?*

At that moment, the front doors burst open, and a man slammed face-first into the floor. As he fought to rise to his knees, he was shoved back down by two officers.

Kostas and Collias.

"This man is under arrest," Kostas announced to the room, stretching his huge chest, "for..." He looked to his partner. "What did we arrest him for?"

Collias shrugged meaty shoulders. "I don't know if we've charged him yet."

"Well, his neighbors said he was an atheist. That'll do."

Virgil watched as the officers hauled the man to his feet. Bruises had already formed on the man's face, and he staggered even with the support of the officers. Virgil decided it might be prudent to wait before speaking to Kostas and Collias.

"Hey, guys," Michaelides said from behind him. "Virgil here wanted to talk to you."

Virgil's heart skipped, but he steadied himself against the counter. "Um, hello."

The officers glared at him. Kostas shook his head. "Virgil Glezos. The guy voted most likely to be the victim of road rage. What are you doing here?"

"Oh," said Virgil. "You all look busy. Maybe I..."

Kostas dropped his side of the criminal, leaving Collias to support the man's entire weight. "Just say it."

"Um." Virgil took a breath. "I was going through Nicholas Manikas's file, and—"

"Already bored." Kostas waved his hand. "Get to the point."

Virgil swallowed. "Why did you two arrest the Manikas brothers?"

Kostas and Collias shared a glance and broke into laughter. Kostas shook his head. "Zeus, that was perfect. Their neighbor called about a noise complaint. So we show up and, right in the front yard, the older brother is sitting on Nicholas's back while the other is punching Nicholas in the head."

Virgil recalled a similar pair of bullies during his school years. For the next week, he'd slept sitting up because laying his head on a pillow sent shooting pain through his skull.

Kostas paused as though waiting for a reaction, then shrugged. "Guess you had to be there. Anyway, we thought it would be funny to have it on Nicholas's record that he was being picked on."

Collias chuckled. "His brothers were pissed about being arrested. I thought they were going to fight us. Their mother told them if they fought police officers, they would bring dishonor to their platoon."

Kostas snorted and kicked the alleged atheist's leg. "They listened to their mother."

Virgil blinked. He was missing some of the humor here.

"We let them go, of course," said Collias. "No charges."

"Yeah. If we charged everyone who picked on someone small, all the strong people would be in jail, and the Alliance would be run by weaklings."

Virgil could see their point. He would make a terrible senator. "Do you think the brothers wanted to kill Nicholas Manikas?"

"Weird question," said Collias.

"Maybe they did." Kostas shook his head. "Maybe not. We didn't ask them."

"Okay." Virgil had at least gotten his first two suspects. Nicholas had gotten into an altercation with his brothers over something unknown, something that could potentially have led the brothers to commit fratricide. More, the brothers hadn't seemed daunted at the prospect of fighting police officers.

"You done?" asked Collias.

"Yes," said Virgil. "Yes. Sorry. I'm done." He turned to go to his office, but was halted by Kostas's voice.

"Hey, Virgil." Kostas grabbed the criminal's arm and jerked him upright. "This is going to be you someday. We're just waiting."

"Yeah." Collias smacked the criminal in the head. "Just give us an excuse to arrest you."

Virgil retreated toward the stairs. "I, um, I'm not going to do that." He hurried to his office.

His office, about half the size of a closet, felt like an oasis within the police department. Whereas the other offices had martial decorations similar to those in Manikas's apartment, Virgil's had only a desk and chair, a few textbooks, his academy participation certificate, and a photograph of his parents' tombstones resting next to each other on a grassy hillside. Simple and nonthreatening.

Virgil set Manikas's folder on the desk and grabbed the gyro from one of the drawers. The smell of yogurt and fresh vegetables permeated the small space as he collapsed into his chair. Years ago, he would have enjoyed the smell. Now, it was just a byproduct of the fuel he needed to survive. He took a bite without tasting it.

Manikas's funeral was in two days. That would be a good opportunity to interview the suspects. Until then, Virgil could study the body in the examination room, look into the brothers' files, and research more rituals for Patroklus to perform.

Michaelides and Tektón seemed suspicious of the priest. Patroklus could have been involved in the murder. His ritual hadn't revealed any clues. Maybe he had sabotaged it.

Virgil had three suspects now. This was great.

Chrysanthe will understand why I have to miss her show tonight, right? I can make it up to her by attending her next show. If I bring justice to a murder victim, but sacrifice doing something for Chrysanthe, does it make me a terrible person?

Probably.

Sighing, he took a last bite of gyro and headed to the examination lab. Then he stopped. He knew how he could see Chrysanthe's show.

THREE

SWEAT TICKED ITS way down Virgil's cheek. The enclosed stadium had no air conditioning, and the combination of summer temperatures and packed people kept the place sweltering. He shifted position. His butt had grown numb from sitting on a stone slab for over half an hour.

His contact was late. Virgil glanced to his right, past the others in his row, toward the aisle. No one approached.

"Virgil Glezos?"

Virgil looked up at the bulky man leaning over him. "That's me. I saved you a space." He gestured to an empty section of stone slab next to him, one of the few remaining vacant spots.

The man raised his voice to be heard over the sound of hundreds of conversations. "Antonio Kaliokles. Principal at the School of Achilles in Arestia." He extended a meaty hand.

Virgil shook the hand. "Virg— Right, you already know."

"Weird place to meet." Antonio gestured to the empty stage many meters below. "A dance show?"

Virgil thought it was clever, meeting at Chrysanthe's show so he could fulfill both his work and familial obligations. He hoped to speak to her afterward.

"The senator is speaking, too." Virgil was curious about the speech, since Senator Kelipapalous had voted to give certificates to the homicide detective students after their professor's murder. Maybe the senator would mention the new profession.

"Yeah, sure, it's still a dance. Why here?"

Virgil remembered Tektón's comments about the priest's potential involvement in the case. He kept his voice low so the people in the row below them couldn't hear. "I'm not sure I can trust everyone at the office, so I thought it would be better to meet somewhere else."

"You into some conspiracy shit, then?" Antonio settled beside Virgil and removed a thin stack of papers from the inside of his coat. "That's cool. I've got the school records for the Manikas brothers, like you asked."

Virgil moved to accept the documents, but Antonio withdrew them. "Sorry," said Virgil. "Wasn't thinking."

After making certain none of the audience members were paying attention to him, he pulled out a thin folder he'd been sitting on and handed it to Antonio. Although Virgil risked a prison sentence for letting a civilian see police records, Antonio had refused to meet here otherwise.

"Great." Antonio handed the papers to Virgil. "I've always hated Dmitry. Can't wait to see what dirt you all have on him."

The stadium lights subsided, flooding the area in darkness. Conversations faded. Virgil looked up as a spotlight popped on, illuminating a tiny section of the stage. A lone dancer, wrapped in a tight toga and wearing a garland about her head, emerged into the light while accompanied by soft drums and a flute. She frolicked until three dancers, dressed in streaming European garments, attacked from the shadows. Drums pounded, the flute became aggressive, and more Greek dancers appeared. Lights burst on in quick succession to cover the entire stage, and a battle ensued. No Chrysanthe yet.

While watching the show with his peripheral vision, Virgil turned to the documents Antonio had provided, squinting to read the text in the pale illumination from the distant spotlight. Grades, discipline reports… He read each page in detail before flipping to the next.

"When is this going to be over?" The man in the row ahead of Virgil didn't remove his eyes from the proceedings during his complaint.

The woman next to him patted his shoulder. "You'll survive, dear."

A man on his other side chuckled. "At least if we're having to watch dancing, we get to look at hot women." The two men shared a laugh, but the woman stiffened.

On the stage, the Europeans had huddled together in a tight form. They broke apart to reveal a bright golden dancer. When the golden dancer spread her arms and leaped forward, the other European dancers formed a mushroom cloud expanding from her.

Oh. Chrysanthe must have choreographed a dance about the Greek Alliance obtaining nuclear technology from the Europeans.

"Anything good?" Antonio whispered.

"Yeah, they're really talented." Virgil flushed and looked down at the papers. "Um, I mean, not yet."

He continued reading. Manikas had received many punishments throughout his schooling, most for disrespecting his elders. His peers had also beaten him many times, resulting in more disciplinary action against him since he hadn't won the fights. His school experience sounded similar to Virgil's.

More interesting were the frequent altercations with his older brothers between classes. It seemed they had a history of assaulting him. *Could their bullying have progressed to murder, perhaps provoked by Nicholas fighting back?*

Virgil turned to Antonio. "Did Nicholas Manikas have any enemies?"

Antonio shrugged. "Probably. Everyone has enemies in school."

And yet, no one knew of specific enemies. Such a lack implied either that Manikas's murderer had struck at random, or that Manikas had secret enemies.

Onstage, the Greeks retreated from the golden dancer as she circled them. Their movements had become cautious, confined, as the golden dancer came ever closer.

Then Chrysanthe burst from the wings in a tight lab coat. She engaged the golden dancer, at first with tentative feints and then increasingly faster turns and steps. The combat continued for several minutes as the Greeks and Europeans surrounded Chrysanthe and the golden dancer in a circle that continually contracted and expanded. Several times, the golden dancer lifted Chrysanthe into the air. Each time, Chrysanthe pushed away, and the attack began anew. When she finally defeated the golden dancer, she placed a garland over her kneeling opponent's head.

A celebration began, with the music cheerful for the first time since the show's beginning. Once the light flute ended its melody, ominous drums rose. The Europeans returned and swarmed Chrysanthe. They carried her from the protesting Greeks and chained her to an imaginary rock. A child dancer entered the stage in a dark feathery costume and swooped toward Chrysanthe. The child reached into Chrysanthe's side and held aloft something that looked like a liver. As Chrysanthe writhed, the lights and music faded to nothing.

Virgil waited for something further to happen, but the orchestra remained silent and the performers seemed to not even breathe. The audience had fallen still, without even the rustle of clothes to mar the purity of the moment.

Then applause erupted, filling the stadium. Virgil joined. They had loved it. They were cheering for his sister. They realized how talented she was.

The clapping continued for over a minute before fading. Chrysanthe led the dancers in a synchronized bow before they filed offstage in a sinuous motion.

Antonio set down the folder. "This was a waste. Didn't find anything interesting. You done with those papers?"

Virgil's grip tightened. "I might keep them. They could be evidence."

"Not happening." Antonio held out a thick hand. "School property. I'm not even supposed to let you see them."

"Okay."

Antonio could pull his punch and still leave Virgil unconscious. They exchanged papers, Virgil sitting on his folder again, as another figure emerged onstage.

"Guess I can't leave yet." Antonio grimaced and settled back onto the stone slab. "People will think I just came for the dance."

A new round of applause greeted City-Priest Argyrios as he strode on stage with his dark-blue robe billowing after him like a storm cloud. He faced the audience with a blank expression reminiscent of Patroklus's.

Why did Arestia's City-Priest agree to introduce the senator? City-Priests are always complaining about the volumes of their workloads, so why did he consider a minor task like this to be important?

"Thank you," said Argyrios in a rumbling voice. "Our guest tonight is Senator Kelipapalous, who has traveled from the current senate chamber in Sparta. He is serving his second term as Arestia's senator and is one of the most influential members of the Appropriations Committee. He has successfully argued for the reduction of funding to the arts, hospitality, and religious research during his tenure. Please give him an appropriate welcome to the stage."

The senator, whose short dark hair and strong chin made him look like an actor or a newly retired soldier, emerged to more applause than Argyrios had received. "Thank you for that warm introduction, City-Priest. I'll take it from here."

Argyrios gave him a curt nod before exiting the stage. The senator straightened his formal toga and cape, and waited until the clapping died.

"Now, folks, I would love to give a speech about how great the Alliance is. I would love to give a speech about our moral purity. I would love to give a speech about how we are strong and that we will conquer any adversary. That would be a pretty good speech, right?" The senator shook his head. "But that speech would be a lie."

Virgil blinked. If anyone else had said what the senator had just said, they would be killed. Most senators probably held similar opinions and worse, but they knew enough to say nothing.

When the senator spoke again, his voice reverberated throughout the stadium. "For centuries, our alliance has been sliding backward. We used to control the world through magic. Europe, Asia, and northern Africa were ours. We built them, gave them infrastructure and the tools for learning. We gave them agriculture and stability. We gave them the salvation of truth, the knowledge of our gods. In short, we turned them from savages into civilized people. And they repaid us by abandoning us, by behaving like ungrateful children.

"How did it happen? How did they rob us of our rightful territory? No offense to City-Priest Argyrios and the temple system, but it wasn't through magic. They have none. No, our enemies did it with technology."

Kelipapalous strode to the left side of the stage. "I would love to give a speech about our technological breakthroughs and how we will overtake our enemies. But you know and I know that would also be a lie. We have been behind for centuries. We didn't get our first car until almost a hundred years after the European Alliance invented them. We didn't build our first plane until over twenty years after the European Alliance invented them. And I don't know about you folks, but I don't always feel safe flying in our planes."

People shifted in their seats, and a low buzz of whispered conversation filled the stadium. Virgil expected them to walk out or shout obscenities or throw rocks. But the audience quieted when Kelipapalous spoke again.

"Who developed the first nuclear weapon? Europe. It took us fifty years before we built our first nuclear bomb. Are you noticing a pattern here? We have been left behind because our technology isn't any good. Until we fix that, we will always be left behind.

"Some of my fellow senators want us to follow the same course that has led us nowhere for the past thousand years. They throw away our tax money on frivolous programs. Now, there are a lot of programs that sound good when those senators manipulate the words and twist the facts, but you know and I know that we don't need those programs. We know they don't make our country better. Even more than that, we don't have the money to waste on those programs. We have been living in dangerous times for centuries, so we need to focus our efforts, and I think you all know by now where we should focus them."

Kelipapalous paced the stage, snapping from one direction to the other so that the bottom of his cloak never touched his back. "We haven't won a war in one hundred and thirty-five years. For a race of warriors, that is beyond pathetic. We are Greeks. We are the favored of the gods.

"The problem, of course, is that our enemies no longer use swords and spears, and we haven't adapted. Instead, my fellow senators have put our tax money into public temples.

"Public. Temples.

"No offense to City-Priest Argyrios and the temple system, but do we need better temples? Will those keep us strong or help us defeat our enemies? They haven't in over a hundred years. My fellow senators have put our tax money into training priests. That has also failed us. And more recently, when the Senate voted on a new use of funds, did they choose to fund something useful, like developing better weapons or more nuclear missiles? They did not. Now there are a lot of examples of wasteful programs I could choose from, but the stupidest, most ridiculous, most pansy-assed, was funding the creation of a new profession: homicide detectives."

Virgil's hands clamped around his legs. But...the senator had voted to give participation certificates to the Academy students in the homicide-detective program. *Why is he reversing his stance?*

"We already have ways of catching the bad guys. The police patrol our streets and have maintained order for hundreds of years. I already felt safe, and I know you all did, too. No offense to City-Priest Argyrios and the temple system, but the temple's support for detectives baffles me. Of course, now that we have detectives, *priests* are more involved in investigations. They've gained more authority in law enforcement. Are you seeing what I'm seeing?"

Is he implying some sort of...power play by the priests? Virgil frowned. And Kelipapalous had not only linked the priests and homicide detectives, he had stoked the crowd's hatred of both groups. Virgil imagined being hunted through the streets by mobs who intended to beat him to death. It would be like school all over again.

Michaelides and Tektón had mentioned Manikas's dislike of the priests. *Did Manikas's outspokenness about priests' roles in law enforcement make him a threat?* Virgil decided he would ask Patroklus to perform another ritual. Either the ritual would work and Virgil would gain more information for the investigation, or it wouldn't work and he would have more reason to suspect Patroklus.

Kelipapalous continued, pounding his fist for each point. "Our alliance is in danger of obsolescence and extinction. We need technology. We need weapons. We need to be able to defeat our enemies.

"My fellow senators would tell you that the Alliance is better for lagging behind in technology, that we compensate by being stronger. They would tell you that we are braver than our enemies. They would tell you that the gods have a plan for us. I would love to give that speech.

"Well, it's partially true. We are braver than anyone else. We're Greeks. How could we not be the world's bravest? And the gods do have a plan for us. But their plan isn't for us to languish while others triumph. Their plan is for us to surge forward, to leave behind anything not directly related to our goals. We can't waste our time or money on useless programs. We must build our military capabilities and strike our enemies mercilessly. We must merge our magic with technology.

"The gods have a plan for us, and that plan is conquest."

Cheering erupted for several minutes, drowning all thought and damaging eardrums. While Virgil's ears still rang in the aftermath, Kelipapalous continued.

"I have proposed, along with some of my more progressive colleagues, a bill to be introduced at the end of the week that will redirect funding from unimportant programs to areas where the Alliance needs change."

At the end of Blasphemer's Week, then, Virgil might no longer have a job. His fate rested in the hands of senators, and a lot of them were just as ignorant as Kelipapalous.

He might have a chance, though. A good counterargument to the bill would be a successfully solved case. If Virgil could find Manikas's murderer before then…

No. I've never succeeded in anything before, and I doubt I'll suddenly start now.

The senator continued, elucidating the points in the bill at length. After his speech, the senator received a standing ovation. Virgil felt obligated to join. The rest of the audience hooted and clapped with ecstatic frenzy, as though they'd already won a war.

"I hope we go after the Norwegians first," said Antonio after Kelipaplous exited the stage. "They've always pissed me off. The whole concept of Ragnarok and a snake as big as the world is ridiculous."

"Um." *Does the senator really want to incite a war? The Alliance hasn't been a military threat in nearly a century, but the senator wants to abandon our uneasy peace and my profession for what? Some kind of dominance contest with our former territories that we're probably going to lose?*

"Well, I'm heading out." Antonio tucked his papers into his tunic. "Interesting speech. Not so good for you, though." He pushed his way through the other people in their row to reach the line heading to the exit.

The topic of war seemed to have excited the audience. Most of the men talked to each other in loud voices, proclaiming their disdain for other nationalities as they began filing down the stone steps to the exit. Virgil shuffled to his place in line and tried to block the jingoism from his thoughts.

A few minutes later, he reached the stadium's lowest level. Chrysanthe stood beside the stage, speaking to a small group of reporters and camerapeople. Even from several meters away, he could hear her chatter at high speed and volume. She'd always been able to charm even the grimmest of listeners.

Virgil approached, stopping behind the circle of reporters. "Chrysanthe!"

She glanced up from her conversation, her eyes widening. "Virgil! You came." She held up two fingers. "I'll be with you in a couple minutes, after these people are done making me famous."

Virgil retreated out of earshot and leaned against the wall while waiting for her to finish. She seemed to enjoy herself, answering questions in a steady stream of pleasant high-pitched syllables that washed over him and reminded him of the few good moments of his childhood.

After she finished having fun talking to the reporters, she would have to talk to him. It would be a big letdown for her. She probably had to put a lot of effort into being nice to him. She was good at it, though. Maybe because of all the acting she had to do while dancing.

When the reporters had finished the interview, Chrysanthe approached him and settled against the wall next to him. "I'm glad you made it," she said in a grave voice, her eyes downcast.

"Yeah," said Virgil. "I am, too."

She continued to slouch for several moments, saying nothing, before breaking into a grin and standing straight with her arms wide. "Were you really planning to keep us standing like that the whole time? You know, some people hug their relatives when they meet. It's true."

Virgil submitted. It was weird that she wanted to hug him. She was probably doing it out of familial obligation.

"I know our Greek traditions are strange and frightening," Chrysanthe said as she stood straight again, "but learning them will allow you to disguise yourself as a human more effectively."

"Okay."

Chrysanthe's face tightened. "I was hoping for a laugh. Or at least a less dour expression. Is something wrong? You're acting stranger than usual."

He always made people uncomfortable.

"Sorry. I'm fine. You did a good job. You really changed the feel of the show when you came out." Virgil waved to indicate the stage. "The choreography was very good, too."

"Well, thank you. I spent a long time on it."

"Why did you agree to do a performance for a senator who doesn't support the arts?" Virgil regretted the words immediately after he said them.

But Chrysanthe laughed. "Wasn't it hilarious? I came up with the plot right after the City-Priest asked our company to do the performance. Since Kelipapalous hates the arts, I choreographed a dance about a recent Greek military success. If he praises the performance, it will be interpreted as praise of dances in general. If he insults the dance, he comes across as insulting the military victory."

Virgil didn't know how to respond, so he tried to smile. He probably hadn't succeeded, since Chrysanthe gave him a strange look.

"Anyway," she said, "it's good to see you. It's been awhile."

"Yeah," said Virgil. "How are you and Matthaios?"

"Great. We're great." She paused a moment, seeming to study his face. "You should come with us to temple sometime."

"I don't—"

"It'll be good for you. There are good people there, and it makes you feel a lot better about your life. It's very healthy to be in touch with your spiritual side."

"Maybe, but—"

"Think about it. We'd love it if you came." She gestured to the stage. "Sorry about the senator's speech. I don't think he likes your profession."

"Yeah," said Virgil. "And a lot of people agreed with him."

"Still, he's only one senator out of a hundred and twenty. Maybe the others will want to spend taxes on kitten orphanages or something. They can't all have massive inferiority complexes."

Virgil thought about his coworkers. "Maybe."

"So how's work going?"

He shrugged. "Better. The chief let me stay on the most recent case."

"Really?"

"Yeah. I think it's because the victim was an ex-police officer. I've been looking at the body and figured out that he died early this morning. I also went through his police records and his school records. So far, I only have three suspects, but I might be able to find more. I still have some files to look into tonight."

Chrysanthe grinned. "This is the most excited I've seen you since…ever, I guess. It sounds like you've found the right career for you."

"Maybe."

"I remember we talked, and I was worried I had pressured you into something you would hate."

"Being a detective was my idea."

"Yeah, but you wouldn't have done it if I hadn't pushed you into going to an academy for *something*. I'm glad it worked for you." She gave him a quick hug. "Mom would be proud. I'll be praying for you."

Virgil grimaced. "That's alright. You don't have to pray for me. I don't th—"

"It'll help. You'll see. Oh, hey, I know Kelipapalous is a moron, but even morons can say something intelligent on occasion. Do you think you can you use technology for solving your case?"

Virgil considered. "Maybe. I don't know if I could get access to nukes, though, and I don't think they would help."

She laughed. "I was thinking more about cameras. That kind of thing." She glanced at her watch.

She's trying to find out if she's already spent a socially acceptable amount of time with me.

"I'm sorry," she said, "but I really have to go. Matthaios and I are meeting some of his coworkers for dinner. He was going to come to the show, but they had some emergency work teaching thing. I guess some guards were high while they were on shift the other night, so the whole lab had to have training on how to not take drugs while they're at work."

"Oh. Okay."

"I'm really glad you came, though. You should stop by our place someday. Any time is fine."

"Okay."

"Hope to see you soon. Good luck on the case." She gave him another hug and hurried to one of the doors behind the stage.

Virgil stood against the wall for a moment, letting the loneliness seep back into its customary place, before heading to the exit. *I'm such an idiot. I'm supposed to be making*

up *for getting Manikas killed, and I spent too much time
here, and I have so much work to do, and if Kelipapalous and
everyone else who lives in this city-state get their way, I don't
have enough time to do it.*

FOUR

WHEN VIRGIL REACHED his cramped apartment in the early morning hours, he thought he would collapse into instant sleep on his threadbare couch. Every part of him wanted oblivion, from his trembling hands to his aching eyes to his stumbling brain, but minute after minute passed, and he still lay on the couch as alert as if he'd downed a liter of tea.

He glanced at his watch: eight hours until his therapy appointment. Not much time, considering he needed to make food for the day, probably shower, and definitely change clothes.

He sat up. *Why do I deserve therapy? Why do I deserve to feel better? Why do I even deserve sleep? It's my fault Manikas died. He's never going to sleep again. Why should I get to?*

I guess I can't avenge him if I don't get sleep.

Maybe, he decided, reading would serve as a soporific. His current book, *A History of Modern Religion*, lay spine-upward, with its back cover wedged between the couch arm and the wall. Virgil reached for it like a drowning sailor grasping for a lifesaver.

Though he had stopped last night at a section about the evolution of sacrificial practices, he remembered reading, a few nights ago, a passage about Blasphemer's Week. His foggy brain couldn't recall the details now, which meant it must have been a boring passage. Maybe even boring enough to induce sleep. He opened the book and squinted in the room's underachieving light, flipping through pages until he found the section.

> A sole reference[12] exists of an annual assembly of the gods within their home atop Mount Olympus. Such unity amongst the Olympians and the various Earth-dwelling deities is not told of in other sources, and yet this belief is the one most adhered to in common practice. Paintings abound, depicting the scene of gods of all types, from mighty Zeus to aloof Athena to debaucherous Dionysus, and even to grim Hades, gathered in some semblance of order in a grand marble chamber or upon the mountain's peak, overlooking humanity. Some mischief-makers even consider this time period from Hera 29 through Eris 5 as a holiday of sorts to engage in pranks or minor blasphemies whilst the otherwise-watchful eyes of the gods are occupied.

THOUGH STATED IN the driest way possible, the passage reinforced Virgil's question about Patroklus's ritual yesterday: if the gods were away, how could magic work this week? Virgil had already set an appointment for the priest to perform another investigative ritual. He could use the opportunity to ask about the foundations of magical power.

Virgil returned to the book. After reading a few more pages, he found himself nodding off. His eyes eased closed, and his head drooped.

Then he snapped to alertness. Sighing, he continued reading. The pattern repeated again. Then again. Then again. He set the book aside.

If he couldn't sleep, he needed to be working the case. But he couldn't do anything until the ritual, and he couldn't concentrate on anything for more than thirty seconds. He softly pounded his head against the couch's arm.

Even when I'm exhausted, I fail at sleeping.

Circumstances might force him to take a sleeping pill, which came with a new set of perils. But not yet. He still had options.

He glanced at the dartboard next to the door. Heaving himself to his aching feet, he collected the darts from the board, stood in the worn spot on the carpet beside the couch, readied the first dart, whispered a quick prayer to Hebe, and threw.

The dart hit the wall.

Another failure. Of course. Normally, he could come close to the spot where he had aimed. He walked to the board, realizing when he arrived that he should have thrown the other two darts in his hand. *Oh, well. Would have missed with those, too.*

Wait. Something was different. The area of the wall between the door and the dartboard…

He rubbed his bleary eyes to make certain they weren't distorting what he saw. But no, the section of peeling paint he now saw was different than the section of peeling paint that was normally visible. Sometime between when he had left his apartment early yesterday morning and when he had returned early this morning, the dartboard's position had shifted.

And his book. When he'd picked it up tonight, the back cover had been wedged between the couch and wall. But when he'd set it down yesterday, it was the *front* cover that had been wedged between the couch and wall.

Virgil checked the bookshelf next to the dartboard. *Titanomachy Without the Titans: Temple Politics* had switched places with *Dionysus Distilled: The God's Influence on Modern Social Functions. Athens and Sparta and the Divided Alliance* stuck out farther than before.

Someone had searched his apartment. Virgil tightened his grip on the darts. *I'm definitely not falling asleep tonight. But who would have searched my place? The killer? Maybe the police?*

Why would they think I'm important or competent enough to bother with?

Whoever had done it, the timing implied the invasion was related to the case. *Are they going to return? Are they still here?*

After a frenzied few minutes of examining potential hiding places, he confirmed his watchers had left. But they knew where he lived. He decided this might be a good night to not take a sleeping pill.

But he needed sleep. He needed to sleep so badly. And nothing else was working. But if he used a pill and the invader returned, he wouldn't hear them. He could be killed in his sleep.

Which, really, is a better fate than I deserve or should expect. The constant fatigue, the perpetual failures, the way everyone looked at him with pity or scorn, all replaced by the peaceful misery of Hades.

There were times, before he enrolled in the academy, when he would stare at the ceiling or floor or wall for hours, imagining how it would feel to cut into his skin and slip into death. Those thoughts had followed periods where he had experienced increasing difficulty falling asleep. He hadn't noticed until just now, but the same pattern had crept upon him over the last few days. A little harder to sleep each night, a little more pain, a little more fog enshrouding his mood, until now, when he could welcome the cool touch of a knife. A little slit, peeling his skin aside. Like Nicholas's chest wound.

Virgil shivered. Those thoughts... He needed that therapy appointment tomorrow. He had probably needed it years ago.

And that was another reason he couldn't take a sleeping pill. It would make him oversleep.

He leaned his head against the bookshelf. Every need's solution contradicted another need.

Then he noticed the magazine on the bottom shelf, concealed between two thick books. He pulled it free, staring at the graphic nudity and feeling emptiness.

Maybe I can get masturbating over with, and that will relax me enough to sleep.

He carried the magazine to the bathroom.

FIVE

VIRGIL WRENCHED THE door open, gasping as he rushed into the office. The therapist, Dr. Perikiades, looked up with distilled irritation.

"Sorry." Virgil took another breath. "I'm really sorry. I was going to be here on time, but I couldn't sleep, and I was so exhausted, I had to take a pill, and I overslept, and—"

Dr. Perikiades raised a hand. "Sit down."

Virgil lowered himself onto the light-green couch, straightening his wrinkled tunic. *Do I smell?* He hadn't had time to shower, but he had put on cologne. Maybe Dr. Perikiades wouldn't notice.

If Perikiades did notice, he said nothing. The therapist, a man of medium build, wearing a dark tailored tunic and slacks, sat in a chair at the far end of the room. He held a pad of paper and a pen over his crossed legs. Paintings adorned his ocean-blue walls, showing a variety of scenes: crowded battles, empty fields, naked frolickers, Zeus atop his throne, and more. A sea-breeze odor permeated the air.

Virgil placed his hands on his lap and leaned forward. Dr. Perikiades was judging him. *What does my posture tell him about me? Would a confident person sit like this? Leaning forward makes me appear self-assured, right? Are my shoulders straight enough?* "Like this?"

Dr. Perikiades raised an eyebrow over the rim of his glasses. "That's fine." He jotted something down on the pad of paper.

I didn't sound confident. I knew it. Maybe I need to speak in a deeper voice.

"We are twenty-five minutes into your session," said the therapist, "so we won't accomplish as much as is customary. Let's see what we can salvage. Why are you here?"

Virgil clasped his hands more tightly. "Should I not have come? Since I was late? I'm sorry. I'll be on time next time."

Perikiades shook his head. "That's not what I meant. Why are you seeing a therapist?"

"Oh. Sorry." Virgil tapped his fingers against his hands. He had arrived late and had given the wrong answer to the first question. If this were a test, he was failing.

Is it a test?

Virgil shifted. "My sister, Chrysanthe, she's been saying for years that I should see a therapist. I would have started a couple weeks ago when I took this new job, but the closest thing they have is a physical therapist, so I—"

"You're answering the wrong question. What is your problem?"

"Oh." Virgil blinked. "Depression."

"I see." The man scribbled something onto his paper. "I've never had a male client before. I'm not sure if my normal techniques will work on you." His eyes traversed the span of Virgil's body. "Then again, they might. You say Chrysanthe has been telling you for years to see someone, but that you haven't done so until now. Why did you choose this time, in particular?"

"I...I guess because of work. I thought it might help if I were more...confident?"

"Hm. What is your job?"

"Homicide detective."

"Good profession. Thinking and evidence over strength and punching." Perikiades nodded. "Keeps the chiefs honest. I guess you know that some chiefs, instead of finding the real killers, convict their senator's political opponents. Deplorable."

"Yeah, I guess so." *Was that the right answer? Is he keeping track of how many questions I answer incorrectly?*

Perikiades gestured to Virgil. "Now, you made an active choice to enter the detective profession. Why do you think you chose that career among all the other possibilities?"

Virgil frowned and looked at his hands while considering. "Well, my father was killed when I was young."

"That's great. That's something." More notes. "It's not great that your father is dead, obviously, unless he died in glorious combat. He didn't, did he?"

Virgil remembered sitting in the kitchen as his mother explained the circumstances of his father's death. Virgil had been seven years old. Old enough to realize he had lost something precious, but too young to know how to cope. Kids at school used the opportunity to further humiliate him. That first day, when Claudius told him a boy growing up without a father would always be a coward, was the first time Virgil had contemplated suicide.

Reliving that experience, Virgil clutched his wrist and forced himself to concentrate on the therapist. "No. He didn't. Dad was stabbed in a robbery."

"Right. So that's unfortunate, but it is good that we have a partial motive for your choice of profession. Note that it's only a partial motive. There is also something deeper about you that made you seek out this type of employment. Some core part of your personality. That means something is capable of giving you purpose. We need to find out what that is and apply it to the rest of your life."

"Is it really that easy?"

"Ohhh, no." Perikiades shook his head. "It will get worse before it gets better. And you'll likely overestimate how much better you're getting. And you might never recover before you make a terminal decision. Many paths lie before you, and I'm curious which you'll take."

Virgil nodded. "Me, too."

The therapist studied him for several moments, then flipped to the next page in his notes. "When was the last time you laughed? A genuine, happy laugh?"

"I..." *At the academy, maybe?* He didn't remember laughing then. Certainly not at his jobs. *At home, when I was a kid?* Maybe before Dad had died. That was so long ago, and Virgil didn't really remember. *As a baby, before I could form memories?*

"Right." The therapist scribbled more notes. "Even worse than my low expectations."

Virgil wanted to slink out the doorway.

Perikiades looked up again. "What drives you, Virgil? What makes you wake up every day?"

Work? Hope that I'll someday find someone to talk to or some meaning to my life? Maybe only because my alarm clock rang?

"I'm sorry." Virgil looked at the floor. "I don't know why I wake up every day. I don't have a reason to live. I don't even have a reason to die."

"And yet, you still go to work. You're trying to find a murderer. You still eat. You still take care of yourself. To an extent. Obviously, you haven't showered this morning."

Virgil felt his face turn red.

"The point is, something about you hasn't completely given up yet. We'll return to this subject another day. Until then, give it some thought." Dr. Perikiades leaned back and placed his arms on the chair's armrests. "Let's delve into the basics. Toward what deity do you feel you have the most affinity?"

Virgil stared at his shoes. He had told no one, other than his sister. Even she had been shocked at his confession years ago. If anyone else knew... He thought of the man Kostas and Collias had arrested, the prisons, the honor killings of family members. "Are my answers confidential? You wouldn't tell any—"

"They are confidential. Unless I deem you to be a threat to others and..." Perikiades pursed his lips and gestured to Virgil. "I doubt that will be my conclusion. So why are you embarrassed? Is it one of the sex gods?"

No, I can't trust him to keep it secret. "Um, no. This week, it's Hebe."

"*Hebe*? The goddess of youth?" Perikiades jotted something into his notebook, shaking his head. "Sorry, Virgil, but you're not that young anymore. How old are you? Late thirties?"

Virgil blinked. "Twenty-three."

"Oh." Perikiades's pen scribbled across the paper. "My apologies. You keep praying to her. Maybe things will work out."

Virgil's eyes moved to the door. *How many minutes have passed?* "I was hoping therapy would let me analyze people better. Suspects and such. And maybe it would give me more confidence, and that would help me find out who killed Nicholas Manikas."

"Confidence?" Dr. Perikiades aimed his pen at Virgil. "Look at the way you're sitting. You're trying to minimize your presence. You're trying to take up as little room as possible."

Virgil looked down. His knees touched, his arms lay across his legs, and he had hunched forward. He forced himself to sit straight, spread his legs out. It felt weird.

"Confident people take up as much space as they can. They're not worried about making space for other people. They want other people to make space for them."

"I just don't know if that's me."

Dr. Perikiades shrugged. "Do you want to continue being depressed?"

Virgil tried to imagine life without depression. *What if I had confidence? What if people liked me? What if I enjoyed going to work or eating or venturing downtown?*

The therapist pursed his lips. "You're uncertain. Not a good sign. Well, let's continue. I think we have a lot we need to talk about. You're an interesting challenge, Mr. Glezos. I like that about you."

To Virgil, it felt as though, with each answered question, he added weeks to the time he would have to spend in therapy. "Do...do you have an express solution? Or maybe something we could do by correspondence? It's just, I'm busy with a case, and I—"

"No!" Perikiades slammed his notebook into his lap.

Virgil blinked and hunched forward. "Sorry! I'll stop being depressed!"

"Look, Virgil, you can't solve your case if you're not confident. You are hunting a murderer. You need to be prepared for what happens when you find that murderer."

Maybe therapy was the wrong decision. *Forcing myself to have confidence would transform me into a different person. If I were confident and likable, what other aspects of me would change?*

But those aspects would die, anyway, if he killed himself, and he didn't know how much longer he could last. Not with the way his thoughts had been going since last night.

Virgil took a breath and faced the therapist. "Okay."

SIX

VIRGIL STARED AT the corpse on the lab table. A thick white blanket covered the body, leaving only the head exposed. Despite Manikas's agonized expression, he still seemed to be having a better morning than Virgil. *Isn't therapy supposed to make you feel better?*

"You were an officer." Virgil leaned over the corpse, keeping his words to a whisper. "I doubt you ever needed therapy."

"You asked to see me?"

Virgil started and slammed into the white tiled wall behind him, letting out a squeak he would spend the rest of the day trying to forget. Patroklus stood, hands clasped, beside the metal supply shelf on the other side of the table from Virgil.

Virgil collected himself and gathered his thimbleful of pride together. "Yeah, Patroklus, thanks for coming."

Patroklus remained motionless as a statue. *Would someone involved in a murder have such an absence of reaction in the presence of their victim?*

"Um," Virgil continued, "I'm sorry to bother you, but I was looking through the catalogue yesterday, the catalogue listing all the spells priests can perform for law enforcement. I found this one, and I think it could work. Also, I've got some leads, maybe."

Virgil decided not to mention that Patroklus was one of the suspects and that this procedure was also a test for him.

"Or," said Virgil, "I have some people to talk to tomorrow. About the case. I think that counts as having leads. Anyway, I thought this would be a good approach. And it sounded as though a soul is required, and Manikas's should still be attached since we haven't coined him yet."

Patroklus's expression remained unchanged. "No apology is necessary. Requests such as these are part of my job."

From within the creases of his voluminous robe, Patroklus removed a thick bundle of cloth, folded with the immaculate precision of a god, and spread it atop the client. Once the cloth had expanded to its full length, the priest lifted the top fold to reveal a large assortment of bone slivers resting on the material in precise rows and columns. The catalogue had not specified the origins of the bones.

"You are correct," Patroklus said, "that this procedure requires the presence of a soul. However, I am uncertain it will be effective on a corpse."

"Okay." Virgil had screwed up again. His professor would have been mortified at the steady stream of failures. "We can still try, though, right?"

Patroklus glanced from Virgil to the bone slivers and back again with an arched eyebrow. Virgil blushed and took a step back.

"You do not believe." Patroklus studied the slivers.

Virgil glanced to the doorway. No one was listening. He replied in a whisper. "What do you mean?"

"You do not believe in our gods." Patroklus spoke at normal volume, and Virgil's stomach tightened. "You do not close your eyes or display proper reverence during these rituals. And yet, you ask me to perform this ritual now. Can you explain the contradiction?"

Patroklus must have seen me opening my eyes during the ritual. How much should I say? How would a priest react to hearing that someone questioned the basic premise of his career? What if Patroklus tells others? Are priests required to report unbelievers?

Virgil remembered the alleged atheist that Kostas and Collias had thrown to the floor. "Oh, I do believe."

That didn't sound convincing, even to him.

Patroklus stared. "You do not. Rather, you are uncertain. You have found no definitive proof either way. Your eyes betray you."

"I—"

Patroklus raised a hand. "Do not worry. Such evidence is inadmissible for law enforcement. Besides, if the police wanted to convict you of a crime, they need not rely on evidence."

Despite all Virgil's precautions, Patroklus knew. "I—"

"I repeat my question. If you have such doubt in the source of my power, why do you trust in my spells?"

"Well." Virgil avoided Patroklus's eyes. "Priests have been performing magic for over two thousand years. There has to be something causing it to work, but it doesn't necessarily have to be the gods. That's what I think, anyway."

"I see."

"And you performed magic yesterday when the gods are supposed to be unavailable. If the gods are required for magic, why didn't your spell fail? I mean, it sort of did since you didn't find anything, but…" Virgil stopped, realizing his words could be interpreted as questioning Patroklus's competence.

"Magic," said Patroklus, "can be performed by calling upon the essences of the gods. Though the gods are not listening, their essences are everywhere. Not even belief is required."

Patroklus extended his hand over the bone slivers. He closed his eyes, and his body relaxed.

"Do you have any evidence?" Virgil asked. "I mean, have you met Athena, or maybe a nymph or something?"

Patroklus opened his eyes and maintained a placid expression while letting his hand drop. "We do not discuss the Mysteries with those outside the priesthood." He gestured to the body. "May I?"

Virgil blinked. "Oh, yeah. Sorry."

Stupid. He had interrupted the ritual and broken Patroklus's concentration. Maybe he had even contaminated the results. Patroklus probably hated him.

The priest raised his hand over the slivers again. Virgil forced himself to remain still and braced himself for the inevitable special effects induced by the priest's powers.

"Mighty Apollo, god of truth," Patroklus said in a deadened voice. The air in the room grew thick, pressing against Virgil's chest and prickling his skin. "We beseech you to grant us knowledge from these vessels."

Unnatural warmth flooded Virgil's feet and traveled through his legs before spreading throughout his body. He shifted and scratched his arms.

Patroklus's eyelids snapped open to reveal pupils draining to pure white. Without moving his head, the priest gathered the cloth and bones together, folding and pressing the material until it was arranged as neatly as it had been after first emerging from his robe. Taking the cloth in both hands, he shook it with economical motion. Four times, lightly, back and forth, before he paused with the cloth poised above the body like an unresolved chord. Patroklus had performed every motion in the exact manner described by the catalogue.

Patroklus's voice deepened by two octaves. "Ask your question of the victim."

Virgil's mind went blank for several long seconds before he remembered the question he had prepared. "Um, who killed you?"

Upon the last syllable, Patroklus flipped the cloth open and let the bone slivers drop. They spilled across the corpse, popping along Manikas's chest or bouncing off each other until settling in their final resting places. Virgil pressed against the table and looked down at the slivers, trying to decipher something valuable from the results, but the bones appeared to be distributed at random.

"Is…is it supposed to look like that?"

The priest's eyes had regained their color. "If meaningful information were available, the slivers would spell words."

"Oh." Virgil squinted at them. He pointed at one grouping. "That kind of looks like a delta, right?"

"No."

Patroklus gathered the bones together and restored them to their precise positions in the cloth. Virgil wracked his brain for another question he could ask of the bones, but Patroklus had already folded the cloth and gathered it into his robe. The priest didn't speak to or acknowledge Virgil before gliding out of the room and passing from sight.

Watching the priest had revealed nothing. Patroklus's behavior remained as inscrutable as always, with never a slip from his impassive expression. Normally, Virgil would have counted two failed rituals as evidence for Patroklus's guilt, especially when the spell catalogue described in such florid language how effective the rituals were, but both failures had several potential explanations. Patroklus might have sabotaged the rituals, Manikas might not know who killed him, or this last ritual might not work on corpses.

Or maybe I did something to screw it up.

Virgil sighed and pulled a candy bar from his pocket while leaning over the corpse. He opened the wrapper, and a loose nut dropped onto the sheet. Virgil wiped the nut onto the floor.

Talking to Manikas's family probably wouldn't yield anything useful, either. But, given the lack of other leads, Virgil knew he needed to try. Maybe he could also examine the kitchen again.

He cursed himself for not taking photographs of the crime scene last night. He would have to do it next time someone got murdered.

He could also try to determine the exact murder weapon. There were several spear tips from previous murders in the evidence rooms in the basement. He could fetch those and compare them to the wound's shape…

"What's up, Super Sleuth?"

"You figure it out? You crack the case?"

Virgil suppressed a curse as Schirra and Stathis swaggered into the room. Stathis crossed his arms and leaned against the metal shelf while Schirra stood at the foot of the examination table and glared at Virgil.

Why do they look so pleased with themselves? Did they hear that the chief is going to remove me from the case soon?

"It...it takes a while to solve these things. I have to gather evidence and examine clues and..." Virgil faltered when Schirra smirked.

"Oh, yeah," she said in her low voice. "Sounds like you've got it all under control." She and Stathis shared a laugh.

Virgil looked at his shoes. "I still have things to try. I'm not done yet. I'm going to compare spear tips to his wound to see if I can determine the shape of the murder weapon."

Stathis cocked his head. "Couldn't you just ask the murderer when you catch him? I don't see why it's important to know what the weapon looked like, anyway."

I always do a terrible job of explaining my thoughts to people. "I'm hoping it will help me find the murderer. Have you seen the chief today?"

Schirra shrugged. "Not yet, but we're meeting him in a few. New crime scene. Another murder. Sounds like you're really busy with this case, though, and we don't need you, anyway."

A new crime could be good practice for Virgil. He could try his new techniques there and maybe not screw it up this time. "I should probably go, too. I'm supposed to be present for cases like that. I—"

"You're taking a long time with this one," said Schirra.

"Yeah," said Stathis. "When you were hired, you were supposed to help us with the investigations, but now that the chief is letting you work on them, all you're doing is slowing things down."

"Well...I mean, these things aren't fast. And I don't think—"

"Whatever." Schirra shook her head. "Maybe consider showering once in a while."

Virgil sniffed his tunic after Schirra and Stathis had strolled from the room. Should have put on more cologne. Everyone had noticed, and now they were going to think of him as the guy who never showered.

He shook his head. The shower comment wasn't the most important part of that conversation. Schirra and Stathis wanted to prevent him from going to the crime scene, but he belonged there. The chief should have ordered him to go. Maybe Virgil's performance on this case had confirmed the chief's opinions of Virgil and his profession.

Chief Dimitriou had made no secret of his preference for the old investigative methods, in which the act of gathering evidence was treated as a mere formality before the officers concocted their own conclusions, presumably from a combination of personal dislikes and made-for-television movies. Maybe the chief planned to prevent Virgil from working on cases in order to fire him for never solving anything.

Virgil's stomach fluttered. *I can't allow that, right? No. I can't. That's what my therapist would say.*

Virgil took a bite of his candy bar and wiped the crumbs from the client's sheet. He would be at that crime scene.

SEVEN

VIRGIL TOOK SHORT, shallow breaths as he clambered up the apartment building's concrete staircase. Paint peeled from the walls, and the overhead lights flickered every few seconds as though the place were auditioning to be a location in a horror movie. It seemed like an appropriate place to murder someone.

The motive was unclear, though. Apparently, the victim had served as a security guard at the Keres Lab, the same lab where Chrysanthe's husband worked. *Why would someone kill a security guard at home?* Virgil decided to take more thorough mental notes of the scene this time, so he didn't miss as many crucial details as he had at Manikas's apartment.

When he reached the second landing, he noticed the doors to Rooms 202 and 204 stood ajar. It didn't surprise him that Room 204 was open; the murder had occurred there, and the officers would have gathered inside. *But why is the adjacent unit open?*

As he paused at the top of the stairs, a crash came from within Room 202. A moment later, a dark shape slammed against the open doorway's frame before sliding to the floor and spilling into the hall. A body, crumpled into a shape no living human could assume.

Footsteps came from within the room. The killer, walking to the door.

Virgil backed toward the stairway, his legs shaking. Almost two semesters of combat training hadn't prepared him for a real fight. He reached for the banister, but his hand slipped, and he collapsed against the railing, banging his elbow. It tingled and throbbed, and he didn't know how well he could use it if forced into combat. A silhouette filled Room 202's doorway, casting a shadow into the hall as the figure emerged.

Chief Dimitriou. Virgil released his breath.

The chief stepped forward and planted a boot atop the body as though conquering a mountain. He smirked and dusted off his hands. "Convicted."

Virgil blinked. "Wait…what?"

Then he realized: the chief must have accused the victim's next-door neighbor in Room 202 of committing the murder and had successfully challenged him to a trial by combat. Standard operating procedure for police departments in the Greek Alliance. Barbaric and stupid.

The door to Room 204 slammed open, and Stathis emerged, holding his nose. "Smells awful in there. Guy must've been dead for more than a day. Ugh."

While Stathis leaned against the wall and took deep breaths, Patroklus seemed to float from the room into the hallway. At least now Virgil knew why Patroklus had left the lab with such haste. The priest halted several steps from the chief and peered at the body of the "perpetrator."

"I see my services are unnecessary."

"Yep." The chief grinned as though he had won an Olympic gold medal. "This is how you solve a case. Keep 'em coming, Zeus. I love this week." He looked in Virgil's direction, his eyes narrowing as though at an uncommon stench. "Virgil. I thought you were already working on a case."

Virgil swallowed. "Yeah. But I—"

"So why aren't you doing your job?"

"Well, this—"

"Solve one case before starting another. You're a homicide detective; I thought you would have known that." The chief frowned. "Nicholas was one of us, and it sends a bad message to leave his death unresolved for so long. You find the murderer by the end of tomorrow, or I'll find him myself."

Virgil stared, mouth open. "Well, I mean, um, I...I think th—"

"After the senator's speech last night, I would have expected you to hurry with your investigation. You might not have much time before you're unemployed."

Virgil tried to ignore the glee dripping from the words. "Okay."

He wondered what his therapist would have thought of his response. It didn't really matter what Perikiades thought, though. He could say all he wanted when he was comfortable in his chair. It was different when you were actually in the situation. Even Perikiades probably wouldn't have antagonized someone who had just finished killing another man.

Besides, maybe the chief was right. Instead of traipsing to every murder scene in the city-state, Virgil could concentrate on the Manikas case and solve it. Then he could move on to other cases. One at a time, like the chief had said.

Why did the chief allow me to work on this particular case, though? Does he know on some level that my method is the only way to find the real murderer? Does he want true justice for Manikas and not the arbitrary justice he normally deals out?

"Stathis!" Dimitriou folded his arms across his chest. "Write down that I conducted the investigation and executed the murderer. Schirra, get out here and clean up this mess."

Schirra exited from 204 and glared at the crumpled body on the floor. "Why am I cleaning this up? I'm one of the most senior members on the force."

"Because you're a woman, and women are good at cleaning."

"I'm a police officer."

"Women aren't real officers. Now get to work. I'll be back at the station." The chief strode to the stairs, jostling Virgil to the side on his way past.

As the sounds of the chief's footsteps faded, Virgil turned to Schirra. She looked at him with something resembling sympathy or commiseration.

"Um," said Virgil. "I'm sorry the chief said that. You're a real officer. You're as much of a bully as the others."

Schirra frowned and seized the dead person's legs. "You always know exactly what to say to make any situation worse."

"Sorry, I..."

Schirra knelt and heaved the body over her shoulders. "Get the fuck out of my sight."

Virgil felt his face redden. She was right, he always made things worse. A perfect summary of his life. He hurried to the stairs before he caused any more damage.

VIRGIL RUBBED HIS sore eyes as he ambled into the evidence room. Rows of shelves filled with baskets and cardboard boxes fought for space between the dingy walls. He made his way to the nearest shelf and peered into the basket labeled, "knives." An accurate description. Various sizes, various stain patterns, various degrees of sharpness, but all knives. There were no notes indicating to which investigations the weapons belonged, or where they had been found, so the room served more as a museum of the macabre than anything functional.

He selected one of the larger knives. It looked sharp. Applying minimal pressure, he ran his finger across the edge. It felt like, at most, a cool breeze, but he noticed the knife had sliced free a thin layer of skin. His thumb played with the skin flap. *How would this blade feel against my...*

No. He dropped it back in the basket. He would just ignore those thoughts and pretend they had never happened.

He located three baskets labeled "spear tips" on an upper shelf, each of them packed to the brim with an assortment of spear tips. Comparing them to Manikas's wound might help identify the brand and model of spear used, which might provide a clue, leading to the murderer. Virgil stacked the baskets and carried them from the room.

Maybe, even if I miss the deadline, the chief might consider a clue like that as sufficient progress, and then he'll give me an extension. Virgil sighed. *Unlikely.*

After walking down several flights of stairs to reach the examination laboratory, Virgil stowed the baskets in the back corner. He retrieved Manikas's body from cold storage, wrestled it onto a cart, and transferred it to the lab table.

The corpse's smell wafted into the air. Its odor had metamorphosed into something strange, but inoffensive. Flowery, maybe. Even dead, Manikas continued to develop as a person.

Virgil pulled back the blanket. "Oh, no."

In Manikas's chest, the original spear entrance had been extended to form the mouth of a smiley face. Two additional holes in the body formed the eyes. Flowers protruded from each hole, with white petals leaning over the fleshy edges. From the mouth, a stick held a note that read, "Happy Blasphemer's Week, Virgil!"

Virgil jerked the note and flowers from the wound. For a moment, he stared at them. Whoever had placed them here had rendered the wound unusable for investigation. Virgil couldn't compare spear tips to it. He couldn't do anything with it. The person playing the gag might have destroyed any chance Manikas had of receiving justice.

Was it a gag, though? Someone had deliberately entered a police headquarters laboratory, pulled out a body, carved holes in the chest, and put flowers in it. The prank wasn't even that funny.

No, this was sabotage. Someone didn't want him to find the killer. Either it was one of the officers who wanted him to fail and thus discredit his profession, or it was someone associated with the killer. Maybe the killer himself.

Virgil tossed the flowers and note into a trashcan, unable to enjoy the thud of their impact. This was his fault.

If he'd examined the body earlier, the sabotage wouldn't have been an issue. He would have already determined the type of spear. Alternatively, if he'd made drawings and measurements of the body, he could still have made educated guesses about the shape and size of the murder weapon. His brief probing of the wound had become hazy in his sleep-deprived memory; he could only recall jagged edges.

Useless. This latest failure wasn't even the saboteur's fault; it was Virgil's.

A notebook would have helped. Something similar to the one his therapist used when taking those voluminous notes during his session. Virgil decided to purchase one today.

Of course, it wouldn't help with the evidence he had already missed or lost. Nothing more could be gained from the body. Virgil covered it and rolled it back to cold storage.

Now, the investigation depended on tomorrow's interviews. His stupid mistake had eliminated all the other leads.

VIRGIL DELAYED RETURNING to his apartment until late that night, in case anyone had decided to search his place again. He wanted to give them enough time to finish before he arrived. Discovering them in the middle of the act sounded like more danger than he wanted to handle at the moment. Although he certainly deserved to be impaled or stabbed for his succession of failures on this case.

When he opened the door, his place seemed quiet. No rustling, no muffled cursing. He tossed his new notebook onto the couch and collapsed beside it.

After purchasing the notebook, he had spent most of the night in the corner of a cafe, filling out the details of the investigation so far: the place of the murder, the victim's family, potential leads, whatever information he could remember. The simple act had organized his thoughts, though he still had a dearth of leads.

He'd retrieved the Blasphemer's Week prank note from the trash. It might serve as a handwriting comparison if the note's author were involved in the murder, but it was probably useless. His only avenue of investigation now was the funeral tomorrow. Manikas's family needed to yield important information, especially if he wanted to find the murderer before the chief's deadline.

Virgil didn't want to arrive at the funeral late, as he had for his therapy appointment this morning. Since there would be no sleep without a pill, he decided to take it in the next few minutes instead of wasting hours trying to fall asleep without it. He also decided to shower tonight, since he likely wouldn't have time in the morning, and everyone today had commented on his smell.

Virgil pulled himself from the couch and strode to the bathroom. Tomorrow was his last day on the case. If he were to have any hope of solving Manikas's murder, tomorrow had to go perfectly.

EIGHT

MANIKAS'S FAMILY MEMBERS had chosen for the funeral a pleasant, peaceful venue that styled itself as the Elysian Fields. The moniker seemed to match: the place had lush grass, leafy trees, the occasional colorful marble statue, and scattered marble benches. Soft music composed of harps and chimes wafted through the summer air from hidden speakers. The bright blue sky and calm breeze further added to the atmosphere of paradise.

Paradise didn't fix sleep deprivation. Virgil failed to stifle a yawn as the mourners gathered before the tallest tree.

No coffin for today's service. Normally, the deceased would be displayed, complete with coins in the mouth, so all attendees could verify that their loved one had made the journey across the River Acheron. These attendees, however, would have to wait another day for that visual confirmation, partially because no one had coined Manikas and partially due to the smiley face on the deceased's chest.

The relatives, all dressed in formal black togas, stood near the tree and the fire pit. They would occasionally turn toward each other or glance over their shoulders to the section of the field where the officers and Virgil had gathered. Chief Dimitriou had ordered his officers to keep a respectful distance and demeanor, so Virgil held his hat and the officers held their spears while standing at attention, maintaining blank expressions due either to professionalism or boredom.

When Virgil had first arrived, Kostas had suggested that Virgil take the place of the corpse in the service, since it was his fault Nicholas hadn't been coined. The other officers had chortled, though they had kept their mirth to a respectful volume. Chief Dimitriou silenced them, but only after they had almost quieted of their own accords.

"Service is starting soon." The chief nodded toward to the relatives under the shade from the tree.

A final pair of stragglers joined the family. Virgil suppressed a sigh and shifted his stance. In this moment, he would trade his life for a chair.

At least the funeral was a convenient opportunity to interview the family afterward. And during the service, Virgil could observe them to see if they moved in a way indicative of someone who murdered a relative.

Though he didn't recognize everyone in the first two rows, some looked familiar. *Is that Manikas's father, Paulus, or...* No, that was the mother, Clymera. Those stout figures to her right in military uniforms must be Boris and Alexandros, Manikas's brothers. The main suspects.

The music faded and, from behind the collection of officers, Patroklus strode forth. He crossed the flowing grass with great solemnity, arms folded across his chest and hands hidden within his sleeves. His red robe rustled in the thin breeze as he walked past the rows of relatives. Upon reaching the fire pit, over which was mounted a dead bull, he produced a torch and lighter from his robe. He lit the torch and set it in the pit. Flames and smoke arose, and the smell of cooking bull floated through the air.

Patroklus walked to the base of the tall tree. When he turned to face the crowd, everyone stopped speaking.

"Welcome, everyone, on this day, the first day of Eris," he said in a soft voice that nevertheless traveled to the most distant attendees. "Let us begin with a prayer."

Why does the priest, or anyone else, bother with prayer during the week when people believe the gods aren't listening? Maybe it was habit, or maybe they thought their words would somehow reach the intended recipients. Or maybe people thought the gods had some kind of prayer mailbox and could sort through missed messages at their leisure.

The relatives and the officers around Virgil bowed their heads. Patroklus paused a moment, stared directly at Virgil, then bowed his own head. *Did he notice, even at this distance, that I didn't close my eyes?* Virgil decided to pretend to pray to avoid dangerous accusations of impiety, but he kept his eyelids slightly open so he could observe the other attendees.

Patroklus began. "All-powerful Zeus, though you cannot hear us now, as you are engaged in activities more worthy of your attention, we express our honor and praise to you. You keep our city-state alive through your mercy and vigilance. You keep us strong and safe. You make the Greek Alliance the strongest power in the world."

Does Patroklus really believe that? Does he think anyone here believes that? The Alliance hadn't dominated the world in centuries. None of the relatives seemed to have reacted, though.

"Ares, namesake of our city-state and the one to whom we look for guidance in the conduct of our lives, we honor you. Your haste for violent action inspires us and gives us the might to conquer our enemies."

If Ares really existed, he had been sleeping on the job. It had been over a hundred years since the Alliance had won a war. *Patroklus should have offered him a sacrifice of caffeine or something.* Virgil shook his head. Dangerous thoughts, even during Blasphemer's Week.

"Hades, who rules our final destination, we honor you as well, as is fitting for this occasion. Though you are mysterious and ill-tempered, you will be our keeper for eternity, and we do not wish to offend you. We dedicate this ceremony to your name."

Heads rose and eyes opened. None of the attendees had acted suspiciously during the prayer. Virgil had hoped for something useful.

Patroklus waited for several moments before speaking again, presumably to allow all that reverence to permeate people's minds and bodies. "Nicholas Manikas is the man we have come to mourn. He died prematurely under tragic circumstances. His body is not here and has not yet been coined, at the request of the investigating homicide detective."

Patroklus waved his hand to indicate Virgil. A wave of murmurs came from the relatives as they turned to face Virgil. They stared for several seconds as though committing every feature of him to memory so they would know the true face of evil. He clenched his hands around his hat and wondered if any of them would be audacious enough to kill him here, in the presence of two dozen police officers. The officers would probably cheer them on.

Why did Patroklus volunteer the fact that I requested not coining Manikas? Does he want someone to kill me? If so, does that fact imply his involvement in the murder, or only a strong dislike of me?

Maybe I deserve to be killed for my transgression. Withholding the coin had so far accomplished nothing other than hurting the victim's family. Manikas's soul might have been necessary for the rituals, but the rituals had revealed nothing to the priest. *Everything I've done so far has been pointless.*

"However," said Patroklus, "we should not dwell on Nicholas Manikas's death, but his life."

With those words, the priest departed the focal point. Striding past the gathered audience without reaction, he rejoined the officers.

A lengthy pause followed, with the relatives glancing back and forth between each other before a middle-aged man shuffled forward to the spot Patroklus had vacated. Paulus, Manikas's father. Upon reaching the tree, he turned to face the attendees and cleared his throat.

"Nicholas was my son," he said in a gravelly voice, "and there can be no greater pedigree than to have me as a father. It will come as no surprise to you, then, that he was a hero. As I served in the military and garnered various honors, including two Valiant Service Medals in the Asian Conflict of '73 and three recommendations for Exemplary Service Medals in the subsequent years, Nicholas also wanted to serve his city-state to the fullest of his abilities."

He continued, giving a somewhat dubious account of the deceased's life. According to Mr. Manikas, Nicholas had lived a life of adventure, heroic deeds, and selfless acts even the most self-denying of people had never achieved. Typical funeral fare. The rest of the ceremony continued similarly, with relatives and coworkers comparing Manikas's actions to those of Perseus, Jason, and Herakles. From the file Virgil had read, Manikas's most heroic act had been to arrest someone who had exposed himself in a produce store. Virgil did not volunteer this information during the service.

Virgil's legs became stiffer and stiffer and his back ached with increasing intensity as the speakers droned on. He needed a chair. Or at least something to lean on. He wasn't as strong as all these other people. After over an hour, the last person spoke, and Patroklus came forward to end the ceremony.

"Nicholas Manikas was well served by your tales of his life," Patroklus said. "Though he will spend his eternity upon the unchanging fields of Hades, rendered insipid and irrelevant by that fate which claims us all, it is good that those who remain remember his better days."

The priest bowed, and the gathering disintegrated. The relatives dispersed from their rows and gathered in clumps, passing around plates of bull meat.

Virgil took a breath, trying to calm himself. Though he had dreaded the upcoming confrontation with the family, the investigation would end today in failure if he didn't speak to them. Returning his hat to his head and pulling his notebook from his pocket, he scanned the clumps and found his target. As he moved to intercept, he heard conversations from the other clumps with topics ranging from the pleasant scenery to the next wrestling competition.

To Virgil's right, a bulky relative strode toward Officer Collias. Without saying a word, the man shoved Collias.

"You pulled me over the other day!" The relative bunched his fists. With his muscles, he looked like he might be a match for the officer.

"What about it?" Collias asked, with equal parts aggression and confusion.

"The fine was huge. I didn't deserve that."

Collias shrugged. "You owe it, either way."

The relative closed the gap between them, standing chest-to-chest with Collias. "Maybe I'll find a way to make it worth paying."

Virgil glanced around for safe cover. He could duck behind a nearby pair of trees, or behind a set of relatives already making bets on the proceedings.

Before Collias or his assailant initiated the fight, Kostas swaggered from the crowd and inserted himself between the two. With one blow, he laid out the relative.

"I don't care if you live or die." Kostas leaned over the man, who groaned on the grass. "But if you don't back down right now, we'll be burying you next to Nicholas today."

The man stood, and for a moment, it looked as though he would take a swing. But he spit blood in the grass beside Kostas's boot and said, "You're not worth it," before spinning on his heel and walking away.

Talking resumed. Kostas clapped Collias on the back, and they strolled toward the other officers, laughing.

Virgil released his breath. He would have hated to see someone killed right in front of him, though it would have been easy to solve that particular case. He continued toward Manikas's father.

"Mr. Manikas?" Virgil asked when he arrived.

The barrel-chested man turned from the woman to whom he'd been speaking. "What do you want?"

"I'd like to ask you a few questions about your son."

"I've already spoken," the man said, his expression akin to that of someone who had swallowed a shard of glass. "Let me grieve."

"I'm sorry. It's just, I'm conducting the investigation into his death, and I wanted to talk to you about what your son was doing his last few days."

The man raised a meaty fist, one with scars and bruises. "If you say one more word to me, just one, I will kick your ass so hard you'll be kissing your own butt. This is my son's funeral, and I must mourn my loss."

Virgil opened his mouth to apologize, but realized his mistake in time. He bowed his head and backed away. The father returned to his conversation, which sounded as though it had to do with gas prices during summer months.

That should have gone better. In his notebook, he wrote, "Paulus Manikas didn't want to talk. Threatened ass-kicking."

As he searched for the older brothers to question them next, he saw the chief approaching Nicholas's father. He wondered how the conversation would go, given Nicholas's dismissal from the police force.

Virgil turned away from that particular storm and located the brothers in a nearby cluster of relatives, their shiny uniforms and thick torsos making them a focal point. They stood on either side of their mother, their backs to Virgil, while the people in the cluster ate and gabbed. The conversation stopped when Virgil approached.

The brothers turned to face him, their expressions stoic. "Who are you?"

Virgil extended his free hand. "I'm the detective conducting the investigation into Nicholas's death."

The mother, a tall, thin woman in a severe black toga, turned. She wept into her hand under her veil. The oldest brother, Boris, set his plate down and folded his arms across his chest. "So, you're the one who ordered him not to be coined."

Virgil shuffled, looked at his hand, and dropped it to his side. "Um."

"Kind of disrespectful, don't you think? How would you like to be stuck on the riverbank, waiting to move on with your existence?"

"Well…" *That actually feels like my life.* "Can I ask you all a few questions?"

From Boris's expression, the idea seemed as welcoming as a bowl of goose dung. "Ask."

"Um. The day Nicholas Manikas was fired, you and Alexandros were arrested for beating him." Virgil didn't add that he thought their motive for beating their brother might be their motive for killing him.

Boris and Alexandros turned toward each other, paused, and laughed in unison. "Yeah," said Boris. "That was pretty hilarious. Now everyone knows we beat up Nicholas."

"Look," said Alexandros, "it was our brotherly duty to beat Nicholas. He was always a wimp. We tried to toughen him up. If we'd done a better job, he might still be alive today."

"So," said Boris, "the only thing we should have been arrested for is not beating him more."

"You have almost the same build as Nicholas." Alexandros eyed Virgil as though contemplating a recalcitrant nail or a particularly annoying weed. "Little flabbier than he was. We could offer you the same services we gave him."

Virgil took a step back. "No, I…I'm fine." He directed his gaze to the ground. "So, where were you two on the night of the murder?"

Boris and Alexandros exchanged a glance again. "It sounds," said Boris, "like you're accusing us of the murder."

Virgil blanched. He was being too obvious. "Well…"

"We didn't do it. I was at a dog-fighting show at the Drowned Sailor." Boris pointed at Alexandros. "He was at a Chronic Death concert with friends."

Virgil wrote down the names in his notebook. "Okay. Can—"

"And now you're done asking questions."

Virgil blinked. "Um, I still have more. I thought you would want to help. I'm trying to find the murderer so he can be punished. And th—"

The other brother gestured to several laughing police officers who had begun walking toward their cars at the edge of the property. "The police have already been doing a good job of that. They typically solve murders in the same day."

"I don't think—"

"Then you come along, slow down the process, and make a difficult time even harder on the family." Boris stepped closer and shoved Virgil. Virgil had to take a step back to regain his balance.

"I'm just trying to—"

"Leave. Or you'll be the next one we talk about under this tree. And I'm sure the stories about you won't be as flattering."

Virgil studied the man's face. Boris seemed capable of following through with his threat. "Okay. I'm sorry."

Maybe this was the end. He wouldn't learn anything else today. He had no leads, and he would have to give up the investigation. Manikas's death would go unpunished, and all the trouble Virgil had caused would mean nothing.

"Wait," said the mother. "Please." Her sons turned to her, mouths gaping.

"Okay." Virgil's heart jumped. Someone wanted to talk to him. "You're Clymera, right?"

"Please, call me Mrs. Manikas." She removed her hand from beneath the veil and wiped it with a handkerchief produced from somewhere within her dress. Her voice seemed on the verge of trembling as she continued. "Someone killed my son, and I want to see them suffer. I'm certain my sons won't begrudge their mother some vengeance."

"No, Mom," said Alexandros. "Of course, we wouldn't."

Boris shook his head. "I want vengeance for Nicholas, too. I just don't think you should be getting involved, Mother. Let the men handle it."

She hugged each of her sons. "That's kind of you. I just want to talk to the detective for a few minutes, though, to answer his questions. Maybe I can sit on one of those nice benches while we talk?"

Virgil looked to the brothers, who appeared confused. Boris shook his head after a few moments. "Mother, this is the guy who didn't let them coin Nicholas."

"Yes." Her voice dropped. "And I hope that proved worthwhile. If no conviction comes from his investigation, we may have some reckoning for the insult."

The brothers appeared pleased at the prospect, eyeing Virgil like a chew toy. He swallowed.

"Thank you, ma'am. That's great. This will be very helpful."

"The bench, please?"

Virgil followed as the two brothers guided their mother between them to the closest bench. It sat under a tree that provided a few square meters of shade. Mrs. Manikas lowered herself onto the center of the bench and crossed her legs, sighing. Virgil envied her. His own legs felt stiff.

Mrs. Manikas looked up, though her face remained hidden by the veil. "Now, what would you like to know?"

"Um." Virgil paused to gather his thoughts. "What was Nicholas like? Who were his friends? How did he spend his last few days?"

The woman clasped her hands atop her lap. "My Nicholas was a gentle soul. Always a kind word for those around him. Always taking care of his poor mother. Then he turned eight."

Virgil nodded while trying to hide his inner confusion. He couldn't reconcile her description of Nicholas with the one the officers had given him.

While Virgil jotted down notes, Mrs. Manikas continued. "You might have noticed that Nicholas isn't built as well as most officers. He's always been on the thin side. Not weak, but thin. This made him a target for the other kids at school. He would come home crying to me about what the bigger kids had done or said to him."

"Mom," said Alexandros. "This guy is a stranger."

"It's okay, dear. This man is going to find out who did this."

Boris gave her a pleading look. "I still don't think Nicholas would want us talking about him like this in public."

Virgil cleared his throat. "I can understand what he might have gone through."

The mother smiled. "I thought as much, judging from your physique and the way you carry yourself."

Virgil shifted position.

"Nicholas changed after a year of being hurt and insulted. He became sarcastic and spiteful. He wouldn't physically harm anyone because he couldn't, but he would eat all the cookies before anyone else had a chance, or leave chores undone, or leave messes for others to clean. No amount of punishment would change him. His sweet brothers even tried to regulate his behavior, but to no avail."

"Mother," said Boris. "We're not sweet. Please don't say that."

"Allow your mother her eccentricities, dear." She turned back to Virgil. "Nicholas's behavior grew worse when he joined the police."

So, Nicholas Manikas's personality had irritated a great many people, including his own family. Not new information, but at least it gave Virgil more insight into what made Nicholas the man he was. "Do you know about any friends he had?"

Mrs. Manikas shook her head. "He swore he had friends, but we never saw any. Nicholas became very private after he moved out and started working. I've never even set foot in his apartment. I suppose, now, I never will."

Poor Manikas. *Maybe, if someone hadn't killed him, he and I could have spoken about our common experiences and offered each other sympathy.*

"After he was fired," said Mrs. Manikas, "he started looking for jobs at various places. He didn't tell me where, just that he would let me know when he got hired."

Motion from the corner of Virgil's eye. He looked up and saw Paulus Manikas striding toward them. Virgil's chest tightened.

Paulus interposed himself between his wife and Virgil. "What are you doing, harassing my family?"

"It's okay, dear," Mrs. Manikas said. "I'm giving him information that will help him find out who killed our son."

The man shook his head. "I make the decisions for this family, and it is absolutely not okay." He stared at Virgil with narrowed eyes. Virgil looked away. "You've caused enough harm already. I just learned from your chief that Nicholas would still be alive if the police department hadn't been forced to hire you."

Virgil swallowed and then backed away when he saw the expressions on the brothers' faces. "Um. That wasn't my decision."

"In a sense," the father said, eyes narrowing, "it could be said that you were the one responsible for my son's death."

Virgil swallowed again. "I don't think that's what my investigation will conclude. I need to get back to the station and keep working. Thank you for your help, Mrs. Manikas."

He didn't wait for a response before striding toward his car. Before he took more than a few steps, something unyielding grabbed his arm and spun him around.

Virgil flailed and stumbled, fighting to keep from crumpling to the ground. He swayed, then regained his balance and looked up to see the chief.

The chief seized Virgil's shoulders and shook him hard enough to rattle his teeth. "What in Hades's name are you doing?"

Virgil staggered again and tried to ignore his spinning head. "Um… Questioning the—"

"That is the family of the deceased. You have no right to be harassing them."

"I'm trying to f—"

"I don't care what you're trying to do." The chief shoved Virgil away. Virgil stumbled several steps, but managed to stay upright. "They have suffered enough already. Why aren't you out trying to find the murderer?"

Virgil took a breath. "I am. I think it might be the brothers."

"The brothers?" The chief turned his gaze to them, his eyes widening slightly. Maybe he noticed their bulging muscles and thick torsos. "Both of them, huh?"

"Yes. They had an altercation with the victim a few days before the murder, which might have led to them killing him."

"And you're thinking of formally accusing them?"

"I'm considering it. I d—"

"I see."

Before Virgil could say anything else, the chief strode away. Maybe the chief wanted to prepare himself for a trial by combat with the Manikas brothers. Virgil didn't want to formally accuse them yet, though, not without more clues.

And he didn't know where to find those clues. He could call the Drowned Sailor and the Chronic Death concert venue to confirm the Manikas brothers' stories. *But what if those leads don't help?*

Virgil glanced back at the Manikas family. Paulus had shepherded his family across the field, likely trying to put as much distance as possible between them and Virgil.

Growing up with Mr. Manikas couldn't have been easy, but at least Nicholas had gotten to grow up with a father. *What would Nicholas and I have become if the situations of our formative years were reversed? What would my home life have been like if I'd grown up with Mr. and Mrs. Manikas and two older brothers instead of my mother and Chrysanthe? Maybe I would have been the one lying in a laboratory storage compartment. Maybe I would have been the one so estranged from my family that they never saw my apartment.*

Thinking about Nicholas's apartment reminded him that he hadn't taken notes while at the crime scene. He had a notebook now and nothing else to do, no leads other than checking the Manikas brothers' alibis. Virgil hurried to his car, hoping this next excursion would yield more clues.

NINE

VIRGIL ALWAYS FELT embarrassed when approaching his car, a Nymph model. While most respectable cars on the road had huge wheels, spiked rims, and colorful paint jobs, his stood at shoulder-height, had all the defensive systems of a limp celery stalk, and only had a paint job if one considered rust an acrylic. Fortunately, he saw no one else on the sidewalk outside Elysian Fields and managed to slide behind the steering wheel undetected. Slouching in his seat, he turned the ignition, let the car rattle to a start, and pulled away from the curb.

Manikas's apartment was on the northwest side of town, several kilometers away. Virgil's car bumped along a road that could be generously described as "'textured," following it through winding uphill streets bordered on both sides by houses of questionable stability crammed together. In the distance, the clean marble dome and spire of the Temple of Ares loomed over the other municipal buildings.

One final hill before reaching Manikas's apartment building. Virgil's car struggled, its engine banging in protest, but it crested the summit and poured downhill. After the car staggered through a couple potholes spanning most of the street's width, Virgil parked alongside the sidewalk, a few meters from the steps to the apartment, a two-story structure with several units side by side.

The cracked concrete stairs led up a tiny weed-covered hill and past yellow police tape to the graffiti-laden front door of Manikas's unit. Virgil reached to turn off his car, but froze in mid-motion. Manikas's door had opened.

As Virgil watched, his breath still, a figure emerged from the apartment, wearing a black hooded cloak. The sight seemed out-of-place in this suburban environment in the daytime, and it became more suspicious given that it occurred when the majority of the police force wouldn't have left the funeral yet. He had found his fourth suspect.

Virgil frowned. A civilian wouldn't visit a crime scene without intending to tamper with it or remove something. Either the man had important evidence in his possession, or he had just destroyed a clue Virgil had overlooked the other day. Another lost piece of information because Virgil hadn't acted sooner or taken notes.

He considered calling the police, but they would arrive too late. His heart hammered. It was up to him. This might be the moment. He could catch the suspect, demand answers, and maybe even solve the case. Right here, right now, within the chief's deadline.

The man shut the apartment door and, with the cloak billowing behind, bounded down the steps. He was of average height. His dark clothing obscured other details.

Virgil remained motionless in his car. *Should I get out and... confront the suspect? Or wait to see what happens?*

The man entered a car several meters ahead of Virgil's. The car looked inconspicuous, a dark blue Titan or Gorgon or similar model with no obvious markings. Black cloth covered the rear license plate. Before Virgil could pull out his notebook, the car rumbled into action and pulled away from the curb.

Virgil swallowed. He had missed the chance to apprehend the man at the apartment by being an indecisive moron, but he could still follow and confront the man at his destination.

Virgil recalled what his therapist had said about him not being ready to confront the murderer yet. Well, that would always be true, and he didn't have any choice in the timing. He squeezed the steering wheel as he turned his Nymph from the sidewalk and began the pursuit.

The street sloped downward, descending to the bottom of one hill before climbing up the next. As Virgil's car crept downhill, he watched the other driver lean to the side. It looked as though the man were changing radio stations, or increasing the speaker volume.

Virgil pushed down on the gas pedal. His car had little reaction to the increase in fuel consumption. Then the downhill slope increased, allowing gravity to further assist with acceleration.

It wasn't enough. The cloaked driver had gained tens of meters already and seemed intent on increasing his lead. Virgil tried to force the Nymph to go more quickly.

Red brake lights blinked on from the rear of the other car, probably because the man felt uncomfortable driving downhill at that speed. Virgil sighed. He wished his car had that issue. At least the other car's braking gave the Nymph an opportunity to regain distance.

To Virgil's dismay, the Nymph continued to fall behind. He pushed the gas pedal to the floor. His car rattled, shaking the mirrors, the seat, Virgil's teeth. It felt as though it could fly apart at any moment and scatter auto parts across the narrow street.

The other vehicle continued to increase the distance between them.

This felt shameful, reminding him of his early years of education and his peers laughing at him while he tried to run the kilometer-long course. He felt his face redden. A quick glance out the window assured him that no one saw his humiliation.

A few seconds later, the other man braked again, then again. Still, the distance between their cars increased. Probably, the other driver didn't even know he was involved in a car chase.

The situation became more laughable when the other car reached the bottom of the hill. It began to climb the hill, slowing noticeably, but Virgil's car could still do no more than maintain the distance between them. Ahead, the driver seemed to adjust his position in his seat. While Virgil's car crept along at what were, for the Nymph, insane speeds, the cloaked man was listening to music and relaxing.

When the Nymph reached the bottom of the hill, it had already fallen half a block behind its prey. As Virgil's car began its ascent, its speed plummeted. He gripped the steering wheel with whitened knuckles, cursing himself for doing something so pointless, but was unable to stop himself.

The other driver rolled down his window and draped his arm on the outside of the door.

Virgil sighed again. The other car had soon put a block of distance between them, then two blocks. Then it crested the hill and disappeared from sight.

Virgil beat his head against the steering wheel. Time to surrender.

He turned the Nymph around and began lumbering downhill to return to Manikas's apartment. It was better this way. If the cloaked man were the murderer, Virgil couldn't have done anything other than deciding whether to die by a spear through his chest or through his back.

As the car reached the hill's bottom and began trudging uphill, Virgil pondered what the cloaked man's purpose at Manikas's apartment had been. *When I arrive, am I going to find a ransacked apartment? If something is missing, I won't know. Diaper-pissing Ares. I should have surveyed the scene better the other morning.*

His car finally reached Manikas's apartment. He pulled up to the curb again and let the engine rattle to a halt. Sighing, he lurched out of the car.

As Virgil strode up the steps toward Manikas's door, the neighbor exited the adjacent unit. Smaller than average height and out-of-shape, the man wore a tight-fitting tunic and wheezed as he walked toward his own set of steps.

Maybe he had seen the cloaked man. Maybe he had even seen the murder.

"Excuse me!" Virgil breathed hard as he hurried toward the neighbor.

The man stopped mid-way down the steps and smiled. "Good morning!"

"Yeah, you too." Virgil cut across the hill to meet the man.

When he reached the neighbor, he extended his hand. The man shook it while appraising Virgil.

"Um," said Virgil. "Sorry to bother you. Did you see a guy in a black cloak come by here today? He just left a few minutes ago."

The man pursed his lips and shook his head. "Don't think so. I heard the door open and shut, but I figured it was just the police coming back. You're not an officer, are you?"

"No," Virgil said. "Homicide detective. I'm investigating the murder."

"Cool," the man said.

"Um, anything you know about what happened here would be helpful. Do you remember anything from the other night? Or anything about Mr. Manikas at all?"

"Not really." The man shrugged. "Didn't talk to my neighbor much. He never seemed in the mood. Didn't hear anything happen next door the other night, either. You're welcome to come in and talk about it if you want. I can make you some coffee and warm up some baklava. I don't think I have anything helpful for you, though."

"Maybe later. Thank you for the offer, though."

"Sure. You have a good day."

"You too."

Virgil watched the neighbor pound down the steps to the sidewalk. Those few exchanges had been the most pleasant conversation he'd had in months, with someone who wasn't his sister. *Is something wrong with that man?*

Virgil adjusted his hat and returned to Manikas's door. Nothing about the door seemed different from the other night. No obvious tampering or vandalism. No forced entry. Maybe the police officers had forgotten to lock the door before leaving, or maybe the cloaked man had a key. The latter would imply a personal relationship with the deceased, which could indicate the brothers.

Virgil tested the doorknob. It turned without resistance. Unlocked. He pushed the door open slowly, then raised his hand as a shield when sunlight from the opposite window blasted his eyes.

When his eyes acclimated, he examined the entryway. To the best of his recollection, it appeared the same as it had yesterday morning. He pulled out his notebook and made a quick sketch of the room, indicating cracks in the tile and door. The drawing would never decorate a politician's house, but it gave the relative locations of the room's features.

In the kitchen, a pool of darkened blood marked the murder location. Virgil walked to the refrigerator, stepping over the blood, and opened the door. A mild aroma of expired food assailed his nose, but he held the door open long enough to satisfy himself that the suspect hadn't pilfered any leftovers or condiments. Manikas's heirs would be pleased.

Letting the door close, he looked down at the spot where Manikas's body had lain. *What were those final moments like?* Virgil tried to imagine himself in that situation, making food one moment and turning to watch a spear impale you the next. Poor Manikas. He'd been abused by family and coworkers his entire life, and then someone had killed him. If Virgil hadn't been hired in his place, Manikas might have had different experiences the previous two weeks and might still be alive.

Virgil grimaced and continued his search. The kitchen counters had no obvious new markings, but some of the drawers were ajar. The first two contained nothing but silverware or measuring cups, while the third held toothpicks. Either Manikas had stored nothing of interest here, or the cloaked man had taken it.

As the rest of the kitchen seemed undisturbed, Virgil jotted down some quick notes and walked to the living room. Though Manikas had a different decoration scheme than Virgil, his apartment felt similarly empty. Maybe the emptiness said something about Manikas. Those weapons on the walls and the lack of personal photographs could indicate that Manikas hid his true self from the outside world even in his inner sanctum. *Did he allow himself to be himself anywhere?*

Despite my many problems, at least I don't hide from my true nature: I'm an awkward failure with little to offer the world. He closed his eyes, then forced them open.

A swift search of the living room revealed nothing. He continued to the bedroom.

The police hadn't left it like this. Drawers in the corner dresser hung half-open, crumpled bedsheets and clothes lay on the floor, and the mattress rested on the bed frame at an odd angle. Virgil slid the drawers fully open one by one, but found only clothes, and no sign that anything else had been there. Lifting the sheets revealed only the floor.

One final place to check. Virgil approached the bed and lifted the mattress. Beneath it lay a blue book.

Why did the searcher leave it? Given the mattress's odd angle, the suspect must have seen the book. Virgil pulled it from its resting place and set the mattress down.

The book had no fancy gold writing or any indication of its purpose, but it looked like a diary. Virgil noticed a gap in the middle and checked: torn shreds of paper marking the remnants of missing pages. After that, only blank pages.

This, then, was what the cloaked man had sought. Probably, the diary had once held incriminating evidence about the murderer.

Virgil groaned. He had been so close. If he'd left the funeral a few minutes earlier or driven a little more quickly, he could have caught the man, or at least have been able to hide and hope for a glimpse of the man's face. Or if he'd performed a thorough search of the apartment the morning of the murder, he could have found the diary. It felt as though everything about this case served only to remind him what he should have done differently.

Why did the man remove only a few pages? Virgil counted the stubs. Seventeen missing pages. The others were intact. *Why not take the entire book and leave no evidence it existed?*

He turned to the last entry. Hera 14. The day before Manikas was fired. That had to be relevant. Something had happened after that day that led to Manikas's death. If events had transpired differently, if the department had laid off a different officer, or if it hadn't hired Virgil…

He shook his head. A lot of things would have been better without him. He needed to concentrate now. Maybe he could find some clues in the earlier portion of the diary. He flipped to the first page.

> **5414 Zeus 1.** *Another new year, another new diary. I burned the previous diary, according to the annual tradition. No need to save those memories. None of them were any good, anyway.*
>
> *Of course, the other officers celebrated last night by making fun of me and hitting me on the arm and pretending they hadn't hit me very hard. They aimed for the same spot every time, and it hurts to wear anything with sleeves. You'd think I would have learned by now not to attend these parties, but I always go and hope it will be something different and that maybe they'll respect me. If I didn't go, though, the other guys would probably do something even worse when I saw them again. I hate parties, and I hate my coworkers, and I hate everyone. They're a bunch of assholes who think just because they have some muscle and a uniform and a spear that they're better than everyone else. Well, they're not. I'm smarter than they are, and I would be a better officer if I weren't always having to worry about what prank they're planning to pull on me next.*
>
> *Anyway, I always celebrate the new year with a new poem. So, here it is:*
>
> *Hoping, watching, waiting*
> *Trapped behind the invisible iron bars of a cage built*
> *   by society*

Trying to break them

Pulling

Begging

Pleading

for them to let me out

But am I in the cage looking out into the world of freedom

Or am I the free one looking at society in the cage?

Probably the first one

Virgil rubbed his eye. He wasn't crying. But that poem was really good. He knew how Nicholas felt, how your options were to either accept the roles society forced upon you or be a permanent outcast.

He closed the book. There would be time to read more poetry later. And to scour the diary for clues, or a cast of characters to question. He slipped it into his pocket.

Though it might provide leads, it also raised questions. *How would the murderer have known about the diary, which was supposedly a private book?* That fact implied a close relationship with the victim. *Was the cloaked man a lover? Was Manikas's death the result of an escalated lover's quarrel?*

Virgil grimaced. He had less than a day to answer all those questions and provide the chief with the culprit, and his only piece of evidence was a book whose most important pages were missing.

AFTER USING MANIKAS'S restroom, Virgil hurried back to the police station. Instead of ensconcing himself in his office to read the diary, he headed to the chief's office. Since Virgil had acquired new evidence, he hoped he could beg the chief for an extension on the deadline.

The chief's office was at the far end of a hall, secluded from the more heavily trafficked areas. Virgil knocked on the door, but heard nothing. A tentative twist of the doorknob indicated the door was unlocked. Taking a final glance to make certain no one saw, Virgil slipped inside.

The office had few decorations, only a ceremonial golden spear mounted on the opposite wall, and wasn't much larger than Virgil's. It would only take three steps for him to crack his knees against the desk. The desk's surface was bare, with the exception of an opened envelope and an unfolded letter. The letter bore the Senate's seal.

Why would the Senate have sent Chief Dimitriou a letter? Virgil wondered if it had something to do with the detective position. Senator Kelipapalous, who represented Arestia, had mentioned introducing a bill that would, among other things, end funding for homicide detectives. *Does the letter have any further insight on the likelihood of the bill passing?*

Virgil glanced down the hallway. No one. He knew reading the chief's mail was illegal and, considering the chief's temperament, lethal. The mail was open, though, and he was just going to take a quick peek, and no one else would know, and the letter probably concerned him.

He closed the door and picked up the letter. It was addressed to the chief from Senator Kelipapalous.

> *We have a problem in common, but a solution presents itself. Your department will be required, by legislative decree, to hire a homicide detective to assist in investigations. I recommend hiring one of the certificate-holders from the short-lived Klasistratos Academy homicide detective program, Virgil Glezos.*

Virgil paused. The letter actually did concern him. Someone had written about him, by name. That was ominous.

*Glezos has the skill level necessary to prove our point
about the ineffectiveness of detectives, though I suggest
you aid him appropriately in order to achieve our goal.
You have done precious little for me compared to what
your counterparts in other city-states have done for my
fellow senators. I expect you to obey me in this instance.
I think you will find your obedience will suit your
purposes as well.*

Your Senator,

Gregor Kelipapalous

They wanted him to fail. *I guess that's unsurprising.* What
was surprising was that they had selected him, specifically, for
this job. Then Virgil realized Kelipapalous's plan: he would use
Virgil's failure to solve any cases as evidence for the uselessness
of homicide detectives in order to pass the bill through the
Senate.

It meant the chief wouldn't grant an extension. It also meant
Virgil had less than a day to solve this case.

Before he set the letter down again, he noticed a handwritten
addition in the corner.

I mean it. —GK, Eris 1.

TEN

VIRGIL SAT AT his desk, staring at the wall and contemplating the senator's letter. It made him feel more important to know the city-state had hired him for the sole purpose of discrediting his entire profession. *I do matter.*

Initially, the chief seemed to have obeyed the senator's request by removing Virgil from every case. Something had changed when Manikas was murdered, though. The chief might, as Virgil had speculated earlier, want true justice for the former officer. Or maybe he no longer agreed with the senator. The most likely possibility, Virgil decided, was that he had let Virgil work the case because he wanted the detective's failure to be even more spectacular. After the series of blunders Virgil had made, he could set back the Alliance's acceptance of detectives by decades.

Virgil sighed. The chief's motives were irrelevant. The deadline for the Manikas case expired tonight, but regardless of how many mistakes Virgil had made, he still had a chance to solve it. He pulled out his notebook and flipped to his last entry.

An hour later, Virgil had made progress of sorts by eliminating two of his suspects. Checking the Manikas brothers' alibis had confirmed their stories: Alexandros had spent the night in question at a Chronic Death concert, and Boris had gone to a dog-fighting ring in the Drowned Sailor's basement. The proprietor had said Boris had been the one fighting the dogs.

The prime suspects were gone. That left only the unknown cloaked man, the man who had desecrated the corpse, and Patroklus as suspects. Of course, Patroklus could have been either or both of the other suspects.

At least Virgil had one other lead to follow: Manikas's diary. Virgil loaded one of his high-adrenaline Rejects of the Sirens albums into his tape player, more to keep himself awake than because he enjoyed their music, and settled into his chair with the book. After picking up the frigid lamb wrap from his desk, he opened the diary to the second entry.

> **Zeus 2:** *I pulled someone over today for speeding. When I told him I was giving him a ticket, the guy just laughed and drove away.*
>
> *Fucker. If I see him again, I'll slash his tires.*
>
> *I wish I could find someone, just one person, that I could share a bond with, or who would at least respect me.*

Virgil knew how that felt, when others demonstrated such a profound lack of respect for you that you wondered if you were a real person. *Maybe Manikas and I could have been fake people together.*

Virgil's stomach rumbled. He bit into the lamb wrap, frowning as he chewed the congealed fat. *It's still food, and I don't feel like walking to the kitchen to heat it, and, anyway, a fuck-up like me doesn't deserve decent food.* He took another bite and continued reading.

Many of the entries elucidated Manikas's opinions of his coworkers, sometimes at great length. Artino, for example, was a "smarmy bully, with a spine made of olive oil and the moral compass of a serial killer," while Schirra was "the worst kind of asshole, one who takes out her frustrations on those around her," and Chief Dimitriou was a "testosterone-engorged, self-aggrandizing half-brain, whose idea of intellectual prowess is beating up a checkers set." Manikas reserved the largest share of his ire, though, for Kostas.

> **Ares 19:** *When I'm chief, I'll force everyone to work overtime during a holiday weekend and make everyone play darts while Kostas holds the dartboard. Today, he told me he was going to tie me to a chair in my parents' living room so I could watch him seduce my mom. She's like twenty years older than him. Disgusting. Then, when I was on patrol, he arrested me on a busy street in front of everyone. He handcuffed me and shoved me in the back of his car. When we got to the station, he led me inside and everyone laughed. Then he took off my handcuffs and told me the charges were dropped.*
>
> *When he left the station again, I pissed in one of his desk drawers.*

Virgil wrinkled his nose. A creative response, if crude. And, he figured, probably ineffective. Kostas didn't use his desk often.

> **Ares 31:** *Heading to the Dionysium for a few days. Never been before. This is going to be awesome. I've heard about it and all the fucked-up shit that happens there. Well, for an entire week, fucked-up shit is going to be my daily routine.*
>
> *Drinking and screwing and eating*
>
> *Sleeping and shouting and running*
>
> *Starting fires*
>
> *Smoking until I can't feel*
>
> *Sauce on my dick, and wine in my ass*
>
> *This is the great escape*
>
> *This is the Dionysium*

An interesting poem, Virgil decided, as he finished his wrap. It described the festival accurately, or at least agreed with the accounts Virgil had heard before. For a moment, he considered attending next year's Dionysium. He decided he wouldn't fit in.

> **Dionysus 8:** *Back! Oh, it was glorious! I was glorious! Enough food and drink for a year, and the quantity of sex I should be getting on a regular basis. Gotta go back next year. I'm not writing everything down; too incriminating.*
>
> *I made a friend there. He's probably the first real friend I've ever had. We were both fucking women next to each other, and he said he recognized me. We started talking, and it turns out he was the asshole who drove off while I was writing him a ticket.*
>
> *We hung out the rest of the week, drinking together and fucking together. It was great. And since Tim lives in Arestia, it won't be a long-distance friendship. Maybe I won't slash his tires.*
>
> *Eating from the same plate*
> *Drinking from the same bottle*
> *Puking into the same hole*
> *Sharing the same women*
> *Ignoring each other's flaws*
> *That's true friendship*

Virgil nodded. So, Nicholas had found a friend, someone to brighten his last few weeks of life. Ordinarily, Virgil would have felt relief for the former officer. Given Nicholas's fate, though, this "Tim" became a potential murderer and someone to question. Maybe Tim was even the cloaked man Virgil had chased this morning. Manikas might have mentioned the diary to his new friend, and that friend had now removed all pages that contained incriminating evidence. Virgil recorded Tim's name in his notebook and returned to the diary.

> **Dionysus 20:** *Tim said we should meet up at this bar, The Ferryman's Oar. He says he goes all the time, so I figured I'd join him. It was pretty fun. He told me to stay away from the dartboard. There's a gang that dominates it, and they're all pretty tough. I told him it wasn't a problem for a police officer. I just walked up to them and said, "Tim and I are playing."*
>
> *A guy who had knives strapped to his arms, legs, and belt, who later told me his name was Malcolm, looked me up and down like he was thinking of fighting me. Then he shrugged and said he wouldn't mind an easy win.*
>
> *He did win, but I think his friends might have been helping him cheat. Anyway, he invited us to play again another night. Probably, I'll beat him then.*

Malcolm. Another associate of Nicholas. Though the diary provided insufficient information for a phone directory search, Virgil at least knew where he could find Tim and Malcolm: The Ferryman's Oar. He could conduct interviews tonight. Virgil checked his watch: 13:41. A few more hours, then. If Nicholas's associates were helpful enough, Virgil might solve the case before the chief's deadline expired. That might give respectability to the profession and upset the senator's plans for him.

It's a nice dream.

Virgil knew he would find some way to ruin the opportunity. And, he realized, the cloaked man hadn't removed the diary pages that mentioned the bar, which meant this new lead would likely yield nothing.

But he had nothing else to try. Maybe visiting the bar wouldn't provide direct evidence, but it might supply an indirect link. Another thin thread to follow.

Manikas had left an inconveniently low number of clues about his death.

Virgil wished they had met, even if Virgil's employment at Nicholas's expense would have made initial conversations awkward. They would have liked each other. They responded a little differently to persecution, but they could have bonded over their shared mistreatment.

Sighing, Virgil returned to the diary. There were several more entries, some of them complaining about Nicholas's treatment at his job, and some of them about the denizens of The Ferryman's Oar. Nicholas had become closer to Malcolm and the others than to Tim. It seemed as though his initial hopes for friendship had dimmed, and he had settled for distant companionship.

After an hour of reading, one final entry remained. Virgil felt as though he knew Nicholas better after reading about the last few months of the victim's life, but it was too late for them to meet. This final entry might be the last chance Virgil had to experience Nicholas.

Hera 14: Maybe I made a mistake becoming a police officer. I thought people would respect me. My parents don't respect me, my brothers don't respect me, the other officers don't respect me, and the civilians don't respect me. It was just a bad idea, thinking I could gain the respect of others through a police uniform. I should have become a soldier instead.

At least this job pays enough to keep me out of the temple charity wards. And if I get good enough at handling weapons, I can gain the respect of others. I'll at least be able to give out tickets without people laughing at me or asking if I'm going to a costume party.

Respect isn't given

It's taken

I will have mine

If I have to rip your heart from your bleeding chest

I will have mine

If I have to smash your car with my bare hands

I will have mine

If I have to hold you in the fire while it eats your flesh

Respect isn't given

But I will have it

Actually, that's kind of creepy. I won't mind burning this diary next year. But that poem makes me sound pretty tough.

Virgil closed the book and rested it on his desk. *At least my parents and Chrysanthe always loved and encouraged me, despite my flaws.* Though his father had died when Virgil was young, Virgil had recollections of the man and knew he had shown his love for Virgil. His mother, despite having to work to support a family of three by herself, had always found time to let her children know she cared about them. Chrysanthe had always listened to Virgil, had always made him feel as though he could succeed.

If Nicholas's family had given him that kind of support, he might have still died, but he would have been happier beforehand. At least Nicholas found friends near the end. Those friendships were his sole meaningful contributions to the investigation of his death.

Virgil realized he couldn't interview those friends without help. *I'll just say or do something stupid. And I'm terrible at telling if people are lying.*

Patroklus could detect lies, though. Yesterday in the lab, he had known Virgil's faith was false. *Maybe Patroklus can use his skills at the bar, maybe in conjunction with another ritual.*

The priest's two previous spells had revealed nothing, though, due either to lack of evidence, incompetence, or Patroklus's sabotage. If a third consecutive spell failed, Virgil decided he would feel confident in a thorough investigation of the priest. If it worked, he would have more evidence to catch Nicholas's killer.

Virgil pulled out his phone and called the priest. There was no answer, so Virgil left a message, outlining his plan for the night. He hoped The Ferryman's Oar would provide answers. Maybe Nicholas's diary would lead the way to the truth.

ELEVEN

VIRGIL KEPT BOTH hands on his car's steering wheel, dividing his attention between the road and his passenger, Patroklus. A continual stream of cars passed them, many of them honking.

"I hope the killer's at the bar tonight," said Virgil. "The chief said tonight is the deadline, and I don't have any other leads. Not real leads."

"I see." The priest sat straight in the passenger seat, eyes forward and face empty.

Virgil gripped the wheel more tightly, trying to think of another conversation topic. It shouldn't have surprised him that talking about himself bored other people.

"So, um," he said, "Nicholas's corpse was desecrated yesterday."

Patroklus had no reaction. "Interesting. How does this affect your investigation?"

"It makes the investigation more difficult. I had wanted to compare spear tips to the wound to see if I could determine what the murder weapon was."

"Clever."

He's right. It was *clever of the perpetrator to destroy evidence.* "Since I couldn't do that comparison, it makes tonight even more important."

"Of course."

Virgil frowned. He would almost prefer conversing with Schirra, despite her barrage of insults. At least she would do more than ask questions or give two-word statements, which seemed to be Patroklus's sole concessions to the practice of socialization. "So, do you think you'll ever make High Priest?"

"An odd question." The silence dragged on long enough that Virgil thought Patroklus had considered those three words a complete response, but then the priest elaborated. "Serving as a priest for the police force is a parallel career path and will not lead to selection as the High Priest."

"I'm sorry." Virgil turned onto the next street, avoiding a particularly large pothole. "But most priests aspire to that, right? I mean, you have to prove you're really good to be High Priest. Does that mean you're not—"

"Perhaps a different conversation topic would be advisable."

Virgil wanted to hit his head against the steering wheel. "Sorry, sorry. You're right." *I always say something offensive. I always make people hate me.* For several moments, he tried to think of something neutral to say. "Why don't priests take a vacation this week? Since there isn't anything for them to do?"

"Priests must prepare for the return of the gods." Patroklus still gave no hints of emotion. "There is much to do."

Virgil hoped he hadn't offended the priest again. He turned right at the next traffic light and felt relief when he saw their destination: The Ferryman's Oar, the bar Nicholas had mentioned in his diary. It was a small space nestled between an automobile repair shop and a children's daycare.

They pulled into the gravel parking lot and clattered to a stop in the first available space. Virgil heaved himself out of the Nymph and stood for a moment, studying the lot. Cars and trucks of various sizes had crammed into nearly every space. Several looked similar to the one he had chased this morning, but were the wrong color. Then he saw it, in one of the spots on the far left. The dark blue Titan or Gorgon. The cloaked man was here.

Virgil knew he could be wrong. The car was a common model and a common color. But this type and color of car had intersected the investigation twice, here at the bar and at Nicholas's apartment, and Professor Lambros had cautioned against believing in coincidences. Since no black cloth covered the license plate this time, Virgil pulled out his notebook and jotted down the characters.

"Another clue?" Patroklus stood behind Virgil, having given no indication of his approach.

"Maybe," said Virgil. "It means someone of interest might be here." When Patroklus gave no response, Virgil gestured to The Ferryman's Oar. "Do you think we should…"

Patroklus inclined his head. Virgil berated himself inwardly. Stupid question. Obviously, that was the next step. He led the way toward the bar.

The bar was made from beautiful white rock slabs, with arched windows cut into the sides. Above the windows, a wooden sign proclaimed the bar's name. Soft strumming drifted from the inside, mixing well with the peaceful night sky. A pleasant sea breeze drifted over the new arrivals and wafted its briny scent through their nostrils. Virgil wished the place had outdoor seating.

He halted before going inside and adjusted his tunic and hat. "Okay." Deep breath. He pushed through the swinging doors and entered, with Patroklus behind him.

Inside, candles sat atop every creaky wooden table, and torches lined the wood-paneled walls. The lights flickered, casting dancing shadows across the room and its inhabitants. The bartender watched everyone from his counter at the back of the room as he polished a glass. Most patrons sat, nursing their wine or playing dice or shouting at the television screen on the wall, but one cluster stood several meters from a target, with darts in hand.

"I like playing darts," said Virgil. "I make lucky throws pretty often."

One of the television-watchers slammed a fist on his table. "We should nuke them all! Stop rolling over like cowards!" At first, Virgil thought the man might be watching a sporting event, but the screen showed the Senate chamber in Sparta.

He wondered if the man were one of the people Nicholas had mentioned in his diary.

Virgil turned to Patroklus. "Do you think we're expected to get drinks if we're just here to question people?"

"I don't drink alcohol."

It had been two years since the time Virgil had spent half an hour in a bar. He looked around the room again and then back to the bartender, who hadn't taken his eyes from them. "Maybe I could just explain what we're doing and see what he says."

Patroklus inclined his head.

Several of the patrons turned to stare as Virgil walked to the bartender. *What gives me away as someone who doesn't belong? My walk, or the way I dress, or some intrinsic quality that sets me apart from other people? My therapist would know.*

When he reached the counter, the brawny bartender stopped polishing and set down the glass. "What'll it be?"

"Um." Virgil shifted. "We're not actually here to drink. We're, well, we're investigating a…a crime. We think… I mean, the victim knew some of the people here. And he came here. So, we were just going to ask a few questions."

"Do what you want. What'll it be?"

"Um." Virgil looked down, then forced himself to meet the man's eyes again. "We were thinking of not drinking. We're sort of on duty. So… Is that okay?"

The bartender's face remained still as stone. "What do you think?"

Virgil blinked. "I—"

"You seem confused, so let me help. You have two options: you can buy a drink, or you can get the fuck out of my establishment."

The bartender looked like someone who worked out at least twice a day. He also looked like someone who didn't get the opportunity to use his muscles as much as he would have liked.

Virgil put his hands in his pockets. "Okay. We'll get something."

"You want something fruity, with an umbrella and a cherry?"

"Uh." Virgil swallowed. "No. Thanks, though. I'll just have some wine, I guess."

"Uh-huh. What kind?"

Virgil eyed the bottles lined up on the shelves behind the bartender, but didn't take time to read any labels since the bartender and Patroklus were waiting on him. "Whatever's cheapest."

The bartender rolled his eyes and retrieved one of the bottles. "This one is only in my stock to serve as a warning that you should never buy cheap wine." He twisted off the bottle cap and poured some of the red liquid into the glass on the counter. After returning the bottle to the shelf, he scooped some ice from the bucket next to him and dropped several ice cubes into the glass. "I do this for kids and other people who can't handle alcohol."

Virgil blinked. "O-okay. Thanks."

"What will your friend have?"

Virgil turned to Patroklus. "What did you want?"

Patroklus made no motion, and his face remained expressionless. "Water."

The bartender nodded. "Him, I can respect. Priests have an excuse for drinking like pussies." He pulled a glass from the overhanging rack and filled it with tap water. "Eight drachma."

Virgil pulled out the bills and laid them on the bar, leaving enough for a tip. "Okay. We'll just be in here, asking questions."

"Right." The bartender dropped the money into the register and began polishing another glass.

Virgil picked up his glass of wine and took a sip, then another. "This is actually pretty good."

"Figured you'd like it," said the bartender.

"Do you think we could ask you questions first? Since you're the bartender, you probably saw Nicholas a lot, and—"

"What do you think?"

Virgil blinked. "Okay. Um, well, thank you, then."

He shuffled away from the counter, with Patroklus following at a sedate pace. After a few steps, Virgil paused to allow Patroklus to catch up.

"I guess," Virgil said, keeping his voice low, "we can start walking around and asking people if they knew Nicholas. Did you need to prepare your spell?"

"Yes. Shall we?"

Patroklus led the way to an unoccupied booth. Advertisements on its wall featured women in bathing suits, posing suggestively with wine bottles in their laps. Virgil took a seat across from Patroklus and set his drink on the wooden table next to an empty libation bowl. He didn't know what the priest would do next. The spell catalogue only gave vague descriptions for some entries, focusing more on the spells' effects rather than how to perform them. Sitting here now and watching Patroklus felt exciting, as if Virgil was witnessing something new in the field of detective work. To his knowledge, no one had ever used this spell for a murder investigation.

The priest angled himself away from the bar's other denizens. Though no one stared directly at the pair, surreptitious eyes peered from mirrors, and peripheral gazes focused on them.

Removing a smooth stone from his robe, Patroklus held it between two thin fingers while using his body to shield it from the views of the other patrons. He waved his free hand in circular motions over the stone and spoke in a low tone, voice no more than a whisper.

"Aletheia, imbue this token with your knowledge and skill. Guide it to reveal lies or deceptions that we may work in your name."

The stone glowed once, a bright orange, before returning to its normal dull color. No one in the room reacted.

Virgil took a sip from his drink. "Okay. So does that mean we're ready now?"

"Almost." Patroklus let the stone rest in his palm, still hidden from the rest of the establishment. "Tell me a truth and a lie."

Right. Make certain the stone worked. "I am a homicide detective."

Nothing happened. Patroklus nodded. "Now the lie."

"People like me."

The stone glowed bright orange for a brief moment before returning to its original color. Patroklus closed his hand around the stone. "It is done."

Good. Now he needed to decide whom to talk to first. Virgil scanned the room. *Whom would Nicholas have spent the most time with? The group drinking in the corner booth? The foursome playing that dice game? The solitary man staring at the ceiling? The two engaged in a hushed discussion? The cluster playing darts? The lutist on the stage next to the bar? How would I even begin the conversation?*

"Where should we start?" he asked.

"I have no suggestion."

"Um." Nicholas had mentioned spending time with a couple groups of people. Virgil stood and shrugged. "Let's try over there." He walked toward the corner booth, hoping the silence behind him meant the priest followed.

The three in the corner booth looked up with narrowed eyes when Virgil and the priest came close. "Yes?" asked the man with long sideburns.

"Um." *I'm annoying them. I annoy everyone.* "Did any of you know Nicholas Manikas?"

The man raised his eyebrows. "No."

"Sorry," said Virgil. "It's just… I'm investigating a murder. So, are you sure you didn't know Manikas?"

"None of us knew him," said a man in a white shirt. "Now leave."

Virgil glanced at Patroklus, who gave him a subtle nod. The truth stone must have agreed with them. "Okay. Sorry for your time. I mean, sorry to bother you, and thank you for your time."

The group's conversation resumed as Virgil retreated to the center of the room. Patroklus looked at him without expression.

"It could have been a worse start," Virgil said. Patroklus made no reply. "Look, maybe this is a bad idea. Maybe we're not going to find anything useful by talking to anyone here."

Patroklus nodded. "That is true. I am unsure what you hope to gain by acting on that possibility, though."

Virgil's stomach twisted. "Sorry. You're right. Um, let's go over there next." He pointed to the people playing darts.

Diaper-pissing Ares. I should have started there. The diary had mentioned dart players.

The four men seemed even less happy at the interruption than the previous group. "What is it?" demanded the one with an array of knives on his belt, arms, and legs. In his diary, Nicholas had mentioned someone who loved knives. Malcolm?

"Hi," Virgil said to Malcolm's knives. "We're investigating a murder. Did—"

"Are you a police officer?"

Virgil shook his head. "No. Homicide detective."

"Good." The man leaned back. "Didn't want to fight to the death at the moment. Although..." He seemed to appraise Virgil. "It might not go too badly."

Virgil blinked and sipped from his glass. "I guess not, yeah. I just want to ask a few questions."

"Is that...?" The man peered closely at Virgil's drink. "Are those *ice cubes* in your wine?"

"Um."

The man shook his head. "Never mind. I was going to make fun of you for it, but it actually takes some balls to walk around with a drink like that."

One of the other men, bald with a goatee, threw a dart that landed in the seven wedge of the target. He grinned. Virgil identified him as Tomas from Nicholas's diary.

It was so odd to meet these people he had read about earlier. Like interacting with cartoon characters.

Malcolm slapped Tomas on the back. "You enjoy your little victory now. I'll have you crying by the end of the night."

"Whatever, Malcolm Greasehands."

"Um," said Virgil. "Did any of you know Nicholas Manikas?"

Malcolm and Tomas stared at each other. They appeared... puzzled.

"He get killed?" Malcolm asked. "When did that happen?"

Virgil gestured in the general direction of Nicholas's apartment. "A couple nights ago. On the twenty-ninth."

"You know who did it?"

"No, that's why I'm here. I—"

Tomas stepped closer, thick wine fumes rolling from him and clogging Virgil's nostrils. "You're trying to accuse us, aren't you? Why do you think we did it? More importantly—"

Tomas pushed Virgil. A light push, but with enough force to show it could have been much harder. "Even if we did do it, how do you think you're going to *prove* it?"

Even if Virgil had done well in his combat training courses, and he decidedly had not, he would have hesitated to apply that knowledge to Tomas. He took a step back.

"I'm not supposed to do trials by combat. That's not my job. I just ask questions."

Malcolm laughed and fingered one of his knives. "You just try to ask us questions. Go ahead."

"Okay." Virgil looked to Patroklus, but the priest responded by drinking his water. "Do any of you know who killed Nicholas?"

The men laughed. No sign of hurt or anger or sadness. *Nicholas thought* these *people were his friends?*

"Nope," said Tomas. "Although, I wouldn't blame anyone for doing it. He was an asshole."

"No, he wasn't."

All heads turned to an older man sitting by himself in a corner. The man leaned forward now, both hands clutching his glass. His eyes drooped downward. "He was a nice guy. I liked him."

The young man wearing the shark-tooth necklace, Artorios, shook his head. "Jakob, Nicholas was always making fun of you and telling you to not be such a coward and to fix your problems. I doubt he ever said anything nice to you. He certainly didn't say anything nice about you."

"I know." Jakob shrugged. "He listened, though. He listened to everything I ever told him. No one else ever did."

"Just means he was bored and lonely." Artorios laughed. "Doesn't mean he was a nice guy."

"Nicholas seemed nice to me," said Virgil. "He just had a difficult time."

Artorios snatched the darts from Tomas's hand. "If you know so much about him, why are you asking us?"

Virgil shifted. "I don't. It's just… He had to have done something nice, right? Malcolm." Virgil tried to ignore the way Malcolm stroked his knives. "Did Nicholas do anything nice for you?"

"He certainly gave me a lot of money." Malcolm laughed. "Wagers on dart games. Guy was terrible, but thought he was Olympics material."

Tomas pointed to a man in a sheer white shirt whose muscles looked equally as deadly as Malcolm's knives. "Nicholas gave money to Caius."

"Yeah." Artorios threw a dart. "Remember what he called you?"

"Called me a beggar." Caius shrugged. "Still lent me the money. And after I paid him back the money, I paid him back for the beggar remark." He flexed his muscles.

Artorios threw another dart. "I remember that. That was hilarious."

"Speaking of that…" Caius sidled over to Artorios and, as Artorios threw his last dart, struck the man on the back. The dart flew wild, striking an advertisement next to a patron's head. "Nicholas owed you money, didn't he?"

The bar patrons sat up straighter, watching the conversation between Caius and Artorios with what looked like trepidation. Virgil noted the exit and the path through the tables he would need to take to reach it.

"Asshole. We're on the same team." Artorios shouldered Caius out of the way and strode to the wall to retrieve his darts. The tension in the bar dropped a notch, but didn't vanish. "He owed a lot of people money. Like Malcolm."

Debt. A prime motive for murder. Virgil wrote the information in his notebook.

"So what?" Malcolm took the darts from Artorios. "He got fired. He needed to borrow money."

Artorios laughed. "Only he didn't call it 'borrowing.' Said he considered it a gift."

"He was going to pay." Malcolm threw a dart. "Not anymore, I guess."

Virgil glanced at Patroklus, but the priest said nothing. No lies so far, then.

Caius turned to the dice players in one of the booths. "Hey! You guys loan him anything?"

The dice players looked up from their game. Three raised their hands, but the fourth shook his head. "Not me."

Patroklus nudged Virgil. From within the priest's sleeve, the stone glowed orange.

"Come on, Tim," said one of the man's friends. "I saw you give it to him."

Tim. Nicholas's friend from the Dyonisium. The person who had first brought him to The Ferryman's Oar.

Tim shrugged and leaned back. "Fine, I loaned him money. I just don't want to be accused of killing him because I gave him some drachma."

Malcolm handed the darts to Caius. "You think Nicholas planned this?"

Caius shook his head. "You mean, did he plan to die so he didn't have to pay us back? It's a bad plan, man. Besides, he said he was looking for jobs." Caius threw his dart, though he seemed less than satisfied with his result.

Virgil swallowed. "What jobs?"

Malcolm glared as if Virgil had interrupted the conversation. "He had big dreams. He was going to be a security guard at a mall. He was going to be a security guard at Pericles Center, or at Socrates and Friends, or Platonic Electronics." Malcolm took a sip of wine. "Never seemed to work out for him."

Caius threw his first dart. "His last night here was hilarious."

"That's true." Malcolm took another drink. "He came in, had four drinks in twenty minutes, and said he was going to go apply for another job."

Virgil took notes. "What time was that?"

"Who does that?" Tomas said, watching Caius. "Chugging wine, getting completely drunk, middle of the night, knocking on some company's door and asking for a job?" Caius threw the dart and the other players cursed. "At least Nicholas went out memorably."

"Was it really the middle of the night?" Virgil asked.

"Yes." Tomas frowned. "I already said that."

"Do you know where he was applying?"

Tomas shrugged. "Don't know. He didn't say. I don't think it matters, really. Going anywhere stumbling-drunk in the middle of the night asking for a job takes some balls."

Virgil wondered what to write about that clue. *Something about Nicholas having balls?*

The dart players kept talking, and Patroklus only showed the orange stone on a few occasions of obvious exaggeration. Everyone had an alibi. No culprits, but at least Virgil knew some places to check next.

Before leaving, Virgil nudged Patroklus and gestured toward Tim. The man had been quiet most of the night and had, for a brief time, occupied a special position in Nicholas's social life. Both were reasons for suspicion.

Tim folded his arms across his chest when Virgil and Patroklus approached. "What?"

"Hi," said Virgil. "Um, our intelligence says you and Nicholas were good friends."

"Yeah." Tim shrugged. "Although it was more like I was his friend, but he wasn't mine."

"Okay. Did you notice anything odd about him in the past two weeks? Any differences in behavior? Did he say anything unusual? Did you two have any arguments?"

"That's a lot of questions." Tim took a drink. "I don't know the answers to any of them, and I don't know why I should tell you if I did."

"Do you have any information that would be helpful in apprehending the person who killed your friend?"

"No."

Patroklus nudged Virgil. The stone glowed orange again. Virgil nodded.

"Tim, we're trying to find out who killed your friend. Someone killed a person you cared about."

"Like I said, he wasn't my friend. I was his friend. There's a difference."

Virgil nodded. "I understand. Still, he has family who care about him. If you died, wouldn't you want your family to know who did it? So they could avenge you?"

Tim laughed. "Don't see how likely it is someone could manage to kill *me*."

One of his companions chortled. "Whatever, man. I've seen you wrestle. Doesn't take much to knock you on your ass."

Tim snarled and grabbed the man's throat. The man slammed his palm into Tim's nose, then elbowed Tim's arm and twisted it behind his back.

Virgil took a step away while Tim's other companions began pounding the table. All other patrons in the bar had stilled their activities to watch.

"Say, 'mercy'!" shouted the man who had pinned Tim.

"Fuck you!" Tim's face had turned bright red.

The man pulled Tim's arm higher. "Say it!"

Tim cried out, but shook his head. When the man pulled the arm even higher, Tim grunted. "Mercy!"

The man released Tim and sat back. "You owe me a drink."

The other patrons returned to their own conversations. Tim coughed and clutched his arm. "Fine. But you just caught me by surprise. Won't happen again."

Virgil wished he had done better in combat training. He hadn't realized it would be useful even when drinking with one's friends. "Tim, please. I could really use your help with this."

Tim's face contorted for a moment. Then he shrugged. "Yeah, fine, I do have something that might help. Just a few pages from his diary."

Virgil blinked. "You... Were you the person leaving Nicholas's apartment the other morning? The guy I was in a car chase with?"

"Car chase? I think I would have noticed that." Tim shook his head. "No, I just happened to find a few pages somewhere."

Virgil glanced at the stone in Patroklus's robe. Orange again. "Are you sure you're telling me everything?"

"Okay, maybe I took some pages out of a diary." Tim shook his head. "But I didn't murder Nicholas. I just thought maybe, since I didn't have an alibi when he was killed, and since those pages probably mentioned me, maybe I should… Well, I didn't do it, and I didn't want to get killed for it."

"How did you even know about the diary?"

Tim laughed bitterly. "Nicholas was drunk at the time. He was telling me he'd written in his diary that he would slash my tires if he ever caught me again. Said he changed his mind after we became friends."

Virgil jotted that information in his notebook. "Do you have the pages with you?"

"They're in the car." Tim stood.

"You still owe me that drink, man," his companion said.

Tim glared. "Yeah, yeah, I know. Fuck off."

Virgil glanced at Patroklus, who nodded. They followed Tim outside. Once in the parking lot, Virgil led the way to the Titan or Gorgon. Tim gave him an odd look, but said nothing.

"Here." Tim reached inside the car and pulled the pages from the passenger seat. Virgil held them close and squinted to read the first page in the dim moonlight.

Hera 15. They fired me. They actually fired me. The bastards. I…

Virgil looked up. This was it. This was the rest of the diary. Nicholas's final days were recorded here. Maybe this book contained the clues that would solve the case.

"Why didn't you take the whole book?" asked Virgil.

Tim shut his car door. "I still wanted you to find the killer. I thought there might be some clues in the first part of the diary. I realized afterward I should have gotten all the entries starting from when he met me. I was going to go back tomorrow."

Virgil glanced at Patroklus, who nodded. It was nice having a magic-wielding priest to help him. Given the success of the spell tonight, Virgil thought he could eliminate Patroklus from his list of suspects.

"Okay. We'll contact you if we have more questions." Virgil raised the diary pages. "Thank you for these. They'll be very helpful." Tim said nothing as Virgil and Patroklus departed.

"That actually didn't go too badly," Virgil said as he and the priest walked back to the Nymph. "Thanks for helping."

"I am here to serve."

"We actually got some good clues. And I was questioning people, just like a real detective. And you were a big part of it. Didn't it feel great?"

Patroklus stopped beside the passenger-side door of the Nymph. He glanced at Virgil expectantly.

"Sorry." Virgil hurried to his door. He opened it and was about to slide inside when he noticed a piece of paper lying on his seat. *Who put it there?* He picked it up and, sliding behind the steering wheel, began to read.

> *Virgil, I am having you watched by someone within your organization. I know every move you make. Cease your investigation while you can. If you fail to heed my warning, death awaits you.*

Virgil frowned. Someone had searched his apartment, someone had desecrated Manikas's corpse, the senator had written to the chief about him, and now this. *Who is spending so much time focusing on* me?

He reread the note. Someone within the organization. That could mean almost anyone within his social circle. Schirra, Stathis, any of the other officers, maybe even…

"What does it say?"

Patroklus.

"Nothing." Virgil pocketed the paper. "Nothing. It's just a blank sheet of paper. Must have fallen out of my pocket earlier."

Patroklus's eyes moved to the sleeve of his robe. The stone glowed orange. His eyes met Virgil's. "I see."

Virgil swallowed. The priest said nothing and turned his face straight ahead, peering out the windshield at nothing in particular.

"Um," said Virgil. "It's kind of late. I should take us back to the station."

TWELVE

THE DRIVE TO the station took place under the most oppressive silence Virgil had felt since first introducing himself to his police officer coworkers. He wondered what Patroklus was thinking as he sat in the passenger seat, staring ahead with his usual indiscernible expression. Even when Virgil apologized for going over bumps in the road, Patroklus stared straight ahead without response.

The note might not have referred to the priest. Any of the officers would have worked with an outsider to prove Virgil's incompetence and that his entire profession had no merit. Kostas in particular might do it for free, and might even throw in an assassination if the requester didn't dissent with too much vehemence.

I probably won't know who wrote the note until he's leaning over me, watching me die.

Patroklus had earned suspicion, though. He had pointed Virgil out during the funeral, as though he wanted people to murder Virgil.

Virgil tightened his grip on the steering wheel. He didn't need to go through Patroklus's numerous suspicious behaviors again.

Should I question him while the stone is visible? No, that would be stupid. If the stone reveals his intentions to kill me, he'll feel forced to act immediately. But I could tail him after I drop him off at the station.

His previous attempt at a car chase, when he had chased Tim from Nicholas's apartment, had been a failure of impressive proportions, but Patroklus seemed like he would be a slow driver. Maybe he would go somewhere incriminating, or visit someone who would provide another piece of evidence. The chief's deadline expired in two hours, so Virgil hoped to find proof before then that Patroklus had committed the murder.

Virgil's car lurched into the almost-empty station parking lot and came to a halt in the spot nearest the main door. Without saying a word, Patroklus exited and floated to one of the few cars in the lot. A Sphinx. Virgil waited, hoping his intentions weren't too obvious. *Is he going to think I'm politely waiting to make sure his car starts, or is he going to suspect me of following him?*

Patroklus gave no indication of noticing and entered his inexpensive but respectable car in the same fluid motion with which he conducted all his affairs. A moment later, the Sphinx's lights flashed on, and the car pulled away from its spot and entered the road. Virgil backed out of his own spot and shoved the gas pedal to the floor, offering a prayer to Hebe that he could match Patroklus's speed.

The Sphinx moved at a sedate pace, gliding up and down hills and making smooth turns. It seemed to pass over potholes, while Virgil's Nymph risked losing its tires as it dropped into each one.

He wondered if he maintained enough distance from Patroklus. There weren't many cars on the road, so Patroklus could easily notice the Nymph following him.

This is such a stupid idea. Like all of my ideas. I should never have become a detective, should never have thought I could do anything.

Virgil took a breath. Those thoughts could wait until he was trying to get to sleep. He concentrated on following the Sphinx.

After a few minutes, Patroklus's destination became obvious. Several intersections later, the Sphinx pulled into the tree-shaded parking lot of the huge Temple of Ares. Lights covered the building, making it bright as day. Virgil drove past the structure to make the priest think Virgil wasn't following him. At the next block, Virgil turned around, switched off his headlights, and drove back to the temple. There were no signs that anyone noticed as he parked in the row, farthest from the temple entrance.

What now? Virgil sat behind the steering wheel, watching the temple. No movement. Patroklus must have already gone inside.

Virgil knew he couldn't follow. If he entered the building, the priests would discover him, and Patroklus would learn of his visit. Maybe he could find a window through which to spy on Patroklus.

He grimaced. He hadn't thought this plan through and hadn't initially expected the priest to drive to the temple, anyway. Coming here made Patroklus's plans ambiguous. *Why couldn't he have gone to meet the murderer, or killed another person, or something else helpful?*

Virgil stepped out of the car and eased the door closed. No sounds other than the rustling of leaves. No movement other than the rocking of tree branches. Good. He was still unseen.

He took deliberate steps, following the outside perimeter of the parking lot. The temple's floodlights shone only dimly here, and shadows from the thin line of trimmed trees along the road gave him a modicum of cover. While most of the grounds beyond the perimeter lay bathed in light, darkness covered the areas to the sides of the temple. Virgil decided those spaces would offer the best chances to observe Patroklus.

It felt wrong to be spying on someone on the hallowed ground of a temple. Maybe this place was sacred and maybe it wasn't, but doing espionage here was so vulgar. Like using the flag to blow his nose.

As a child, he had thought of temples as sacred, mysterious, magical. Exactly the way priests wanted you to view them. When he grew older and more distrustful, temples had come to symbolize secrets. He sometimes wished his parents had given him to the priesthood so he could have learned those secrets and determined whether the gods existed.

It was probably for the best that his parents kept him for their own. He probably didn't even possess the aptitude for magic.

Virgil quickened his pace. Maybe attempting surveillance here was pointless. Maybe he—

"What is your purpose here?"

"Diaper-pissing Ares!" Virgil's legs went wobbly as he turned, one step at a time, making no sudden movements. A priest stood behind him, enshrouded in a gray robe. A tiny silver pin, in the shape of a sword, was fastened to his breast. The man's face appeared as impassive as Patroklus's. He folded his arms across his stomach, each hand disappearing into the opposite arm's sleeve.

"I'm sorry!" Virgil clutched his chest, as though he could somehow tame his racing heart. "For the curse, and... I shouldn't say things like that, I know, and please don't hurt me, and... I mean, it's Blasphemer's Week, so maybe it's okay, but probably it isn't..."

The priest said nothing, but he also didn't seem inclined to perform some kind of harmful magic, or call the police.

"So I was, I just got lost, and..."

Virgil's voice trailed off. The priest wouldn't believe that. *What are the consequences for wandering through the temple parking lot?*

Temples were technically public property, but those in charge of enforcing the rules didn't always agree on the conditions under which the rules should be enforced. The priest might have him arrested. Kostas would love to throw Virgil into the back of a police truck. Better to tell the truth and hope for mercy than risk telling lies the priest could unveil.

"I was following someone, and—"

"Following whom?"

Virgil blinked. "Um, Patroklus. He's a priest, too. He came here, and he's been helping me with my investigation, but I got a note, and I'm worried he might be spying on me. So—"

"So you came to this holy place to spy on him." The priest stood rigid, his muscles unmoving and his face stone.

"Yes." It sounded bad when stated so baldly. Virgil looked at his shoes. *What's the priest going to do? Can he excommunicate me?* Virgil remembered the only excommunication he'd heard of, remembered reading about it in the papers and imagining what the poor woman was experiencing. They had tattooed her cheek so that everyone would know the temple had forbidden anyone to employ her, or sell her anything, or offer her succor. He often wondered what had happened to her after that day. The same fate would befall him if anyone discovered the shallowness of his belief, and if the judge were feeling exceedingly kind. In case the priest could determine Virgil's thoughts from his expression, Virgil concentrated on keeping his face blank.

The priest gave no indication he had noticed anything unusual. "What do you wish to know about Patroklus?"

"Um." *Is it really going to be this easy? Is he really going to just answer my questions?* "I guess, just, is he planning to kill me or anything?"

"I see." While most people would have used the ensuing pause to consider the request, the priest appeared to do nothing beyond staring at Virgil.

"Do...do you know if he's planning anything like that?"

"Patroklus is inscrutable even amongst his brethren." A twitch at the priest's mouth, the first indication of any emotion. "Or his near-brethren, I suppose. You know he is a priest and not a Custodian-Priest, yes?"

"Um, I knew he wasn't on the career path to be High-Priest."

"Yes, that is the polite way to say it. During his acolyte period, he displayed no affinity toward any particular god. Most priests do and are assigned to temples accordingly when they become Custodian-Priests." The priest tapped his sword pin. "As Patroklus has no affinity toward any god, a very rare condition, his thoughts are more difficult to discern."

"Okay," said Virgil. "So you don't know his intentions, either. But why isn't he in line to be High-Priest? Not matching a specific god doesn't mean he's not any good, right?"

The Custodian-Priest inclined his head. "You are quite polite and have a kind heart. Unfortunately, those conditions are concomitant with naiveté. Consider this: if no god wanted him, how good could he be?"

"Well, maybe all the gods wanted him."

"No, such is not the way priests are selected. That is why he was assigned to law enforcement. To sate your curiosity as to his purpose at our temple, he sleeps in the dormitories with the real priests." Another twitch of his mouth. "Pardon. I must be more vigilant about maintaining the illusion that all priests are equal. Patroklus sleeps in the dormitories with the Custodian-Priests. He is therefore unlikely to conduct any suspicious activities while here."

"Okay." Those answers helped, at least. Disappointing, though, that one more investigative path had ended in failure.

"Now that your questions have been answered, even your unasked question, will you vacate our premises?"

"Oh." Virgil glanced at his car many meters away. "Um, sure. Yeah, I'll do that. Thank you."

The Custodian-Priest inclined his head and disappeared without sound into the shadows. The night felt undisturbed, as though the priest had never stood here.

Virgil headed back to his car. The venture hadn't been as complete a loss as most of his ideas. He still didn't know if Patroklus wanted to kill him, but at least he had learned that no one else knew, either.

Virgil opened the door to his apartment. After the encounter with the Custodian-Priest, his mind had sifted through all his observations of Patroklus. All the law enforcement priest's behavior could be interpreted as deliberate deception, or harmless incompetence, or as the simple result of unavailable evidence. Maybe Virgil would never know Patroklus's intentions until the priest killed him. Or until his death from old age, or pneumonia, or a tiger attack, or another event unrelated to Patroklus.

He sighed as he lowered himself onto the couch. It groaned its familiar groan, and he began the familiar routine of his lonely night.

Despite the nebulous possibilities surrounding the priest's immediate goals, Virgil felt sorry for him having to spend every night in the dormitories with people who had so little respect for him. *Maybe under other circumstances, Patroklus, Nicholas, and I could have formed a support group. All of us know what it's like for others to hate us, and to dread returning home at night.* Virgil didn't have to endure the ridicule of dormmates, but he knew the loneliness of an empty apartment.

At least he had Chrysanthe. Patroklus didn't have anyone. Nicholas didn't, either. Nicholas didn't even have the friends he thought he had.

Even if Virgil couldn't help Patroklus, he could avenge Nicholas and give the poor man's spirit some peace. Assuming he determined the murderer's identity in the next hour.

One set of clues remained, a tenuous hope for justice. Virgil pulled the diary pages from his pocket and unfolded them, realizing that by reading them he was counting down through Nicholas's final days.

Hera 15. They fired me. They actually fired me. The bastards. I couldn't believe it. They fired me, after all those years I worked for them. After all I put up with. They hired some asshole to play detective and then said they couldn't afford me, too, and that I wasn't a real officer, anyway. I was a real officer. I was a lot better than any of them. I made my share of arrests. The only reason I didn't have stats as good as Kostas or Tektón or Schirra is because they never gave me the good assignments. They were setting me up for failure, and I went along with it. I was too innocent to see what they were doing.

I will never forget Chief Dimitriou's expression when he told me. He smiled. He thought it was some big joke that he was throwing me out on the streets after all my years of service. I wanted to punch him in the face, but civilians can't get away with that kind of thing. Actually, officers can't, either, not with the chief.

I hate them all, and I hate the guy they replaced me with.

Thrown away like trash

Left to drift in the wind

place to place, never resting

Never feeling happiness again

If they knew what it was like,

if they knew the pain and the sadness

and how lost I feel

they would do it again and just laugh louder

But I won't fall

I won't fail

I won't falter

I will rise up again

I am strong

Though I have a mouse's body,

I have the strength of a lion

A full-grown one, not a cub

An asshole. That's what Nicholas thought of him. And he was right to think so. It had already been three days, and Virgil still hadn't found the killer. In fact, he was so incompetent that even a *senator* had heard about his incompetence. He continued reading.

I went to my parents' house to tell them. They'd find out eventually, anyway, and I thought they might have some ideas for jobs. Boris and Alexandros were there. Of course, they started insulting me and telling me I was

*worthless since I didn't have a job. They insinuated that
being a police officer wasn't a real job, that it was what
people did when they weren't good enough to be soldiers.
I told them that at least police officers hadn't lost every
war for the last hundred years. So, they beat me up.*

*Kostas and Collias showed up a few minutes later. I
guess someone had called the police because of a noise
disturbance. Collias said the neighbor had described it
as a, "squealing sound." He asked me to demonstrate. I
told him it was like the sound his mother made every
time I stuck it to her, so he hit me in the stomach and
kicked me in the ribs. It was worth it.*

*Then they arrested my brothers and made a big deal
out of questioning me to find out the cause of the
disturbance. They were laughing the whole time and
referring to me as a civilian. I wanted to punch them
all in the throats.*

The rest of the diary was mostly a list of Nicholas's hatreds
and his activities during the days of his unemployment. He
seemed to spend most of his time between job searches at The
Ferryman's Oar. Tim's name appeared in several entries, never
in an incriminating way.

The entries contained complaints about not having enough
money to buy food. Nicholas would have to pay rent at the end
of the month and didn't know how he would manage.

Virgil flipped to the next page. The last entry had been written only three days ago, only hours before Virgil had arrived
at Nicholas's kitchen to examine the man's lifeless body. Virgil
sighed and began to read Nicholas's last recorded thoughts.

Hera 28: *Visited my parents again for Hera's Day. Always
a mistake. I hate that house and all the reminders it has
of my childhood. Those were the worst years of my life,
and the ones that followed weren't much better.*

Dad barely spoke to me. That's normal, but he spoke even less this time. He's never seemed happy with me, and I think he wishes I had never been born. I don't know what's wrong with me, why I didn't turn out like my brothers. They're big and muscular, and I never have been. I guess they always took my food away and taunted me before eating it. They were always assholes, and they were my parents' favorites.

During the visit, Mom told me I was "precious" and a bunch of other bullshit. Said I was sensitive. She said she wasn't surprised I'd been fired, that I wasn't strong enough physically or mentally to be a police officer, and that maybe I should consider being a hairstylist. I almost walked out right then, but stayed for dinner because I'm running out of food at home.

They never liked me, always thought I was a waste. I disappointed them every day.

I needed a drink, of course, so I went to the bar, and then went to apply for another job. Big mistake. Don't want to talk about it. The guard there took my ID card, threw me outside, and then threw my ID at me. It made a mark on my forehead.

I thought becoming a police officer would finally make my parents proud of me. It didn't work.

Virgil closed the diary and rubbed his eyes, wiping away the stray moisture that had somehow accumulated there. That was it. Nicholas's last recorded words, the last things he would ever say to the world. Nicholas was a man whose life was full of pain, someone who hurt just as badly as Virgil. And someone had seen him and decided he should die.

As Virgil set the pages next to him on the couch, he realized something: none of the bar's denizens, other than Tim, knew where Nicholas lived. But when Nicholas applied for a job during his last night alive, the guard there had taken his ID, and the ID had his address. It couldn't be a coincidence that the guard had encountered him only hours before his murder and also knew his address.

Unfortunately, Nicholas had neglected to mention the most important piece of evidence: the guard's employer. Virgil stood and began pacing the frayed carpet. If he wanted to find where Nicholas went on that last night, he would have to drive everywhere in the city-state.

Someone had sent Virgil threatening notes, though. Someone with access to the police department. Determining the identity of that spy might lead to the killer. Maybe he could ask Patroklus to...

No. Virgil had no hard evidence against the priest but plenty of facts left him suspicious. Patroklus had access to the station, could have placed the note on Virgil's car, could have sabotaged the spells...

In fact, magic had revealed few clues in this investigation. Maybe Senator Kelipapalous and Chrysanthe were right: maybe it was time to try technology. Virgil knew the equipment he needed, but he couldn't purchase it before the stores opened in the morning. After the chief's deadline.

Virgil's mouth tightened. The deadline didn't matter. Even if the chief removed him from the case, Virgil would solve it. Nicholas had suffered and would receive little comfort for it, but he would at least be avenged.

THIRTEEN

AS VIRGIL ENTERED the examination room with his shopping bag, the room's familiar chill washed over him like a northern wind. Though the air stung his skin and smelled of decay and sterility, he felt more relaxed here than anywhere else. *What does that say about me, that I only feel comfortable in a room designed for corpses?*

As he walked by Nicholas's shelf, he paused and placed a hand on it. "I'll try to find out who did this," he said in a whisper, wondering how Nicholas would have responded. "I know it's not much, but it's all I can do. I hope it will make you feel more at peace."

He lowered his shopping bag onto the examination table, careful to not break the bag's contents. The equipment had been expensive, costing him his entire savings and several hard-to-find books from his collection. He removed two items from the bag: a motion detector and a camera. The electronics store clerk had said it would be easy to figure out how to make the two work in combination, but even the clerk had looked as though he didn't believe it.

Leaning over the devices, Virgil picked up the motion detector and turned it in his hand. Several slots on each side looked as though they connected to...something. Maybe the camera had a corresponding slot or a wire or—

"What are you doing now?"

Schirra.

She and Stathis sauntered through the doorway, their faces more creased than normal. Schirra folded her arms across her chest as she stopped in the room's center, her eyes hidden by the sunglasses she wore even indoors. Whatever reason the officers had for coming, Virgil knew he wouldn't enjoy it. Not that he ever enjoyed much of anything.

"Oh, I, uh, nothing." Virgil fumbled the detector, but managed to set it on the table without dropping it.

Schirra strode forward, boots clacking on the tile. She snatched up the camera, turning it in her hands. "Look at you, the hot-shot homicide detective, here to revolutionize how we fight crime."

"It's a camera. I—"

"I know what it is." Schirra's mouth twisted. "It's the fifty-fifth century. I've seen a camera. *Zeus*."

"It doesn't matter, anyway," Stathis said. "You're off the case."

"Yeah, I know the deadline was midnight last night," Virgil said. "I've got an idea, though, and I thought the chief might—"

"The chief is dead." Schirra bowed her head, and Stathis followed her lead.

Virgil blinked. "Wh…"

The chief is…dead? Virgil remembered seeing him yesterday at the funeral, bombastic and angry. To imagine the chief now lying motionless on the ground, like one of his victims, felt surreal. Chief Dimitriou had survived eleven years in his position. Compared to the normal life expectancy of police chiefs, he had been practically immortal.

Why didn't I hear before now? He hadn't, he supposed, spoken to anyone other than the store clerk this morning. Last night, he'd slept soundly enough that he might have missed a call, despite not taking a sleeping pill for the first time in days.

"When? What happened?"

"Like you care." Stathis snorted. "Bet you're even happy about it, since the chief was on your ass to do your job on time."

Of course, Stathis didn't know Virgil hadn't planned to abide by the ultimatum. "I didn't… This…" Virgil shook his head. "How did it happen?"

Stathis shrugged. "He found out who killed Nicholas."

"What? He did? Why didn't he tell me?" Then Virgil realized what had happened.

"He did it the old-fashioned way," Stathis said, confirming Virgil's fear. "None of your detective mumbo jumbo. He decided one of the neighbors did it and challenged him to single combat yesterday afternoon."

Yesterday afternoon? Before the deadline expired? Why?

Schirra shook her head. "But Ares wasn't on the chief's side, and…"

"I don't think Ares had anything to do with it," Virgil said.

"Shut up!" Schirra looked as though she wanted to tear him in half.

Virgil's face reddened, and he looked to the floor. He had said the wrong thing again. With every conversation, he managed to make someone angry.

Schirra hadn't finished being angry. "You sound just like my heathen brother, attributing everything to Odin or Loki or some other false god! Your detective methods aren't helping this case at all. You think you're so much smarter than we are. You look down on us and tell yourself we couldn't possibly understand how to track down a murderer. You just use that as a shield, hiding behind your rules and books, because you're too scared to face a killer. Well, Chief Dimitriou wasn't afraid, and you had better not say anything to tarnish his memory."

"Yeah!" said Stathis. "All you do is slow things down. You're a coward!"

Virgil nodded. "I know I'm a coward. But I'm not slowing things down. This is the right—"

"Shut up!" Schirra said. "I can't believe you have the audacity to question the actions of someone who has done more to punish crime than anyone else in the history of our police department."

"Yeah!" said Stathis. "Your teachers were stupid cowards, and so are you! You just sit here all day and play with your cameras because you don't have the balls to fight."

Did cowardice motivate my choice of career? He swallowed. "No, this—"

"Chief Dimitriou was a real man, and he died like a real man."

"It's just… It doesn't make any sense to handle a criminal investigation like this. You just randomly decide who you think the murderer is and then fight them to prove that you're right?"

Stathis raised his thick fists. "You'd better watch it, Virgil. I've had enough of your shit."

Virgil took a step back. "I'm not trying to be rude, so please don't hurt me, but what conclusions would you draw from the fact that, since the chief has taken office, the average height of convicted criminals has dropped by almost thirty centimeters?"

"You shut up!" Stathis charged forward.

Virgil couldn't dodge before Stathis shoved him in the chest with both hands. Virgil had the briefest sensation of backward motion before slamming into the lab table behind him. His spine screamed while he slid down the table to the floor. Throbbing waves of pain cascaded through his back, rising and falling. *Did I break anything? Am I going to be paralyzed?*

I deserve this. I deserve this.

Stathis loomed over him with bunched fists. "Chief Dimitriou was the best police chief we've had in years! He killed over five hundred murderers!"

"Anyway." Schirra put a hand on Stathis's shoulder and pointed to Nicholas's shelf. "Case closed. Let's coin 'em."

"Wait," croaked Virgil as the two began to remove coins from containers on their utility belts. If he wanted to try magic again, either with Patroklus or another priest, he couldn't let the officers separate Nicholas's soul from the body.

Stathis slid open Nicholas's shelf. Icy fog rose from the compartment.

"Stop." Virgil placed both hands on the floor and pushed himself up. Pain washed over him, but he could move. "Please. I'm not done yet."

Schirra's eyebrows rose as she turned to Virgil. "You look done to me."

"Besides," Stathis added, "the chief already found the murderer. Investigation's over."

Virgil winced as his muscles spasmed. "No, it's not. The chief put me in charge of this." He clutched his back. "Besides, the chief lost the fight, which means that, legally, he didn't find the murderer."

Stathis held a coin in his hand, only centimeters above Nicholas's mouth, and looked to Schirra for confirmation. If she made even the slightest nod, she would cripple or destroy the investigation. Virgil watched her, hoping she would understand.

For a moment, she stared forward without expression. Then she sighed and waved Stathis away. "Whatever, Virgil. You can keep working on it until you give up. At least it'll be fun watching you make a fool of yourself."

Virgil nodded. "Thank you."

"You might want to hurry, though. I could change my mind at any moment."

The two officers returned the coins to their containers. Stathis turned to Virgil and sneered. "Look, Virgil, maybe the neighbor didn't really kill Nicholas, but the point is, nobody cares. If it weren't for you, we'd have already picked the killer."

Schirra smirked. "Kinda like what would've happened if *you* were the one who got killed."

Virgil knew they spoke the truth. The chief likely wouldn't have bothered to avenge Virgil's death in any real way. Virgil would have died and been buried, unmourned by anyone except Chrysanthe. The Elysian Fields service would have looked ridiculous with only one attendee.

Schirra shook her head and looked at Stathis. "Anyway, we need to go to the conference room; we're choosing a new chief." She turned to Virgil. "You can watch, but if you say anything disrespectful, I won't save you from the consequences."

VIRGIL STEPPED INTO the sweltering air of the crowded conference room, which stank of the sweat and farts of thirty men, and immediately received an elbow to the gut. He doubled over, coughing, but Michaelides stared straight ahead with an innocent expression and a twinkling eye. Virgil grunted and shook his head; even if he'd felt inclined to demand an apology, he knew Michaelides wouldn't grant it. Instead, Virgil maneuvered his way to the side wall, well away from the gathering of officers and the table that occupied the center of the room.

All of Arestia's police officers had gathered in this room. That meant the person who left the notes on the corpse and in Virgil's car was likely here. Maybe tomorrow, that person's face would show up on the film from the cameras. Virgil wondered who it would be.

Schirra and Stathis, who had entered several steps ahead of him, forced their way through the morass toward the front of the room. The other officers didn't seem willing to budge, resulting in awkward battles fought with shoulders and elbows.

"Sorry there's not a dress version of the uniform for you, Schirra," Tektón said as Schirra bulled her way past him. Tektón was spiteful and cruel enough to have desecrated the corpse, or to agree to monitor Virgil. A suspect, then.

Galanos chuckled. "Yeah. A lady like you would look a lot prettier in a dress. Or maybe with a couple of your top buttons undone." Galanos had the requisite cruelty to impede the investigation, but not the intelligence.

Schirra frowned, but said nothing. Despite how she treated him, Virgil felt a pang of sympathy for her. *She isn't the kind of person to clandestinely sabotage an investigation. If she wanted me to stop, she would arrange my compliance with her fists. Besides, she already had the opportunity a few minutes ago in the lab.*

Stathis shoved his way toward Galanos. Schirra halted her partner with a hand on his shoulder. He glared, but relented and let his hands fall to his sides.

"Come on, Schirra, lighten up," Galanos said. "It's just a joke. No need to get all mad."

"When you have to tell someone it's a joke," Schirra said in a frosty voice, "it's probably not a good one." She elbowed past him, with Stathis following in her wake.

Other conversations continued throughout the room. Near Virgil, two officers were discussing the latest episode of *Spies For the Alliance: Sparta* in which the SFA tracks down a pair of European militants attempting to destroy an orphanage. Only feverish political manipulation by the European government prevented a righteous war the Greek Alliance would surely have won. Stupid stuff, but people seemed to enjoy it.

"I haven't told you about that day?" Kostas was saying as he entered the room with a pair of officers. "Yeah, so some guy at temple was eyeing Collias's wife. Giving her a good, long, up-and-down, like he wanted more than just a piece. Collias was busy praying, he's a good guy like that, but I saw it. So I stood up, walked down the row, grabbed the guy by the throat, and said so everyone could hear, 'You so much as glance at my partner's wife again, your eyes are going straight up your ass.' Guy kept his face planted on the floor rest of the service, and from what I heard, started driving all the way across town every week just to go to another temple instead."

Kostas's audience laughed. Virgil stepped out of Kostas's way as the officer pushed past and took a seat at the head of the conference table.

Kostas cleared his throat and raised his hand. *He's the kind of person who would have volunteered to hinder the Nicholas investigation and would have* begged *for permission to threaten me.*

While Kostas stood motionless, the other officers shuffled into their final places. Tektón and Galanos, glancing over their shoulders, backed up until they had pressed Virgil against the wall. He had to peer over Tektón's head to watch the proceedings.

"We're here on this second day of Eris," Kostas said, "to vote for a new police chief after the sad loss of Chief Dimitriou in the line of duty." Most people in the room bowed their heads. "Dimitriou was an inspiration, killing five hundred and twenty-seven murderers during his tenure, beating the previous record by one hundred and six."

Virgil thought about the man he'd seen Chief Dimitriou toss into the apartment hallway two days ago. It didn't sound like an honorable legacy. At least Nicholas's neighbor had survived the trial-by-combat. It was weird, though. The guy seemed nice, but it seemed implausible that he could have killed the chief. Maybe he had just gotten a lucky shot.

The officers stamped their feet. "That crazy Malakas was just getting started," said one of them from the middle of the room.

"Kill 'em all!" said another.

"Kill the guy who killed the chief." Bitter laughter throughout the room.

Kostas raised his hand again. "First, we must say the requisite prayer to Ares. Bow your heads."

Virgil watched as the others followed orders. He'd never witnessed this particular ceremony before. Given the youth of most of the officers and the length of the chief's tenure, it seemed likely most of the others here had never seen a vote for a new police chief before, either. It was interesting, in an anthropological sense.

Kostas intoned his words with a grave solemnity he typically reserved for descriptions of his sexual exploits. "Ares, watch over the brave warriors of your city-state. Guide our hands in combat and help us slaughter our enemies. Make us strong so we do not need to rely on strategy.

"We speak to you on this day because one of your own has died. We use the bowl and blade to mingle our blood with his in recognition of the bond between us and you."

Everyone raised their heads. Kostas picked up a bowl from the table and placed it in front of him. According to the rules, Kostas must have placed some of Chief Dimitriou's blood in the ceremonial vessel before the meeting. Drawing a knife from his belt, the man held the blade aloft for a moment before running it across the top of his arm, near his wrist. A thin line of blood welled up, and Kostas held his arm high, allowing several drops of brotherhood to dribble into the vessel. When Kostas pulled his arm away, Artino took the bowl and contributed his own blood before passing the bowl to the next person in line.

Virgil's legs trembled while he watched the vessel's progress. He imagined the knife slicing into his skin, the flesh peeling to each side as blood gushed from the wound. He remembered Nicholas's spear wound the other night, jagged and uneven and gross.

As the bowl traveled from one officer to the next, Virgil wondered how it would feel to hold the blade poised above his arm, having to make the incision while everyone watched. *Will it hurt? Of course it will.*

When the bowl and blade came to Tektón, who stood closest to Virgil, the officer made his offering before looking over his shoulder. His eyes met Virgil's.

Virgil froze. Even if it meant bonding with his coworkers, he didn't know if he could cut into his own arm.

Tektón passed the bowl to the next officer, smirking. Virgil blinked. *That was good, right, not having to cut myself?* It didn't feel like a victory.

The bowl came to a rest on the conference table again, and Kostas raised his hand. "Let's hope that keeps Ares's bloodlust in check for another few years," he said with a light chuckle. "I'm sure Chief Dimitriou wouldn't want us to mourn for him overlong. He would want us to continue his proud tradition of killing the wicked and preserving the honor of our police force. So, let's get to it.

"Before our vote, we'll have the arm wrestling contest. The nominees will face each other and we will then vote accordingly."

The more senior officers strode to the conference table. When Schirra approached, though, Kostas held up a hand. "Not you, Schirra. The men are busy here."

"She's an officer, too," said Stathis.

"I have just as much right to participate as anyone else here." Schirra eyed Artino. "More right than most of you."

"Uh-huh." Kostas shook his head. "As deputy, I'm in charge, and you are not allowed to compete. Of course, the officers can still vote for you."

Schirra snorted. "Sounds like someone's scared."

"Not scared. Just don't want to damage your dainty little arms." Kostas grinned. "Now, take your place, officer."

"Yeah, *Schirra*," said Tektón. "It's called a brotherhood, not a sisterhood. You're on the outside until you can grow a dick."

Schirra stepped to him, until the two were standing face-to-face. Tektón stood several centimeters taller, but Schirra didn't back away.

"You might have a dick," she said, "but it doesn't do much growing."

"Ooooooo," said the officers in the room.

Kostas raised a hand. "Let's have some quiet in here. This is a dignified ceremony, Schirra."

Schirra tensed, and Virgil wondered if she would attack Tektón. After several moments of silence, she stepped back, and the room's atmosphere eased.

Over the next few minutes, pairs of men arm wrestled. After each contest, the loser would storm away to the guffaws of his fellows, while the winner received loud applause. In the end, Tektón defeated his final opponent. He bowed to the shouts of his fellows and, with a jagged grin on his face, returned to his spot near Virgil.

"Well, that was informative," said Kostas after the noise had dissipated. "Time to vote now. We have several deserving candidates, some more deserving than others." He gestured to Tektón, who received another burst of cheers. "So, please fill out your written ballots for your candidate of choice. Turn them in to me, and I'll tally the results and let you know who our next chief is."

Kostas's eyes locked onto Virgil's. "You're not an officer, Virgil, so don't even try to vote. I'll know which one is your handwriting. I don't know what your handwriting looks like, but I'm sure it's weak and full of flowers."

Virgil blinked. *Did Kostas really say that?* After his surprise at the deputy's odd statement, it took Virgil several moments to realize the deputy had forbidden him from participating in the vote. Not that it mattered, given the choices.

"Now let's get this out of the way so we can get started on the memorial feast for Chief Dimitriou."

In silence, the officers passed note cards and pens around the room. Most of the officers finished scribbling down their votes within seconds and flung their cards into a pile on the conference table. Schirra paused for a moment, her mouth tightening, before writing something and setting the card firmly on the table. Two minutes later, everyone had voted.

Kostas began counting, making tallies on a separate sheet of paper. His face remained impassive throughout. Schirra and Stathis exchanged a glance. No one spoke.

Kostas laid down the last card and looked up. Virgil felt his heart pound. *Who's the next chief? Will the elected be more lenient toward me than Dimitriou has been? Or worse?*

"Schirra had two votes." Kostas paused, then grinned. "Come on, people, we're not voting on the most frigid bitch."

Most of the room laughed, some turning to Schirra. She didn't seem to share their mirth. Beside her, Stathis bunched his fists again.

Kostas raised his hand, and the noise died. "Calm down, Schirra, it's just a joke. Let's keep going. I had four votes. Thanks, guys. Artino had seventeen. And Tektón had thirty-two. So we have our winner. Let's give a hand to Chief Tektón."

Applause erupted, people pounding the floor or each other, clapping, shouting. Artino's face twisted at the announcement, his only contribution to the applause a sullen expression. Schirra and Stathis kept their arms to their sides and spoke heatedly. Virgil couldn't hear them at this distance, but he could guess the gist of their words.

Tektón. The man seems like a typical cop, all bluster and testosterone and little patience. My best strategy is to avoid notice. As evidenced by Chief Dimitriou, though, that strategy didn't always work.

Tektón shoved through the ranks and jumped atop the table, raising both arms. "My subordinates!" he said to cheers. "During my tenure as your chief, I promise you only one thing: I am going to kick some ass!"

More cheering and feet pounding the floor. It sounded like a stampede.

"There are a lot of criminals out there who think they can get away with doing their crimes. Well, we're the only thing standing between them and our loved ones, and we can't afford to be soft. Chief Dimitriou knew that. We can't afford to question what we're doing. We can't afford to take months to figure out who committed a crime. We have our instincts, our gut feelings, our massive testicles that let us know in our very bones who the guilty party is.

"Chief Dimitriou was on a streak. Five hundred and twenty-seven convictions. That's a big number. Which means it's no coincidence that the chief died when he did, after letting a *homicide detective* do his work for him."

An ominous direction for the speech to take. Virgil eyed the exit. Too far for him to reach unnoticed.

"Now, the previous chief was a good guy. But he went wrong at the end, and the gods punished him for it."

Virgil blinked. The gods were, according to tradition, ensconced on Mount Olympus for their annual meeting. Even if they existed, they wouldn't have seen the chief's actions.

"Well, I'm not going to make the same mistake. I'm going to be proactive and enforce our senator's bill before it's passed. We're going to start phasing out Virgil."

The officers looked over their shoulders at Virgil. He had seen those looks before on the faces of every classmate who had ever shouted an insult or stolen his books or beaten him until he crumpled into a ball.

"Virgil, clean out your office. The rest of you, remember, we're not just Greeks. We're not from just any city-state in the Alliance. We have Ares on our side. We are Arestia! Now, let's do some feasting and then get back on the streets and bust some heads!"

Tektón leaped to the floor and led the others from the room in a wild charge. For several minutes, Virgil stood in place.

Nothing ever changed, nothing ever improved. Despite attending an academy to learn a valuable profession, he was still treated the same as when he was a child. Everyone still hated him, and his life was still terrible.

He headed upstairs. Maybe he could clean out his former office and set up his equipment before Tektón and the others came back.

A LATE RETURN to his apartment again. Virgil walked to his couch and set down the box containing his personal effects. One step closer to losing his job and, especially since he had donated his savings to the investigation, one step closer to losing his apartment.

A sigh slipped through his lips as he sat on his couch. At least he had figured out how to connect the cameras and motion detectors. After several test runs to verify the equipment worked, he had set up one combination facing the lab door, one facing the records room door, one facing his office, and another facing Patroklus's office. All hidden, to prevent both detection and theft. Tomorrow morning, he would take the film to the developer and look through the resulting photographs to see if any of the cameras had seen the spy. Then he would repeat the cycle every day until he found his target, or until the end of the week, when he would lose his job.

It felt as though everyone wanted him to fail. *What is the point of any of this?* Every time he got something, someone tried to take it away. Everything he did, someone tried to undo. Instead of giving him purpose, this job made him realize nothing he did would ever matter.

And why should it? I have never mattered, so why should my actions?

He picked up *A History of Modern Religion.* Though he needed to sleep now, he knew his body wouldn't let him. And he had to wake up early for another therapy session, where the therapist would undoubtedly tell him all his suspicions about the world were true. Another night for sleeping pills. Virgil set the book down and headed to the medicine cabinet.

FOURTEEN

VIRGIL'S HEAD STILL felt foggy from the sleeping pill, but he had arrived at his appointment on time. He studied the paintings in the room and wondered what the developed film would show when he retrieved it from the cameras and took it to the shop.

Dr. Perikiades leaned back in his chair and tapped his notepad. "Nothing specific you wanted to talk about, then? You could have just said 'no' instead of staring at me."

Virgil forced himself to sit forward on the couch. Then he wondered if that were the wrong thing. *What did Perikiades say last time about sitting?* Virgil sat back and pulled a cold gyro from his pocket. "Sorry."

Perikiades wrinkled his nose when Virgil unwrapped the gyro. "What did you put on that thing?"

Virgil paused with his food halfway to his mouth. "Is it bad? I don't really think about it much."

"Well, I wouldn't eat it. But if you want to subject your body to that, continue. Your profession will probably kill you before your diet does."

The therapist stood and opened the window behind him. A soft breeze ruffled the paper in his notepad.

Perikiades sat again, closer to the window than before. "Speaking of profession, we'll start with that, since you have nothing else to say. A profession is the most important part of a man's life."

Virgil nodded. "Makes sense." He certainly had nothing to offer the world in any other aspect of his life.

"What made you decide to be a homicide detective?"

Virgil noticed his legs had clamped together, so he forced them apart to display confidence. *Why does this room feel even less comfortable than the last time?*

"Um." He took a slow bite of his breakfast. "Chrysanthe told me I should do something different."

"There's a theme there." The therapist frowned. "Chrysanthe seems to be your catalyst."

"Yeah, I guess so."

"Did Chrysanthe tell you to become a homicide detective?"

Virgil shook his head. "That was my decision."

"Right. Now, a man's self-worth is tied to the quality of his work. And the type of work he does. So, what made you choose that particular profession?"

Virgil stopped chewing. "I...I don't know. Why did you become a therapist?"

"To meet women."

"Has it helped?"

"Yep." Dr. Perikiades tapped his pen against his knee. "Yep. Did you have any aptitudes earlier in your life? In school?"

Virgil shifted position on the couch, leaning closer to the arm. "I don't know. I wasn't really that good at anything in school. I kept trying out for the wrestling team, but the coaches said my performance made me basically an extra layer of the mat."

"What about math and science?"

Virgil looked up and shrugged. "I don't... Actually, I think I did make good grades in those classes. I stopped taking them, though."

Dr. Perikiades wrote in his notepad. "Do you feel the eureka moment? I do. If you were good at math and science and not at wrestling, why did you continue to try out for the wrestling team?"

Virgil opened his mouth and then closed it.

Dr. Perikiades paused for several moments. "Exactly. You want to fail. There is something about you that doesn't want you to succeed. This is our eureka moment."

"So, you're saying I should change careers? That I should go into wrestling so I can fail like I want?" *I am such an idiot.* "No, sorry, you're saying I should go into math or science."

But giving up now would prove everything the police officers had ever said about him, and would confirm everything he had thought about himself, and would mean he could never make amends for Nicholas's death.

"Too late for that now, don't you think?" The therapist jotted down notes without looking up. "You've let other people dictate your life choices. The wrestling team, Chrysanthe. So it's no surprise that you've failed at all of them. And because you have failed, you have destroyed your self-esteem."

Virgil put the last bit of gyro in his mouth. "I don't think there was any self-esteem to destroy."

"If you wake up every day thinking you have a good chance of walking down the street without breaking your legs or that you can drink water without choking to death on it, you have at least some self-esteem. That, or you're quite the gambler." Dr. Perikiades tapped his pen against his knee. "Given your previous history with your life choices, you now have only one option."

"Quit?"

Perikiades frowned. "Get better at your job."

"Oh. I'm not sure I can."

"I know you're not. I know. That's why I'm going to cancel one of my appointments tomorrow and have you come in then, too."

"Oh. Okay." Virgil concentrated on keeping his legs in position. He was so bad at living, he had to have twice as many therapy sessions as other people in order to become normal. He crumpled the gyro wrapper and stuffed it in his pocket.

"For now," said Perikiades, "let's continue talking about your predilection for failure. You have chosen a career which is new, which means you can be fired in two different ways: either the job itself is eliminated, or you are fired for personal ineptitude. What do you think of that?"

Virgil's hands squeezed his knees. "I don't think that's why I started. I think—"

"You probably don't think you have sufficient skills." Perikiades shrugged. "A valid concern. But you need to make certain you solve the case, to show yourself you can accomplish goals when you put in effort. I'm sure the victim's family is interested in justice, and that's important, but solving this case is vital for you personally. And from what you've told me, you're not on track for success."

Virgil bowed his head.

FIFTEEN

VIRGIL RETURNED TO police headquarters after his therapy session and found the station in uproar. Throughout the lobby, officers chattered in groups or pairs. Some drew unintelligible diagrams on the dry-erase board on one wall, others demonstrated combat moves on their conversation partners, and others lowered their heads with convincing solemnity. Michaelides and Collias leaned against the front desk, staring at the far wall with distant expressions.

"He was there for me," said Michaelides.

"Yeah," said Collias.

"Couple months back, he and I were called to stop a robbery at a bank. One of the guys had a gun. Don't know how he got it, but he pointed it right at me. Woulda shot me straight in the heart. Tektón stepped in front of me, between me and the gun. Guy pulled the trigger. Gun made some kind of clicking noise, and nothing happened, but Tektón would've taken the bullet. He grabbed the gun and beat the guy in the head with it."

"Yeah," said Collias. "Great partner."

"The best."

Virgil tried to escape their notice as he walked past them to the corner where Schirra and Stathis spoke. They didn't glance in his direction when he stopped several paces away.

"This wouldn't have happened if they had chosen me." Schirra glared into her coffee mug as though its contents had choked a beloved relative. "No one else has the arrest record I do. No one else trains as hard as I do. I'm better at criminal investigations than the rest of them. The records prove it, but no one wants to admit it. I should have been the chief."

Stathis nodded. "Maybe this time."

She snorted and took a sip from her mug. "Yeah, sounds about as plausible as Zeus keeping his dick in his pants for a week."

Virgil wondered why she stayed in the police force when she faced so much opposition. Perikiades had told Virgil he needed to solve his case in order to prove his self-worth. Maybe Schirra felt a similar pressure.

Galanos brushed past Virgil and slapped Schirra in the ass. Her face hardened as the officer laughed and danced away. Stathis moved to pursue, but Schirra put a hand on his shoulder.

"I want to be the one to kill him," she said in a whisper, eyes narrowing. "In the daylight, when he's surrounded by family, when he thinks he's safe."

Virgil stepped closer. "What happened?"

Stathis glared. "Galanos grabbed her ass. He does that every chance he gets."

Virgil blinked. "No, I mean, why is everyone so excited?"

Stathis snorted. "So you're just dismissing the daily harassment?"

Schirra shook her head. "It's okay. I'm used to people looking the other way. Or laughing."

Virgil shuffled and felt his face redden. He had dismissed Schirra's mistreatment the way others dismissed his.

What should I have said instead? Should I have challenged Galanos, despite the personal injury that would have resulted? He forced his hands to remain still. *I wish I didn't exist.*

Schirra turned to him. "Last night, we got an anonymous tip about another murder."

"Who?"

"Don't interrupt me, and you might find out. I don't know who the victim was. No one important. Some security guard from the Keres Lab."

"Really? The Keres Lab?" The lab where Chrysanthe's husband worked. "When did he die?"

"We're guessing about five days ago. Look, these aren't the important details."

Virgil looked down. Professor Lambros had told the class that a true detective intuitively knew the correct questions to ask in any given situation. Virgil had thought about that lesson after therapy this morning and how he never asked the correct question, and had written his resignation in the parking lot. Then he had crumpled the paper and thrown it on the floor, realizing he owed Nicholas vengeance.

"Sorry," he said. "Sorry for wasting your time. What are the important details?"

Schirra sighed. "Tektón was trying to prove himself, and he challenged someone to trial by combat." She gestured to the activity within the office. "The accused won."

"Oh." Virgil closed his eyes for a moment. Tektón had never treated him well, but the thought of him lying dead brought Virgil no comfort. "I guess the chief didn't do any kind of investigation beforehand."

"Did you take a class in how to say the exact wrong thing in every situation?" Schirra shook her head. "Is that what they taught you in homicide school? It sounds as though he went to the apartment complex where the murder took place and picked the biggest guy he could find." Then she glared at him. "What do you know about it, anyway? You wouldn't understand real police work. You're just a homicide detective."

Stathis smirked. "Whatever that is."

Virgil stared at Stathis for a moment, wondering how seriously to take the comment. "I th—"

"Everyone!" Kostas entered the lobby. The officer stood in the entryway with his thumbs in his belt, his face blank.

"Another tragedy has struck our police force," said Kostas. "This morning, we lost Chief Tektón in the line of duty. This is doubly painful because it comes so soon after the death of our previous chief.

"Tektón was a good chief and a strong one. Though he did not serve long, he compensated for his lack of tenure with his bloodlust.

"He requires no more eulogizing, though. Tektón would not want us to mourn overlong. He would want us to choose a new chief and continue with our sacred duty of protecting our community. We will gather in the conference room in thirty minutes."

Without any further words, Kostas left the lobby, and the talking began anew. Most conversations centered on potential candidates for the next chief. Virgil began walking to the lab. No chief was likely to be sympathetic to him.

Schirra placed a hand on Virgil's shoulder and forced him to face her. "You might want to hurry and solve your case," she said. "If you're capable. The next chief might not be so soft on you. I know I wouldn't be."

"But why not?" Virgil backed away when she released his shoulder. "I'm trying to find the actual person who killed Nicholas. You know trials by combat don't work. Two chiefs—"

Stathis stepped forward and folded two thick arms across his chest. "Watch it, Virgil. 'Ares works his will through our hands,'" he said, quoting the opening passage of the police officers' handbook, "'and guides us in ascertaining the criminal. How could the reasoning of a mortal, shortsighted by his lower consciousness, compare to that of a god?'"

"The priests say police chiefs are often used to assassinate political enemies for their senators."

Schirra glared. "You'd better get back to your lab before you piss me off even more."

Virgil watched her hands clench into fists. "Sorry. You're right. That's a good idea."

Turning, he dodged past the other officers who milled about. No one would miss his presence. He headed to the hallways to retrieve his film from the cameras.

AFTER LEARNING OF the unfortunate selection of Artino as the new chief, Virgil had spent the rest of the early afternoon refilling his cameras, scouring the diary again, and trying to sort through the scant evidence he'd collected between involuntary naps on the table in the examination lab. As expected, he had discovered nothing new, and the naps had only made him feel as though he'd gotten even less sleep.

Before Virgil had fully succumbed to his fourth involuntary nap, the developer had called to report that the photographs were ready. Virgil collected them from the shop, reminding himself the photographs would likely offer no insights. Every other approach in the investigation had yielded nothing, so this one should be no different.

Virgil opened the folder from the camera shop and removed the first photograph. A delightful picture of Kostas and Collias walking past the lab, dragging a disheveled figure between them and laughing. Virgil tossed the photo onto the examination table and pulled out the next one. There were several more shots of Kostas and Collias walking past the lab, still dragging the same figure.

In the photographs of the door to his former office, Virgil saw himself moving out his personal effects. He held one of the pictures closer. *Do my clothes really fit that poorly? I guess my hat compensates somewhat. Do I really look that weak?* He shook his head and dropped those pictures onto the pile.

The pictures of Patroklus's office were last. Most showed Patroklus's own arrivals and departures, but two showed a man in a dark blue uniform that Virgil didn't recognize. The photograph of the man's arrival showed his back, and Virgil could see no identifying features other than short dark hair. When the man departed, though, the front of his uniform showed a name tag.

Virgil squinted, but couldn't read the letters. *Maybe if I had something to magnify the image...* He remembered seeing a microscope in the evidence storage room the other day.

Minutes later, he returned from the evidence room with the microscope under his arm. Judging from the bloodstains on its base, someone must have used it at least once.

Virgil set the microscope on his desk and slid the photograph under the clips on the stage. He peered through the eyepiece and adjusted the photograph's position until the strange man's name tag occupied the center of the field of view. Then he twisted the focusing knobs, sharpening the words on the name tag until he could decipher the blurry letters.

Pappas. The man's name was Pappas. A common enough name that it provided no meaningful clue. Another thrilling success story in the long line of successes Virgil had enjoyed in this investigation. He took hold of the photograph's corner to remove it from beneath the clips, but then noticed more writing under the man's name.

"Keres Laboratory." The Alliance's main military laboratory, located at the edge of town. A facility that manufactured weapons of any variety: physical, chemical, biological, nuclear, and magical.

Chrysanthe's husband, Matthaios, worked in the bio warfare department at that lab. *And the murder Tektón had tried to solve, hadn't the victim worked at that lab?* Three days ago, Chief Dimitriou had killed a murder victim's neighbor and then declared the crime solved. *Did that victim also work at Keres Lab?*

After returning the photographs to the folder, Virgil hurried downstairs to the records room. Before entering the camera's field of view, he adjusted his hat and tunic. Adopting a straighter posture, he walked to the records room door, picked the lock, and began searching through the cabinets.

Several minutes later, he had procured the murder report on the body found on Hera 30. As Virgil had suspected, the man had worked at the Keres Lab and had been killed early on Hera 29, the night before the neighbor had reported his death. The same date as the murder Tektón had tried to avenge, and the same date Manikas had died.

It was technically possible that the murders of three people on the same night were a coincidence, despite two of them working at the same laboratory and the third applying for a similar job at an unknown place. And it could be an even more fantastical coincidence that Patroklus had met with another man who worked at that same laboratory. Virgil allowed himself a moment to acknowledge the possibility of a universe with that much whimsy, and then his thoughts returned to reality.

Something must have happened at the Keres Laboratory late on the night of Hera 28. Nicholas must have applied for a job there. Later, he and two security guards had been murdered in their own homes. *Did Nicholas see something he shouldn't have?*

Virgil nodded. Another avenue of investigation. His most plausible yet, one which required the fewest leaps of deduction. While Patroklus had connections to the lab and might have sufficient authority to gain Virgil entrance, Virgil didn't know if he could trust the priest. Matthaios worked there, though. If necessary, Virgil could ask for his help.

Tomorrow, then. After his therapist appointment, he would go to Keres Laboratory, determine Pappas's relationship with Patroklus, and uncover what happened the night of Hera 28. *This case is coming to a close soon.*

SIXTEEN

VIRGIL STUDIED THE tan carpet in Dr. Perikiades's office, noting the shapes formed by patches of light and dark. In-depth examination of the floor allowed him a respite from the therapist's piercing eyes.

At least I didn't make him angry by arriving late again. Virgil hadn't taken a sleeping pill last night. He hadn't needed to, despite his excitement.

He actually had genuine leads on the case. Those cameras were awesome. Maybe they would actually solve the murder. *I should have set them up earlier. They're much better detectives than I am.* He had spent last night calling the families of the murdered guards, although despite Virgil's pleas about how the information would help solve Nicholas's murder, the families had refused to discuss the victims.

Dr. Perikiades cleared his throat. "Having difficulty answering?"

Virgil looked up. "Oh. Sorry. Just lost in thought. What was the question?"

Perikiades rolled his eyes. "I have many better ways of wasting my time than you paying me to watch you stare at the carpet. In the future, answer my questions promptly. Now, again, give me a list of goals, activities, or material goods that make you happy."

"Happy?" The unfamiliar word stumbled across Virgil's tongue. "Well, I think solving the case might make me happy. It's going really well right now. I think whoever killed Nicholas killed other people, too, and I think they work at the Keres Lab."

Dr. Perikiades coughed and sat up straight. "The Keres Lab? Really? So you think you've uncovered some kind of conspiracy? Are you certain you're capable of surviving?"

Virgil blinked. "Oh. I guess I hadn't thought—"

"I mean, solving a murder already sounded above your ability level, right? And now you're trying to expose a network of violent criminals in the highest levels of the military who want to remain secret?"

"Well, I guess—"

Perikiades held up a hand. "That's your decision, of course. We'll work with that. Let's assume that, somehow, through the intercession of the gods or pure luck, you manage to navigate their web of intrigue, find Mr. Manikas's killer, deliver the conspirators to justice, and survive the experience. Can you imagine that?"

Virgil closed his eyes. He could only see the mocking laughter of his coworkers, the disappointed glare of his deceased academy professor, and his body lying dead in his apartment. "Yes."

"Great. Now imagine what happens afterward. You return home to your empty apartment and proceed through your normal routine. Which is..." Perikiades flipped to previous pages in his notebook. "Locking your door, sitting on your couch, reading a book, wishing you were doing something else, trying to hit your dartboard, wishing you had some sort of talent at anything, masturbating if the idea didn't seem too boring at the moment, and taking sleeping pills." The therapist glanced up at Virgil. "When you imagine doing this, are you happy?"

"No."

"Good, because that sounds worse than having a mosquito colony on your dick. You need to find something beyond your work that will give your life meaning. Why do you wake up in the morning?"

"Habit?" Virgil sighed. "I don't know. Sometimes I think the only reason I haven't killed myself is that I know that what might come next is even worse."

"Right. Anyone in your situation would feel the same. Now, you said before you've never had any friends."

"Right. I thought someone was tolerating me once, but I was wrong."

Dr. Perikiades adjusted his glasses. "Friends are good. I recommend them, if you're capable. They'll insult other people to make you feel better about yourself, and can make you feel less lonely for a couple hours at a time. Remember, a lone building doesn't make a city."

"Okay. That sounds nice." Virgil wished Nicholas hadn't died. Maybe under other circumstances, they could have become close. They had similar difficulties fitting in to society and a similar lack of friends. Those commonalities sounded like good foundations for a friendship. "There is a guy, I guess. He's dead, but I feel as though I've gotten to know him. Do..."

Dr. Perikiades's eyes widened. Virgil's hands tightened on his legs again.

Perikiades shook his head. "You realize how pathetic that sounds, right?"

Virgil's face flushed. "Yes. I guess so."

"Thank Zeus. Didn't want to have to explain that." Dr. Perikiades jotted something in his notebook. "Well, maybe we're going a little too fast here, but I'm going to suggest you try to find a friend. That can be your goal for next week. I want you to come in here and tell me about a friend you've made, or at least about your progress toward friendship with someone. Assuming you survive your conspiracy investigation, of course."

Virgil looked at his shoes. *Maybe I can build a mountain from scratch, too.*

"How does that feel? To have a goal, something to work toward?"

"Daunting."

The therapist pursed his lips and made more notes. "Your response shouldn't have surprised me. Well, it's often good

WHEN THE GODS ARE AWAY 151

to face our fears. Unless they kill us, of course. But making a friend shouldn't be lethal, even for you. Give this task appropriate consideration. You will never find any solace in life unless you do this."

Having solace would feel so weird. *Do I even want that? Do I deserve it?*

"Okay." Virgil stood. "Can I go now?"

SEVENTEEN

THE CAR PUTTERED to a stop in the visitors' section at the rear of the Keres Laboratory parking lot. Virgil opened his door and stepped onto the asphalt, gazing toward the distant building. It loomed ahead like a fallen Titan, sprawling to the limits of his vision. Arches and pillars, pure sparkling white, separated the domed partitions and made the lab look like a great leader's tomb, or a temple to a popular god.

And it was a long way from the rear of the parking lot. By the time Virgil arrived at the oaken front doors, sweat soaked his tunic and forehead. He wiped his face off as best as he could and offered a prayer to Hebe for success, another data point for his weekly experiment. After the quick supplication, he entered the building.

Virgil gasped at the lobby's opulence. A high, domed ceiling capped the spacious marble room. Mosaics covered the ceiling and floors. In the hands of some artists, the depictions of the wretched Keres spirits swooping amongst the dying and hopeless could have looked bold and gaudy, but this artist had made them appear tasteful and elegant. Sunlight poured into the room through the series of windows on both levels, making it as bright as a beach. Broad curving staircases led to the top floor, and glass doors along the walls led to hallways. Virgil hadn't seen such beauty and craftsmanship in many years, the last time he'd attended temple.

"May I help you?" A woman sat at the front desk, stacking papers into a pile.

Virgil blinked and came closer. In his peripheral vision, he could see two burly security guards watching him from near one of the staircases, several meters away. He appreciated them considering him a threat.

"I have some questions to ask," Virgil said. "I don't know whom to ask, though."

"You ask me first. Then I tell you if you can ask someone else."

Virgil looked at the desk. "I'm a homicide detective, and I'm conducting a murder investigation."

"Oh, yeah? How exciting." She didn't look excited. "That isn't a question, though."

"Okay." Virgil struggled for a moment to organize his explanation. "Someone was murdered the other day. Nicholas Manikas. And two guards, Petrides and Tantalo. I'm wondering if our priest was involved, and he was talking to someone named Pappas from your organization."

The woman stared for a long moment before responding. "While you still haven't asked an actual question, it sounds as though you're requesting information on one of our employees. We don't offer personal information to the public. I'm certain you understand."

Virgil's breath caught. "Well, I'm not really the public. I'm a h—"

"Are you contradicting me?" The woman gave him an insincere smile.

"No, no, I…I don't do that." Virgil coughed. *What now?* Then he remembered Chrysanthe's husband. "Um, I know someone who works here. Matthaios Vallas. He's in Bio Warfare. He'll vouch for me. Could you tell him Virgil Glezos is—"

"No." The woman leaned forward. "We do not disrupt the work of our scientists here. They have much more important things to do than attend to the needs of demanding *tourists.*"

Virgil's mouth remained open for several seconds before he remembered social niceties and closed it. He didn't know exactly what information he needed, but he knew it was here, within this lab.

"I really don't mean to bother you," he said, eyes downcast, "but this is important. I'm trying to find a murderer, and..."

His voice trailed off as she gestured to the two burly guards. They lumbered forward, folding their arms across their broad chests when they reached him. Virgil's forehead didn't reach their shoulders.

"Agnes," said one of them as his nostrils flared, "is this boy bothering you?"

Virgil looked at his arms. He guessed, from some angles, he could be mistaken for a boy, but—

"Yes," said the woman. "I've asked him to leave, and he refused."

"Hm." The man turned to Virgil. "You're being annoying. You need to leave. Now."

Virgil swallowed. "Sure, but I—"

The other guard grabbed Virgil by the shoulders and hoisted him into the air. Virgil's feet dangled, kicking, though he made certain not to kick the person holding him. This guy could kill him. No one would care about, or even mourn, Virgil's death. They would only express shock that it hadn't come sooner.

Perikiades was right: I don't belong in this field, and I'm not prepared to track down a murderer. I've failed my sister, my professor, and all one of the people in my life who have ever believed in me, and I guess I just counted that person twice.

Virgil tried to push away, uncertain what he would do if he managed to escape the guard's grasp. Instead of loosening his grip, the guard pulled him closer, and Virgil could smell the rankness of the man's breath. Like raw meat left on a counter overnight.

The man smiled. "You will leave on your legs or on your face. Which will it be?"

Virgil knew which option the guard would prefer. "Legs," said Virgil. "I choose legs."

With a disappointed expression, the guard released him. Virgil crumpled to the floor. Trembling, he regained his footing.

Virgil gestured to the door. "I'm just going to go now. If that's okay."

Silence. Virgil took that as acceptance. He squeezed past the guards, who refused to move for him, and wobbled out of the building. The door slammed with resounding force behind him.

That was pathetic. Because of Virgil's ineptitude, he couldn't do anything with the key clues to this investigation. Hebe had failed him. Or maybe she had just realized how pointless it was to help him.

During the long walk back to the car, he couldn't bring himself to lift his head. He didn't belong here, not in this profession. Really, he didn't belong anywhere. The officers were right to mock him.

I needed to question the people at the lab, but I let them eject me from the building. I should resign. I'm never going to solve this case. I'm never going to solve any case. It's just not in my nature.

He opened the car door and slid behind the wheel, letting the shame well up within him. For several moments, hopelessness and despair performed their normal dance routines as they led him to contemplate the meaninglessness of his life. *What have I ever accomplished, what joy have I ever brought to anyone, what meaningful contribution can I ever hope to make?* The usual questions, the ones that didn't make him question his worth as much as they made him fully realize his worthlessness. Then he remembered an idiom: *Sisyphus never gives up.*

Virgil sighed. Maybe he could gather information another way. Even if the receptionist wouldn't cooperate, even if he couldn't speak to Pappas, he still had some clues from the photograph. If this lab operated like other companies, the uniforms corresponded to the departments. Pappas had worn a dark blue uniform. If Virgil could determine which departments used dark blue uniforms, he would know where to search for Pappas. Matthaios might let Virgil visit the laboratory as a guest the next day, or within the next few days.

It wasn't much, but he didn't have anything else to try. Virgil took a breath and pulled himself from the car.

Ducking behind parked vehicles to avoid notice by any watchers from the entrance, Virgil made his way, row by row, to the rear corner of the colossal building. He crept to one of the windows and peered inside. Posters in the hallway featured techniques for obtaining information from unwilling subjects, the tamest of which showed diagrams of pressure points on or inside the human body. It was probably the interrogation department. The corridors were empty, though. He debated waiting for someone to pass by, but decided to continue to another window a few meters away.

Through the next window, he could see two people in red uniforms stride by. No posters, though, so no indication of the activities within the hallway.

As he continued searching for indications of the department's identity, he felt two heavy fingers tap his shoulder. Swallowing, he straightened and turned around. One of the security guards from earlier stood with an amused smirk.

"Seriously?" the guard asked. "We just threw you out a few minutes ago. We just threatened to hurt you if you stuck around. You squealed. It was embarrassing for you. And now…" He gestured to the window. "What did you think was going to happen here?"

"Um." Virgil's knees began to shake as he wondered how it would feel to have his teeth knocked out. He could imagine them being torn from the roots and… He shook his head. "Can I have a redo?"

The guard snorted. "No. I'm going to make sure you don't come back again." He raised a fist, but dropped it as an impish smile replaced his smirk. Reaching into a pocket, the guard withdrew a phone.

Virgil watched him dial. "W-who are you calling?"

ALMOST AN HOUR later, the police truck rumbled toward the laboratory building while the security guard pressed a hand into Virgil's chest, pinning him against the wall. Virgil's heart raced as the vehicle came to a halt several paces away. On the side of the truck, the Arestia police department's skull-and-spear logo leered at him.

For a moment, the truck was still, and Virgil wondered which officers had come. He couldn't see through the tinted windows. Then the two front doors swung open.

Kostas and Collias. Virgil's knees wobbled again, and he only remained standing because of the pressure of the security guard's hand against his chest.

The officers nodded to the guard as they swaggered toward Virgil. "I've been waiting for this for a long time." Kostas removed a pair of handcuffs from his belt. "Virgil, you're under arrest."

EIGHTEEN

VIRGIL'S SHOULDER ABSORBED the brunt of the impact with the front door of the police headquarters. With his hands cuffed behind his back, he couldn't catch himself as he spilled to the floor. His cheek slammed into the tiles, the force rattling his teeth and filling his vision with red.

As his tongue checked the stability of each tooth, he groaned and maneuvered his knees underneath his chest. That allowed him to push himself to his feet and turn to face the door.

Kostas and Collias strutted into the lobby then, their arms raised to the ceiling. "We're back!" Kostas announced. Collias shoved the still-unbalanced Virgil, sending him sprawling back to the floor.

For a moment, Virgil remained stationary on the tile. His shoulder hurt, his mouth ached, he could taste blood, and sharp pain ran through his knees. He looked up to see the dozen or so officers frozen in mid-motion in the lobby, some of them leaning against the counter, others facing each other, and still others holding baklava to their mouths. Several officers began to eye him the way they would watch their food cooking. Virgil was surprised they didn't lick their lips. From their perspective, this was probably incredibly funny. Police officers had arrested their local homicide detective and would lock him away until they "solved" his case for him. Amusing, if one had poor taste.

He almost didn't bother standing again, knowing Collias might shove him once more. Kostas and Collias stared at him, waiting, and Virgil realized he had no choice but to let them continue their joke. He struggled to his feet again. Kostas approached him, and Virgil flinched.

"Relax." The officer chuckled as he grabbed Virgil's arm and swung him around. Virgil teetered for a moment before steadying himself. Kostas lifted Virgil's forearm and inserted a key into the handcuffs. As the handcuffs dropped to the floor, Kostas stepped back. "All is forgiven."

Virgil rubbed his wrists. It didn't help, but he didn't know what else to do. "Why?"

"Because, deep down, I'm a really nice guy." Kostas sauntered toward the lobby desk and slouched against it.

Moments passed without speech. Eyes remained trained on Virgil, scrutinizing him. The officers had something odd in their expressions, something beyond the dislike to which he had grown accustomed, but he couldn't interpret it. After meeting the gaze of everyone in the room and not receiving an answer, he started toward Schirra and Stathis. He approached them not because they were any more kindly disposed toward him than the others, but because he was accustomed to their particular brand of abuse. *Does that mean we're friends? Did I accomplish the goal my therapist gave me?*

Before he reached them, a new shadow appeared on the lobby floor. Everyone turned to watch as Chief Artino swaggered toward the front desk, his hands gripping his bulky belt and a thick sneer across his face. He stopped, pretending not to take notice of the attention he received, and faced Virgil.

"Virgil Glezos," he said, "I formally accuse you of the murder of Nicholas Manikas."

The instant froze, each component of the scene suspended like particles in water: Artino's words, the leers of some officers, the uncomfortable averted gazes of others, Virgil's distant realization of this event's implications. Virgil felt nothing. Not his breath, not his heart, not the clothes against his skin, nor the bruise on his cheek, nor the aches in his wrists, not the sounds trickling into his ears. It was as though he were looking at a photograph of the scene before him, experiencing only the sight and none of the other senses.

Then every sensation rushed forward, engulfing Virgil. Blood pounded in his ears, and his arms shook.

"What... But... No, I..." A formal accusation meant...

"We will begin the trial by combat. Do you need a moment to prepare?"

I need many moments. A lifetime's worth. The police officers watched him, some with teeth bared like wolves and others with embarrassed expressions. *How have I never seen this? How have I missed their...I guess it's not hatred, but it's a lack of any more empathy for me than they would have for an insect.* Shoving him in meetings, insulting his profession, threatening to beat him... He had known it was cruel, but it was still better than in school. But this... This was something beyond. Now they thought it would be funny to kill him.

They wanted him dead.

"This is ridiculous!"

Everyone turned to Schirra, who stepped forward from the far wall. "There's no way Virgil could have killed Nicholas. Do you really think he'd have the stealth to sneak up on Nicholas? Or the strength to drive the spear through Nicholas's chest? Or the courage to even try?"

The officers looked at Virgil and laughed. He had never appreciated mockery before now.

Virgil pointed to Schirra. "She's right. Listen to her."

His only hope was with her. He couldn't fight Artino. He couldn't fight anyone. Artino was going to pulverize him, beat his face in, leave his body broken and bleeding. Virgil could imagine lying on the ground, dying, while grinning officers gathered around and peered down at him as they waited for the remaining life to seep from his body.

Artino waved Schirra away with a huge hand. "Does anyone seriously think *Schirra* knows what she's talking about?"

The laughter stopped. Artino smirked.

Schirra's face turned red. "You're a coward if you challenge Virgil, especially when you know you're wrong."

Artino frowned. "Little lady, you sound like someone who's thinking of committing murder. Probably very soon. Fortunately, the legal system has a way of handling that."

Schirra smiled. "I will enjoy seeing what someone with testicles as shriveled as yours considers fighting."

"My testicles dropping in your face will be the last thing you see." Artino turned to Virgil. "Back to the resolution of our present case."

"Please don't." Virgil's knees shook. Maybe Schirra would continue arguing and convince Artino. The chief had to see that killing Virgil would solve nothing, would only satiate some temporary desire to humiliate someone weak. "I really didn't do it. I'm not any good at fighting." He thought of the blows that would follow, of the pain, of his consciousness fading to nothing. At least that would be an end to his succession of failures.

For a moment, no one said anything, and Virgil began to hope he had swayed them. Then Artino laughed, joined by most of the other officers. They laughed while Virgil stood alone, the noise echoing throughout the room like the police station's version of the bells tolling for new arrivals in Hades.

"You don't have to do this, Artino," Schirra said. "You're better than this."

"The day I need advice from a woman," Artino said, "I'll hang up my testicles. Remember your oath, Schirra. Everyone here swore to obey the police chief, whether you agree with my decisions or not. Stand down, officer."

Virgil hoped Schirra would make some further effort, but she clenched her fists and said nothing more. *She was my last chance.* He felt faint. The room wavered, and Artino's words floated from a distance.

Artino unbuckled his weapons belt, letting it clatter to the floor. "You know the rules." He cracked his knuckles one by one. "No weapons. No allies. No proxies. Just the two of us, and the fight only ends when one of us draws his last breath."

Shit. This is really happening. These are really the last seconds of my life.

Artino's muscles bulged through his uniform. Virgil's buried themselves within extra layers of skin to avoid detection. He could already feel every blow of Artino's fists and boots, hitting him over the head, or in the chest or the legs. Bones breaking, organs bursting, consciousness slipping away as though pulled along by the flow of the Acheron itself.

Schirra's face had tightened, her eyebrows furrowed and her mouth downturned. Stathis frowned, his muscles tensed. Several meters away, Kostas's mouth opened in an anticipatory grin while his brethren leaned forward around him.

Artino faced Virgil. "On this, the fourth day of Eris in the year 5414, I challenge Virgil Glezos to trial by combat."

The official challenge had been issued and couldn't be withdrawn.

Virgil could picture the aftermath. Chrysanthe would receive the call tonight telling her Virgil had been found guilty of murder and had been executed. She would remain calm for the duration of the conversation, then hang up and cry on Matthaios's shoulder.

"He has been accused of murdering Nicholas Manikas on the morning of Hera 29, an act so foul that only his blood will sate the demands of justice."

On Virgil's eighth birthday, his mother had invited some of his classmates to his party. Later, he found she had bribed their parents. It hadn't worked, or at least not the way she had hoped. His classmates had organized a wrestling tournament and ignored him. Chrysanthe, only six at the time, had let him join her in playing with dolls.

"I, Chief Artino, the representative of the law of Arestia and the Greek Alliance and the gods themselves, will face him in combat."

Virgil had spent two years delivering gyros. Simpler times, in which he had only been threatened with death in certain neighborhoods.

"There will be no weapons. There will be no reprieve. There will be no break. There will be no mercy."

He remembered reading every night, falling asleep late to adventure stories, or to scholarly texts about the gods. He remembered playing darts, sometimes in public and more often alone in his home. He remembered the day he had received a certificate of participation from the Academy, a symbol that he had achieved something, or had at least tried.

"We will fight until one of us is dead. Then we will know the verdict of the gods on the case of Virgil's guilt. Let Ares guide us to the truth. In the name of the mighty war god, let the trial by combat begin."

He remembered Chrysanthe after her performance the other day and how happy she'd been to see him.

Artino raised two thick fists and smiled. "Okay. Let's have some fun."

Virgil bolted from the room.

He didn't know what was happening, hadn't consciously thought through anything. One moment, he faced Artino's flashing eyes, and the next, he had spun and flown past the other officers as he raced through the front door. Now his wobbling legs propelled him along the walkway to the parking lot.

As he dropped from the walkway to the asphalt, he heard the station door slam open and the footsteps of the entire force pounding after him. He wouldn't get far.

Artino shouted from behind. "Come back here and let me kill you!"

Virgil's lungs heaved, aching as they choked in what little air he could gather in his headlong flight. With each step, his legs threatened to crumple. Somehow, possibly because he was running for his life, he forced himself to continue, and made it past the rows of parked cars to the grass separating the parking lot from the road. The footsteps behind him sounded closer, and he could feel himself slowing. He could measure his remaining lifespan in meters.

A stumble as he reached the concrete of the road, but he recovered. No time to check for traffic; the others were right behind him. He passed the yellow lines dividing the lanes, wind rushing past his ears and drowning all sound. The other side lay only a few meters farther. He didn't think reaching it would save him, but it would give him a few more moments of life, a few more moments to—

A loud honk came from behind him, followed by a sickening crunch and a liquid sound. Virgil's foot hit the grass on the other side of the road, and he turned to see a huge car squealing to a halt. A bloody figure in blue slid from the car's hood to the street, then lay still.

The other officers stood on the grass on the opposite side of the road, eyes wide as they surveyed the remnants of their former chief. They glanced at Virgil and then to the remains, repeating the cycle over and over in a loop of confusion.

Kostas cleared his throat. "This is…highly irregular."

Artino was dead. Virgil stared at his opponent, comprehending more fully with each second that Artino would not rise again. Another dead police chief, another family without a husband or father, another failure of law enforcement.

Also, no more trial by combat today.

Virgil's breathing began to soften, and his heart to slow. *I survived. I survived.* He should have been dead or dying now, but random circumstances had saved him. Unfortunately, those circumstances also killed the latest chief of police.

Other cars had stopped by now, forming a line behind the car that had struck Artino. Cars farther back honked, and drivers leaned out of their windows to shout incomprehensible insults to those ahead of them.

A man emerged from the car that had killed Artino. Slamming the door shut behind him, he sauntered toward the police with a slight limp. Blood ran down his forehead, and he adjusted his tunic over his medium frame. He stopped several paces away and glanced from Artino's body to the police. "What seems to be the problem, officers?"

Kostas thrust his chest forward. "You, sir, have just interfered with a trial by combat."

The other officers remained silent, their grins from earlier replaced by dropped jaws and blank expressions. Virgil stood still, unable to leave the scene. He felt the same as the time he had broken one of his mother's vases as a child. His mother had found him still standing there minutes later, awaiting punishment.

The driver looked at the gore. "Are trials by combat being done in the middle of the road now?"

"No." Kostas closed his eyes and shook his head. "Fucking shit, Virgil. You ruin everything."

Virgil opened his mouth to apologize, then caught himself. He concentrated on standing in a way that expressed confidence without belligerence. Just like Perikiades had said. Legs farther apart. Take up space.

I'm probably not succeeding.

Schirra folded her arms across her chest. "Artino ruined everything by being a coward and a moron. Looks like the gods gave him what he deserved."

Kostas glared. "Artino was our chief, our comrade, and our friend. If you speak that way about him again, I will smash your face in."

Schirra shrugged. "I challenge you to try."

Kostas blinked and hesitated before responding. "If you continue insulting my fellow officers, I just might accept that challenge."

"Whatever."

Galanos pointed at Virgil. "This is your fault, Virgil. You should have been the one getting hit. When I'm chief, I'm going to accuse you and finish what Chief Artino started."

Schirra gestured to Virgil, who twitched in anticipation of fleeing again. "Virgil's safe now."

Kostas shook his head. "Virgil didn't win that fight. He ran like the coward he is. And Artino died by being hit with a car. This entire thing..." He indicated the scene. "It's just pathetic for everyone involved."

"That's true," Schirra said. "But Virgil can only be accused of the crime once."

Kostas clenched a fist. "Damn it."

Virgil's muscles released. A technicality. He had won on a technicality. He would get to live another day.

The other officers displayed various combinations of disappointment, relief, and sorrow. Virgil decided it might behoove him in the future to spend more time away from the police station. He had won this fight, sort of, but he could accidentally fall down the stairs, or accidentally impale himself with a spear, or accidentally stick his head in the microwave. And as the note the other night had said, someone still had orders to kill him.

Unless the note had referred to Artino. Virgil stared at the remains. Maybe the chief had challenged him at the orders of the murderer.

Either way, he didn't want to stay here any longer. "Can I leave now?"

Kostas glared. "I don't give a shit. You're not worth killing, anyway." He turned to the other officers and waved them toward the station. "Let's head back. We need to vote on a new chief now. Again. Schirra, you gather the remains. You can cast your vote when you're done."

Most of the officers began walking away while Schirra remained behind, standing beside Artino. Virgil joined her. He noticed Stathis approaching from headquarters, carrying a canvas bag, gloves, and cleaning solution. The man cocked his head when he noticed Virgil.

"Thought these would be for you," Stathis said when he arrived. He shrugged.

Schirra glanced up. "Thanks for bringing supplies. Do you have any plastic bags?" Stathis nodded and showed her the contents of the canvas bag.

Virgil stared at Artino's remains, wondering what he should be doing now. It was his fault Artino had been hit.

While Stathis held a large trash bag open, Schirra hoisted Artino's body over her shoulder and dumped it into the sack. The bag strained, but held.

"They're not going to vote for me," she said.

Stathis nodded and tied a knot in the bag.

Schirra opened the bottle of cleaning solution. "Even though I'm the most experienced one left. Even though they keep getting themselves killed for stupid reasons. Even though I have the best record in every aspect of the job. Apparently, a uterus keeps you from performing the duties of a police chief. And it apparently means you only deserve sixty percent of the paycheck of someone with testicles."

Why are people referencing testicles so much today? Virgil felt sorry for Schirra, but he didn't see that aspect of society changing any time soon. He certainly couldn't do anything to change the culture.

The driver, who had stayed silent until now, shrugged and edged toward his car. "I'm heading out now." He clambered inside and, within seconds, had driven off. The line of cars followed, keeping a wide distance from the bag of Artino's remains.

Virgil turned to Schirra. "Thanks for trying to protect me."

Schirra hesitated, then shrugged. "I was doing it for Artino, not you. There's no honor in killing someone as weak as you."

Virgil nodded. "I understand. I still appreciate it." *Why did she hesitate? Does she find the situation as ludicrous as I do?*

Stathis glowered. "You owe her. You never defend her against the other officers."

"I…" Virgil looked at the road and remembered the times the officers had insulted her, or grabbed her, and how he had said nothing. Stathis was right. "Yeah."

"Don't worry." Schirra poured cleaning solution onto the bloodstained road. "I'll make sure you repay me. Right now, though, all I can think about is how I'm having to clean up your mess. Please leave."

"Oh. Okay." Virgil stepped back toward the police station. He began walking, this time paying attention as he crossed the street.

As he walked, he thought about the note in his car the other night. *Did it refer to Artino?* It could have referred to the former chief, or most of the other officers; they all wanted to see Virgil dead. Maybe he had assumed Patroklus's guilt too quickly. *I owe him an apology.*

VIRGIL FELT AS though he had interrupted something important when he entered the priest's police station office. Patroklus sat in a lotus position atop his chair, with hands folded in his lap, his eyes opening as Virgil walked forward. Patroklus placed his feet on the ground and pulled himself toward the desk.

"I'm sorry," said Virgil. "Were you busy?"

Patroklus's expression didn't change. "I am always busy. I didn't expect to see you. Your actions the other night hinted at a lack of trust on your part." Patroklus placed his hands atop the desk, which he had organized with inhuman meticulousness.

"I know." Virgil put his hands in his pockets and looked around the room, noting the worn religious texts and various implements on shelves. "I'm sorry about that. I—"

Patroklus waved toward the empty chair in front of the desk. Virgil attempted a smile and sat.

"I lied about the paper on the car seat the other night." Virgil couldn't bring himself to meet the priest's eyes.

"We both know that I know that."

"Right." Virgil looked at his hands. "It was a note. It said someone in our organization was going to kill me if I continued the investigation. I thought it might be you. I'm sorry."

Patroklus steepled his fingers. "I see. What made you conclude otherwise?"

"Chief Artino tried to kill me today."

Patroklus nodded. "He seems to have failed."

No flinch, no almost-imperceptible motion of an eyelid or eyebrow or cheek. Virgil wondered what Patroklus thought. *Does he not care about my near death, or did he train himself to hide emotion so well that even news like this leaves him unfazed?* Maybe he spent so much time communing with the gods, or with what he described as the gods' spirits, that mortal concerns had ceased to have any meaning for him. That's how other priests explained their imperturbability.

"Yeah, he failed. He got hit by a car and died." Virgil's mouth tightened. "Kostas and everyone else seemed to be disappointed."

"Unsurprising. Perhaps Kostas's mistreatment during his school years has hardened him against the plights of others."

What? Kostas was picked on at school? A bully like that? "Oh. I didn't—"

Patroklus gestured to the door. "Thank you for your apology. However, I'm busy now. Unless there is something else, please allow me to return to my meditation."

"Oh. Okay." Virgil stood. He had probably made the situation worse. "Um, I hope your work goes well." He began to close the door as Patroklus folded himself back into the lotus position, but then remembered the Keres Lab.

"Actually," said Virgil, "I had another question."

Patroklus raised an eyebrow. "What is your question?"

Virgil paused to organize his thoughts. "The other day, I placed a camera with a motion detector near the ceiling, facing your door. It's still there, actually." Patroklus said nothing. "I saw a picture of someone from the Keres Lab visiting your office. Why would—"

"An astute question. I commend your diligence." Patroklus placed one hand atop the other. "Priests are often called upon to bless weapons for military laboratories. This employee, Mr. Pappas, works in the Nuclear Weapons department and brought me paperwork for blessing one of their warheads. I can understand how such an activity would appear suspicious."

"Okay." A simple explanation. He should have questioned Patroklus before driving to the laboratory. That thought reminded him of something else. "Um, since I was arrested, my car is still at the Keres Lab. I don't think anyone else here would be willing to give me a ride, and I'm not sure it would be safe to accept one from them, either. Would you mind...?"

Patroklus folded his hands in his lap. "I have no business there at the moment. I would suggest taking the public transit system. The blue line seems most appropriate."

"Oh." Of course. It was a long drive to the edge of the city-state, and it had been rude of him to ask. "Sorry. Um, bye." He escaped the room.

ONCE AGAIN, VIRGIL returned home late at night. While Arestia had public transportation in a technical sense, the system had loose guidelines for punctuality. At least he had gotten to the laboratory and retrieved his car. The car had, as expected, been vandalized, with the rear left-side window shattered, and a brake light removed with surgical precision.

Sighing and shutting his apartment door, Virgil plucked the darts from the board and walked to the throwing position next to the couch. Unbidden, the memory of Artino's challenge flashed before him. He saw the cruelty in Artino's eyes, remembered trying to come to terms with his own impending death.

No. That was over. The police couldn't accuse him again until the next murder. He steadied himself, took aim, and let the dart fly.

It hit the board. Two more shots, both of them hitting the board. *I'm improving. Best to quit for the night and savor my success.*

He sighed and dragged himself to the dilapidated couch, collapsing onto its firm cushions. Nothing here but his book. Perikiades was right: even if Virgil successfully solved a case, afterward he would only come back here again. Alone. Today, he didn't even have victory to make him feel a little better.

Artino's leering face floated within his mind. Virgil heard his own voice pleading again, then heard Artino make the formal accusation. The scene played, ending with the sight of Artino's body smeared along the road. Then it restarted.

Virgil rubbed his temples. Every remaining clue in the case resided in a laboratory that had denied him access. The families of the victims refused to speak to him. Every time he followed a clue, something terrible happened. And it had all culminated with Artino trying to kill him.

Sadly, it wouldn't have mattered if Artino had succeeded. Virgil would never solve this case. *I should have known from the beginning.* Even the senator, whom Virgil had never met, knew about his incompetence. It was even Virgil's fault Nicholas died.

He stared at his hands. *These useless hands.*

I don't deserve to be here. I don't deserve my job. I don't deserve therapy. I don't deserve happiness. I don't deserve anything. I'm

*a waste. I'm stupid, I'm weak, and all I do is make other people's
lives worse. The world would be better if I weren't in it.*

Standing, he shuffled to the bathroom without considering
why. Head down, reliving his failures. He stepped into the small
room and grabbed the razor blade from the counter. Held it
before him for several seconds. Placed his arm on the counter,
wrist upward. Lowered the razor. Gently applied pressure.

No.

Virgil dropped the blade before it cut into his skin. The
blade bounced off the counter and onto the floor. His hand
shook. *No.* He hurried from the bathroom and stood in the
living room, staring at the wall. *What was I thinking? I don't
want that.*

His hands still shook. *I need to get away from this place.*

Chrysanthe. The one person who could tolerate his presence.
He could visit her. She had said he could stop by her house any
time. *I need to talk to someone who cares.*

Adjusting his hat, Virgil walked out the door and ventured
into the night.

NINETEEN

VIRGIL'S HANDS STILL shook from the razor incident as he walked toward the thin two-story house. No lights were on, not even the porch lights, so he approached with caution. During his previous visit, several months ago, he'd tripped on a loose board and smashed one of Chrysanthe's clay Tyche idols. This time, he stepped over the offending board and made it to the front door without mishap.

He rapped twice against the wooden door, then wondered if he should knock more. *How many times do people usually knock?*

For several moments, nothing happened. He put his hands in his pockets and rocked on his feet while contemplating the appropriate length of time before another round of knocking. Then, a light appeared from the window to his right. The door opened a moment later to reveal his sister standing before a softly lit interior. She wore a fluffy blue bathrobe festooned with colorful octopuses and matching bunny slippers, the same outfit in which she had been married.

"Virgil?" Her eyes were half-shut. "What are you doing here? This late? Come in!"

Before he could move, Chrysanthe leaned forward and hugged him. Hugs always felt odd, like being squeezed with pillows. The last person to have hugged him, other than Chrysanthe, was their mother.

Giving him a light pat on the back, Chrysanthe withdrew and beckoned him inside. Virgil obeyed, shutting the door behind them as he entered the sanctuary. A blanket of warmth enveloped him, somehow comfortable despite the rising temperatures of the summer.

Chrysanthe padded through the hall and past the stairway into the wooden-floored living room. She gestured for him to sit on the plump black couch against the left wall. "You'll best match the décor if you are at the far left, maybe three centimeters from the edge." Her eyes twinkled.

Virgil attempted to smile as he squeezed past the table and sank where she indicated. Chrysanthe lowered herself into the cushion at the other end.

She must have redecorated since his previous visit. Several new figurines and ribbons had made their ways onto the Terpsichore shrine next to Chrysanthe's end of the couch, simple white paper lamps now stood in the corners, and a blank white canvas faced the couch from the opposite wall. "Looks nice."

"Thanks." Her voice sounded bright. "How are you? You look…depressed again."

"I guess so." He looked at his shoes and rubbed his wrist. "But would you trust a cheerful homicide detective?"

She gave him a wan smile. "I don't know, but I'd like to see a cheerful Virgil. Although I'm worried smiling would make your facial muscles cramp up."

"Sorry. I guess I should try to smile more."

"I'm teasing. I'm just worried about you. What's the occasion for the visit? You don't come over very often."

"It's just been awhile." He clasped his hands, turning to the table to hide his wince at the memory of earlier. "And I've had kind of a bad day. I thought I'd stop by. If that's okay?"

She laughed. "Usually, that's the sort of question people ask *before* they show up at someone's house in the middle of the night. It's fine. It's good to see you."

Virgil grimaced. He should have called first, or maybe scheduled a time to see her later in the week. Maybe she didn't want him here right now. Still, even though he'd only been here a few minutes, it was already the best night he'd had in weeks. And after those moments with the razor... He couldn't leave yet.

"Thanks for coming to my show the other night. I know dancing isn't really a hobby of yours."

"Sure. It was... I really—"

Chrysanthe laughed. "That's okay. You don't have to pretend you liked it. I was still glad you came."

"Okay." Virgil tried to lean back, decided it made him look awkward, and sat forward again. Then he noticed his legs brushing against each other and forced them farther apart. "I started therapy, like you recommended."

Chrysanthe chuckled, and Virgil's face grew hot. "I recommended that three years ago. I'm glad you started, though. I think it will help. I don't want you feeling so down all the time."

"I don't, either. Maybe being depressed is helpful, though. It means I'm more likely to take risks, since I'm less concerned about the consequences. That could be good for my job."

For a few moments, Chrysanthe seemed to force herself to remain composed. "That's a horrible thing to say. You're going to get yourself killed if you think like that." She shuddered. "You need to keep going to therapy. It obviously hasn't helped yet."

Virgil's hands gripped his legs more tightly. "Okay."

"So, what has your therapist said?"

"Last time, this morning, he said I should try to find a friend."

"That's a good suggestion. I think that would be really good for you. One effective way to meet people is to join a temple group. That's where I met Matthaios."

Going to temple sounded horrible. He hadn't gone since moving out of their mother's house, and he'd wanted to stop attending long before that. "I don't really get along with those people. They're too certain about everything."

Loud clomping from the staircase interrupted Chrysanthe's response. Virgil craned his neck to look past her as a pair of hairy legs came into view, followed by the rest of Chrysanthe's husband. Matthaios shambled across the hallway floor toward them, dressed in shorts and a tight white tank top. He scratched his stomach and stared blankly as he thudded past

Chrysanthe and flopped into the couch's middle seat. After adjusting his muscular frame for a moment, he put his arm around Chrysanthe and kissed the top of her head.

"Hey, Matthaios," Virgil said.

"Hi, Virgil." Matthaios made it sound like a grunt.

Virgil shifted. "So, how are you two doing?"

"Great!" Chrysanthe beamed. "Matthaios is up for a promotion, and I'm taking on two new students. And I'm thinking of entering the competition this fall. The show's over, so I have more time to prepare personal material."

Matthaios rubbed her back. "You're going to win this year."

"That's good." Virgil's voice had risen an octave. He racked his brain for something else to say and noticed the urn on the table. "You've still got Mom's ashes set out."

"Yeah," Chrysanthe said while Matthaios stared straight ahead. "It makes it feel as though she's still with us. And it's the least we can do for her, since she raised us by herself after Dad was killed." She paused and then fixed Virgil with her lecturing gaze, the one that could be serious or joking. "You know, you could take her, too. Or we could split her. I can scoop some of the ashes into a baggie for you."

Virgil stared at her, still uncertain if she were serious. "I don't think she would find that funny."

"Sure, she would." Chrysanthe laughed. Then she paused. "No, you're right, she probably wouldn't. Still, you could take her now and then."

"She's dead," Virgil said. "I don't think she even—"

"I think it's cute." Matthaios hugged Chrysanthe and kissed her again. She smiled in return. Matthaios faced Virgil. "Actually, we were just about to turn in, so…"

"No, that's all right," Chrysanthe told Virgil. "You can stay. It's always good to see you."

"Even in the middle of the night?" Matthaios said. Virgil winced.

Chrysanthe swatted Matthaios and stood up. "I told him he could come by any time." She turned to Virgil. "Can I get you something to drink?"

"Um, sure." Virgil resisted glancing at Matthaios and instead stared at the floor.

"Talk amongst yourselves while I'm gone." Chrysanthe walked to the kitchen. "Red or white?"

"Um, red." Virgil took a breath. "Can…can I get ice in it?"

Matthaios frowned. "That's disgusting."

Virgil felt his legs clamp together again, but this time let them be. "Okay, I don't need ice."

"It's fine. You can have ice," Chrysanthe called out from the kitchen.

Matthaios leaned back, closed his eyes, and rested his head against the couch. Virgil squirmed in his seat, wondering if he should excuse himself. He stared at the floor, then the table, and continued moving his eyes between the two.

He shouldn't have come. He was ruining their night, just like he ruined everything.

"Um," said Virgil, "that's cool about your promotion."

Matthaios shifted position. "Yep. It is."

"So, what will you be doing now?"

"I'm the new Principal Investigator of the Weaponized Bacterial Infections Unit in the Bio Warfare Department."

"That sounds cool. What w—"

"Do you mind?" Matthaios slouched more. "I'm tired and not in the mood for talking. To you."

"Oh. Okay." Virgil wanted to fold in on himself and disappear. He shouldn't have expected solace. He didn't deserve it. He made everyone's life worse.

Chrysanthe returned. She carried three wine glasses divided precariously between two hands, but the liquid contents didn't shift position as she moved.

"Refills will be coming shortly," she sang while handing the first glass to Matthaios and the second to Virgil. She rejoined them on the couch.

The cool liquid soothed his throat, and a layer of tranquility rolled over his thoughts. Nice and chilled, the way the bartender had made it. He raised the glass to his lips for another sip…

"Virgil." Chrysanthe stretched her arm across Matthaios to hold the aluminum libation bowl for Virgil. "I'd appreciate it, when you're in our house…"

"It's Blasphemers' Week," said Virgil. "The gods aren't paying attention."

"Not an excuse. It's a terrible holiday, anyway." She shook the bowl. "Please."

"Sorry. Sorry." Virgil acquiesced, wasting several drops of perfectly good wine by pouring them in the bowl.

"Thank you." Chrysanthe and Matthaios added their own drops to the bowl before she placed it under the table.

Virgil took another drink. "Doesn't it ever bother you that your religion condones the mistreatment of women?"

Chrysanthe's face hardened. "We are not discussing that again."

Matthaios glared at him and, while sitting up straight, elbowed him in the ribs.

"Ouch," said Virgil. "Sorry." He stared at the blank canvas on the opposite wall. *I said the wrong thing again. Maybe I shouldn't have stopped with that razor.* He shuddered.

"Did you want to look at the photo album?" Chrysanthe asked.

"What?"

Before he could make a decision, she stood up and darted across the room. He didn't know she'd put together a photo album.

"Have you seen it?" Virgil asked Matthaios.

Matthaios nodded without looking at Virgil. "I have to take a shit." He stood and plodded toward the staircase.

Chrysanthe returned a moment later with a thick green book adorned with streaming ribbons. "The ribbons are so that I know it's the photo album instead of our receipt book." She reclaimed her seat. "Also, the receipt book is smaller and blue."

"Looks nice," said Virgil. "Are you sure you all want me here right now? It looks as though—"

"It's fine." She opened the book and flipped past the first few pages, then angled it so Virgil could see.

The next several pages gave an overview of their childhoods. Chrysanthe sitting at a table with her birthday cake, surrounded by twelve other kids. Chrysanthe and her friends in a line for a roller coaster. Chrysanthe and her friends performing a dance routine she'd choreographed before turning twelve. In contrast, Virgil's pictures showed him alone or with Chrysanthe. Their parents were sprinkled throughout the pictures, sometimes sitting with their children or sometimes in the background. Eventually, their father stopped appearing in photographs, but the trend with Chrysanthe and Virgil continued. Chrysanthe always had a flock of admirers, while Virgil sat alone.

"That's what I wanted to show you." Chrysanthe tapped the page.

Virgil looked up from the book. *She wanted to show me she had more friends than I did?*

Chrysanthe must have seen his expression. "I'm sorry; I didn't mean it like that. It's just, do you really want the rest of your life to be like this? You haven't changed since I've known you. And I've known you for a long time. I worry about you. I think your therapist is right. You do need a friend, and I want to make sure you take it seriously, and that this time, you don't wait three years to start trying something someone suggests."

Virgil looked at the floor and took a sip of wine. "Okay. I'll see what I can do." Probably, he was capable of accomplishing nothing in that respect, and failures made the pain deeper.

"It's just that you seem really depressed and that won't change until you do something about it. And really, consider temple. I know you don't think much of it, but it can change your life. You know the saying: 'the goats don't know the gods, and one can see their lot in life.'" Chrysanthe shook her head. "Well, I'll stop harassing you."

She closed the book and set it on the floor beside the couch. Immediately after she did so, Matthaios's heavy footsteps pounded against the stairs.

Matthaios settled into place between the two of them without saying anything and retrieved his wine from the table. He took a sip, leaned back, and placed his arm around Chrysanthe's shoulders. "The wine's good."

"Thanks." Chrysanthe leaned over Matthaios to look at Virgil. "So, how's work?"

Virgil grimaced. "Could be better. The chief accused me of murdering the victim."

"Wait, what?" Her eyes widened. "*You*? But…doesn't that usually mean a trial by combat?"

"Yeah." Virgil looked at the floor. "So, that happened."

"Virgil, I'm so sorry. I can't imagine what that would be like." Chrysanthe looked confused, as though she had heard something incorrectly.

Matthaios straightened. "You won a trial?"

"Technically." Virgil remembered the formal accusation and running and turning to see Artino's remains on the road. A shudder ran through him. "I ran into the street during the trial and the chief followed and got hit by a car. So, I don't know if I won, but I at least can't be accused of the same crime again."

"Oh." Matthaios leaned back again.

"That's terrible." Chrysanthe clenched her fist. "You should have said something earlier. I can't imagine people doing something like that to you. They knew you didn't commit the crime." She stood and began pacing the room. "That place isn't safe for you. If they did it once, they're going to try again. You need to get a job somewhere else."

"You're probably right." Virgil took another sip. "Maybe my death would be good for the profession, though. If everyone knows how dangerous it is to be a homicide detective, more people will want to be one."

Chrysanthe wrinkled her nose. "That's a terrible thing to say. Are you sure you're okay?"

He could see his bathroom again, his arm on the counter, the razor held against his wrist. "I'm fine."

She seemed skeptical. "Did anyone even stand up for you? When you were accused?"

"Schirra did, but no one listened to her." At least Chrysanthe cared about what he had gone through. Patroklus hadn't seemed to. *Would Nicholas have expressed sympathy? Probably not, but he would have felt it on the inside.* "And our chiefs keep dying. We've lost three in the last three days. It's so stupid. They're throwing their lives away. But it's probably the only reason I'm still allowed to investigate Nicholas's murder. The chiefs die before they have time to remove me from the case."

"They had families, right?"

"Yeah. All three of them had a wife and kids."

"Such a barbaric custom." Chrysanthe returned to her place on the couch. "Those chiefs are spouses and parents, and no one thinks anything of them dying. And then they accuse you just because they can. Thinking of you being killed like that... It's infuriating that our modern police force still chooses to handle criminal investigations in such a stupid way."

"I think it's a good idea." Matthaios took another gulp. "It prevents the blood feuds that we had before the police were created."

"It's the fifty-fifth century. Surely there are better ways of preventing blood feuds. Like maybe having an effective method of investigating crime instead of crossing your fingers that you're killing the right person." Chrysanthe looked back to Virgil. "You really need to get out of there. I suppose the decision is being made for you. You heard they're voting on Kelipapalous's bill in three days and they expect it to pass?"

Virgil grimaced, remembering the senator's speech. "Yeah. Whatever they decide, though, I owe Nicholas. He was a good guy, and his death should be avenged. I want the actual killer to be punished, not just whichever random person the police pick. That's worth the risk."

After a long pause, Chrysanthe prompted, "So, do you have any leads?"

"Sort of. Most haven't worked." Virgil swirled the wine in his glass. "Our priest performed two rituals. I've read Nicholas's diary. And I've spent two days tracking down people who knew Nicholas. He apparently owed money to some people at a bar and to someone he met at a Dionysium."

"Oh, I love the Dyonisium!" Chrysanthe said. "All the wine and orgies."

Matthaios grinned. "Good stuff. So many memories."

"If you still have the memories, you're doing it wrong." Chrysanthe and Matthaios laughed.

Virgil blinked, deciding he didn't want to know if they were joking. "Nicholas borrowed money from people since he didn't have a job. He kept applying for jobs, but no one would hire him. Mostly, he was looking into security guard stuff. I thought our priest might be involved, and he was doing something with the lab where you work, Matthaios. Oh, and a couple guards who worked there were killed recently. Petrides and Tantalo. I went by the lab today, but no one told me anything. They just kicked me out."

Matthaios grunted and paused for a moment before his face cracked and he burst into laughter. "I heard about that," he said after his guffaws had subsided. Chrysanthe stared at him. "Everyone at the office was talking about it, how some guy came into the lobby and the guards picked him up and tossed him around. 'I choose legs! I want to leave on my legs!'" He laughed again, then abruptly stopped and straightened his face as he turned to Chrysanthe. "Sorry, I didn't realize at the time that was him."

Virgil blinked. "Yeah, that was me."

Chrysanthe kept her gaze focused on Matthaios. "It doesn't sound that funny."

"Hm. Yeah." Matthaios's mouth twitched. "Guess not."

Chrysanthe didn't appear mollified. "Did you know those two guards who were killed?"

"Petrides and Tantalo?" Matthaios shrugged. "They were the two who were on drugs the other night. The reason I had to go to that meeting and missed your show. They got fired. Didn't know they got killed, too."

"Oh," said Virgil. "That's good to know. That might mean something."

"Hey." Chrysanthe patted Matthaios's leg. "Why don't you escort Virgil into the lab tomorrow?"

Matthaios grimaced. "I don't—"

"Thanks, dear." Chrysanthe turned to Virgil. "Do you have anyone else to talk to? I mean, witnesses or suspects?"

"No."

Matthaios smirked. "Have you tried questioning the corpse?"

"Hey." Chrysanthe swatted Matthaios on the shoulder.

Virgil considered Matthaios's words. Matthaios was joking, but questioning the body would make solving the case ridiculously easy. There wouldn't really be any way, though, other than Patroklus's casting of bones, and that hadn't worked.

Maybe I could... Yes! Patroklus could help and would likely come tonight if requested. With any luck, Virgil could unearth some clues from a conversation with Nicholas. *What should I ask?*

"Virgil?" Chrysanthe asked with concern. "Are you okay?"

"That's actually a good idea." Virgil sat up. "I'll see you all later. I need to try this." He set his wine glass on the table and stood. As he walked, he pulled out his phone to call Patroklus.

"Virgil!" Chrysanthe called when he reached the door. "Are you going to do something stupid?"

As Virgil stepped outside, he heard Matthaios saying, "It's Virgil. Of course, he is."

TWENTY

ONCE AGAIN, NICHOLAS'S pale body lay upon the examination table under a thin blanket. His eyes stared at the ceiling, seeming to beseech the gods for help that had not come. Virgil leaned over the corpse to say something, but paused. In a short time, instead of this one-sided interaction, he would be having a real conversation with Nicholas.

Weird. Virgil felt even weirder realizing he would be talking to Nicholas in the land of the dead.

Virgil rubbed his arms. For the first time, the room's chill felt uncomfortable.

He checked his watch. Patroklus should arrive at any moment, and then they could discuss how to proceed. Virgil had never heard of anyone attempting this line of inquiry before, but the priest should know what to do. Virgil checked his watch again.

How long will it take Patroklus to reach the station? Should he have already made it? Virgil tapped his foot and glanced at the doorway, then back to the client.

"You asked to see me?"

Virgil started. Patroklus stood less than a meter behind him.

"Yes." Virgil sputtered and tried to conceal his startled expression. "Yes, sorry. I'm really sorry it's so late, but this is important."

"More important than my sleep, apparently." Patroklus remained expressionless.

"I'm really sorry about that, but…I want to go to Hades."

"Okay. Now I'm angry."

Virgil put his hands up. "I can explain. This makes sense." He paused, looked down at the client, and organized his thoughts. "If I go to Hades, I can talk to Nicholas. He saw his attacker, so he knows who killed him. Nicholas was stabbed in the front. That makes sense, right?" He looked up at Patroklus, searching those blank eyes for some hint of agreement or scorn or almost anything other than the nothing on display.

"You are uncertain about the existence of the gods, yet you believe in Hades?"

Virgil glanced around the room to make certain no one else could hear. In a whisper, he asked, "Haven't people traveled to Hades and returned?"

Patroklus spoke at normal volume. "That is true."

Another glance, and Virgil whispered again. "So, we know Hades exists. We don't know who created it or why, but we know it's there."

Patroklus inclined his head. "I presume your request implies trust in my intentions."

Virgil flushed. "Um, yes. I'm sorry for not trusting you earlier. I—"

Patroklus raised a hand. "Apologies are unnecessary. What do you hope to learn that you did not learn from the previous rituals?"

"Well…" *Good point. I already asked the victim about the murderer.* "Maybe Nicholas didn't know who killed him, but he could still have information that will help me find the murderer. Or…maybe there weren't enough bone slivers for him to fully explain. Maybe he needed more than one hundred and forty characters, or whatever the maximum number of words is that you can make with those."

Patroklus arched an eyebrow. "Bone casts are not text messages."

"Well, I don't know. But there could be something he can tell me." Virgil wondered how he could find one person out of so many. *Should I wander around, shouting Nicholas's name? If I can get there quickly, Nicholas won't have traveled far.*

"Do you know how difficult and dangerous it is to travel to Hades?"

"No, but I have to try. This is important." Virgil glanced down at the victim again. Murky circumstances surrounded the man's death, but none of those circumstances would have evolved if the police department hadn't fired Nicholas in order to afford hiring Virgil. *It was my fault.* "Is there a specific entrance? Do I have to climb a mountain or something?"

"No. Hades is the next world. It is accessible anywhere, if the right words are spoken and the right conditions are met."

"Great. That sounds easy." No long journeys, no hiking or camping or anything unpleasant. The hard part, then, would be finding Nicholas after arriving.

"It is not easy. Otherwise, everyone would do it. You must be near death, in true danger of dying. Then you must speak the words, 'Hades, Hades, Hades.'"

Virgil watched Patroklus for several seconds, but saw no deviation from the priest's normal staid expression. "Um…"

"The boundary between our world and Hades will become porous in your physical vicinity. You will feel the pull of Hades and will be drawn into it, weakened because of your near-death state."

Virgil blinked as Patroklus's words registered. "Wait, I'm not sure about this near-death state."

"It is a necessary condition."

Virgil thought of Nicholas. Near death wasn't actual death, and Patroklus could drive him to a hospital if necessary. The priest drove so slowly, though. "Okay."

"Spirits in the underworld will feel your weakness and try to take you. If they succeed, you will remain in Hades forever, as though you had actually died. And you may still die due to your body's near-death condition."

Virgil nodded. "So, I may have to fight off some spirits when I get there."

"There will be no fighting the spirits." Patroklus produced a blue plastic bowl and several small square herb jars from his robe. Holding the bowl in one hand, he deftly sprinkled the herbs into it with his other hand. "You will be weak and there will be billions of them. Everyone who has ever died. You will be helpless."

"So, this is a bad idea?"

"I can assemble a charm for you." Patroklus returned the herb jars to his robe and pulled out a bright gold necklace, which he laid in the bowl. "To ward off the spirits, you must wear the charm at all times and keep it in direct contact with your body. It will not hide you from the spirits, but it will prevent them from harming you." He began to stir the bowl's ingredients with a wooden spoon. "But I must caution you, the charm will become an anti-charm if the wearer possesses murderous intent."

"So, if I try to kill someone while I'm in Hades..."

"If you try or even intend to kill someone once you have dissolved the borders between the two worlds, the charm will become a lure, drawing the spirits to the charm's holder. They will take you, and you will remain forever in the land of the dead."

Virgil narrowed his eyes. "Okay, so I won't try to kill any dead people."

"Or anyone in our plane of existence."

While Patroklus continued stirring the mixture within the bowl, Virgil removed two coins from his pocket and turned to Nicholas. It was time.

Virgil leaned over the body. "I hope the rest of your journey is more pleasant than the start. I'll see you soon."

He gripped Nicholas's upper and lower jaws, pulled them open, and reached inside. Holding the tongue against the roof of Nicholas's mouth, he set the coins next to the bottom teeth. Then he lowered the tongue to prevent the coins from sliding down the throat. Although choking no longer concerned the victim, Nicholas would need access to the money. Virgil put a hand beneath the jaw and gently closed Nicholas's mouth. It was done. He wiped his hands on his pants.

At that moment, Patroklus returned the spoon to his robe and extracted the necklace from the bowl. Its interlocking gold links draped over his fingers as he passed it to Virgil.

Virgil stared at the necklace. "Well, I guess I should put this on." Patroklus said nothing.

Virgil removed his hat and, seeing no better resting place, set it on Nicholas's head. It looked good on him.

"You must truly be in danger of dying, and you must know this in your heart," Patroklus said from behind him.

Virgil released the top button from his tunic to loosen the collar, then put the necklace over his head and let it slide under his tunic. A surge of energy traveled throughout his body as the necklace touched his flesh. He smiled, feeling giddy for a moment, barely listening as the priest continued.

"I will not help you. I will not call anyone to help you."

Virgil put his hat back on. It matched the necklace pretty well. He turned to Patroklus, who now stood close enough that their breaths mingled. Then he realized what the priest had said. "Wait, you're not…"

Virgil gasped. Sharp pain burst through his side as he looked up at Patroklus. The priest had no expression. Coldness crept through Virgil's belly, and lightheadedness swept over him. Pain billowed, and tiny tears formed in his eyes.

Patroklus retracted a bloodstained knife. He turned and, without a backward glance, wisped through the doorway and out of sight.

The coldness had now spread to Virgil's chest. Red soaked his tunic, expanding from the wound and popping crimson flowers across his belly. He put a hand to the red and stared in confusion. His arms and legs grew cold, and he felt wobbly. His legs gave way, and he tumbled in slow motion to the floor, cheek resting against the warm tile. No one else was here. He was alone.

Maybe I was wrong about Patroklus not wanting to kill me.

That note… After the trial, Virgil had assumed the note in his car must have referred to Artino or another officer. *Why did I assume that? There wasn't any reason not to believe Patroklus didn't also want me dead.*

Maybe he considers this some bizarre form of aid. What instructions did he give me?

For a moment, Virgil feared they had slipped into the foggy portions of his fading mind. Then he remembered. There was something he was supposed to say. Simple words, shouldn't be hard, but what were they? The lightness in his head threatened to float him away. He needed to do something before he went. From a great distance, faintly, it came to him.

"Hades." It came out as a grunt. He hoped the spirits or the world or whomever was in charge would find the word intelligible.

As though from a distance, he could hear voices. Their words were indiscernible. Faint blue wisps appeared.

Something prodded his mind. *More. There's more I'm supposed to do. More words.* Everything felt so calm and cold, though. *Why bother putting in the effort to say the rest?* "Hades," he forced himself to say out of some kind of moral obligation.

The voices grew louder, and the wisps morphed into hands, then from hands to torsos, then to faces, flowing in and out, becoming more and more solid. More appeared. The hands seemed to reach for him, evaporating into mist when they came too close.

More. I have one more thing to say. Do I really need to finish, though? Why not just drift somewhere comfortable, into this lightness that's beckoning? Wouldn't that feel nice? Everything feels so heavy now, and I could use the rest. Earlier today, someone tried to kill me, and then I tried to kill myself. Wouldn't it be fitting to let myself die now? Wouldn't everyone else be happy? Everyone but Chrysanthe hates me, and she would be relieved of the burden of taking care of me. The world would be better without me.

But he had more work to do.

Gathering strength, he forced a third, "Hades," just before his eyelids collapsed and he floated from existence.

TWENTY-ONE

VIRGIL FLOATED AMIDST darkness as pure spirit, without weight or form. The darkness was as devoid of sensation as the universe must have been before its creation. Nothing existed outside his thoughts, not even his own flesh. *Maybe I am the universe now.*

Maybe this is how it feels to take drugs.

Does this mean I actually died? Were all those first-person accounts and descriptions and geography lessons of Hades just lies? Is the afterlife nothing more than being alone with your thoughts for eternity? He would have cried if he could have; he could imagine no worse fate than to continually re-experience the torments from his coworkers, or how it had felt when his father died, and then his mother, and the way everyone had treated him throughout his entire life.

A bell tolled in the distance, and an overpowering heaviness pulled him down, like an anchor dragging him to the sea bottom. His body had returned. Every cubic centimeter of him felt like an oppressive weight.

His eyes were closed, and he saw nothing but more darkness. None of his senses seemed to work: he could hear nothing, smell nothing, feel nothing. Though he had no sensation of falling, he also had no sensation of support. Before, the entire perceivable universe consisted of nothing but his thoughts; now, it had expanded to consist of nothing but his body.

He tried to open his eyes, but they remained as stone. His arms lay stiff at his side. His legs didn't budge, no matter how he willed them to shift even a millimeter. *Am I paralyzed? Am I even breathing?* Virgil tried to swallow, but his throat refused to respond. *How can I tell if I'm suffocating, if I can't see or feel anything?*

The bell tolled again, its low tone ringing his teeth. His mouth opened, and he gasped for breath, gulping in the chilled air and feeling it scrape through his throat. An unearthly wind swept his body, raking his clothes and threatening to steal his hat. He still couldn't move his arms.

The bell rang once more, and his eyes snapped open.

He was in Hades.

A dark night sky, devoid of stars or clouds, loomed overhead. Mist veiled his vision, blanketing the terrain and obscuring the view from all sides but above. Silhouettes of indiscernible shapes wavered through the mist in the nearby darkness, held at bay by the pale glow of streetlamps lining the well-trodden dirt path on which he lay. Occasional bright sparkles flickered just beyond the silhouettes, disappearing and reappearing at random as though warning him something lurked there.

He knew he should move, should finish his task. *But what if something terrible is out there?* The dead were everywhere around here. He could feel their essences within the ground, even within the air around him.

He sat up, flexing his fingers and blinking. *Why did I insist on coming? What's going to happen when I walk down that path? What will happen if I don't walk down that path? Patroklus should have explained better. Maybe he didn't intend for me to succeed or even return.*

The wind slipped beneath his collar and sliced across his chest, causing goosebumps to sprout across his arms. He rubbed them, savoring the slight heat provided by friction. While doing so, he noticed a slit marring his white tunic. A closer examination revealed the bloodless wound in his belly, reminding him of his travel method. *Perhaps, before visiting Hades, it would have been edifying to have questioned Patroklus further about the details of the procedure required to get here.*

How much time do I have here? Somewhere, his parents wandered this world, together or separately. Maybe he could visit them.

No. He had come to find Nicholas and didn't know how much time remained before he returned to the real world. There wouldn't be further opportunity to interview a firsthand source during this visit, and he didn't think he could take another stabbing, not tonight.

Besides, his parents might not want to see him. They loved him, sure, but maybe they were happy to be free of him now. Maybe they would be ashamed of what he had become. Best to focus on this task and not invite any painful revelations. Grunting, Virgil hoisted himself to his feet.

Another flicker in the distance. *What causes those flickers? Spirits? Some other supernatural phenomenon?* Either way, it wouldn't hurt to avoid them. Reaching beneath his tunic collar, he squeezed the necklace until his trembling subsided. When he had calmed somewhat, he let the jewelry return to its resting place against his chest.

The wind swirled past him again, reminding him that he should begin moving. *Where would Nicholas have gone? Where do spirits usually go after arriving in the afterlife?*

Though the path seemed the obvious choice, and those sparkles beyond the streetlamps on either side of the path discouraged idle exploration elsewhere, no signs indicated which way to go, and the path faded into abyssal darkness in either direction. From the direction he faced, came the sounds of trickling water and of faint waves pressing themselves against the shore. One of the rivers of Hades.

What's waiting for me there? He wished he'd paid more attention in his academy geography courses. *Will spirits see me when I step into the open? Where is Cerberus?*

Virgil took a breath and, though he didn't quite swallow his fears, he did tuck them into the back corner of his mouth to chew later. Adjusting his hat with unsteady hands, he started toward the river and tried to assume he hadn't actually died.

The path crunched beneath his shoes as he walked. He hoped it wasn't made of crushed bone or anything macabre like that. It felt like dirt. Probably, it was dirt.

At the edge of his vision, the path dipped downhill and faded into the mist. Only faint wisps of ground emerged ahead, although occasional twisted voices wafted through the air. Maybe Nicholas's was accompanying them.

Virgil found himself looking forward to meeting the ex-officer. Maybe his idea of friendship with Nicholas wasn't as sad and pathetic as Perikiades had implied. Sure, Nicholas and he might not have much opportunity to develop any emotional connection for the next few decades, but maybe they could lay a foundation for when Virgil returned.

Okay, Perikiades was right: that sounds pathetic.

After Virgil spent several minutes trudging near-blind through the fog, a river poked through the misty veil with pinpricks of distant light reflected in the water. The path dissipated before the river, yielding to flat colorless vegetation. And there, along the riverbank, stood a group of people gazing around in despair, or muttering to themselves or their companions. None of them looked like Nicholas.

Should I attract their attention or hide? The charm Patroklus made for me should protect me if the group notices me, right? The longer Virgil stayed here, the more questions he wished he had asked the priest.

Why are these people waiting, anyway? Why don't they just disperse and wallow in the misery of the afterlife? Or enjoy it, or whatever their preference is? Then he remembered: they still had to cross the river, which meant...

Almost as one, their heads turned to peer even farther down the riverbank at something Virgil couldn't quite make out through the dark fog. The way the people began to gasp, though, he thought he knew what to expect. Something began to emerge, haze and shadow enshrouding it like a dark robe. Then a bright bald head broke through the darkness, appearing almost skeletal in the thin light. Its stone expression could have terrified a battalion, and probably had; every trace of mercy had been eradicated from its surface. As the head advanced, a body formed beneath, dressed in pure black. Arms and legs moved confidently, like juggernauts toward their target. Small round sunglasses hid the eyes, and a cape billowed behind, writhing in the wind as though in the agony of the damned.

"Charon." Virgil spoke the name with reverence. He hadn't even thought about the ferryman when planning the visit here. *If Charon exists, what does that mean about Apollo? Ares? Zeus? More germane to the moment, what will the ferryman do if he finds a living person waiting on the shore of one of the rivers?* Virgil eyed the shadows beyond the path and, weighing the risk, stepped out of Charon's view.

"I see you."

The voice resonated, as loud as though spoken from a distance of mere centimeters. Virgil swallowed and glanced toward Charon to see the ferryman staring directly at him.

Virgil considered his options. He could run down the path, retracing his steps. He could flee into the shadows and brave whatever unknowns awaited there. Or he could plead his case to Charon and hope empathy lay somewhere within that Hadean soul.

Will Charon listen, or feed me to Cerberus? Or possibly drown me in the river? Drowning might not be a bad way to go, and then I'd already be right here at the riverbank, ready for my turn on Charon's boat.

The ferryman spoke again. "You're still alive."

Virgil glanced down at his wound, which remained unchanged. "That's good, I guess."

"You are intruding in my realm. What business do you have here?" Charon stood near the line of people, but his sunglasses did not waver from Virgil. The ferryman's cape fluttered behind him.

Virgil stared at the hard-packed ground, then decided he only had one choice. *I came here to find Nicholas, but the ferryman won't allow me to leave unharmed if I try to run.*

Virgil began walking toward Charon, pulling his hat forward on his head. "Um, I want to talk to someone. He's in Hades."

"Oh, yeah?"

No one in the line seemed able to decide whether to watch Charon or Virgil. Virgil tried to ignore the eyes on him, tried not to worry about his likely fate. "Yeah. I'm a detective in charge—"

Charon held up a pale hand. "Let me stop you right there."

Virgil took the words literally and halted several paces from Charon. *How much longer before I return to the overworld and lose my chance to speak to Nicholas? And lose my chance to give credibility to my profession? And lose my chance to bring justice to a victim?*

"Not only is it not in my job description to deal with the living, but do you see this?" Charon waved to indicate the line.

"Do you mean all the people?"

"Yeah. I've got a huge line of dead people who got here ahead of you." Charon glanced back at them, and they squirmed. "You all just hold on. Pretend you're in line for a roller coaster."

Despite Charon's demeanor, several moments had passed since Virgil's discovery, and Virgil remained unharmed. Maybe Charon wouldn't blast him into nothingness or kill him in some other grotesque way.

Virgil rubbed the back of his head. "I'm sorry, I don't mean to cause problems. It's just, I went to a lot of trouble." He racked his brain for something to offer. Nicholas might have had the fee for passage across the Acheron now that Virgil had coined him, but Virgil hadn't thought to bring coins for himself. *Maybe...* Virgil produced his wallet and removed a paper five-drachma bill before returning the wallet to his pocket. "Um, maybe you could just look the other way or something?"

Charon plucked the bill from Virgil's fingers and eyed it with repugnance. "Look the other way while I take you across the Acheron? Sound plausible to you? What if you were my boss, and I tried to lay that kind of story on you? 'Oh, you know, sir, I was just looking the other way and he snuck past me. My bad.'"

Virgil adjusted his hat and tried to think of a response.

"And what am I supposed to do with this money, anyway?"

"Well..."

"Take a look around." Charon waved his hand to indicate the shadowy world around them. "You notice any shopping malls? Movie theaters? Nail salons? Not a lot of merchandise to be had. What am I supposed to use this for?" He waved the bill in Virgil's face. "Making paper airplanes?"

"Um," Virgil managed to say while Charon tucked the bill into a cloak pocket.

"And do you know what the dead are going to do to you if I even did decide to take you across?"

"Right!" Virgil reached under his tunic and pulled out the necklace, making sure to keep his hand on the charm itself. "I've got this charm—"

"Yeah, I'm sure you do." Charon's voice dripped with the kind of condescension reserved for a hated enemy or child. "Everyone's got a charm. You know how many people come down here with fake charms, smiling and whistling like they're perfectly safe just seconds before they get nabbed? The fake-charm business is booming up there."

"Um." Virgil put the necklace back under his tunic. *Patroklus wouldn't have cheated me, right? The priest would have made the charm correctly, wouldn't he? Sure, he was irritated about the late-night call, but not so much that he would have set me up to be trapped in Hades. Although, Patroklus did stab me. Maybe he actually was angry about his interrupted sleep, or maybe he really was working for Nicholas's murderer.* "I… The guy who gave me this… He didn't ask for money…"

"Well, whatever. Even disregarding that, you must have done something stupid to get down here." Charon leaned forward, examining Virgil. "What'd you do, stab yourself?"

Virgil shook his head. "*I* didn't."

Charon nodded, again with condescension. "So, you get points for desperation. It's pretty important you talk to this person, then? More than a chat about the latest fashion trends in Athens?"

"Yeah," Virgil said. "It's prob—"

"Cool. Look, it's not like I get a lot of people who actually want to be here. No one ever comes to visit me or anything. And the people who do come down here… Well, they're not exactly the *life* of the party." He seemed to stare at Virgil expectantly.

"Look, I really need—"

Charon sighed, looking more peeved than when he had first noticed Virgil. "Okay. Fine. You're desperate, and I don't have a lot else to do. Or, at least nothing that I won't already be doing until old age gets me, anyway."

"Oh." *This might really work.* "Thanks!"

"Yeah, you owe me. Come on." Charon spun to return to the mist, his cape twirling about him. Before the cape had fully settled, Charon called out to the line of souls. "Wait here. You guys are next."

In a quieter voice, Charon said to Virgil, "Can't take anyone else this trip, since I don't want a lot of witnesses seeing me break the rules." He began striding quickly along the river-bank without bothering to see if Virgil followed. Virgil stared at the line of souls for a moment and then hurried after the ferryman as quickly as his protesting lungs would allow.

"So, where's your boat?" Virgil asked, wheezing, when he caught up.

"Boat?" Charon snorted. "That might have been fine six thousand years ago, but we keep up with the times down here."

They passed through a curtain of mist dividing the waiting area from the rest of the river's edge and emerged into a dark clearing to see, parked along the muddy waterfront, a large yellow bus. Mud spattered its tires and the bottom third of its exterior, and black paint labeled it as "Hades Route 1."

Virgil blinked. "You've got a bus."

"Yep."

"Charon is a bus driver."

Charon frowned. "It's a lot more efficient than a taxi, and a lot better than rowing a ferry back and forth all day."

Virgil blanched. "Yeah, yeah, it's great. I was just surprised." Not a good idea to piss off Charon.

"Hm. Well, get in."

They walked to the door at the front of the bus and climbed in. Charon took his spot behind the steering wheel, and Virgil slid into the seat directly behind him. The bus rumbled to a start, a tremor passing along its body, and the low-quality speakers blared into action with one of those songs Chrysanthe liked, something with harmonies and ridiculous devotional words:

It's Blasphemer's Week, my child

When the world's allowed to grow wild

And when the gods are away

The killers come to play

It's Blasphemer's Week, my daughter

When flames of violence grow hotter

Because when the gods are away

The wicked won't pay

"Not too bad, huh?" Charon asked as the bus bounced its way along the riverbank.

"I don't like the song," Virgil said. "Can we listen to something else?"

It's Blasphemer's Week, my son

No place to run, no help will come

For when the gods are away

Even the faithful can't pray

"Oh, yeah?" Charon snapped the radio off with more force than necessary. "You have any other requests? Want me to shave your testicles or something?"

"No!" Virgil shook his head and glanced down at the bus's sticky floor. *What is it with people talking about testicles today?* "Sorry. You can put the song back on. I don't mind."

"Whatever."

They rode in silence. *Has anyone ever questioned the musical tastes of the ferryman to the underworld before?* Virgil wondered if he should say something to alleviate the awkwardness, but the right words didn't come. Instead, he stared out the window as the river rolled beside them. The water looked like a sheet of darkness, a mirror to the featureless sky above. Even if a sun shone down on this dark world, Virgil doubted he could have seen the bottom of that thick river. No wonder people preferred to pay Charon's price rather than risk swimming.

"So, what do you use the obol for?" he asked the ferryman.

"'Obol?' '*Obol?*' Just say 'coin', dude; it's not the second century. Shit." Charon shook his head. "You know, we use it for various things. Gas money, maintaining the roads, keeping the rivers clean, solstice pizza parties. It all goes to a good cause."

"Gas money?"

"Well, yeah. What do you think the bus runs on? Hopes and dreams?" Charon shook his head. "I've got a place up top I go regularly. Nice, quiet place in Athens."

"Did you use the coins to get your cape?"

"You like that?" Virgil could hear the pride in the ferryman's voice. "I got it used, but it's so awesome. Everyone's gotta have their 'thing,' and this is mine. If you don't remember anything else from your time down here, remember this: the cape might be optional, but looking cool is not."

"I'll keep that in mind." Virgil wondered if he had ever looked cool. *Would my coworkers have trusted or respected me more if I had a different hat? Or maybe a cape, like Charon? Likely, anything I did would serve as more fodder for humiliation.*

"You know," Charon said as they continued through the darkness, "you're a little more on the quiet and demanding side than I usually like, but I tell you what, you got balls coming down here. Most people would be too scared of what Hades would do to them."

"Oh." *Does the god Hades wait across the Acheron to deal punishment to presumptuous chthonic travelers?* Another lapse in information flow from Patroklus. Virgil's stomach tightened. The gods had never shown their presence before, had only been stories from childhood. Charon existed, though, and if Charon existed, maybe the gods could, too. And those gods were not beings who suffered foolishness or disrespect. Virgil didn't want to carry the world on his shoulders or have his liver eaten for eternity, and had never seriously considered the possibility before now. "Is that something I should be concerned about?" he asked, trying to keep his voice steady.

"Eh." Charon shrugged, showing the nonchalance of one who didn't potentially face an existence comprised entirely of pain and suffering. "Just between you and me, I'm not sure Hades even exists. I mean, Hades the place? Sure. But Hades the dude? I dunno."

"Good." Virgil felt his shoulders relax. "I've always wondered if the gods really exist."

"Well, whether they do or not, it's the threat of Hades that keeps people in line. Makes my job easier and keeps the back-talk down. My imposing presence doesn't hurt, either, huh?" Charon turned to grin at him. "And between the threat of Hades, fake charms, and botched near-death experiences, the riffraff stay out. The living ones, anyway. You have no idea how many stupid academy kids end up dead when they try visiting here. Sometimes it's like a fucking frat party on the riverbank."

Virgil nodded, but couldn't think of an appropriate response. He stared out the window. After a few moments of silence, Charon spoke again. "Anyway, my point is that you're in a good mental position if you're this brave right now. Once you get to the afterlife, you don't change at all. I mean, I'm not dead yet, so I still change. All these other people, though? Just the way they were when they left real life. That's what some of my coworkers told me, so I talked to some of the old-timers and it's true. You might learn something here or there, but your personality stays the same. Really sucks for the depressed ones. Can't even escape by killing themselves. Not something you have to worry about, though."

"Yeah, I guess not." Virgil declined elaboration.

Through the darkness and haze ahead of them, a structure emerged. It grew and came more into focus with each meter traveled until revealing itself as a large metal bridge crossing over the Acheron. The bus slowed and turned onto the bridge, going over a slight bump as they transitioned from the river-bank to the clanging metal. Virgil was crossing the river now, on his way into the realm of the dead. Trying not to become overwhelmed by the idea, he distracted himself by peering past the iron railings to the dark waters below. He imagined the bus toppling into the frigid river, him struggling to break through a window and swim to the surface, and then him surrendering to the inevitable. A good impediment for people who might otherwise view the afterworld as a tourist destination, or who wanted a continuing relationship with loved ones.

"Bridge is not pedestrian-friendly," Charon said. "Magical barriers. You know."

"Okay." Some places didn't have the infrastructure for walking or biking.

"Yeah, it's pretty lonely down here. Don't really get to talk to people much except coworkers on occasion. Not sure how my predecessors did it. The hiring agency sold it to me as a glamorous job, like it was all kinds of exciting."

Predecessors? "It's not exciting?"

"No, dude, not at all. Everyone I'm giving rides to is either quiet and contemplative, or just bitching about being dead. It's like, get over it already. Or, if you want to complain, wait until we get across the bridge, because I certainly don't want to hear it." Charon shrugged while the bus reached the bridge's apex. "I was sympathetic at first, but when you hear your thousandth sob story that's exactly the same as the other nine hundred and ninety-nine, you start getting a bit inured to it all."

"Are there at least any good parts to the job?"

"Elysian Fields, bro!" Virgil could see Charon's broad smile from the man's profile. "I just have to give up spending my mortal life in the world above, and I get a free ticket to the Elysian Fields. No boring normal afterlife for *this* guy!"

Virgil shrugged. "That sounds okay, I guess."

"*Okay?* Not everyone gets to go to the Elysian Fields when they die. You know who does? Heroes. And I'm gonna be right there with 'em, chummin' it up with fuckin' Herakles and Achilles and shit."

At least Charon had a happy afterlife awaiting him after a lifetime of boredom and misery. Virgil couldn't say the same.

It struck Virgil that he'd actually enjoyed this conversation. Charon treated him somewhat like an equal. Only Chrysanthe had ever treated Virgil like that before. It was unfortunate he had to travel to the underworld to experience that treatment.

The bus went over another slight bump, signaling that they had left the bridge and emerged onto the opposite riverbank. He was really here. He was really in Hades.

That reminded him. "Um, I have a question."

"No surprise there," Charon said. "You seem like the kind of dude who always has a question."

"Yeah." Virgil's fingers tightened about his knees. "How do I find Nicholas?"

Charon laughed. "Oh, man, that's a tough one. Yeah, Hades is pretty big. Your guy could be almost anywhere by now, and you probably don't have a lot of time before you wake up."

"Oh."

"Unless you don't wake up. But then it won't really matter whether you find your guy or not."

So stupid. Virgil had risked his life for nothing. There was no way he would be able to find Nicholas in the vastness of Hades before waking up. He cursed himself for putting the coins in Nicholas's mouth; if he hadn't, the officer would have been wandering around near the riverbank, and Virgil would have already found him. The coins hadn't been in place long, though. "Well, he just got here a few minutes before I did."

"Really?" Charon shrugged. "What's he look like?"

"Dark hair, thin, medium height. He had a spear wound in his chest."

"Think I know your man." Charon grinned. "Look at me, saving the day. Yeah, your buddy was here for several days. We'd talk now and then. Kind of a jerk sometimes, but it was nice to see a recurring face. He just got his coins a little bit ago, like you said, so I figured it was fair to jump him to the front of the line since he'd been here so long. Took him in the load right before I saw you. He was sitting right where you're sitting. I told him he ought to check out the forest, since it looks pretty cool and people seem to throw a lot of parties there. Looked like he was considering it, so that's probably your best bet."

Virgil nodded. Maybe not a wasted trip, then. Maybe he would actually get the information he needed. "I'll try that. That's really helpful."

"That's my job. Customer service for the afterlife. Like a department store greeter and a chauffeur in one package." Charon nodded, smiling. "Oh, yeah, you'll want to look out for Cerberus, too."

Virgil blinked. He'd forgotten. "What...? Will my charm work?"

"Nope, not on living beings." Charon shook his head. "You know, not to be a dick or anything, but you seem to have gone into this venture woefully unprepared."

"Yeah." Yet another item to bring up with Patroklus. "What do I do? How do I avoid him?"

"Them. 'How do you avoid *them?*' The first Cerberus actually was a three-headed dog, but he was just a mutant. After that, management started using three wolves and collectively called them 'Cerberus.' You know, to keep the three-heads thing going." Charon shuddered. "Honestly, I'd be a lot less scared of some mutant dog than a pack of wolves."

"Will they know I'm here?"

"They'll know soon as you step off the bus. You've probably got time before they get here, though."

"What will they do when...if..."

Charon made a face. "They're hungry, and they've been conditioned to hunt people, so they're not going to do anything good."

Virgil put his head in his hands. Such a stupid idea. All of it. He should never have suggested it. *Why did Patroklus agree if he knew all the risks?*

Maintain a steady breathing rate. Don't panic. Just be prepared. He would have to run as soon as he left the bus. *Then what?* It wouldn't matter if he found Nicholas, if the wolves found him in the middle of their conversation. He needed a moment to think, to plan his moves.

The bus pulled to a stop. "Here we are." Charon flipped the door open. "You might want to run."

Virgil blinked, and his stomach twisted. "Wait, what do—"

"Just get out." A pause. "And if anyone asks, I never saw you."

Virgil clambered down the steps and jumped out. "Thanks."

Before the door had even fully closed, the bus began to circle around toward the bridge. As it crept toward the metal archway, Virgil could hear Charon call out, "See you later!"

Considering the ferryman's job, that actually sounded pretty ominous.

The bus disappeared into the mist, and Virgil was alone again.

TWENTY-TWO

VIRGIL TURNED, EXAMINING his surroundings for signs of movement. Cerberus would have already begun the hunt, catching their quarry's scent after Virgil had disembarked from the bus. No wolves yet, but the forest stood a short distance away.

Time to run, then. He sent a silent prayer to Hebe to prevent the wolves finding him, and then sprinted toward the forest, keeping his eyes to the shadowed ground. Uneven patches caused him to stumble every few steps, but he never completely lost his footing. Each breath squeezed his chest as though a building column had fallen across it. His side began to cramp. Tendons in his knees stiffened. Glancing up, he saw he had only crossed half the distance to the forest. At least no wolves had appeared, and his stomach wound remained oddly silent.

A few moments later, he stopped and leaned over, panting. He couldn't run anymore, not with his lungs on the verge of collapse and his body threatening mutiny. Running twice in one day was too much, especially when his life had depended on it both times.

Despite his gasping lungs and aching side, he managed to hobble to the edge of the forest and crouch behind one of the trees. He peeked through the underbrush to the open field from which he had come. Nothing. Probably, the wolves wouldn't strike from that direction. They knew which direction travelers came from, so they would strike from the rear. Maybe they had already arrived. Maybe—

Something cold brushed his arm.

Virgil's shriek filled the still air. He clamped his mouth shut. A translucent blue shadow flitted past him and into the darkness of the forest. Goosebumps covered his skin where the shadow had come into contact with him. *Did it do something to me? Was that the first step toward the spirits trapping me here? Did it take away a piece of my soul or my essence?* He rubbed his arm, then pulled his hand away. *Is that part of my skin infectious now? Did I just spread the contagion to my hand?*

Virgil forced himself to take a breath. Nothing seemed different. He felt exactly the same as before. Everything was fine. Maybe the charm had repelled the spirit. Still, he decided it would be wise to avoid contact with any more of those things since he didn't know what they could to do to him or even how spirits could physically interact with the living.

He wished he had more information on this world. *Do all priests explain situations as poorly as Patroklus?*

No more shadows floated nearby, or at least none he could see, but the wolves knew his location now if they hadn't before. He strained his ears, but could hear nothing. *Maybe I have a few more moments before they arrive. Time to start the search.* Charon said Nicholas would probably be in the forest somewhere.

"Nicholas?" he called, unsure how to proceed, but knowing he had to try something. No response. "Nicholas Manikas?"

With great trepidation, he strode deeper into the forest. The branches and leaves seemed to cling to his sleeves and pant legs, as though to hold him in place for Cerberus. At each step, he had to pluck himself free.

Another shade flew along the ground near him, disappearing into the underbrush after a few seconds. Then another and another, always several paces away. None paid him any notice, and Virgil patted his charm, thinking positively of Patroklus for the first time since arriving in Hades.

"Nicholas?"

Nothing. Only the sounds of trees and the wind whistling through them.

Then he heard the crackling of a leaf to his right. A pair of eyes peeking from within the underbrush. Cerberus had arrived.

Wolves are clever hunters, right? They likely have me surrounded. His heart raced. *What do I do now? What does one do when being hunted by wolves?* Whichever way he walked, he would be headed toward one of them, until they lunged and killed him in a frenzy of teeth and claws. Water welled in his eyes. This wasn't how he wanted to die. *Patroklus should have said something. Charon shouldn't have left me like this. I should never have tried to solve this mystery or ever believed I had something to offer the world.*

Another crackle. The wolves were coming closer, getting ready to make their moves. *Why are they bothering to be so crafty?* They didn't need to put in any great effort to kill him. Maybe they were savoring the rare opportunity to hunt.

Virgil looked up. *The trees.*

He wrapped his arms around the trunk closest to him and tried to shimmy up. As he lifted his arms to raise himself another few centimeters, his legs slipped, and he toppled away from the tree, landing on his butt.

The wolves are laughing now.

He eyed the lowest branch above him. It looked thick enough to support his weight, but it was just out of reach. He jumped, grabbing hold of it. His legs swung, and his hands threatened to slide off, and his arms threatened to just surrender unconditionally, but his feet managed to find purchase against the trunk. Holding onto the branch, he walked his legs up the trunk until he was parallel to the ground, and then rotated himself around the branch so he was lying on top of it.

A rustle came from below. A wolf stood at the base of the tree.

Virgil whimpered and squeezed the branch tightly. The wolf settled directly beneath Virgil, sitting on its haunches. It seemed to smile at him, as though it knew he could go nowhere. Thick white and gray fur, piercing eyes, and sharp, sharp teeth.

The other wolves emerged from the underbrush, taking up positions around the tree. They had trapped him, leaving him no way to seek Nicholas. *My desperate, unplanned attempt has somehow failed.*

After taking a moment to allow his heart to calm, Virgil slid himself backward along the branch, then pulled himself into a sitting position, with his back against the tree trunk. His legs dangled well above the predators. The branch felt steady. *It should hold.*

What now? Do I wait here until I either return to the world of the living or until I die? That would make his experience in Hades pointless. He needed to search for Nicholas, and he couldn't even leave this tree.

Maybe Nicholas would come to him, since spirits didn't have to worry about Cerberus. "Nicholas Manikas?" His voice sounded thin and higher-pitched than normal, but it embarrassed him less now than it usually would. "Nicholas?"

Below, the wolves cocked their heads.

At the edge of his vision, a shade headed straight toward him. *That's a really straight path. It has to have sensed me. Is it Nicholas or something else? Did the charm fail? Did I drop it?* Virgil fumbled under his shirt for the necklace and clutched it with one hand until his knuckles seemed ready to pop from his skin. Still the shade approached.

It has to be Nicholas, right? Virgil shifted position. If the shade were unfriendly, if it could somehow get past the charm's ward, Virgil would have to choose between death by ghost or death by wolves. *Death by ghosts would involve fewer teeth.*

The spirit was only meters away now. *What is it going to do? Am I going to die?* He closed his eyes and shielded his face with an arm...

Nothing, not even the coldness from physical contact with a shade. Virgil opened his eyes and saw the shade hovering in place a meter away, an amorphous form floating above the branch. Lowering his arm, he watched as the fuzzy blue mist coalesced into human form. Colors began peeking through the blue translucence. It never fully solidified, but Virgil soon recognized it and found himself nose to nose with…

"Nicholas." Virgil's heart beat quickly.

"Yeah, that's me." Nicholas still wore the house tunic in which he had been murdered. His bare legs looked incongruous in this setting. "You're making a lot of noise and being really annoying. Who are you?"

"Um…" The last time Virgil had seen Nicholas, the former police officer had lain motionless on a table in the sterile lab at the station. Watching him speak and move seemed inappropriate somehow, like snooping through someone's diary.

"Hey, you're still alive." The ghost of Nicholas cocked its head. "You're filled out, solid. Weird. Guess that's why Cerberus is so interested in you. What are you doing here?"

Virgil tried not to stare at the gash in Nicholas's chest. "I'm a homicide detective."

"Are you that asshole who replaced me?" Nicholas now appeared as angry as every ghost in every horror movie Virgil had ever squealed his way through. Virgil understood why everyone had labeled the ex-officer a jerk. He had to find Nicholas's softer side, the one Nicholas hid inside his diary.

"It wasn't really…"

"I hate you," Nicholas snarled. "I bet I could make you fall off this branch. You'd better have a pretty damned good reason for being here."

"Um," said Virgil, "I know this isn't you, Nicholas. All this rage you show to the outside world. I know there's a different person on the inside. I think the two of us are actu—"

"What are you talking about? You're just pissing me off even more."

"I…I read your diary." Virgil's heart sped up. He would have moved his legs farther apart into the position of confidence his therapist had told him about, but then he would have fallen from the tree.

Nicholas's face twisted into a horrible mask that could have gotten him a job as a gargoyle. "What did you just say? It sounded as though you said you read my diary." He looked down at the waiting wolves.

"I had to, for the investigation." Virgil did not look at the wolves. This meeting hadn't turned out the way he had expected. He should have known Nicholas wouldn't open up to a stranger in the first few minutes of conversation. "It was for professional purposes. And I...I liked it. A lot of things you said are things I've experienced. And your poetry was really good."

"I know it was good, but it wasn't meant for anyone else to read." Nicholas folded his arms across his chest. "And now you're here, and if you die for real, you won't be able to destroy the diary. It will just be sitting out there, waiting for someone to find. That's the only reason I haven't made you die, by the way."

"Um," said Virgil. "I don't think that's the only reason. I've read your diary, remember? I know your inner thoughts and—"

"It's the only reason!"

"Okay." Virgil tightened his grip on the branch. "Well, keep thinking about that reason. It's a good one."

"So, you traveled all the way here, to Hades, to rub it in my face that you read my diary."

Virgil's eyes went wide. "No! No, that's not why I came. I came for the investigation."

Nicholas's expression showed all the hate that must have fermented within him throughout his life. If Charon were right about how people didn't change once they arrived in Hades, Nicholas had a miserable eternity ahead of him.

Not that I have much more to look forward to.

"So," said Nicholas, "despite the fact that your hiring caused me to be fired and then killed, you came here to ask me to help you do your job?"

Virgil blinked. The wolves still sat below, unwavering eyes trained on him. "Well, I'm trying to find out who murdered you."

Nicholas smirked and waved it off. "About that? I'm over it now. I just talked to the chief a few minutes ago, and he said he took care of it. You'll have to do better than that."

Virgil swallowed. "I don't think he really did take care of it." He studied Nicholas's reaction before continuing. "Unless your next-door neighbor killed you. Even—"

"No, it wasn't Antony." Nicholas shook his head. "Although he was kind of a dick. I'm glad the chief killed him."

"Actually, he didn't—"

"Wait." Nicholas paused, and his eyes unfocused for a moment. "You're alive, but you're in Hades."

"Yeah, you said that before," Virgil said. "But about the guy who k—"

"You don't hear about regular people coming down here. You know who does stuff like that?" Nicholas leaned forward. "Herakles. Orpheus. It's a pretty big deal."

"Oh." Virgil turned that idea around in his head. "I guess—"

"So, a real-life hero risked coming to Hades to talk to *me*." Nicholas smiled. "That's *awesome*. I'm legendary now. People are going to be talking and writing about me for centuries. I'm going to be famous. Do you think ghosts can have sex? Because if so, I'm going to be getting a lot of it." He pumped his fist. "Yeah. You need my help. I've got inside information. I'm a key witness."

"Yeah." Virgil didn't know how much time he had before returning to the real world. "I was hoping we could get to that. What—"

"Lay it on me." Nicholas rolled his shoulders, maintaining his manic grin. "I'm going to earn being in this legend. How can I help? What do you need to know?"

"Well...do you know who killed you?"

"No, not really."

Virgil slumped, though Nicholas still seemed way too enthused for someone who didn't know the answer. The risks Virgil had taken, the wound he had suffered, it all meant nothing.

Nicholas shrugged. "I know it was one of the guys at the Keres Lab. You know, the military lab at the edge of town."

Virgil felt something strange. *Triumph?* It felt different than he had expected. "Yeah, that's what I thought. I found several clues pointing to that lab. But who did it? And why? I thought you were just applying for a job there."

"I know, right?" Nicholas shook his head.

"So...what happened?"

"Oh, yeah. Funny story." Nicholas's threadbare chest billowed, and his hands gesticulated while he spoke. "I was kind of drunk when I went. I was tired of the guys at the bar hounding me about some money they had given me, so I figured I'd just apply for a job right away. If you show up asking about jobs after hours, it shows initiative and desire and whatever else companies are looking for."

Virgil raised an eyebrow.

"So, I get to this lab place, and it's supposed to be all big and important. You know, they do all kinds of secret stuff there. But at first, no one's waiting by the front door. Then, I hear this stupid laughing. You know, the kind that just irritates you and makes you want to kill the person doing the laughing? You probably laugh like that."

"Um." Virgil couldn't remember ever laughing.

"So I walk around the reception desk and see these two guys in guard uniforms. They're laughing and telling fart jokes or something. I didn't pay much attention, because if a person laughs like that, they probably don't have anything important to say."

"Petrides and Tantalo," said Virgil.

"What?"

"The two guards. They were... Never mind." Virgil settled back against the tree trunk and hoped Nicholas would hurry. *How much longer before I return to the overworld?*

Nicholas shrugged. "Whatever. So, I told them I was looking for a job and they needed to tell me who to talk to. They were scared of me, so they jumped up and said they'd do it. I hope you remember that part when you're writing this story. They were scared of me."

"Um..." Virgil resisted the urge to glance at his watch or tap his foot.

"Anyway, so they took me to this meeting room in the lobby area. A bunch of guys in suits and lab coats were in there. I walked in, figuring these people would give me an interview, or maybe just hire me right away. They were sitting around some table and there was a map on the wall. It showed the Alliance and Europe, and some cities were marked."

"Why w—"

"I don't know, okay? That's not the important part. It's just a detail, to make things more interesting." Nicholas shook his head. "You don't know how to tell a story, do you? Anyway, these guys seemed kind of surprised to see me and started yelling at me to get out, so I told them they were a bunch of cock-sucking sheep-fuckers for not offering me a job after all the initiative I showed, and then I left. I guess I made them mad or something, because one of them killed me that night. Which is embarrassing, because a lot of people around here are wandering around in battle gear, and I have leisure wear." He gestured at his house tunic and bare legs.

Virgil looked at his hands. "I thought one of the guards got your ID and threw you out."

Nicholas glared at him. "I left. On my own."

"But, in your diary, it says th—"

"I left on my own!"

Virgil tried to back away, but the tree trunk pressed against his spine. "Okay, okay. You left on your own. So, do you think they killed you because you heard what they were talking about?"

"That's the impression I got. The guy just impaled me; he didn't really give me a monologue beforehand."

"So, what were they saying?"

"I didn't hear anything clearly. They were talking about a nuclear missile and mentioned Blasphemer's Week and the gods or something." Nicholas shook his head. "It was pretty weird."

That didn't make much sense. Virgil needed to think about it further. Later, though, when he had more time. "What did your killer look like?"

"You're just rattling off these questions. I like it." Nicholas spent a moment in contemplation. "Hm. Short dark hair.

About my height. Gold-rimmed glasses. Kind of an angry expression." He furrowed his brows and bared his teeth in demonstration.

"Okay." Virgil nodded. He had hoped for more, but he had still received more useful information than the rest of his investigation had provided. If he made it back to the real world, he would have a good chance of determining who committed the murder. This case could prove that homicide detectives had a place in law enforcement and could give Nicholas some justice. "That's good. That will help."

"Sweet. Glad I could be of assistance." Nicholas beamed and pumped his fist again. "I am a friggin' legend! People are going to be telling their kids stories about how Nicholas Manikas and that short detective with the stupid hat solved a big murder mystery."

Virgil winced. *Is my hat stupid?* It was the only thing he had from his father. Maybe it... Virgil shook his head. No time to dwell on Nicholas's comment now. *Does Nicholas think so poorly of me, though?* He didn't seem to feel the same connection that Virgil had. *Maybe it will take time. Maybe—*

"You'd better destroy my diary when you get back."

"Um, sure. I can do that."

"If you don't, I'll know. And I will make your afterlife miserable." Nicholas looked around. "More miserable. I might do it, anyway. I don't like you, Virgil. You annoy me, and we are nothing alike. Look at you." He paused as though to allow Virgil a moment for introspection. "You're skittish. I bet I could just shout in your ear, and you'd jump off this branch. I spent every day working with the other police officers and I never broke, no matter how hard they tried. You're ugly, and I'm a lady-killer. I'm actually good at what I did, and you couldn't figure out your case without firsthand evidence. Please don't ever compare yourself to me again. It's embarrassing. Not for you, of course, but for me."

"Um."

"Anyway, when are you leaving?"

Virgil stared at his hands, not knowing if he could face Nicholas. Nicholas was right: the two of them were nothing alike. *I'm a failure in all aspects of my life, and no one will ever want to be friends with me. Chrysanthe wouldn't care about me if we weren't related. I'm stupid and ridiculous, just like everyone tells me.*

"I asked you a question. When are you leaving?"

Virgil shrugged. "I don't know how to get back."

"Okay. Well, I might take off then. I still don't really know my way around here, and Charon said there were cool parties in this forest, but I don't hear anything. Remember your promise. I consider it a binding oath."

"Okay."

Before Nicholas turned to leave, Virgil felt a tingling in his left arm. *Is that where the shade brushed me earlier?* His right hand grabbed the tingling area, but felt nothing strange. Then his leg began to tingle, then his chest. Bright yellow spots popped around him, like the spots in one's vision after staring at the sun too long. Tingles danced across his body. *Is the charm's charge depleted? Did the spirits discover me?* "What's happening?"

"Looks like you're going back," Nicholas said. "Go get 'em, guy. Tell the world my story and make me famous."

Virgil felt his body fading out, and the dark world was speckled with pieces of a plain white wall and a laboratory table. The last thing he heard before Hades disappeared was Nicholas's voice: "I am so *awesome.*"

TWENTY-THREE

PAIN. BRIGHT LIGHT. Queasiness. Cold. Something jabbed Virgil's arm.

"Ouch," he said.

"Virgil?" A familiar voice. His eyes snapped open.

The night sky rolled by overhead, and he realized he lay atop a stiff padded board on a gurney. A tube, resting along his arm, traveled somewhere behind him. Medical technicians grabbed the railings on either side of the gurney as they hustled him across the parking lot in the direction of flashing red and blue lights.

He wanted to sleep. Everything felt so heavy, so far away, so postpone-able. His eyelids drooped.

"Virgil? Are you awake?"

"Chrysanthe," he croaked. His eyelids fluttered open.

His sister peered over a railing. Tears moistened her cheeks. "What did you *do*?"

Virgil grunted. "I've been stabbed." The stretcher went over a bump, and a sharp pain shocked his stomach.

He had felt so much better in Hades. He remembered lying in the police laboratory, clutching his wound while spirits surrounded him, and then waking up in the afterlife. So much nicer than this stretcher and this wound and this tube in his arm.

Chrysanthe kept pace with the stretcher. "I was worried about you when you left the house, so I decided to check on you. We came here and none of the officers wanted to see if you were okay, so we went in, and... And we found you like this. I called the hospital and I prayed to Apollo to keep you safe and..."

"I talked to Nicholas."

"W-what?"

"I found out who killed him."

Virgil felt the stretcher leave the ground, and the world swayed. The medical technicians were lifting him into the ambulance. As he passed its doors, he caught a glimpse of Matthaios in the distance, drinking a soda.

"Ma'am, do you and your husband want to ride to the hospital? We need to hurry. This man has lost a lot of blood."

Virgil closed his eyes, and sleep overtook him.

VIRGIL LEANED AGAINST the checkout desk's chipped wooden counter, trying not to show too many outward signs of the fire lancing into his side. The receptionist clacked away on her keyboard, performing some task with her outdated computer that he couldn't seem to care about. Chrysanthe stood next to him, watching him as unwaveringly as Cerberus had. Matthaios was probably around somewhere.

Previous events seemed so hazy. *Did I really travel to Hades? Did I really speak to Nicholas and the ferryman? What is Charon doing now? Probably his job. Is he thinking about me at all? Probably not.*

Does Charon really drive a bus?

Virgil yawned. His unconsciousness in the hospital was the best sleep he'd had in months.

"Okay, ma'am," the receptionist said in a high-pitched voice, looking away from her computer. "He's cleared to leave. He should be fine to return to work tomorrow."

Chrysanthe's jaw dropped. "He just had surgery for a *stab wound*. Isn't that pretty serious? Shouldn't he be lying in bed for several days?"

The receptionist adjusted her glasses and turned to Virgil. "Does it still hurt?"

Virgil's side screamed, and he could feel the stitches moving every time he shifted position. He nodded.

"Well, shake it off. You'll be fine."

Chrysanthe's nostrils flared. "This is my brother. He has just had surgery, and he is going to get some painkillers at the very least."

The receptionist narrowed her eyes at Chrysanthe. "I've heard about people like you. Are you just trying to get a prescription so you can sell the pills?"

"No!" Chrysanthe looked as though she wanted to pull the woman from behind the counter and fling her across the room. "Look, Virgil's not the kind of guy who lets you know when something's wrong. I'd just feel more comfortable knowing he has something to prevent him from suffering."

The receptionist turned back to her computer. "Well, our doctors are too busy to write any prescriptions. You'll have to find your happy pills somewhere else."

Virgil stood straight, trying to ignore the pain. It felt like weasels chewing his skin. "It's okay. I'll be fine. Let's just go."

Chrysanthe put Virgil's arm over her shoulder. "Fine. But we'll try to find something at the store."

VIRGIL LEANED ON Chrysanthe's shoulder as she opened the door to his apartment. Everything felt hazy, far away, similar to his out-of-body experience before arriving in Hades. The sensation was actually pleasant. A nice contrast to the worries and anxiety of normal life. *Maybe I should consider taking up painkillers as a hobby.*

Something brushed against his leg, and he realized they had reached the couch. Chrysanthe lowered him onto one of the cushions while he clutched his side to prevent his stitches from bursting. *Can they burst?* They felt as though they could. He didn't want to test the hypothesis. He settled himself into a reclining position as Matthaios strolled into the room and closed the door.

Virgil found it hard to believe he had visited Hades only last night. Or early this morning. The journey, and speaking to Charon and Nicholas, seemed as though it had happened weeks or months ago. He recalled Nicholas's words during their brief conversation.

"Is my hat stupid?" Virgil asked.

Chrysanthe looked incredulous, but shook her head after a moment. "No, your hat is pretty cool."

"Yeah." Matthaios nodded. "It's actually the only cool thing about you."

Chrysanthe swatted him.

The two stood for several moments, glancing back and forth at each other, while Virgil tried not to show how his wound throbbed every second. When would they leave? He needed a glass of wine, and then he could return to the investigation with the clues Nicholas had provided.

"It's okay," he said with a strained voice. "I'll be fine."

"No, we're staying." Chrysanthe folded her arms. "I don't trust you. It's nice that you're passionate about solving this case, but you're being reckless."

"Yeah," Matthaios said. "*Stabbing* yourself? Just to solve a case?"

Virgil shook his head. "I didn't st—"

"Whatever." Chrysanthe waved her hand. "Your priest stabbed you. But you asked him to do it."

"Not exactly." Virgil winced as another wave of pain rolled over him.

"I wish we could prosecute him," Chrysanthe said. "I don't like the priesthood's immunity to law enforcement."

Virgil still wondered whose side the priest was on. *Did he stab me in an unorthodox attempt to aid the investigation, or was the wound meant to be fatal while providing plausible deniability for his motives?*

"Okay," Virgil said, "but I'm fine. I'm just going to sleep it off."

Chrysanthe laughed. "You don't sleep off a knife wound. You just want us to leave so you can get back to work. Well, the case can wait. Nicholas isn't going to get any more dead. He has reached the maximum possible level of deadness." She turned to Matthaios. "Dear, can you get him some water?"

Matthaios sighed. "He was released from the hospital. He should be well enough to get his own water."

"Please?"

Matthaios grumbled and headed to the kitchen. Chrysanthe turned back to Virgil.

"Look, you're worrying me. Again. After Mom died, you fell apart. You were oversleeping and missing work and getting fired. I had to start calling you every day to make sure you didn't miss your shift and lose another job. I was hurting, too, Virgil, but I had to take care of you."

Virgil bowed his head. "I know."

"Then you left for the academy in Athens, and I was happy. Partly because I didn't have to take care of you anymore and could concentrate on my own life. Mostly because I thought you were better, though. You certainly seemed to be. So when you came back after getting your certificate, I didn't think I needed to check on you anymore. And just tonight, you said you were going to therapy, and I thought, 'This is great. Virgil is finally growing up.'

"But last night, you were *also* talking about how you dying would make more people want your job and other crap. So when you ran off, I thought I needed to check on you. And you're right back where you were before, unable to take care of yourself, except this time, you're not just missing work, you're asking people to stab you."

Virgil blinked. He had ruined Chrysanthe's life. It was bad enough he couldn't contribute to society in any meaningful way, that his life had no value to anyone. Now, he knew he had a net negative impact on Chrysanthe's life. *She should have let me die in the examination lab.*

Cabinet doors slammed open in the kitchen.

Chrysanthe looked up, then bowed her head. "I'm so sorry, I shouldn't have said that. That's not what you need to hear right now. I just get so frustrated. I don't understand you."

"I'm sorry." Virgil was unable to meet her eyes. He wondered if he should say more. *I should, but I can't. Not now.* "Sorry.

This... It's not just about the case now." He tried to sit up, but his wound protested. "I think Nicholas stumbled into something big, but I don't know what. The killer came from the military lab where Matthaios works."

The activity in the kitchen paused. "What about my lab?"

"Nicholas overheard some talk about a nuclear missile." Virgil's sentence was punctuated by the high-pitched sound of water pouring into a glass.

"There's supposed to be another nuclear missile test tonight," Matthaios said from the other room.

"Right!" Chrysanthe's face lit up. "They've been talking about the launch all over the news. Other countries are calling it reckless since its flight path takes it over so many heavily populated areas. And they say it makes no sense, because the missile has to go against the Earth's rotation to fly across Europe. They say the Alliance is being provocative."

Tonight. Something would happen tonight. Nicholas was killed to hide the truth, and that cover-up would be successful if Virgil didn't do something. And even though describing the available evidence as "circumstantial" was generous, his conclusion felt right. Professor Lambros would have encouraged him to pursue his hunch.

The flowing water stopped, and Matthaios emerged. "This isn't the first time we've done one of these tests. Other countries keep complaining, and nothing changes. They need to realize it's the only possible way for us to conduct missile tests. It's not as though we can just fire it into the Mediterranean, and Europe has better ocean access than we do." Matthaios took a sip from the glass before handing it to Virgil.

Virgil took the glass. "So, whatever Nicholas saw, it has something to do with the test."

Matthaois grunted. "I don't see how. The missile is being fired into the middle of the ocean. Nothing out there but a bunch of fish. Maybe Poseidon."

"Well, no," said Chrysanthe. "This is the week when all the gods have their annual meeting at Mount Olympus. So Poseidon should be safe."

"Well, there it is." Matthaios shrugged. "Unless you're a fish-rights activist. You know, all those 'stop nuking the whales' groups."

"Maybe that's why this launch date was chosen," said Virgil. "Today is the last day the gods are supposedly away. Maybe the people launching it want to hide their actions from the gods. And they killed the witnesses, so no one else will know until it's too late."

Chrysanthe nodded. "Did you learn anything else?"

"Nicholas described his killer to me, in a vague way. The guy had short hair, was about medium height, and had gold-rimmed glasses."

Matthaios rubbed his head. "And probably in the Nuclear Warfare Division... That might be..." He paused, and his face tightened.

Chrysanthe put a hand on his shoulder. "What is it?"

"The guy who started our nuclear program." Matthaios swallowed. "No one else could understand the documents we obtained from the European program, so he's one of the most valuable people in the Alliance. They won't allow us to speak his name outside of the lab. Shit, he was the one who named the lab. I've seen him in the hallways, but..."

Chrysanthe looked at Virgil, then back to Matthaios. "You can say his name now, though. Since he's wanted for murder."

Matthaios stared at the ground. "It doesn't matter if he killed someone. If he wanted to dabble in murder as a hobby, I doubt the authorities would question him."

Virgil closed his eyes. He ruined everything. Even when solving a simple homicide, he had to uncover conspiracies best left hidden. The police department would love hearing him accuse the shadowy head of the Greek Alliance's nuclear warfare program of murdering an unemployed police officer.

Chrysanthe tightened her grip on Matthaios's shoulder. "Dear, this is important. We need to know his name. Please."

Matthaios's mouth pursed and contorted. Finally, he whispered, "Frederick Nyx."

Virgil took a sip of water. His side protested at the motion. "So, why would he kill someone who saw plans for a missile test that isn't a secret?"

"Maybe he's changing the target coordinates of the missile," Chrysanthe said. "Maybe so that it hits a city." She shook her head. "I know that's a strong accusation, but what else would motivate murder in that situation?"

Matthaios took a breath. "We don't have any evidence of that."

"Not yet," said Virgil, "but I think she's right."

Nicholas and the guards overheard plans to destroy a city, causing the would-be perpetrators to kill the witnesses to preserve their plan. The missile would overfly several cities on the European continent while traveling to the Atlantic Ocean. Any one of those cities could be a target. It made sense, or it would at least make sense to a madman.

"That's what he's doing," said Virgil. "You heard that speech Senator Kelipapalous made about how the Alliance isn't as powerful as Europe. I bet a lot of people feel that way, and Nyx is probably one of them. This is their way of demonstrating the Alliance is as formidable as anyone." He tried to push himself upright, but collapsed in the attempt. "I have to stop him."

"Remember what happened last time you went to that lab?" Chrysanthe said as Virgil began to ease himself into a sitting position. "Besides, you just got stabbed. You're in no condition t—"

"People are going to die," Virgil said. "There isn't time."

Not only would the people in the target-city die, the other countries would declare war on the Alliance. Maybe those countries would even use their nuclear weapons. *Does Nyx really want that? Global nuclear war? The destruction of the Alliance? Why?*

Chrysanthe seemed to look inward for several moments. "Fine. You're right. When and where is the launch taking place?"

"I don't know the exact time," Matthaios said, "just that it's in the closing hours of Eris 5. Tonight. The launch site... I don't know; that part is secret. There are several places it could be: Mystras, Heraklion, Mykonos, Galatas, Thessalonika… And others." He looked concerned. "Maybe we should tell someone. Maybe our district representative."

"I don't think anyone would listen to us," Chrysanthe said. "Not politicians or people at Keres. We don't have any evidence. We might have to stop this ourselves, crazy as that would be."

"We don't know where the launch site is, though," said Virgil.

Matthaios paced the room. "If the pattern holds, before they head to the launch site…" He hesitated, then continued. "Nyx and the others will be doing last-minute work at the lab. We can try to find evidence about what they're going to do, and tell someone before they leave. Or, maybe, we can confront them there, and stop them before the launch takes place. Then, we won't have to worry about finding the specific site."

"That's a good idea," said Chrysanthe. "And if we don't find them, maybe someone at the lab knows which site it is, or maybe we can find the information ourselves. We should leave soon."

"This is going to be dangerous," Virgil said. "You can't go. I don't want you getting hurt. I can just go by myself."

"That's very noble of you, but it also wouldn't work," said Chrysanthe. "You're not even in condition to get a glass of water for yourself, so I can't imagine you'd be able to fight the security guards."

"I could have gotten the water."

"I'm sure. That doesn't change the fact that we're still going with you. Matthaios can get us in. He was going to escort you there today, anyway."

Virgil forced himself to stand. "Okay." His limbs felt heavy, his mind foggy. "I'm going to need some caffeine pills." They had less than sixteen hours to save whichever city had been targeted.

TWENTY-FOUR

KERES LAB LOOMED ahead of them, the distance more daunting than it had been yesterday. Virgil suppressed a groan and concentrated on putting one foot in front of the other as he clutched his stomach. One step at a time, one excruciating breath at a time, one fervent curse of Patroklus at a time.

The painkillers had worn off during the car ride, and he hadn't thought to bring more. Though Chrysanthe allowed him to lean on her, the stitches in his side felt strained almost to tearing, and the pain had matured into several complex flavors. Without the caffeine pills, he might have collapsed. *Maybe the hospital shouldn't have released me yet.*

Matthaios had taken the lead, striding with purpose and not glancing back to see if Virgil and Chrysanthe kept up. "It's like you two aren't familiar with the concept of treason."

"I'm well aware of the concept of treason," Chrysanthe replied between grunts, increasing the pace to even more uncomfortable levels. "As long as we succeed, we won't have to worry about it. 'The law favors the victor.'"

"Well, you've never seen someone drawn and quartered before," said Matthaios. "I have, at an employee orientation, to demonstrate the consequences of disloyalty. I will never forget the way that traitorous bastard screamed."

Virgil shuddered at the image. He had heard of the government's predilection for the punishment, but had never witnessed it.

Chrysanthe shifted position as she walked, jostling Virgil. "Drawing and quartering is only used when the prosecutors can prove cowardice was demonstrated. I don't think they'll be able to claim that in our case."

"They can prove anything they want." Matthaios shook his head. "Besides, hanging is the other option, and I don't want that, either."

"That's a reasonable desire. You don't have to come, Matthaios."

"I'm not letting you go without me."

They walked for several minutes before reaching the laboratory's entrance, and Virgil experienced every single one of those minutes acutely. The pain was like a third traveling companion, an imaginary friend. *But Dr. Perikiades probably wouldn't accept it as fulfilling my assignment.*

Chrysanthe stopped, and Virgil looked up from his shoes. He stood before the oaken doors and contemplated the wisdom of returning to the military laboratory, particularly when he had been so thoroughly humiliated yesterday. Matthaios, in the vanguard of their diminutive formation, grabbed the massive door handle.

Chrysanthe put a hand on his shoulder. "We need a moment."

Matthaios nodded and released the handle. Chrysanthe held out her hands to Matthaios and Virgil.

Great. A prayer. Even if the gods are there to listen, they should understand the time constraint. "Um, this is the time of year the gods are—"

"I know." Chrysanthe's brows furrowed. "Do it anyway. It's polite."

Virgil blinked, but said nothing further. He took Chrysanthe's and Matthaios's hands to complete the circle. When the others closed their eyes, Virgil paused, then did the same. Though he doubted the effectiveness of prayer, especially at this time, it also wouldn't hurt.

"Ares, namesake of this mighty city-state," Chrysanthe said, "I know I rarely pray to you. I apologize, but I don't often have the occasion in my line of work. Maybe I should be praying to thank you for that. Today, though, we are here to do your work, to protect your city-state and the entire Alliance. Please guide our mission and help us save your people. We have worshiped you and honored your strength. Help us maintain your legacy and bring further glory to your name. As you favor the brave, see our bravery in undertaking this task, and help us succeed. We go, as ever, in your name."

It seems illogical to pray to Ares to prevent a war. Maybe, if Ares exists, he'll appreciate the fact that stopping the war will likely require violence.

Virgil opened his eyes to see Matthaios and Chrysanthe share a quick kiss. He released their hands and resumed his place in front of the door.

Matthaios swung the door open to reveal the laboratory's opulent lobby. Though sunlight had poured throughout the room on his previous visit, now the dim morning light was supplemented by fluorescent lighting from ornate chandeliers. It somehow made the cavernous space cozier.

The receptionist peered at them from her desk and appeared surprised. "You," she said to Virgil. "What in Zeus's name did you think would happen if you showed up here again?"

She remembers me! Virgil counted that as a victory. "Um…"

"He's with me," said Matthaios. The words sounded apologetic. "I'm escorting my wife and brother-in-law on a tour. Wanted them to see my office. Maybe the library."

The receptionist narrowed her eyes. "Hm. I suppose that's technically permissible. Okay, Dr. Vallas. I'll get badges for them, but there will be some restrictions."

This is much easier than yesterday. Maybe I should have requested Matthaios's help before coming here yesterday. Or, I should have asked Chrysanthe to request Matthaios's help.

The receptionist knelt behind her desk for several moments before emerging wit two generic badges and two bright orange vests. She slid them toward Virgil and Chrysanthe.

Virgil took one of the vests, which smelled of thick body odor. On the front and back, it was labeled, "Nonessential Civilian Visitor." He looked up at the receptionist, who smiled and gestured for him to don it.

Virgil grimaced while Chrysanthe helped him slip on the vest. Then he grabbed one of the badges and clipped it to his tunic collar.

The receptionist lifted a handheld radio to her mouth and stared into Virgil's eyes as she spoke. "Attention, security. We have two visitors entering the building. If they are found in unauthorized areas, intercept and kill. Detainment is unnecessary."

Her radio crackled. "Understood."

Virgil blinked. While he hadn't expected any passing security guards to allow him into unauthorized areas, he also hadn't anticipated them actively looking for him.

Chrysanthe frowned. "You all don't get many guests, do you?"

"Nope." The receptionist smirked. "You're free to go in. Enjoy your visit."

"Thank you." Matthaios gestured for the others to follow him. Virgil put his arm over Chrysanthe's shoulders, groaning, and the two trundled from the front desk.

"Quite a workplace," said Chrysanthe as they walked. "I know it's a top-secret lab, but I don't think everyone here should be so cheerful about killing people. Even the receptionist is getting into it."

"I don't mind the vigilance when I'm one of the people they're protecting." Matthaios gestured to the glass door ahead of them. "That leads to the hallway closest to my office. It connects to the other hallways, so we can get wherever we need to."

Virgil couldn't see anyone through the glass door. Maybe the patrols would be sparse enough to allow them access to Nyx's office. At least the receptionist hadn't requested that a guard escort them through the building. *I doubt the three of us could overpower a guard, and even if we did, it would probably just result in alarms and more guards.*

When they reached the door, Matthaios placed his badge against the square card reader. The reader blinked green, and Matthaios held the door while Virgil and Chrysanthe hobbled through.

Clicking footsteps came from a nearby hallway. Unseen doors opened and closed in hallways farther ahead. Distant conversations drifted toward them. The sounds seemed no different than what one could find in any hallway, in any office building in the Alliance. Even the bright tiled floor and plain white walls would have felt familiar to any office worker. And yet, an intangible vibe imbued the corridors with an evil ambiance. *How does Matthaios work here?*

Chrysanthe looked back and forth. "Where now? You know where Nyx's office is, right?"

Matthaios winced at the name. "Yeah. It's to our right in Hallway Sigma. Just after Incendiaries and before Interrogation. We should be fine in the hallways. But if they catch us in his office…"

Chrysanthe squeezed his shoulder. "Lead the way. Remember, we don't have much time."

They set off again, with Virgil feeling as though he were embarking on an epic journey, as though he were one of the characters in the Argonauts story. One of the useless characters, one who didn't contribute anything to the plot beyond adding to the body count.

Chrysanthe had formulated the plan and Matthais had access to the lab, but Virgil had nothing to add. He didn't belong here. *If I had come here by myself like I originally planned, the continent and everyone on it would be turned into a charred radioactive wasteland before tomorrow. It seems like a high price to pay for my ineptitude.*

He grimaced. Those thoughts didn't help.

A sign hung from the ceiling at the first intersecting hallway. "Hallway Alpha." In smaller text below, it said "Hallway Beta— 20 Meters, Hallway Gamma—40 Meters, Hallway Delta—60 meters." That put Hallway Sigma, assuming the pattern held, three hundred and forty meters away. He sighed.

Chrysanthe looked at him, pity in her eyes. "I guess the distance sounds a lot worse when you have a serious injury."

Virgil grunted. "I'll be fine." He wouldn't be, and she probably knew it. Chrysanthe said nothing.

As they reached Hallway Delta, footsteps approached from around the corner. Chrysanthe stiffened, and Matthaios looked back.

We haven't broken any rules yet. We should be okay. Virgil didn't believe it.

The guard who came into view looked surprised when he saw them. "Your friend okay?" he asked Matthaios.

Virgil shifted position to stand taller, but didn't think it helped. It also hurt more.

Matthaios gestured back at Virgil and Chrysanthe. "My brother-in-law got stabbed last night. I'm taking him on a tour of the Bio Warfare Department to cheer him up."

"Yeah, that's what I always say about knife wounds," said the guard. "Just walk 'em off." As he strode past them in the direction of the lobby, he looked over his shoulder. "Nice vests."

Once the man disappeared from view, Virgil took a breath. Chrysanthe tilted her head to indicate they should continue.

Minutes later, they stopped. Virgil looked up to see a welcoming sign. "Hallway Sigma." *We made it. Even better, no one can see us, and there aren't any nearby footsteps. For once, circumstances are aligned in our favor.*

Something's going to go wrong.

Matthaios led them past the first four doors. The door to the next room stood ajar to reveal an unlit office. The label on the wall beside it read, "Nyx."

"Why is it open?" Virgil asked. *Did someone set an enticing trap to catch me?* If they started searching the office, a guard could conveniently pass by and have the authority to execute them.

Chrysanthe turned to Matthaios. "He doesn't typically leave his office unlocked before he leaves the lab, does he?"

Matthaios shook his head. "I hope not. He should be locking it any time he leaves it, even if it's just to use the restroom."

Chrysanthe peered inside the office. "You don't think we were meant to find it like this, do you?" She shook her head. "No, that wouldn't make sense. Nyx wouldn't have expected anyone to realize the plan."

Matthaios grunted. "Maybe he left it open because he doesn't think anyone would be foolish enough to snoop in his office."

If so, Nyx has a good point. The penalty for being caught would deter most people. Maybe he even set up alarm systems.

"I wish he'd been here," said Chrysanthe.

Matthaios nodded. "Yeah. We could have just beaten a confession out of him, or tied him up in a closet and locked the door. I bet no one would have found him until after the launch."

Chrysanthe looked down each side of the hallway and turned to Virgil. "Can you stand guard while we search the room?"

If Nyx or anyone else turned the corner of the hallway, a warning wouldn't give Virgil or the others sufficient time to find cover. They would be unable to reach the closest intersecting hallway before someone spotted them, no statues were conveniently placed to conceal them, and there probably wouldn't be anywhere to hide in the office, other than behind each other.

At least standing watch would make him feel less useless, if only for a short time. He nodded and removed his arm from Chrysanthe's shoulders and lowered himself to the floor, leaning against the wall. Still uncomfortable, but it put less pressure on the wound.

Chrysanthe gave him a concerned glance before entering the room and flicking the light switch. After Matthaois followed, Virgil twisted to peer inside.

Nyx had a simple office: a desk that held a computer and scattered papers, two wooden chairs in front of the desk, and a few photographs of family scenes on the walls. The smell of ocean-breeze air freshener, quite different from an actual ocean breeze, drifted from the room.

Matthaios walked behind the desk and sat in the chair. Chrysanthe stood beside him and began shuffling through ˌpapers on the desk. She frowned at each one.

"Just a lot of equations and dense text," she said. "I wish I'd been allowed to take maths and sciences classes. I'm sure this is all very interesting."

Virgil took a quick glance down the hallway, but saw nothing and heard only distant conversations and footsteps. Nothing warranting an alert. He returned to watching the search.

Matthaios typed something on the computer keyboard and waited with an expectant look. After a few moments, he shook his head. "I can't figure out his password."

"That's probably good," said Chrysanthe, "considering his computer probably has a lot of information about the Alliance's nuclear program." She grabbed another stack of papers. "Oh!"

"What is it?"

"It's an itinerary. For tonight and tomorrow." Her eyes flitted across the page. "Okay, there's no manifesto on here, where he admits to wanting to nuke a city, but it says the launch site is Galatas."

Matthaios whistled. "The opposite coast of the Peloponnesus from us. That's a long drive. We haven't gone on a road trip like that since our honeymoon when you wanted to go penguin-watching on the peninsula."

Virgil remembered her talking about that. Afterward, she said they hadn't found any penguins, but it was more about the journey than the destination.

Matthaios kissed the top of Chrysanthe's head. "Your weirdness is one of the things I love about you."

"You loving me is one of the things I love about you." She rubbed his back. "According to the itinerary, Nyx and the others are supposed to leave in half an hour."

Virgil made another quick check of the hallway. Nothing. No sounds of anyone approaching.

Matthaios frowned. "We still don't have evidence that they're altering the test in any way."

"That's true," said Chrysanthe. "I don't think we can find it here, though. I've already gone through all the papers, and you can't log in to the computer."

"Maybe we can wait here for him," said Matthaios. "Ambush him when he steps into the room. He left the door open, so he should be coming back."

Chrysanthe shook her head. "The itinerary lists several other people. If he comes back to his office, they might be coming with him."

Virgil closed his eyes. Another failure. He knew Nyx was planning to do something. Without proof, though, even if they did manage to stop him, they would be executed.

Our deaths don't matter. Millions of lives will be lost if we fail.

"We have to stop him. It's either here at the lab or at Galatas."

Matthaios rubbed his forehead and sighed. "Okay. We can go to the library. That should have information on the Galatas site. Blueprints, directions, and such. And if Nyx is still in the building, he might be there. Maybe we can lock him away somewhere without anyone noticing."

Chrysanthe nodded. "I imagine that's the best we can do." She grabbed something from the desk. "VIP badges. These might help."

Before Matthaios stood from the chair, he looked underneath the desk. "A safe!"

Chrysanthe started walking to the door. "If you couldn't guess his computer password, I doubt you'll be able to crack his safe."

"Probably not, but I should try while we're here." Matthaios knelt under the desk. A moment later, something flashed.

Virgil looked at the ceiling. Alarm lights began to blink red. "Um."

The alarms weren't confined to this hallway. Reflected flashes came from the other hallways, too. *Everyone in the building will know someone attempted to break into something. With our bright orange vests, Chrysanthe and I are going to be the most reasonable suspects.*

Virgil's arms began shaking. Images of Artino chasing him through the parking lot were interspersed with images of Keres security guards pounding after him through the hallways.

Chrysanthe ran to Virgil's side. "Come on!"

Matthaios raced after her. "Stupid, stupid. I should have known. They are going to draw-and-quarter us."

Virgil grunted as Chrysanthe helped him to his feet. Confused shouts came from the main hallway. Guards would arrive soon. Virgil doubted he could move quickly enough to avoid detection, but Chrysanthe forced him to hurry beside her. He clutched his side as they ran in the direction opposite the voices.

The guards are going to find us. The police will arrest us. The government will execute us. This is my fault. I am getting my sister and Matthaios killed. Everything would have been better if Artino had killed me, or if the spirits had taken me in Hades, or if Patroklus's knife had killed me, or if I had killed myself in the bathroom.

"We need to get to the library," Matthaios said. "They'll be looking for intruders, but they won't necessarily suspect us. If we get there, we can claim we were there the entire time."

They rounded the corner before anyone could see them fleeing Nyx's office. Voices and footsteps still echoed through the corridors, but Matthaios kept moving. Virgil struggled alongside Chrysanthe as best as he could.

They crossed several hallways, leaving the voices somewhere behind them. Red lights flashed. Virgil and Chrysanthe followed Matthaios as he turned left toward the center of the building. At the far end of the corridor, the library awaited.

It took several minutes to reach it because of Virgil's injury, but then they stood before the golden doors of their sanctuary. Below the ceiling, "Library" was written in bold letters. Thin windows were inset in the doors. Virgil leaned forward to peer through the closest.

The window provided a limited view. He could see that no one stood in front of the door, but little else. No nearby sounds of footsteps behind them.

"Move," said Matthaios as he opened the door.

When no one shouted or tackled them, Virgil surmised the library was safe. He stepped inside, along with Chrysanthe, relieved that his mistakes hadn't cost her life.

The library's interior was even more extravagant than its doors. Its entryway reached to the domed ceiling, the morning sunlight streaming through slit-like windows. Soft sounds of strings played from hidden ceiling speakers.

Meters away, a spiral staircase led to the second floor. Large bookcases, with accompanying ladders, lined the walls. Wide spaces throughout the room were occupied by long tables or decorations. Marble statues stood on pedestals, each statue a beautiful rendition of a horrendous creature preying upon soldiers. Other pedestals supported nuclear bombs, which were hopefully inert. A mosaic of an embattled General Klasistratos covered the far wall.

"Wow," said Chrysanthe. "This is the most beautiful library I've ever seen."

Virgil wondered if the decorations enhanced reading comprehension, or had any useful purpose in a library. He doubted Chrysanthe or Matthaios wanted to hear the question.

Matthaios leaned closer and whispered. "The launch site material should be on the first floor, to the left. I don't know if anyone else is in here, so be careful. It would look suspicious if anyone saw us in that section, since there was an intruder alert in the office of the head of the Nuclear Warfare Department."

They walked past a column with raised lettering that proclaimed, "Knowledge Can Kill," and asked, "Do You Know Someone Who Knows Too Much?" Then they veered around the statue of a soldier being attacked by a woman whose skin was covered in boils and open sores, turned behind the spiral staircase, and found themselves in the Nuclear Warfare section. It consisted of two towering bookcases that contained leather-bound tomes, magazines, and binders full of loose papers.

Virgil disengaged from Chrysanthe and sat at the base of the nearest bookcase. It looked intimidatingly tall from this angle.

Chrysanthe and Matthaios busied themselves searching the upper shelves of the bookcase, while Virgil concentrated on the ground-level shelf. This section seemed more technical than he needed, filled with studies on the operation of nuclear bombs and trajectory analyses of missile flight paths. He didn't bother opening those books, knowing they contained incomprehensible combinations of symbols that would make hieroglyphs seem like easy reading. After dragging himself along the floor to the second bookshelf, he discovered titles with more relevance: *Establishment of Arestia's Nuclear Program, Evaluation of Potential Launch Sites, Infrastructure for Galatas Missile Launch Site, Blueprints for Galatas Launch Site.*

"Found it," Virgil said.

Chrysanthe and Matthaios soon stood over his shoulders, reaching around him to snatch books from the shelf. He managed to stay out of their way and minimize his impedance of their investigations. After they had selected books, he grabbed one about building roads from the mission control center to the launch pads. It had detailed accounts of pricing, construction techniques, and day-to-day activities. *My keen detective skills tell me this book won't help.*

"I think we should keep this one." Chrysanthe held up a book containing blueprints.

"Good find." Matthaios squeezed her shoulder.

"Virgil was the one who found the section."

Matthaios glanced down at Virgil with a flat expression. "Oh."

Voices came from outside. Virgil held still and listened. A loud conversation, then someone's hand upon the door. The ambient sound from outside drifted in as the door opened.

Virgil looked up to see Chrysanthe already holding a hand out to him. *Have the guards come? Or Nyx? Will we be able to capture the scientist, or will we be executed on the spot?* Virgil took Chrysanthe's hand and stood as quietly as he could, then peered past the staircase.

The man who came through the doors looked like Nyx: short dark hair and gold-rimmed glasses. The man who had killed Nicholas. Virgil looked at Matthaios, who nodded. *Success.* Virgil started to move forward.

Then two bulky security guards followed Nyx into the room.

Matthaios's eyes widened. "Shit."

TWENTY-FIVE

VIRGIL COULDN'T MOVE. He stood in the open, waiting for the enemy to discover him.

The spiral staircase was between the new arrivals and Virgil right now, but since Nyx was in the library, he would probably want to use the Nuclear Warfare section, and then he would see Virgil and the others. Chrysanthe and Matthaios could beat Nyx in a fight, but those security guards could tear a person in half. Virgil recognized the one who had found him sneaking around the lab yesterday. He hoped to never learn how the guard would react to seeing him here again.

He had to find cover.

The first hiding place he saw was a small statue of a skeletal woman devouring a battlefield casualty, which stood only meters away beside a reading table. It was a questionable hiding place at best, and it wouldn't even hide everyone.

Behind the statue, though, was the first bookshelf in the Ballistics section. It faced the Nuclear Warfare's reading area and would block the view from anyone inspecting the books on launch sites. Virgil turned to tell Chrysanthe, but she was already gesturing to the same shelves. She took his arm and helped him hobble past the creepy statue and behind the bookshelf.

When they reached their destination, Virgil hunkered down beside the others where the books were tallest and thickest. A small gap, between the top of the books on the first row and the bottom of the next shelf, allowed him to view the Nuclear Warfare section. Chrysanthe and Matthaios angled themselves to peer through the gap, as well.

Nothing yet. Virgil offered another prayer to Hebe, though he couldn't figure out how to make the situation fit her area of expertise.

Nyx strode into the section, and Virgil's mouth tightened. There was something strange about this whole situation, meeting a murder victim after their death and then seeing the person who had killed him.

The scientist didn't look frail, exactly, but he also didn't look like the type of person who could physically kill another. A toughness about the eyes and the set of his jaw indicated strength of spirit, but those arms didn't indicate strength of muscle.

The two guards who followed must provide all the muscle Nyx needed. Virgil remembered how it had felt yesterday when they had held him aloft, helpless. His knees wobbled in memory.

Three other men, wearing maroon uniforms, fanned out from behind the guards and looked to Nyx. Matthaios might know what the maroon signified. Blue was for Nuclear Warfare. The guards were hanging out with Nyx, so maroon likely had something to do with...ballistic missiles. Virgil cursed silently. *Maybe this is not a good hiding place.*

Nyx stood before one of the Nuclear Warfare shelves and began running his fingers along the spines of the books with a familiarity bordering on disturbing. The guards watched as though he were the most fascinating person in the world.

"Let's wait a few minutes to allow the business with my office intruder to settle," Nyx said in a strong baritone. "There was nothing in that safe. I thought any intruder would be unable to resist attempting to open it, though."

Beside Virgil, Matthaios shook his head.

"Still," said Nyx, selecting one of the books, "this gives me the opportunity to retrieve some documents, and we'll be safe here. Athas, fetch my car and move it to the rear entrance."

"Yes, sir." One of the men in maroon walked to the exit.

If Nyx had his people prepositioning the car, they would be leaving for Galatas soon. Chrysanthe hadn't had time to formulate a plan for infiltrating the Galatas launch site, and it appeared she wouldn't get much more.

"You have the tunes, right?" Nyx tossed the book to another man in maroon. "Something energetic? I hate listening to the radio on road trips. All that talking and 'slow jams,' and whatever raucous sheep-bleating the record companies pretend is music these days."

"Yes, sir," said the man. "Your secretary had some suggestions. Some old-school Beached Whales, some Writhing Deceased, and the new Perilous Paranormal Paramour album."

"Great. Put that one on first; I haven't had time to listen to it yet, what with all the commotion going on here and all our improvisations to the plan." He paused. "We will need to exercise more caution, of course. The fact that someone snuck into my office means someone knows of my plans."

Virgil and the others would not have surprise on their side, then. Nyx would be expecting them.

Virgil heard the library door open again, though he couldn't see who entered until they rounded the staircase. A long, red robe flicked into view. A priest. *Why does Nyx have a priest working with him?* Virgil adjusted the angle of his head to get a clearer view.

Wait. Virgil recognized that face. He stiffened.

Patroklus.

So, Patroklus *had* been working for Nicholas's murderer. Patroklus had been watching Virgil the entire time, trying to thwart the investigation. *Did those first spells really not provide useful information, or did Patroklus purposely make them fail? Maybe he never intended me to survive the trip to Hades. And all that time, he looked me in the eyes, spoke to me as a colleague, and never revealed his true intentions or the fact that he might kill me if I got too close to the truth.*

Of course, the evidence was all circumstantial. Maybe Patroklus was simply incompetent with those first spells. Or maybe he told the truth, and there wasn't anything useful to be gleaned from them. Maybe he had stabbed Virgil only because Virgil had unknowingly requested it.

But why is he here, then? Is he a double-agent, pretending to work for Nyx while reporting to another agency?

While Virgil tried to process this new information and keep his breathing under control, Patroklus's face inclined downward and turned toward the bookshelf where Virgil and the others hid. Those piercing blue eyes seemed to penetrate the books and bore directly into Virgil.

Virgil reached for the charm in his pocket and squeezed it. *Can Patroklus actually see me? This angle should make it almost impossible. Did he use a detector spell, or can he hear us breathing? Or do priests have some kind of extra-sensory perception? Will he tell Nyx and destroy the last chance our continent has at not being blown up?*

The moment passed, and Patroklus looked away. Virgil didn't know if the priest had seen them and decided not to reveal their presence, or if he had seen nothing. Virgil closed his eyes for a moment, trying to will his heart into slowing.

Patroklus crossed the distance to Nyx. "You have made your final decision?"

"Yes." Nyx plucked a binder from the shelf. "During his visit this morning, the senator insisted upon proceeding with the plan, but I would have done it even without his approval. We have invested too much effort to withdraw now. It was foolish of him to believe I would even consider the possibility of doing otherwise."

Patroklus inclined his head. "The senator fears unfavorable public opinion more than expended effort."

"If we all had to rely upon public approval, we would never accomplish anything." Nyx removed some of the loose papers from the binder and returned it to the shelf. "I suppose I have all I need from here. A rental Havoc paid for by the taxpayers, snacks paid for by the taxpayers, identification documents paid for by the taxpayers, some sweet tunes, and my stunning intellect that surpasses that of even Athena."

His cronies exchanged worried glances.

Nyx raised his eyebrows. "It's okay for me to say that. It's not hubris if it's true."

Before the others could respond, Nyx swept out of the section. The others followed, with Patroklus gliding out last. Moments later, the library door closed again.

Silence. A minute passed without even the sound of breathing. Virgil waited, wondering if Nyx and the others would return.

And Patroklus... *I thought he didn't hate me. Maybe that note in my car really was referring to him, even though he made me feel guilty for implicitly accusing him.*

Matthaios stood and spoke in a whisper. "I think they're gone now."

"It really is tonight," said Chrysanthe. "They're really going to do it. We weren't wrong."

She looked as though she were about to start giving orders. Before she could say anything more, Virgil spoke.

"Patroklus was with them."

"Who?" asked Chrysanthe.

"The priest," said Virgil. "I'm worried he might be working for them."

"Is that why he stabbed you?" Chrysanthe's voice faltered at the end of the sentence.

Virgil's hand went to his stitches. "I don't know. He might have been trying to kill me. There was this note. But he might have been trying to help with the investigation. He did give me that charm to ward off spirits while I was in Hades. I—"

"I think the important thing to remember here," Chrysanthe said, a note of exasperation in her voice, "is that he stabbed you and left you for dead. I don't care if he was helping with the investigation. I don't care if he houses orphans and donates all his money to health care for the elderly. I won't forgive him for what he did, and I don't trust him."

"He's a priest," said Virgil. "He doesn't have any money."

"Not the point." Chrysanthe gestured to the reading section. "Besides, you saw him with Fred Nyx. They're co-conspirators."

Virgil looked at his hands. "Unless Patroklus is only pretending to work with Nyx and actually plans to stop him."

Chrysanthe frowned. "I doubt it."

Matthaios put a hand on her shoulder. "Chrysanthe is probably right. We can't be certain, though. Maybe he's working with the bad guys and maybe he isn't. But it's more dangerous to trust him and be wrong than to not trust him and be wrong. We have to assume he's the enemy until we know otherwise."

Chrysanthe shrugged. "I am okay with any plan that vilifies him in an actual or hypothetical sense."

Virgil stared at his hands. He wished he had the conviction of the others. *What if distrusting Patroklus leads to us failing? What if Patroklus is working for Nyx and saw us behind the bookshelf, and we've already failed?*

"Patroklus isn't our only concern, though," said Chrysanthe. "Nyx mentioned the senator. I assume he means Kelipapalous. Why is the senator working with Nyx and a rogue priest?"

Matthaios shrugged. "He probably knows he's losing popularity compared to the temple. Maybe he thinks starting a war will give him more political power."

"Makes sense." Chrysanthe shook her head. "As much sense as possible when your plan is to nuke a city."

Matthaios frowned. "Well, I didn't vote for him."

"Neither did I, so I guess we'll both have clear consciences in the radioactive aftermath." Chrysanthe extended a hand to Virgil. "Sorry you're having to move around so much. This can't be good for you after the night you had."

"It's not." He took her hand and let her help him to his feet.

"Tonight, then," said Matthaios. "And we have a long drive to the launch site. Do we have a plan?"

He and Virgil turned to Chrysanthe.

TWENTY-SIX

VIRGIL CLUTCHED HIS side as Matthaios's car hit another pothole. Matthaios and Chrysanthe, sitting in the front seats, bobbed in the air for a second, but seemed otherwise unaffected.

Galatas lay hours away, and they hadn't even started for it yet. Virgil checked his watch again: 11:14. They wouldn't have much time when they arrived, but Chrysanthe insisted the detours were necessary. She and Matthaios had grabbed formal wear from their house, and Virgil would collect his suit when they arrived at his apartment.

Though he trusted his sister, and knew her plan would give them the best possible chance of success, he also knew the three of them couldn't infiltrate the launch site by themselves and stop Nyx. Not with Nyx's guards. Virgil pulled out his phone. "I'm calling for backup."

"Backup?" Chrysanthe turned from the passenger seat to look at him. "You mean those officers who tried to kill you yesterday?"

"We might not get past the security guards by ourselves," he said. "Besides, the police won't try to kill me now. They'll understand what's at stake."

Before Chrysanthe could protest further, Virgil dialed the number to the station. The phone rang several times before someone picked up.

"Arestia police department. This is Officer Michaelides speaking."

"Hey, Michaelides. This is Virgil. I've got a problem, and I'm calling for backup."

Michaelides chuckled. "Oh, yeah? This oughta be good. I'm putting you on speaker phone."

Virgil looked up at Chrysanthe, who shrugged. *I hate my coworkers.*

"Hey, guys," Michaelides said. "Virgil's on the phone calling for backup. Sounds serious." The laughter of the other officers came through the phone with exceptional clarity. "Okay, Virgil. Go ahead. Everyone's listening."

Virgil closed his eyes, realizing the reaction he would get. "There's a nuclear missile test tonight. We're worried that someone is going to change the target coordinates so it hits a city, so we're going to Galatas to stop it. Meet me at my apartment."

Distorted laughter came through the phone's speaker.

"Virgil Glezos, the homicide detective who saved the world." Michaelides cleared his throat. "Sure thing, buddy. The whole force'll be out there real soon." A click from the other end silenced the laughter.

Virgil looked at Chrysanthe. "I don't think they're really coming."

"I gathered. Those are some enviable coworkers you have." She shook her head. "It's probably better this way; I don't trust them after what they tried to do to you."

Virgil didn't trust them either, but he knew how enthusiastic they could be for any cause that involved violence. They weren't ignoring this request because they couldn't rally behind this particular cause. They were ignoring it because they didn't trust him, because they didn't want to be associated with him. If he were more competent, or if there were even anything likable about him, they would have come. *Once again, the situation is my fault.*

Chrysanthe stared out the windshield for several minutes before turning back to him. "Virgil, you're not in any condition to be fighting."

They hit another pothole. It felt like a knife driving into his side again. Virgil groaned. "I know."

"You're obviously in pain," Chrysanthe continued, "and I'm worried that you'll slow us, or that something might go wrong and your injury will prevent you from getting away."

"Yes, but—"

"It's okay, Virgil. You've done enough to get us the information, and there's not really much more you can do now, anyway. I know you have self-esteem issues and this conversation isn't helping, but I also don't think this is the time to work on your personal growth, not with the world's fate at stake. When we get to your apartment, we'll just drop you off."

Chrysanthe was right: Virgil would slow them down and probably screw something up. Attempting to prove his competence to himself meant nothing in the face of nuclear war.

But he *had* found the information leading them to Nyx. Despite numerous setbacks and failures, he had brought them this far.

Besides, I'm worried about what I'll do if I'm left alone.

"I'm coming. You want to disguise us as aides. The more aides you have, the more important you'll seem. The receptionist and guards are going to make an initial assessment when they see us, and we'll need everything we have to seem legitimate enough to pass that assessment."

Chrysanthe sighed and closed her eyes. "Virgil, I'm worried about you. But you're right."

Matthaios grunted. "There's a police truck parked in front of your apartment."

Virgil leaned forward to look out the front window. A white truck with the skull-and-spear logo. No one stood outside. *Which officers did they send? Does it matter?*

"We might have to fight." Matthaios looked back at Virgil. "Or run."

Matthaios parked behind the police truck. Virgil waited for Chrysanthe to help him from the car, and then the three of them approached the truck.

The truck doors opened, and Virgil stopped. His muscles tensed. After the conversation with Michaelides, he doubted the officers had come to help.

Schirra and Stathis emerged from the vehicle. They slung their spears over their shoulders.

"Did you come to arrest us?" asked Virgil.

Schirra shrugged. "Heard you needed backup."

Virgil stared for several moments. None of the other officers had shown up, but Schirra and Stathis had believed him. *They're willing to risk their lives because of something I said.*

I hope I don't get them killed. "You came."

Schirra and Stathis swaggered toward them. "Obviously," she said with a mischievous smile.

"I didn't think anyone was coming. Did you bring anyone else?"

"Nope," said Schirra. "The others are all a bunch of assholes, and they're incompetent, anyway. The two of us can handle anything you need handled."

"Yeah." Stathis brandished his spear.

While Matthaios folded his arms and watched from several paces away, Chrysanthe stepped between Virgil and the police officers. She glanced over her shoulder at Virgil. "Are these the ones who tried to kill you earlier today?"

Virgil shook his head. "Schirra stood up for me. She tried to stop the chief."

Chrysanthe narrowed her eyes, seeming to take a closer look at the officers. After several moments of scrutiny, she said, "You're a woman."

Schirra snorted. "How perceptive of you."

Storms rolled over Chrysanthe's eyebrows for a moment, but they dissipated, and her shoulders relaxed. "I've always prided myself on my keen observation skills. Thank you for trying to save Virgil. It means a lot to me."

Schirra inclined her head. "So what are we looking at? Someone's aiming a nuke at a city?"

"Yeah," said Virgil. "And if that happens, there might be a nuclear war. The Greek Alliance would be wiped out for certain, and probably all of Europe."

Schirra smiled. "High stakes. I like it."

Stathis set his jaw and nodded. "Me, too."

"Yeah, that's what attracted me to this venture," Chrysanthe said with an unhealthy dose of sarcasm. "You two are definitely police officers."

"Yep," said Schirra. "So, what's the plan?"

"We're heading to Galatas," said Chrysanthe. "We'll be disguised as aides. You'll need to get your formal wear. I'll doctor some IDs on the way. We'll avoid any guards, find Fred Nyx, and keep him from changing the coordinates of the missile's target."

"With violence?" asked Schirra.

"If necessary."

Schirra grinned. "It'll be necessary."

Chrysanthe shook her head. "Definitely a police officer. We're only confronting Nyx directly if he's isolated. You and your friend might be good at combat, but the rest of us aren't."

Matthaios grunted. "I'm not bad," he said under his breath.

Chrysanthe walked back to Virgil, and he accepted her proffered shoulder with great alacrity. *Not a good day for saving the world.*

"Well," said Chrysanthe, "you two and Virgil need to get your suits. Then let's go. We don't have much time."

TWENTY-SEVEN

"I'M SENATOR KELIPAPALOUS'S Chief Advisor on Advanced Technological Warfare." Matthaios extended his hand to the closest security guard. "And these are my assistants and our security detail."

Standing behind Matthaios in the small lobby of the Galatas Launch Site's Operations Center, Virgil adjusted his leather briefcase and hat. He hoped the layer of sweat hadn't bled through his suit. He also hoped his blood hadn't bled through. Chrysanthe had re-wrapped his wound with a liberal application of bandages, but the stitches strained and loosened with each shift of a shoulder or twist of his waist. If they did split and allow the knife wound to blossom blood, they would draw attention to him and jeopardize the plan. *And it will be my fault for allowing Patroklus to stab me.*

He fought the urge to tap his foot, or put his hand in his pocket, or tighten his tie as he stared forward, trying to concentrate on the sparkling marble wall behind the receptionist's desk and the low-hanging, intricate chandeliers throughout the room. *Anything but the way my shoes are biting into my feet, or the way my suit feels tighter than when I wore it last, or the air-conditioning cold enough to preserve a glacier, or the handful of caffeine pills I took to remain awake and that are making my fingers twitch uncontrollably, or the fact that the slightest misspoken word from me could doom the entire continent to a nuclear winter.*

I guess the last one is the most important. And what will happen if the senator's real aides show up?

If Chrysanthe had the same thoughts, she didn't betray them. She stood beside Virgil in a dark business-like blouse and dress, her posture as rigid as Patroklus's at his best, with an expression worthy of a genuine assistant to a senator's genuine Chief Advisor on Advanced Technological Warfare. Schirra and Stathis were behind Virgil, probably standing at attention, with the butts of their spears on the ground, in standard military parade rest.

The craggy-faced guard glanced over the entourage while his partner loitered several paces behind and made threatening faces. The guard's smile displayed a set of mangled teeth as he leered at Schirra.

"Why is one of your aides carrying a spear? Nothing sexier than chicks with spears, but aren't you worried she'll trip over it? Or maybe drop it when she sees a bigger spear?" He grabbed his crotch while his partner laughed.

"Either of our *guards*," said Matthaios, dropping the smile and giving his dark suit two quick tugs, "are fully capable of kicking your ass. Now, we are here to view the launch as Senator Kelipapalous's representatives. Which way is the mission control room?"

For a moment, the guard said nothing as he peered deep into Matthaios's eyes. Matthaios remained as stationary as a column. Virgil held his breath. *What does the guard see? Can he determine that we're impostors from a simple stare-down?* Virgil had to fight the urge to drum his fingers against his leg.

Then the moment passed, and the guard spoke. "I would love to have a wrestling match with your little groupies, but I'm busy at the moment." He waved his hand to indicate the receptionist's desk. "You'll have to check in before you can continue to the control room."

"Very well." Matthaios adjusted his suit and strode toward the desk.

We made it past the front door. Virgil's heart raced, and he had to prevent his muscles from relaxing. *We have many steps left before we confront Nyx in the control room, but we passed the first test.* Virgil matched Chrysanthe's pace as they followed Matthaios to the receptionist.

A loud slapping sound came from behind him. Virgil's head whirled to see the guard in the aftermath of smacking Chrysanthe's ass. His mouth opened. *That's my sister.*

He knew he should defend her, that custom and honor required it. But he couldn't. Not only did he not possess the strength to defend Chrysanthe, any attempt to do so would bring unnecessary attention and jeopardize the mission. He closed his mouth, face flushing as he lowered his eyes to the floor.

Before Virgil could take another step, Schirra threw down her spear and launched herself at the guard. The man's eyes widened, but he had time for no other reaction before Schirra slammed a fist into his nose. He tried to wrap her in a wrestling hold, but she twisted with him and dropped him to the ground like a sack of rice. Then she sent a boot into the underside of his jaw, and his body went slack.

"I hate it when men grab women like that," she said.

Virgil stared at the unconscious body lying on the floor. Maybe Schirra's comments about her ability weren't bluster. Maybe she should have been chosen as chief. *This isn't the time I wanted to learn that, though.*

Her demonstration might have destroyed their only chance to save the Alliance and the Mediterranean region. Any moment now, the alarms would sound, and guards would swarm through the doors, or maybe burst from the ceiling vents. He looked to Chrysanthe and Matthaios, whose wide eyes and open mouths didn't instill confidence. Schirra stood over her victim, smirking without remorse.

"Hey!" The other guard raised his spear and took two steps toward them, but Stathis stepped forward to block him.

"He was out of line. Don't make us do the same to you."

The guard frowned and fingered the walkie-talkie at his belt. Virgil watched as the man and Schirra stared at each other for several moments. Thoughts crossed the man's face in slow motion, as though running upstream in deep water.

Will he call for help? If he does, civilization will be over.

"Fine," the guard said with a contemptuous expression. "Let's not have any further incidents."

Virgil relaxed. The guard was claiming dominance in order to preserve his ego, but their group could allow him that for the sake of the mission.

"I would love a further incident," Schirra said.

Virgil winced. Chrysanthe, acting in a more constructive fashion, collected Schirra's spear from beside the fallen guard and put a hand on Schirra's shoulder. She gave the officer a gentle push forward. The remaining guard, who must have chosen to ignore the implied challenge, stood over his unconscious comrade and nudged him with a boot.

"Get up," he said.

"Come on," said Chrysanthe in a low voice to Schirra, handing her the spear. "No need to cause too much havoc." Schirra made no reply, but allowed Chrysanthe to guide her to the receptionist's desk.

"Hi, there!" the receptionist said in a cheery tone, her face pale. "That was quite an entrance. I hope the rest of your visit is less eventful. Please hand over your weapons and other items. I will also need to check your IDs."

Matthaios, as the chief advisor, carried no accessories, so he stood to the side while the others came forward. Virgil heaved his briefcase atop the counter, wincing as the stitches pulled against his side. He took a step back and watched as the receptionist slid the briefcase toward her. He hoped she didn't give the contents too much scrutiny. Although it didn't contain anything as obvious as books stolen from the library, it did contain the launch site's blueprints scattered amongst random papers from Matthaios's office. Virgil locked his arms to his side and tried to keep his fingers still and his face from tensing. His hand closed around the charm in his pocket. He'd brought it for good luck. It had protected him before and allowed him to gather an essential clue. It was luckier than he'd ever been.

Chrysanthe placed her own briefcase on the counter with a professional flourish. "Please be careful with it. This is my favorite one. I named it 'Theodore.'"

The receptionist coughed. "Okay. I'll treat Theodore with the utmost respect."

Chrysanthe's face turned red. "Thank you."

To avoid seeming overly interested in the results of the examination, Virgil studied the room while the receptionist rifled through the briefcases' contents. As expected, elegant paintings and sculptures decorated the lobby. Large windows gazed out into the night sky. Plush couches formed a semi-circle around the waiting-area table. From the wall behind the receptionist, Senator Kelipapalous's portrait smiled upon them with a friendliness its real-life counterpart likely did not share.

"All done with these," the receptionist sang. "Everything looks fine."

She snapped the briefcases shut and slid them across the smooth counter. Once Virgil and Chrysanthe had collected them, the receptionist turned to the disguised police and said, "Weapons are next. I'm afraid I can't return those to you until you leave."

Schirra stepped forward and dropped her spear on the counter. It rattled against the hard surface before vibrating to a halt. "I'm only turning it in," she said, "because I don't need it."

"Me, too." Stathis set his own spear next to Schirra's.

"Okay, okay, you all are tough." The receptionist failed to hide an annoyed expression. She placed the spears on labeled racks along the wall, next to several other weapons. Then she turned back to Virgil and the others. "Now your IDs, please."

Virgil produced his identification card from his pocket and waited in line behind the others. Chrysanthe had grabbed several old VIP badges from Nyx's desk before Matthaios had triggered the alarm and, during the long car ride, she had altered them with pictures of herself and the others. *Is the receptionist going to notice some minuscule discrepancy? Or a glaring one? Maybe there are expiration dates, or a magnetic strip or something, that will reveal the forgery.*

The receptionist eyed Virgil, and his pulse began pounding. He swallowed.

She ran her eyes from his hat to his dress shoes. "Two meters tall, huh?"

Chrysanthe hadn't altered the writing on the IDs, only the photographs. Before Virgil could respond, the receptionist smirked.

"Men always exaggerate their size." She held the badge out to him.

Virgil blinked and tried not to look too relieved as he accepted it. As he returned it to his pocket, the receptionist handed the other IDs back to their owners. She pointed to the door next to her desk.

"You all can go through here to reach the main hallway. The visitors' room will be all the way to your right. I hope the view is to your liking. There's nothing more beautiful than a night launch."

"I'm sure it'll be great," said Matthaios. "We've never seen a night launch before."

"Visitors are only allowed in limited areas of the launch operations complex, so please proceed directly to the visitors' room."

Virgil nodded and followed Matthaios and Chrysanthe, the briefcase banging against his hip. Even considering Schirra's incident, Chrysanthe's plan was working more smoothly than he had expected.

And now his part was done. He had provided another warm body to make Chrysanthe and the others appear more impressive as Kelipapalous's aides. Since he had no talents beyond being a warm body, he could accompany the others and watch how competent people did things.

Matthaios opened the door and strode into the hall, followed by Chrysanthe. Virgil took a breath.

Nyx is waiting. For the others, not me.

TWENTY-EIGHT

THEY ENTERED A long marble hallway, each end capped by floor-to-ceiling windows spilling night into the building. Paintings occupied every wall, battles from history or legend interspersed with portraits of wizened old men in heroic scenes. Sculptures of humans, beasts, and abstract objects stood atop pedestals against the walls at regular intervals.

As soon as the door closed behind them, Virgil let himself fall against the wall. He put a hand to his wound, but the pressure didn't reduce the pain.

The hall was silent. Virgil strained his ears, but couldn't hear approaching guards, or whispered conversations, or even the hum of machinery. Despite that, the hall bristled with all the tension of an executioner's blade poised to fall. He shivered.

Chrysanthe stepped forward and turned to address them. "I'm sorry for naming my briefcase," she said in a whisper, face reddening again. "I realized right afterward that I shouldn't be doing anything to draw attention to myself, but it was instinct."

Matthaios put his arm around her. "Your inappropriateness is one of the things I love about you."

"That's good, because it's not going to stop after we finish saving the world." Chrysanthe turned to Schirra. "I appreciate you standing up for me like that. It was very noble of you, but please don't do it again. This mission is too important to risk getting caught."

Schirra grimaced. "We'll see. I'm not swearing to it. I'm tired of looking the other way when a man takes advantage of a woman."

Virgil flushed. He would have allowed the guard to escape with impunity despite the fact that the guard had assaulted his sister. *I should have been the one attacking that guard, whatever the cost to myself. I am a coward.*

Chrysanthe shook her head. "Whatever. Let's keep going. The control room is a right at the next hallway, and then a left, then another left." Her mouth twisted into a rueful grin. "We're really doing this, aren't we? We're really going to try to stop the launch of a nuclear missile."

"Yeah," said Schirra. "It's about time my talents were used appropriately."

"Look." Stathis pointed to a digital display hanging from the ceiling. It counted down time in bright red numbers.

1:09:14.

"Oh," said Matthaios.

Sixty-nine minutes to find the control room and convince the mission controllers to stop the launch. Virgil's hands twitched.

Chrysanthe knows the way to the control room, but how long will it take to persuade the controllers and then to actually halt the launch? If I were working in this building and saw five random people burst into an area where they didn't belong, while they shouted about a conspiracy theory involving a nuclear apocalypse, I might be a little skeptical.

"I didn't realize we would be cutting it this close." Chrysanthe shook her head. "Come on."

Schirra stepped forward. "Wait. Stathis, take rear. I've got point." Once they had arranged themselves, the group began walking.

Virgil heard a doorknob turning ahead of them. Next to a portrait of Fred Nyx leading the Keres onto a battlefield, a door opened, and a guard strolled into the hallway. Catching sight of them, the man paused and stared.

Virgil had expected something like this. The five of them couldn't enter the launch facility without encountering guards. He tried to clear his face.

How would a senator's advisor's assistant act? Obsequious? Scared? Disinterested? Haughty? Virgil hoped the guard was satisfied with a convincing portrayal of confusion.

The guard remained stationary as they continued, his hard eyes seeming to examine every facet of Virgil and the others. Virgil concentrated on keeping his arms still and walking in a human-like manner.

How far apart are people's legs when they walk? Are feet supposed to move straight ahead, or should their placement have a slight angle? I've never thought about how I walked before, and this is a terrible time to become so conscious of it. Keeping his eyes forward, he passed the guard. Moments later, receding footsteps came from behind them. Virgil sighed.

Chrysanthe stopped at the next intersecting hallway. "Okay," she said, her face strained. "We take a right here. The control room isn't much farther. I really wish Fred Nyx's secret plan consisted of giving free kittens to everyone."

Schirra snorted. "I prefer the nuke. This is the most fun I've had in years."

Chrysanthe shook her head. "Is everyone ready?"

Virgil reviewed the plan. Schirra, Stathis, Chrysanthe, and Matthaios would tackle Nyx. They would then offer a quick explanation for their actions to the flight controllers and, using Nyx as a hostage, would obtain the evidence from the computer systems to back up their accusations. Virgil would watch. He nodded. *I am absolutely capable of fulfilling my responsibilities.*

"Ready," said Schirra with a feral grin.

"Yeah," said Stathis.

Matthaios squeezed Chrysanthe's shoulder. "I would follow you into Tartarus."

"That's sweet, but I'm not asking that. Maybe we can work up to it." She shrugged. "Well, let's go."

Matthaios straightened his shoulders and continued. Schirra and Matthaios rounded the corner first, disappearing from view. When Virgil and Chrysanthe caught up to them, the other two had stopped. Virgil glanced up and cursed.

A thick, locked metal door blocked their way.

A card reader was next to it, the same design as those in the Keres Lab. Virgil leaned forward, putting his hands on his knees. "Can we try Matthaios's access card?"

Matthaios grunted. He had already pulled out the card. As Matthaios strode to the door, Virgil tried to believe it would work. *It would feel too convenient if it worked, though. Nothing about this investigation has been simple or easy.*

Matthaios held the card against the reader. Virgil held his breath and...

A red light blinked once. Matthaios held the card to the reader again, with the same result. "Shit."

Virgil stared at the floor. They had come this far, and something as simple as an electric lock was stopping them. All the threats, all the frustrations, the missteps, the sudden revelations, the stabbing, all of it meant nothing if they couldn't reach the control room. *But what can we do?* The only option that came to him was to bang his head into the door over and over again. He glanced at one of the clocks in the hallway: 1:01:23.

"Do you want me to break the lock?" Stathis's eyes twinkled.

Schirra shook her head once. "Bad idea. Alarms would go off, and if someone caught us sneaking around in here, w—"

"Someone like me, perhaps?"

Virgil recognized that voice, had feared encountering it here. He turned and saw Patroklus standing before them, alone. As always, the priest's face had the impassivity of a wooden chair, his motives and desires hidden. He rested his hands, one atop the other, over his stomach.

Virgil slipped a hand into his pocket and clutched the charm. *Why did Patroklus bother making it for me if he meant for me to die during that trip to Hades? Or if he planned to report me to the guards now? Maybe Patroklus arrived to help us? Does it even matter if he wants to help?* He recalled Patroklus's previous method of helping.

The priest seemed to study Virgil. *Did my survival surprise him? Does he care either way about my fate?*

"Patroklus," Schirra said. "You need to leave."

Chrysanthe's eyes narrowed into a glare that could have frozen fire. "Wait, you're Patroklus? The one who stabbed Virgil?"

"I am." Patroklus inclined his head. "Did he explain why it was necessary for me to stab him?"

"He explained. It doesn't excuse you. You almost killed my brother. You're supposed to work the will of the gods, not kill millions of innocent people. *Not stab people.*" Chrysanthe's voice cracked on the last sentence, but she strode forward and brandished her briefcase as though it were a stout oaken club.

Matthaios grabbed her by the shoulders. "He's a priest. You don't know what he can do to you."

For a moment, Chrysanthe looked as though she wanted to shove her husband aside and continue her advance. Then her face softened, and she relented.

Virgil sent a silent thanks to Chrysanthe for trying to stand up for him, even though he hadn't stood up for her earlier, and to Matthaios for preventing her. *They're braver than I am. For all they know, Patroklus has some magical way to kill her instantly. Of course, an instant death might also be preferable to whatever the priest plans to do with us, or to dying from radiation poisoning after Europe retaliates for Nyx's nuclear strike.*

For several moments, no one said anything. Schirra and Stathis remained tense, and Stathis's hands trembled every few seconds. Priests did not often use combat magic, but when they did, it was effective and painful.

"I presume," Patroklus said in his monotone voice, "you have discovered or deduced some of the information about what is taking place here."

"That's right," said Chrysanthe. "And we're not going to let you get away with it."

"You do not seem to be in a desirable position relative to your goals." Patroklus turned to Virgil. "I applaud you for coming this far. To have deduced these plans with so little information or opportunity is impressive."

Virgil blinked. *Is he complimenting me? Why? Is it a ploy to distract me?*

"Unfortunately," Patroklus said, nodding to the door, "you are lacking an item essential to your mission. It is a pity, after all your travails, to fail due to something so small." He produced a walkie-talkie from his robe.

"He's calling security!" said Chrysanthe.

Schirra raised her fists and took a step toward the priest. Stathis did the same.

Patroklus didn't flinch or attempt to move away. He only raised a hand, palm outward. "Let me assure you, your attempts to incapacitate me will be futile." Before anyone could speak further, his thumb held down the walkie-talkie's button. "Squad Six, we have five intruders in Section 1B-7."

"Acknowledged," came the reply. "En route."

Patroklus returned the walkie-talkie to his robe. "Perhaps your punishment can be minimized. Depending on your level of cooperation, of course."

Saying nothing further, the priest turned and walked away. Virgil watched him turn down the intersecting hallway and leave their view.

The five of them exchanged glances. "He just left us here by ourselves," Chrysanthe said. "There has to be a reason he wouldn't stay to guard us."

"He doesn't think we'd get far," said Virgil.

A loud clanking sound came from behind them. The security door slid open to reveal several bulky guards in crimson uniforms.

It's over. We've lost. Even if they somehow survived the European retaliation while being at the launch site of the preemptive strike, even if Patroklus vouched for them and managed to reduce their sentences to life in prison, they would be living in a world of nuclear warfare. Despite everything, the investigation, the trial with Artino, the trip to Hades, breaking in to Keres, they had failed.

"Cooperate, or you will be killed." The leader of the guards stepped through the doorway, his crooked grin leaving no doubt as to his preference. His muscles rippled beneath his tight uniform. "You are trespassing in a top-secret military facility. We will detain you until the authorities decide what to do with you."

Virgil thought about rushing the guards, but his best effort wouldn't even bruise their knuckles. *Being caught like this is my fault. If I had solved the mystery of Nicholas's killer sooner, Chrysanthe would have had more time to make preparations and would have obtained a key card that would have given us access to the mission control room. Instead, we're going to wait for the final moments of the countdown in a prison cell, our sole consolation being the fact that we tried to stop it.*

"Um." Virgil blinked, surprised he had said anything and aware of the others' eyes on him, but forced himself to continue. "I know this sounds implausible, but we think Fred Nyx is planning to divert the missile so that it hits a city."

The leader guffawed. *Not the response I wanted, but the response I deserve.*

"Oh, no," said the leader, "that doesn't sound implausible at all. Especially when your crack commando team consists of a guy in a suit, a short guy in a hat, a moron, and two girls."

"I'm not wearing a suit," said Stathis.

"I'm not a girl," said Schirra. "I'm a police officer who can kick your ass."

Virgil's arms and legs trembled. *Violence is about to happen.*

Chrysanthe bowed her head and closed her eyes. "Zeus, hear my prayer. Deliver us from the hands of these guards. Help us do your work."

Well, at least prayer won't hurt. Virgil admired Chrysanthe for never abandoning her gods, even when the gods gave scant evidence they existed, and even less evidence that they would be willing to help her.

A guard with a scar across his cheek laughed. "It's Blasphemer's Week. The gods are all off on Olympus, and none of them are watching what happens here. We can do whatever we want to you. Philipides, take the little one."

One of the guards, presumably Philipides, tore the briefcase from Virgil's fingers and hurled it against the wall. "I'm going to tell you not to struggle, because I have to say that, but I want you to struggle."

Philipides grabbed Virgil's arms with far more force than required and pulled them behind Virgil's back. Virgil's shoulders made a creaking sound as he coughed and leaned forward, trying not to succumb to pain. Metal clacked against metal behind him as the guard produced handcuffs. Unnecessary in his case, but he appreciated Philipides considering him a sufficient threat to warrant their use. Philipides pulled Virgil's right arm even farther behind his back. Virgil suppressed a yelp, though it felt as though the guard had nearly yanked the arm from its socket.

Schirra approached the leader, who laughed. "What?" the man said. "Is the little girl g—"

Schirra swung a fist at him. The guard managed to dodge, but Schirra landed a heel on his leg in the direction of his momentum and sent him sprawling to the ground. Another guard charged her, but she ducked to his side and tripped him as he went past.

The others began struggling with their own guards. Matthaios and Chrysanthe wriggled within the thick hands of their assailants. Stathis broke free and head-butted his guard. As Stathis slammed the guard into the floor and unconsciousness, another guard came from behind and delivered a nasty blow to the back of the officer's head. Stathis dropped to the ground, unmoving.

Virgil willed the man to get up, but nothing happened. *Is Stathis unconscious? Did the guard actually kill him?* Stathis didn't deserve to die. He had showed up to help Virgil despite the other officers ignoring the detective's call to action. Stathis was always loyal to Schirra. He…

Virgil didn't know much more about him except that he'd brought a bucket and some trash bags to clean Virgil's remains from the street outside the police station. *But he must have his own story, his own views of the world, his own hopes and related failures. Are those gone now?*

Virgil pulled forward, twisting to each side, even though the motion wrenched at his wound, but his arms were still held tightly by the guard. Philipides regarded him for a moment, snorted with an almost physical manifestation of contempt, and released his grip to join the fray against Schirra.

Stathis's guard circled her now, as did Philipides and the two she had previously dropped. She gave them a thin smile. Virgil couldn't be certain, but he thought it was false bravado.

Virgil turned to watch Chrysanthe, who still faced her own guard. She bobbed on the balls of her feet, staying out of range of fists and boots, but didn't go on the offensive. *Maybe she's waiting for an opening that is never going to come.*

When Virgil glanced back to Schirra, he saw an unconscious guard on the floor nearby. Two guards, each with visible injuries, had tight grips around Schirra's arms, but she clutched the neck of one.

Virgil glanced around, but saw nothing that could be used to help. *Maybe something from the unconscious guard?* He hobbled closer to the fray as one of the guards landed a blow to Schirra's midsection. The unconscious man's belt had a small baton. *Maybe Schirra can find a use for that if she fights free.* Virgil slid it from its holster. When he looked up, Schirra twisted loose from the guards.

"Schirra!" Virgil tossed her the baton, wincing as his side protested.

She turned, her mouth open in surprise, but extended her hand for the arcing baton. Before it reached her, the leader stepped forward and caught it. Virgil cursed. *I always make situations worse.*

Chrysanthe continued dodging her guard, who appeared frustrated. He lunged at her, but she bounced to the side.

When Virgil looked back to Schirra, she held the baton and cracked an approaching guard in the face. Blood spurted from his nose as he cried out. She feinted another punch to his face, while sending a kick to his knee. Her next blow connected with his jaw, knocking him out. He joined a pile of bodies on the floor.

After that, dispatching Chrysanthe's and Matthaios's guards took Schirra even less time. "That is the most fun I have had in my life," she said, wiping a trickle of blood from the corner of her mouth.

"I suppose being punched in the face does have a certain amount of charm," said Chrysanthe, panting. "But I don't think I ever want to do that again. Thank you for helping us."

"Yes, thank you." Matthaios gasped in deep breaths while rubbing Chrysanthe's shoulder.

The other three exchanged congratulatory glances, but Virgil couldn't join them. He had done nothing. He had watched while the others struggled. Sure, he could have contributed little, and his injury lowered his effectiveness to even more negligible levels, but he should have tried. Instead, he had given a weapon to one of Schirra's assailants.

Chrysanthe was right: I should never have come.

Then Virgil's eyes darted to the floor, where Stathis lay motionless. *Is he dead? Or unconscious?*

The others had noticed, too. Schirra rushed to Stathis's side and felt his wrist. Her face seemed to relax as she released the wrist and let it fall to the floor. Then she slapped Stathis's cheek. Then again, harder. Then again, with even more force. This time, Stathis groaned. Virgil's shoulders dropped, and he felt a release of pressure in his chest. Stathis had survived.

The officer raised his head and looked around. "Oh. We won."

"Yep." Schirra stood up. "Hurry and get up. We still have work to do."

Virgil glanced at the nearest digital display: 47:19.

TWENTY-NINE

"THE GODS WILL help us stop Nyx in time," said Chrysanthe. "They've helped us so far, and they wouldn't let someone like Patroklus win."

Virgil refrained from commenting on the ambiguity of their help and watched as Schirra forced Stathis to stand. Stathis swayed to the side, but Schirra placed her hands on his shoulders and steadied him.

Matthaios pulled something from the unconscious leader's belt. "Found some weapons." He showed them four darts.

Virgil felt his heart jump. He could throw a dart. *Maybe I'll actually have an advantage in this confrontation.*

Is this what confidence feels like?

"I think they're tranquilizer darts," said Matthaios. "Some of the guards at my lab carry them, although I think they prefer using their fists."

"No surprise there." Chrysanthe knelt next to the leader and pulled the badge from his uniform's chest pocket. "At least now we can get through the door."

Virgil shuffled to the wall and collected his briefcase. *I don't expect I'll need the blueprints or any of the other documents in here, which means I probably* will *need them.*

Matthaios offered the darts to Schirra and Stathis. Both officers shook their heads.

"Nope," said Schirra. "I've already got the two best weapons in the Alliance." She flexed her arms.

Matthaios shrugged. "Okay." He handed two darts to Chrysanthe and kept the remaining two.

"Thanks." Chrysanthe tucked them into her pocket and strode to the heavy security door. She placed the guard's badge against the card reader while Virgil held his breath. Once again, their mission was susceptible to a single point of failure. If the card didn't work...

After an interminable pause, the reader's green light blinked on, and a click sounded. The door rumbled open, sliding into the wall.

Virgil's stomach flipped. Almost time. They were about to face Nyx, the man who wanted to bring nuclear war to the Alliance, and the one who had killed Nicholas.

"Let's go!" said Schirra, with the kind of enthusiasm Virgil couldn't imagine experiencing. She and Stathis steamed through the door first, Stathis still unsteady on his feet. Chrysanthe slipped through after them, followed by Matthaios. Virgil hobbled through last, a moment before the door started sliding shut again.

They had entered another hallway, one identical to the previous. Another clock counted down the remaining time: 43:12.

Chrysanthe turned to Virgil. "Are you okay? Can you keep going?"

Virgil nodded and put a hand against the wall. His side throbbed, and he expected his intestines to break through at any moment. "I'm fine."

Chrysanthe didn't look convinced, but didn't comment. "Okay. The control room is down the hallway to our left. We're alm—"

Six more guards appeared from the right hallway. "It's the intruders!"

Matthaios clenched his fists. "This is bullshit!"

We barely made it past the previous guards and now we have to face more? Before Virgil could decide whether to charge or flee or enter an endless loop alternating between the two, Schirra held her hand up.

"We'll handle this," she said. "You three keep going."

"Um," said Virgil. They wouldn't get far without Schirra.

Chrysanthe grabbed him by the shoulder. "Come on. We don't have time to argue!"

Schirra and Stathis burst forward to engage the guards, Stathis lurching more than charging, while Matthaios dodged around them to the hallway Chrysanthe had indicated. Chrysanthe took Virgil's arm and placed it over her shoulder. Bracing himself, he leaned against her and tried to keep pace while they followed Matthaios. As they stumbled forward, his side screamed obscenities in its own special language. Shouts and sounds of boots crunching into flesh came from behind as Chrysanthe dragged Virgil around the corner.

"There!" Chrysanthe pointed. The control-room door lay only paces away. 40:32. *Enough time to tackle Nyx and force the controllers to believe our accusations, and then stop the launch.* Virgil slid from her arm and leaned against the wall, trying to regain his strength for this last confrontation.

Chrysanthe sighed. "Everyone ready?"

No. "Yes," Virgil said.

Matthaios squeezed her shoulder. "Ready. I love you."

Chrysanthe smiled. "I love you, too."

She pulled the door open, and Matthaios rushed past her with a grim expression. Chrysanthe followed, and Virgil hurried after them, clutching his side with his free hand.

They had entered at the back of the dimly lit room. Screens against the far wall showed glowing images of the missile waiting on the launch pad, each displaying the view from a different angle: a distant side view, gazing upward from its tail fins to its peak, looking down over its conical nosecone. Floodlights illuminated it, the bright metal shining against the dark background of the new night sky. It looked poised for flight, like a living thing impatient for its journey to begin.

It also looks like a penis.

Computer consoles were arranged in several rows in a stadium-seating configuration, each of them displaying what looked like blinking or scrolling strings of text and numbers. Men occupied each console, wearing headsets. Most had turned to see the intruders, freezing mid-motion.

Virgil scanned the room's occupants. No one looked familiar.

"He's not here," Virgil whispered.

Where is Nyx going to observe the launch from, then, if not the control room? Is he kilometers away, watching from a secret location? If so, they didn't have time to prevent him from tampering with the target coordinates.

"Should we talk to them?" Virgil noticed several of the controllers had tensed.

"I've got an idea." Chrysanthe stepped forward and addressed the controllers with a raised voice. "This is a drill. We are pretending to be intruders to simulate an invasion of the launch site during a launch. Remember your training. How do you respond if someone enters the control room?"

As one, the controllers removed long knives from their boots.

Virgil choked, and Chrysanthe blanched visibly even in the low lighting. They backed toward the exit.

"Great!" said Chrysanthe in an enthusiastic voice. "Perfect! The drill is over. We'll go test another room now. Good luck with the launch and blowing stuff up."

The controllers watched with knives unsheathed while Chrysanthe led Matthaios and Virgil into the hallway again. Virgil felt relief when the door shut, relief tempered by the realization that they had failed.

"I'm sorry," said Chrysanthe. "I thought they would run out the door, or duck for cover or something. If we go back in there, they'll call security on us. They might already be calling security. I really messed that up."

Matthaios placed a hand on her shoulder. "Now you know how Virgil probably feels all the time."

Virgil hoped she didn't feel that bad. *She deserves better.*

"Still," said Matthaios, "it was a good idea, especially when you had to adapt so quickly."

Chrysanthe gave him a wan smile. "We only have thirty minutes left. I need somewhere to look at the blueprints."

Virgil turned. He pointed to a door with a drawing of a stick-man. "What about there?"

Chrysanthe nodded. "Good idea."

They hurried across the hall and ducked into the restroom. Bright fluorescent lights shined from above, illuminating the fresh white tile floors and the dark marble counter. Each stall had patterned wooden doors reaching from the floor to the ceiling. A spotless mirror stood behind a counter with evenly spaced shiny metal faucets and sink bowls.

Images of his razor next to his sink flashed into his head. Virgil shuddered and tried to push away the thoughts.

Chrysanthe held her hand out. "You still have the blueprints, right?"

Virgil gave her the briefcase. Chrysanthe lifted it onto the counter and undid the latches. After she leaned the top of the briefcase against the mirror, she dug through several papers.

"Good." She removed one of them and unfolded it, spreading the blueprint across the counter. "If Nyx isn't in the control room, he has to be somewhere with access to the communications so he can send updates to the missile's on-board guidance computer. We just need to trace the wiring diagrams to see where that would be. The wires should be connected with the control room."

As Virgil watched her poring over the paper, he wondered what Chrysanthe could have done under different societal conditions. *Would she have become an engineer or a scientist? Or would she still have wanted to dance? At least she would have had the choice.*

Chrysanthe ran a finger along thin lines marked on the page, moving from a box labeled as the "Mission Control Room" through twists and bends in the walls. Her finger stopped at a small box with no label.

"Here," she said. "He has to be here."

"Where is that?" asked Matthaios.

"The next hall to our left, then downstairs. It should be un-marked, I guess. Clever." She looked at the papers. "We don't need the briefcases anymore, and I don't feel like carrying mine. Let's hurry."

She led the way out of the bathroom and toward their destination. Virgil clutched his side and glanced up at the nearest clock: 28:13.

When they turned down the next corridor, Virgil cursed. More crimson-uniformed guards awaited. Under normal circumstances, it would have been good for a nuclear missile launch facility to have such high security, but it was inconvenient right now. During their previous encounter, they had escaped through luck and Schirra. This time, their main advantage was that they were no longer slowed down by their briefcases.

Chrysanthe turned and put her hands on Virgil's shoulder, halting him from his pointless charge. "Let Matthaios and me handle the guards. We've got darts and… Well, we'll figure something out. We'll try to make it to you afterward. Stall Nyx until we get there. Just stall him. If it gets too late, though…"

She pulled one of the tranquilizer darts from her pocket and pressed it into his hand. "Go."

"But—"

"Go!"

She pushed him, almost knocking him to the ground. He regained his balance as Chrysanthe and Matthaios ran toward the guards. *She's right to send me away. I would only be useless again.*

Virgil headed to the stairwell on the right, making sure not to poke himself with the dart's sharp tip. *It would be just like me to accidentally knock myself out when I'm trying to save the world.*

After several excruciating moments descending the stairs, he exited the stairwell and reached the unlabeled door in a hallway with concrete walls. *This is it.* Before opening the door, he glanced up at the digital display: 24:46. *Right.* He pulled more caffeine pills from his pocket and swallowed them, then turned the doorknob and entered the room.

The room was larger than Virgil's apartment, with overhead fluorescent lights and a digital display at the far end. Sturdy cabinets lined the thick concrete walls. A man in a lab coat leaned over a desktop computer, with a disk in his hand.

Fred Nyx.

THIRTY

"UM, STOP." VIRGIL raised his dart as he watched the man in the lab coat.

"Ah. Virgil Glezos." Fred Nyx straightened and turned around, adjusting his gold-rimmed glasses. "So you put all the clues together. I'm impressed."

Another compliment. *Today has been odd.*

"I am, however, surprised to see you alive. Patroklus led me to believe his clever assassination attempt last night would work. Apparently not."

Another piece of evidence pointing to Patroklus as a betrayer, depending on Nyx's credibility. All the evidence, on both sides, was circumstantial, though. And Patroklus had been emotionally supportive of Virgil throughout the investigation. *Kind of. So he might still be on my side.*

Virgil hated how much he wanted that statement to be true.

"Yes, your assassination attempt failed." Virgil shook his dart at Nyx as he imagined Schirra might have done in this situation, but the motion sent a lance of pain through his side, and his pained expression probably negated whatever threat the gesture held. "So don't move. Are you expecting anyone else to come here?"

Nyx shrugged. "Not until after the launch. Other than masterminding this entire scheme, my only role was to send the updated coordinates to the missile from my bunker. My compatriots have fulfilled their duties and are in the viewing room now."

Virgil's side ached, and his legs wobbled. Several simple cots stood near the far wall, but the room had no chairs. For several seconds, he urged himself not to show weakness in front of the enemy. One didn't have to be a general or a Schirra to know one couldn't do that. But after several seconds, he realized he couldn't hold himself up. He leaned against the wall, gritting his teeth at the new pressure against his side.

Nyx raised an eyebrow. Virgil tightened his grip on the dart. The dart gave him the advantage, and he only had to stall Nyx long enough to prevent him from uploading the coordinates to the missile. *Twenty-one minutes until it's over, and then it won't matter what happens to me.*

Nyx pointed to the dart in Virgil's hand. "I didn't anticipate you would be this much of a threat. Had I known, I would have had a full retinue of guards. Not that you can always trust them. You are here tonight because of incompetent guards."

"Okay." Virgil's stomach fluttered as it had the day the police station hired him. He was stalling Nyx, just like Chrysanthe had requested, and he wasn't even having to work hard to do it. "What do you mean?"

"On the night of Hera 28, the two night-shift security guards at the Keres Lab were ingesting drugs. I don't know or care what kind, or what delivery mechanism they used, but it impaired their reasoning. Unfortunate, but such things happen at military laboratories across the Alliance. When your friend, Mr. Manikas, entered the building and insisted on speaking to their boss, who was in a meeting with me, the guards didn't stop to think that perhaps we didn't want our top-secret meeting interrupted by an unemployed police officer."

Virgil frowned. "Nicholas told me about that. I don't understand why you had to kill him. He didn't hear anything, or not enough to be suspicious."

Nyx shrugged. "Pity. I could have spared him, then. Such things happen. Of course, had I known there would be an investigation into the death of Mr. Manikas, I would have found some other way of disposing of him. Given the police department's typical operational mode, though, I think I can be forgiven for assuming they would not do anything constructive."

So, Virgil had only stumbled across the conspiracy because of Nyx's miscalculation. If Nyx had chosen a less public way of killing Nicholas, no one would have discovered the plan to divert the missile until afterward. *Even with Nyx's mistake, I almost didn't discover the plan in time.*

Nyx had stopped talking and instead peered at Virgil with a penetrating gaze. *How long before Nyx makes another attempt to load the coordinates, or until he attacks me?*

Stall. Keep stalling. Nineteen minutes left.

"Um," said Virgil, "I know about your plan to divert the missile test."

"You do not." Nyx gave him a patronizing smile. "Or at least not fully, or you would have made no attempt to obstruct me. In fact, once I explain, I'm certain you'll allow me to continue with my plan. You will be quite fascinated with the results."

"No, I won't." Virgil frowned. "I know you're going to use it to destroy a city and start a nuclear war. That's not something I—"

Nyx brayed, startling Virgil, and thumped the wall with his free hand too vigorously for a genuine reaction. "An amusing conclusion. At least that explains why you have been so intent on stopping me. But no, you are incorrect. A better target exists. Think. Who is having their annual meeting as we speak?"

Virgil stared at him. "I…"

Chrysanthe's dance company had their annual meeting next week. Arestia's police department held one toward the end of the year. Matthaios's team had an office party every month. None of them sounded like activities Nyx might have wanted to nuke.

Nyx sighed. "The Olympians."

"Oh, right!" The whole point of Blasphemer's Week. "So, you're going to use their distraction to—"

"We are going to nuke Mount Olympus and destroy the gods!"

Virgil blinked.

Destroy the gods?

Can a nuclear missile do that?

Is there anyone to destroy? What would happen if there is?

He pictured the muscular bodies of Zeus and Ares, and the voluptuous bodies of Hera and Aphrodite, remembered them portrayed in so many paintings in museums and temples around the Alliance, then imagined those bodies vaporized in an instant. *Can a god really die like that?*

"That's crazy!"

"But it's not!" Nyx's eyes expanded, focused on something beyond Virgil, maybe even beyond reality. "We are freeing ourselves! The gods have controlled us for millennia. They have whimsically interfered with our lives and, with their jealous rivalries, have ruined everything they have touched. It is time for them to be destroyed so we can be set free. And when they are gone, I will emerge from my bunker to lead."

Nyx bounced where he stood.

"The Alliance has relied on magic for thousands of years," Nyx continued. "We haven't matured or learned new things. Europe has. They focused on developing technology, and now they are stronger than we are. They had their first cars a hundred years before we did, their first plane twenty years before we did, and their first nuclear bomb fifty years before we did. Our dependence on the gods has hindered us. Only by destroying them and forcing ourselves to fully embrace technology can we return to the dominance we once had. I am doing this for the Alliance."

Virgil blinked. "The senator said something similar."

Nyx grinned. "Yes, he did, and who do you think gave him his ideas? The senator, like so many others, is my game piece. By using him, I can restore the Alliance's former glory."

Fifteen more minutes to stall. *Chrysanthe would be proud of how well I'm doing. And probably horrified about everything Nyx is saying.* "Okay. Um, I guess I see what you're saying, but—"

"You don't believe in the gods, do you?" Nyx shook his head and smiled. "Of course not. Your entire existence is based on questioning everything. You know no other way. You see, I know you, Virgil. I studied your file. You don't know whether I will be eliminating those troublesome gods from our lives or comically firing a nuclear missile into the side of a mountain. My plan works either way, though, from your point of view. That's the genius of it. If the gods exist, I destroy them. If they don't, I make others believe they are dead. The mountain itself serves only as a symbol, a symbol of everything that keeps us from greatness."

Virgil thought of his sister and her faith. Despite the terrible things the gods were said to have done, she still believed they could be called upon in times of need to aid those who deserved it. She had prayed for Virgil's safety, and her prayer had been answered. She had called to Zeus when their situation had grown dire. She believed so much, that she was confident of success even when circumstances offered little hope.

"No," said Virgil. "They are symbols that inspire us *to* greatness."

Nyx grimaced. "No, definitely n—"

"They are. People believe that if we try hard enough, the gods will intervene to help us accomplish a task we ordinarily would have been incapable of. And even if the gods aren't really there, they're a symbol for the people who believe, something that encourages them to try despite the odds."

Nyx smirked. "Your reasoning is flawed. And quite condescending. You sh—"

"No, listen. I don't like having the beliefs of the majority forced on me. We both know what happens to unbelievers in the Alliance. But I don't think I should force my beliefs, or my lack of beliefs, on others. I don't want others to live under the same oppression I do. The oppressed become the oppressors. It happens in every culture, on a societal and individual level." Virgil looked at the floor. "I...I think that cycle should stop."

Nyx waved his hand. "You are complicating the issue. The senator and I, among others, have examined what the gods have done to us, and we have the perfect opportunity to free ourselves from their clutches. They have become weak, complacent over time. That is one reason relying on them has ruined the Alliance. Consider this: though I made no plans in the open, wouldn't a worthy god have seen my ambition? Wouldn't they have discovered my plan, as you did? If the gods were truly powerful and all-knowing, why didn't they strike me down before I destroyed them?"

Virgil shrugged, then winced at the pain in his side. "Maybe they sent me instead."

"Cute. The real answer is that I have outsmarted them. *I* did. A mortal, albeit a brilliant mortal. The age of gods is at an end."

Thirteen minutes left. *When are Chrysanthe and Matthaios going to get here? Will they? Stalling Nyx would be much easier if Chrysanthe and Matthaios were here.*

"What happens if the gods do exist?" Virgil shifted position against the wall. "If you destroy them, what happens? Maybe nothing. Maybe the universe continues as it always has. But what if it doesn't? Without the gods to perform maintenance, there might be no more sun. The ocean will be uncontrolled, and no one will be around to guide the heavens. Eventually, everything will fall apart and the world will end. Do you really want to take the chance of that happening?"

Nyx grinned. "Yes. Absolutely."

The grin held no mirth. It was more like that of a hyena about to feed. Virgil tried to stand straighter, but slipped and slid down several centimeters.

Nyx didn't seem to notice. "It will be the grandest experiment of all time, an exciting gamble with the highest stakes. And only a handful of people will understand what is happening when the very fabric of the universe falls apart around them."

Virgil tried to picture what it would look like. Would the sea and sky and ground crumble away like dried mud, or would objects begin to blink out of existence, or would everything disappear simultaneously, without time for thought?

Nyx shrugged. "Of course, the universe appears to run without problems when the gods are away during Blasphemer's

Week every year. I expect it will continue along its normal course, and I will be in charge of the Alliance. Also an interesting outcome. Besides, a universe in which the Greek Alliance is not in its rightful position of dominance... Is that a universe that deserves to exist?"

However events unfolded after the destruction of Mount Olympus, something would end. Maybe the universe, maybe magic, or maybe just the Greek religion. But in any of those outcomes, people would suffer.

"Um, I can't let you do this."

"You can, and you should. I know you, Virgil. I know you're curious, and you want to see what will happen just as much as I. Why do you think I'm explaining this to you?"

"To gloat. Whom else will you be able to brag to?"

"Good guess, but wrong. You seem a reasonable sort, and you have a decent head for logic. You've made it here, after all." Nyx indicated the bunker, or possibly the launch site. "You would be a useful ally for any future endeavors."

"That's... I can't join someone who sees the potential destruction of the entire universe as an acceptable risk."

"Virgil, it's time for you to face a sad fact: you can't stop me. I could upload the coordinates right now, and you could do nothing. Do you know why you haven't attacked me yet? It's not because you're physically incapable. It's worse than that. It's self-doubt."

Virgil glanced at the dart in his hand. He could have thrown it at Nyx at any time and avoided the discussion of motivation. If he had believed in his aim, he wouldn't have needed to stall Nyx. But he hadn't thrown the dart.

Nyx is right: my lack of self-confidence is the problem.

Still, he had served his purpose by preventing Nyx from loading the coordinates. Ten more minutes, and Nyx's plan would fail. Or Chrysanthe and Matthaios would arrive to stop Nyx.

"You are perceived as weak, Virgil. From Patroklus, I heard about your raid on my Keres Laboratory. If you were seen as strong and confident, you could have convinced Arestia's police department to join your raid. You would then have captured me before I left for the launch site. Or, the police would have supported your investigation throughout and helped you gather clues that would have led you to me sooner. But you're weak, and they know it. They laughed at you, Virgil.

"You have only come this far because of help from your friends. Where are they now? Not here, not available to aid you in these final moments. Without them, you are nothing. You have logic skills, I grant you that, but you have traveled as far as logic will take you."

Virgil lowered his eyes. Nyx was right: Virgil had accomplished nothing without help. It didn't matter, though. Soon, Chrysanthe and Matthaios would come, and then Nyx would be truly finished.

"If you join my team, though, you won't be alone. You have valuable contributions to make, Virgil. You can help the Alliance recover its greatness in technology, in science, and in military might. It is your patriotic duty. Join me."

Virgil raised his eyebrows. *No one wants* me *to join their team. Nyx is smarter than that. So what is his plan?*

Then Virgil understood. When Virgil entered the room, Nyx hadn't been leaning over to put the disk in the computer and upload the new coordinates. He had already uploaded the coordinates and was leaning over to remove the disk from the computer.

I haven't been stalling Nyx; Nyx has been stalling me.

"You tricked me," said Virgil.

Nyx laughed. "You finally figured it out. Bravo. Not that it matters. You are incapable of stopping me."

A futile attempt at saving the world is better than watching without resistance. Probably. "Um, I'm not letting you do this."

"Whatever. If you try to stop me, I will have your sister killed. Gutted, then burned alive."

Virgil thought of Chrysanthe and how much she had cared for him over the years when no one else had. He shuddered, thinking of her screaming while being gutted, and then again as her skin melted away.

"That's right," Nyx said in clipped tones. "That's the kind of guy I am. I do that kind of thing."

Wait, why is Nyx threatening me? I'm the one with the tranquilizer dart.

Virgil glanced at the display: 7:48. There wasn't time to wait for Chrysanthe and Matthaios. He had to act now.

"No," said Virgil. "I'm not letting you get away with this."

Virgil squeezed his dart. *Nyx is standing closer than the standard distance for targets. This should be easy. I've practiced for years, and I usually hit the targets. Now, when the world and my sister are relying on me, I know I can do it. I can summon the focus to aim the dart true.*

He relaxed, planted his feet in the standard pose, one foot forward, straightened his back despite the agony in his side, let his fingers find their spots on the dart's grooved grip, focused on the center of Nyx's chest, and let the dart fly.

Nyx didn't even move. The dart clattered against the wall next to him and dropped to the floor.

"That," Nyx pronounced, "was pathetic."

Fate had given Virgil a chance, one opportunity to save the world, and he had failed. *Is my ineptitude ever going to end?* As Nyx approached him with arms raised, Virgil decided that, yes, his ineptitude would probably end in about the time it would take Nyx to strangle him.

Someone else should have been here. Chrysanthe would have come up with some clever way to defeat Nyx, something the scientist would never have expected. Schirra would have beaten him up, which he would have expected but couldn't have prevented. Stathis probably could have beaten him up, too. Even Matthaios could have done something more useful than I could.

Nyx grabbed Virgil by the shoulders, pulled him closer, and slammed him against the wall. Something in Virgil's side ripped, and a horrendous pain shot through him. He gasped as Nyx punched him where Patroklus had stabbed him. It felt even worse than the initial cut. An involuntary yelp escaped his lips.

"Look, Virgil," Nyx said while Virgil slid down the wall into an undignified heap. "I am bigger than you, I am stronger than you, and I have fewer moral scruples than you. I will win any contest between us."

Virgil clutched his side and felt something sticky.

Is Nyx really going to do that to Chrysanthe?

"Don't be stupid, and I might suffer you to live." Nyx patted Virgil's hat and returned to blocking Virgil's path to the computer.

As Virgil huffed and tried to regain his breath, Nyx never took his eyes off him. Those eyes studied him, the way a sociopath would study a dying dog. Virgil's side hurt, his back hurt, and his head hurt, but he knew he had to stop the scientist.

Chrysanthe would want me to, despite the risk. She's depending on me. The Alliance is depending on me. Maybe even the gods are depending on me. He forced himself to his feet under Nyx's amused gaze.

"This is sad," said Nyx. "It's like watching preschoolers attack a veteran legion."

Virgil swallowed. He had no plan, no idea what to do, except attack Nyx. *Maybe I can figure out the rest if the attack succeeds.* He charged, uncontrolled, off-balance, and with flailing arms.

Before Virgil could tackle the scientist, Nyx reached forward and grabbed Virgil's throat. Virgil's momentum gave him no time to dodge, and he found himself shoved against the wall again, with fingers tightening around his neck. He tried to breathe, but nothing came. His neck screamed, and his lungs cried out, and his head began to pound.

"You should not have opposed me, Virgil." Nyx's eyes were vacant as he squeezed the life from him.

Virgil pulled at Nyx's hands, but couldn't pry them free. *Nyx is gloating, and I can do nothing. My final vision is going to be of him laughing at me.*

"You are weak in body and character," said Nyx. "Your existence has no meaning and brings no one joy."

Darkness crept into Virgil's vision, and spots speckled Nyx and the opposite wall. Virgil's palms beat at Nyx's arms, each blow feebler than the last.

For brief moments, Virgil had thought he could stand up to his enemies, that he could protect other people. Nyx had shown him the error in his thinking. Even now, Nyx was proving how much of a failure Virgil would always be.

Nyx increased the pressure on Virgil's throat. "Ponder that while you wait for strength and happiness that will never come, while you suffer for eternity in Hades."

Charon told me that no one changes after going to Hades. I'll be like this forever: skittish, incompetent, and weak. This is how it was meant to be.

Wait. Charon. Hades. The charm!

Virgil stopped trying to pull Nyx's hands away and instead removed the charm from his pocket. It felt warm.

"Hades, Hades, Hades," he croaked through his constricted windpipe.

As the last word escaped Virgil's throat, a wind rustled the air. Nyx's coat fluttered. Faint wisps appeared, and thin voices came from all around them, the same as when Virgil had clutched his knife wound in the examination lab before his trip to Hades. The featureless void that preceded Hades flickered into view. The bunker returned. Then the void reappeared, and the two views oscillated, fighting for control of his vision.

It would have been so easy to float away and rejoin that void. Part of him longed for that peace. *No. I will go there someday, but now, Nyx has to be stopped.*

Nyx seemed captivated by the lights. "What?"

Virgil shoved the charm under Nyx's shirt collar.

"What are you...?"

Nyx never finished his sentence, unless the following scream could be considered a grammatically correct way to complete a question. Blue translucent hands crept from nowhere and clutched at Nyx's arms, his legs, his coat, his shirt, more and more of them appearing and grabbing until the scientist was covered in half-visible hands. The scientist struggled, trying to tear them from his body, but for every hand he managed to remove, two more appeared, writhing like snakes and pulling with inhuman force. Virgil watched, horrified, as Nyx's thrashing form faded from view until nothing of him remained.

The charm clattered to the floor. Virgil could breathe again.

"Damn," said a familiar voice. Virgil turned to see Matthaios enter the room, followed by Chrysanthe, Schirra, and Stathis. "That was some shit, Virgil."

THIRTY-ONE

1:23.

The missile would launch soon, still loaded with the coordinates for Mount Olympus. If it launched, it would impact the mountain in under four minutes. A mushroom cloud would burst upward from the home of the gods, portending fallout. Or worse. Darkness would spread, either from the cloud's own shadow, or from the world disintegrating as the gods no longer held it together.

And that event would be locked into place in less than a minute. Virgil didn't know how to stop the launch. Even if he knew which program to run to change the coordinates, he couldn't make the update in the time remaining. And if he called the control room and ordered them to abort the launch, they would have a long discussion about his credentials for authorizing such an action.

0:57.

"What's going on, Virgil?" Chrysanthe's forehead was wreathed with blood.

Virgil tried not to think about what blows the guards had landed on her. He didn't have time. "I don't know."

0:50.

Virgil lurched to the computer desk, trying to find anything that would help. The regular keyboard offered nothing. To the side was a console with headset links, indicator lights, and…a big red button labeled, "Abort."

Virgil flipped up the safety cover over the button and pressed it.

Nothing happened. No change in sound, no lighting change, no change in the indicator lights. The wall clock continued to count down, each glowing number an indictment of Virgil's ineptitude.

0:22.

0:21.

0:20.

Why do they have an abort button if it doesn't do anything?

"Did it work?" asked Chrysanthe.

"It should have." Virgil grabbed a power cable on the desk. He was about to yank it from the wall, when the countdown stopped.

0:11.

Virgil stared for several seconds, waiting to see if the numbers would resume their downward march. Seconds turned into a minute. Still no change. Then the numbers on the clock disappeared.

"I think it worked." He leaned against the desk leg and closed his eyes.

We did it. Depending on what actually held the world together, they had either saved the world or a scenic mountain. Either way, Virgil felt good having accomplished something. Despite the odds, they had succeeded.

This elation was better than he'd expected, better than he'd imagined when he had sat in the therapist's office. Virgil didn't know what consequences they would face for breaking into a military launch site and killing the head of the nuclear warfare program, but at least he had this moment.

Virgil opened his eyes and held the power cable closer. It led from the computer monitor to the wall. If he had yanked it, as he had planned earlier, he would only have turned off the monitor.

"You're bleeding."

Chrysanthe rushed to him. Before Virgil could say anything, she knelt beside him and applied pressure to his wound. He gasped.

"I'm bleeding, too," said Matthaios. "And they jabbed me in the eye." He pointed.

"We're all bleeding," said Schirra. "Virgil's just the loudest complainer."

Chrysanthe frowned. "He's also the only one recovering from a stab wound." She nodded toward the door. "Maybe we should get out of here. This isn't the best place to treat injuries, and it's the worst place to be caught."

As Chrysanthe placed one of Virgil's arms around her shoulders, Matthaios lowered himself and took Virgil's other arm. Together, the two lifted him to his feet. Virgil gasped again, feeling his side tear. He had gained a new pain, too: his neck felt sore where Nyx had almost strangled him to death. *Elation comes with a price.*

The three staggered to the door, and Stathis held it open, stepping aside to let them pass. When they emerged from the small room into the hallway, Patroklus awaited them.

Virgil stared. *What now?*

The priest's expression showed nothing. No disappointment, remorse, sympathy, or anger. His display of emotion would have been appropriate for contemplating a sidewalk. Virgil stared at him, wondering if the priest's facade would crack, or if it were even a facade.

Schirra and Stathis pushed forward to position themselves between their companions and Patroklus, raising their fists. "We can handle him," said Schirra.

Chrysanthe raised her head to glare at Patroklus. "What do you want now?"

Virgil wanted to throttle the priest, too, but didn't see how it would help. Of more interest than the temporary satisfaction of violence was the answer to why Patroklus had assisted Nyx. Maybe Patroklus wanted revenge on the priesthood for relegating him to a dead-end job. Or maybe he had been working against Nyx the entire time and had really aided Chrysanthe and the others. Thinking about the priest confused Virgil, and he didn't want to do it, not now, with his side and neck throbbing.

"There will be no launch today," Patroklus said. "It has been aborted, and the master computer has been shut down. The coordinate change will be discovered and corrected. You have accomplished your goal, so there is no further need for fighting. Perhaps we can discuss the best way to present your actions here today."

"You gave us to the guards," Chrysanthe said. "How do we know you won't do the same thing again?"

Patroklus maintained his placid expression. "I could explain my actions. However, if you already distrust me, you are unlikely to believe my explanation."

"I want to hear it anyway," said Schirra.

Patroklus inclined his head. "While performing rituals at the Keres Lab, I discovered the plot to destroy Olympus. I introduced myself to Fred Nyx and gave him a plausible explanation for my motives in aiding him, though my intent was to sabotage his plans. Upon the murder of Mr. Manikas, Nyx requested that I monitor Virgil's progress and hinder him, by force if necessary. I assisted the investigation when called upon to do so, telling Nyx that I must avoid suspicion. Sending Virgil to Hades gave him clues to Nyx's identity while giving the appearance that I had left Virgil for dead. When I discovered you in the hallway here, I realized you had no access card to reach the control center. I therefore arranged for you to be taken by guards who had an access card, expecting you to overpower them. Officer Schirra is quite formidable. If at any point you had failed in your mission, I was fully capable of halting the launch, either by confronting Nyx or disrupting it at another location within the facility. Having the second option your group provided, however, made our success more likely."

"Makes sense," said Schirra. "He had to know I would defeat the guards."

"Here's what I think happened." Chrysanthe pointed an accusatory finger at the priest. "You purposely sabotaged your rituals to give Virgil bad information, threatened him, stabbed him in an attempt to kill him, and tried to get us captured, all while maintaining plausible deniability."

Patroklus nodded. "That is an alternate interpretation."

"It's okay, Chrysanthe." Virgil made a mental note to investigate the priest later. "He doesn't have anything to gain by betraying us now. And I think, so he doesn't get arrested, he'll want us to say that he wasn't working with Nyx."

Patroklus needs us as much as we need him. Maybe that's how you decide whom to trust.

THE RECEPTION AT the police station was bewildering. As soon as Virgil and the others stepped through the door, applause erupted, and thick hands thumped his back. He had never experienced this sort of thing before, had only seen it in movies, or happening to someone else.

He hadn't wanted to come to the station. The incident the other day had made him realize his coworkers wanted him dead. Patroklus, though, had said Virgil's appearance at the station tonight would ease his future dealings with the officers and would ensure more support against the bill eliminating homicide detectives, so Virgil had acquiesced.

Everyone wanted to hear the story in detail. Chrysanthe obliged, and the officers mostly cheered in the appropriate spots. They laughed at Schirra's anger at Chrysanthe's treatment by the guard and found Virgil's near-strangulation hilarious, but seemed impressed with the group's conduct as a whole.

"That was great how you killed Nicholas's murderer." Chief Galanos patted Virgil's back. "Not the manliest of methods, but the important thing is that you killed him. You're one of us now."

Virgil tried to smile, but doubted he succeeded. Galanos proceeded to reminisce about the first person he had killed in the line of duty.

Later, after Virgil finished calling Nicholas's parents to explain the resolution of the investigation, Schirra and Stathis approached the chair where he sat. They stopped before him.

"Hi." Virgil tried to reduce the strain in his side as he returned his phone to his pocket.

"I guess you're the hero now." Stathis folded his arms across his chest. "Even though Schirra did most of the work."

"I know," said Virgil. "I'm sorry about that. I'm glad you two came, though. Without you, we wouldn't be here now. I'm sorry no one's giving you credit."

Schirra's smile seemed superficial. "I'm used to that." She put a hand on Stathis's shoulder. "That's why we're leaving the police force. I'm going to start a security-guard company. Stathis is going to be my second-in-command."

"Oh." Virgil stared for a moment. "That's great. It's a great idea."

They would do well, he knew, once the city-state discovered Schirra's abilities. But he would lose his only true allies among the police force.

"I'm sorry you're going, though."

"Yeah, well, it's time. We'll let you know when we have the details worked out." Schirra gestured to the room. "Enjoy your party."

She and Stathis drifted away. Throughout the rest of the room, police officers knocked back wine and shared stories. Several had cornered Patroklus, guffawing and shouting whenever Patroklus gave a curt nod. Chrysanthe and Matthaios stood against the wall, nursing their own drinks and tapping their wounds.

Virgil pushed himself to his feet. They looked ready to leave, too.

VIRGIL HOBBLED THROUGH his apartment doorway, supported between Chrysanthe and Matthaios. They lowered him to the couch and placed a pillow beneath his head. Though his wound throbbed, Chrysanthe and Matthaios had at least re-wrapped it to prevent blood from staining the furniture.

"Are you comfortable?" Chrysanthe rubbed her crimson-stained headband.

Virgil pointed to his side. "I've been stabbed."

Chrysanthe laughed. "Good point." She paused. "I guess it's not that funny."

"What about you?" Virgil asked. "How's your head? And Matthaios's eye?"

"Good enough."

Matthaios shrugged. "I've had worse. Actually, that's not true."

Chrysanthe suppressed a yawn. "Do you really think Patroklus will follow through on his promise?"

Patroklus had vowed to speak to the priesthood and the media to oppose the bill eliminating the Alliance's homicide detective programs. With his support, and with the release of the details of Virgil's investigation, the priest thought the bill would fail.

"I guess we'll see." Chrysanthe shrugged. "Are you going to be okay alone this time? No more pressing need to get stabbed or choked?"

Virgil shifted position, then winced. "I'll be fine."

"Cool," Matthaios said. "Call if you need us."

His sister and brother-in-law eased the door closed behind them, leaving Virgil alone once again. Dartboard on the wall, book beside him, magazine in the bathroom. The same as every night. After everything that had happened the last couple days, nothing had changed.

My reward for saving the religion of so many people is to be in my apartment alone again, to contemplate the fact that I killed someone.

Those ghostly blue hands clutching at Nyx's arms and chest and face, as though pulling him underwater. Nyx's body fading more quickly than his scream.

Virgil shuddered. He wanted to talk to someone, but there was no one. Other than Chrysanthe, who had her own problems now, there was never anyone.

The best I've gotten along with anyone other than Chrysanthe was when I was talking to Charon.

But visiting the ferryman required... He glanced in the direction of his bathroom. The razor would still be lying on the floor.

He shuddered. *No. There are sleeping pills, though. If I took enough...*

Virgil closed his eyes. *Why am I thinking about this? This isn't the way.* But he couldn't have a friendship with Charon otherwise.

Would anyone truly miss me if I did it?

After several long moments, Virgil forced himself to rise from the couch.

VIRGIL FOUND HIMSELF enjoying the confused expression on Charon's face.

"What are you doing here?" The ferryman of the dead held the handle of a gas pump at an Athenian gas station.

Virgil leaned against Charon's bus. "Thought I'd come visit. If that's okay."

For a moment, Charon said nothing. He stood still, his dark imposing figure with billowing cloak a contrast to the bright summer day and the other gas station patrons. Then he smiled. "You are a strange motherfucker. You got a couple hours?"

For most of the day, Virgil rode with Charon while they dropped off passengers across the Acheron. They discussed their pasts and how Virgil had resolved the Nicholas case. It felt like a genuine friendship, or at least the beginning of one, or at least how he imagined the beginning of a friendship would feel.

"So," said Charon as they stood on the bank of the Acheron for one of Charon's breaks, "how did you know where to find me without almost killing yourself?"

The ferryman of the dead threw a stone, and Virgil watched as it skipped once, twice, three times before sinking into the dark waters.

Virgil readied his own stone, constraining his motions to minimize the pain in his side. "You mentioned using the obol—*coin*—to get gas for the bus."

"Right," said Charon. "No gas stations in the underworld. Good observation. Weird place to meet Hades's ferryman, though."

Virgil threw his stone, wincing at the twinge in his side. The stone sank without skipping. "You mentioned Athens. And you mentioned getting your cape. I didn't think you would be allowed to travel far while you were getting gas, so I looked for gas stations near costume shops. There weren't too many."

Charon chuckled. "Nice."

Virgil threw another stone. This one skipped once before sinking. *I'm getting better.*

"You know," said Charon, studying Virgil, "you really had no business saving the world. You're kind of annoying, and you definitely aren't the most qualified. You had everything against you, including yourself, but when it was the last second and you were the one there, you did it. Pretty cool. Maybe when we're both dead, you and I will be chilling together."

The absurdity of the statement struck Virgil, that someone thought he could spend eternity with humanity's heroes. *Actually, maybe that idea is kind of plausible. I could be hanging out, swapping war stories with Charon, Herakles, Achilles, and Odysseus, and they might be interested enough to listen.*

For a moment, Virgil stared at Charon. Then something bubbled up inside him, something strange and unstoppable. Something pleasant.

For the first time he could remember, Virgil laughed.

ACKNOWLEDGMENTS

I WOULD LIKE to thank my wife, Julie Rowe, and my friends and family for their love and support over the years. I'd also like to thank everyone who has given me feedback on this story and others, particularly the people at critters.org, Russell Adams, and Amanda Fox. Thank you also to Rob Carroll of Dark Matter INK for taking a chance on an unknown author.

This story started in 2009 as a script for a poorly produced movie I made with friends. I'd like to thank that cast. I didn't base the characters on real people, either with personality or appearance, but I did picture these people as the characters while I was writing. Thanks to Amanda Fox, Matt Kay, Stephen Logsdon, Chris Moore, Dale Morris, Taylor Morris, Khunya Pan, Jessica Riojas, and Kevin Welch.

—Robert E. Harpold

ABOUT THE AUTHOR

ROBERT E. HARPOLD has been writing stories since he was seven years old, and most of those stories will be shown to no one. In previous jobs, he traveled to Greenland and Antarctica and operated spacecraft. Now he designs spacecraft trajectories, which is his *realistic* dream job. His dream job is the same as everyone else's: astronaut. He is married to the most amazing wife, and they have a wonderful daughter and son.

Also Available or Coming Soon from Dark Matter INK

Human Monsters: A Horror Anthology
Edited by Sadie Hartmann & Ashley Saywers
ISBN 978-1-958598-00-9

Zero Dark Thirty: The 30 Darkest Stories from Dark Matter Magazine, 2021–'22 Edited by Rob Carroll
ISBN 978-1-958598-16-0

Linghun by Ai Jiang
ISBN 978-1-958598-02-3

Monstrous Futures: A Sci-Fi Horror Anthology
Edited by Alex Woodroe
ISBN 978-1-958598-07-8

Our Love Will Devour Us by R. L. Meza
ISBN 978-1-958598-17-7

Haunted Reels: Stories from the Minds of Professional Filmmakers Curated by David Lawson
ISBN 978-1-958598-13-9

The Vein by Steph Nelson
ISBN 978-1-958598-15-3

Other Minds by Eliane Boey
ISBN 978-1-958598-19-1

Monster Lairs: A Dark Fantasy Horror Anthology
Edited by Anna Madden
ISBN 978-1-958598-08-5

Frost Bite by Angela Sylvaine
ISBN 978-1-958598-03-0

The Bleed by Stephen S. Schreffler
ISBN 978-1-958598-11-5

Free Burn by Drew Huff
ISBN 978-1-958598-26-9

The House at the End of Lacelean Street
by Catherine McCarthy
ISBN 978-1-958598-23-8

The Dead Spot: Stories of Lost Girls
by Angela Sylvaine
ISBN 978-1-958598-27-6

Grim Root by Bonnie Jo Stufflebeam
ISBN 978-1-958598-36-8

Voracious by Belicia Rhea
ISBN 978-1-958598-25-2

Abducted by Patrick Barb
ISBN 978-1-958598-37-5

Darkly Through the Glass Place by Kirk Bueckert
ISBN 978-1-958598-48-1

Beautiful Ways We Break Each Other Open
by Angela Liu
ISBN 978-1-958598-60-3

Chopping Spree by Angela Sylvaine
ISBN 978-1-958598-31-3

The Off-Season: An Anthology of Coastal New Weird
Edited by Marissa van Uden
ISBN 978-1-958598-24-5

The Exodontists by Drew Huff
ISBN 978-1-958598-64-1

Saturday Fright at the Movies
by Amanda Cecelia Lang
ISBN 978-1-958598-75-7

The Threshing Floor by Steph Nelson
ISBN 978-1-958598-49-8

Club Contango by Eliane Boey
ISBN 978-1-958598-57-3

Psychopomp by Maria Dong
ISBN 978-1-958598-52-8

Little Red Flags: Stories of Cults, Cons, and Control
Edited by Noelle W. Ihli & Steph Nelson
ISBN 978-1-958598-54-2

The Divine Flesh by Drew Huff
ISBN 978-1-958598-59-7

Frost Bite 2 by Angela Sylvaine
ISBN 978-1-958598-55-9

Disgraced Return of the Kap's Needle
by Renan Bernardo
ISBN 978-1-958598-74-0

Soul Couriers by Caleb Stephens
ISBN 978-1-958598-76-4

Dark Matter Presents: Fear City
ISBN 978-1-958598-90-0

Part of the Dark Hart Collection

Rootwork by Tracy Cross
ISBN 978-1-958598-01-6

Mosaic by Catherine McCarthy
ISBN 978-1-958598-06-1

Apparitions by Adam Pottle
ISBN 978-1-958598-18-4

I Can See Your Lies by Izzy Lee
ISBN 978-1-958598-28-3

A Gathering of Weapons by Tracy Cross
ISBN 978-1-958598-38-2